FROM THE PAGES OF
THE ENCHANTED CASTLE and
FIVE CHILDREN AND IT

The children stood round the hole in a ring, looking at the creature they had found. It was worth looking at. Its eyes were on long horns like a snail's eyes, and it could move them in and out like telescopes; it had ears like a bat's ears, and its tubby body was shaped like a spider's and covered with thick soft fur; its legs and arms were furry too, and it had hands and feet like a monkey's.   (from *Five Children and It*, page 17)

I daresay you have often thought what you would do if you had three wishes given you, and have despised the old man and his wife in the black-pudding story, and felt certain that if you had the chance you could think of three really useful wishes without a moment's hesitation. These children had often talked this matter over, but, now the chance had suddenly come to them, they could not make up their minds.   (from *Five Children and It*, pages 20–21)

"I was always generous from a child," said the Sand-fairy. "I've spent the whole of my waking hours in giving. But one thing I won't give—that's advice."   (from *Five Children and It*, page 77)

"Friends, Romans, countrymen—and women—we found a Sammyadd. We have had wishes. We've had wings, and being beautiful as the day—ugh!—that was pretty jolly beastly if you like—and wealth and castles, and that rotten gipsy business with the Lamb. But we're no forrader. We haven't really got anything worth having for our wishes."   (from *Five Children and It*, page 126)

"Why, don't you see, if you told grown-ups I should have no peace of my life. They'd get hold of me, and they wouldn't wish silly things like you do, but real earnest things; and the scientific people would hit on some way of making things last after sunset, as likely as not;

and they'd ask for a graduated income-tax, and old-age pensions and manhood suffrage, and free secondary education, and dull things like that; and get them, and keep them, and the whole world would be turned topsy-turvy."   (from *Five Children and It*, page 182)

And they were at school in a little town in the West of England—the boys at one school, of course, and the girl at another, because the sensible habit of having boys and girls at the same school is not yet as common as I hope it will be some day.

(from *The Enchanted Castle*, page 191)

"Well, don't let's spoil the show with any silly old not believing," said Gerald with decision. "I'm going to believe in magic as hard as I can. This is an enchanted garden, and that's an enchanted castle, and I'm jolly well going to explore."   (from *The Enchanted Castle*, page 204)

There is a curtain, thin as gossamer, clear as glass, strong as iron, that hangs for ever between the world of magic and the world that seems to us to be real. And when once people have found one of the little weak spots in that curtain which are marked by magic rings, and amulets, and the like, almost anything may happen.

(from *The Enchanted Castle*, page 345)

The moonbeam slants more and more; now it touches the far end of the stone, now it draws nearer and nearer to the middle of it, now at last it touches the very heart and centre of that central stone. And then it is as though a spring were touched, a fountain of light released. Everything changes. Or, rather, everything is revealed. There are no more secrets. The plan of the world seems plain, like an easy sum that one writes in big figures on a child's slate.   (from *The Enchanted Castle*, page 409)

It is all very well for all of them to pretend that the whole of this story is my own invention: facts are facts, and you can't explain them away.

(from *The Enchanted Castle*, page 412)

THE ENCHANTED CASTLE

AND

FIVE CHILDREN AND IT

Edith Nesbit

ILLUSTRATED BY H. R. MILLAR

WITH AN INTRODUCTION
BY SANFORD SCHWARTZ

GEORGE STADE
CONSULTING EDITORIAL DIRECTOR

BARNES & NOBLE CLASSICS
NEW YORK

𝒥𝓑

BARNES & NOBLE CLASSICS
NEW YORK

Published by Barnes & Noble Books
122 Fifth Avenue
New York, NY 10011

www.barnesandnoble.com/classics

Five Children and It was first published in 1902.
The Enchanted Castle was first published in 1907.

Published in 2005 by Barnes & Noble Classics with new
Introduction, Notes, Biography, Chronology, Inspired By,
Comments & Questions, and For Further Reading.

Introduction, Notes, and For Further Reading
Copyright © 2005 by Sanford Schwartz.

Note on Edith Nesbit, The World of Edith Nesbit,
Inspired by The Enchanted Castle and Five Children and It,
and Comments & Questions
Copyright © 2005 by Barnes & Noble, Inc.

The Enchanted Castle and Five Children and It
ISBN-13: 978-1-59308-274-1
ISBN-10: 1-59308-274-6
LC Control Number 2005926182

Produced and published in conjunction with:
Fine Creative Media, Inc.
322 Eighth Avenue
New York, NY 10001
Michael J. Fine, President and Publisher

Printed in the United States of America
QM
1   3   5   7   9   10   8   6   4   2
FIRST PRINTING

EDITH NESBIT

Edith Nesbit, a pioneer of twentieth-century children's fiction, was one of the major authors of the "Golden Age" of children's literature, which included Lewis Carroll, George MacDonald, Louisa May Alcott, Rudyard Kipling, Beatrix Potter, J. M. Barrie, Kenneth Grahame, and Frances Hodgson Burnett. She was born in 1858, the youngest of six children. Her childhood was disrupted in 1862 by the sudden death of her father, the head of a small agricultural college in South London. For several years, Edith's mother ran the college on her own, but when Edith's sister Mary contracted tuberculosis, Mrs. Nesbit began moving the family to various locations in England and France in an ultimately futile effort to find a suitable climate. The energetic and sometimes mischievous Edith was sent off intermittently to boarding schools, where she was often unhappy. At other times, she was allowed to roam freely through the countryside around the homes the family rented. She began publishing poetry in her teens, and though her lasting reputation is based on her children's books, she aspired to become a major poet throughout her life.

In 1880 Edith married the dashing and politically active Hubert Bland and soon afterward gave birth to their first child. Four years later the couple joined Sidney and Beatrice Webb, George Bernard Shaw, and several others as founding members of the Fabian Society, an influential circle of progressive intellectuals who would play a major role in the formation of social policy over the coming decades; Bland edited the society's journal. Since he was an uncertain breadwinner, Edith began to support the family by her writing. For nearly two decades she composed (in addition to her verse) a multitude of essays, short stories, adult novels, and tales for children, often working at top speed to keep the family afloat. At the same time, she adopted the image of the so-called New Woman, cutting her hair short, wearing loose-fitting "aesthetic" clothing, and assuming what was then the exclusively male prerogative of smoking cigarettes. Tall, athletic, and by all accounts highly attractive, she also responded to her husband's incessant womanizing by conducting affairs of her own, including a short-lived romance with George Bernard Shaw.

After twenty years of prolific publication and modest critical success, Nesbit finally achieved acclaim with the release of her first children's novel, *The Story of the Treasure Seekers* (1899), a family adventure story. It was the start of a remarkable period of creative activity. *The Wouldbegoods*, a sequel to her first novel, appeared in 1901, followed by *The New Treasure Seekers* (1904). During this time, she also wrote her first fantasy novel, *Five Children and It* (1902) and employed the same "five children" in two sequels, *The Phoenix and the Carpet* (1904) and *The Story of the Amulet* (1906). In 1906 she published one of her most enduring family adventure tales, *The Railway Children*, and in the following year *The Enchanted Castle* (1907), which many regard as her most mature work of children's fiction. Inspired by H. G. Wells's *The Time Machine* (1895), she then produced two time-travel romances for children, *The House of Arden* (1908) and its sequel, *Harding's Luck* (1909), and several other works of fantasy—*The Magic City* (1910), *The Wonderful Garden* (1911), *The Magic World* (1912), and *Wet Magic* (1913). Her output declined dramatically after Hubert's death in 1914. At the time of Edith Nesbit's death, on May 4, 1924, her literary reputation had ebbed, but it recovered in the 1930s, and ever since she has been regarded as one of the seminal voices of modern children's literature.

TABLE OF CONTENTS

THE WORLD OF EDITH NESBIT AND
THE ENCHANTED CASTLE AND
FIVE CHILDREN AND IT

1858 Edith Nesbit is born on August 15 in Kennington, South London, the sixth and youngest child of John Collis and Sarah Green (née Alderton) Nesbit. Her family lives on the campus of an agricultural school founded by Edith's paternal grandfather; her father is the headmaster and teaches chemistry.

1862 In March, John Nesbit dies at the age of forty-three, and Edith's mother takes over the running of the college.

1863 Charles Kingsley's pioneering work of children's fantasy *The Water-Babies* is published; along with subsequent books by Lewis Carroll and George MacDonald, it marks the beginning of a golden era of children's fantasy and of children's literature in general.

1865 Lewis Carroll's *Alice's Adventures in Wonderland* appears.

1866 Edith's sister Mary contracts tuberculosis, and the family moves to the seaside in search of a healthier climate. Edith is briefly enrolled in boarding school, where she is bullied.

1867 Sarah Nesbit takes Mary and two of the other children, including Edith, to the warmer climate of France. The Nesbits travel throughout the country, never remaining in one place for long.

1868 The first part of Louisa May Alcott's *Little Women* appears.

1870 The Nesbit family moves to a Brittany farmhouse; the children are allowed to roam freely. A reluctant Edith is sent to various boarding schools and at one point a convent in Germany. Sarah Nesbit takes Mary back to London, where Mary becomes engaged to Philip Bourke Marston, a poet who is a member of the Pre-Raphaelite circle.

1871 In November, Mary Nesbit dies. George MacDonald publishes *At the Back of the North Wind*. Lewis Carroll's *Through the Looking Glass and What Alice Found There* appears.

1872 The Nesbits settle in Kent, renting Halstead Hall, where the children find many diversions, including railroad tracks that run through the property. Edith enters a period of great happiness. MacDonald's most enduring book for children, *The Princess and the Goblin*, is released.

1875 Edith's first published poems appear in a local paper, the *Sunday Magazine*. The family moves back to London.

1876 Mark Twain publishes *The Adventures of Tom Sawyer*.

1877 Edith meets Hubert Bland, a young writer and political activist.

1880 Hubert Bland and Edith Nesbit are married. Their first child, Paul, is born two months later.

1881 A second child, Iris, is born.

1882 Nesbit meets Alice Hoatson, who will have an ongoing affair with Bland.

1883 Scottish novelist Robert Louis Stevenson publishes *Treasure Island*. George MacDonald publishes *The Princess and Curdie*.

1884 Bland and Nesbit help found the Fabian Society, a circle of progressive intellectuals committed to gradual social change through democratic reform. Nesbit is invited to write pamphlets for the group. The society attracts notable figures, including writers George Bernard Shaw and, later, H. G. Wells. Nesbit also adopts the image of the so-called New Woman of the late nineteenth century: She cuts her hair short, smokes cigarettes, and abandons her corset. Mark Twain's *Adventures of Huckleberry Finn* is published.

1885 With Bland, Nesbit coauthors the novel *The Prophet's Mantle*, a conventional romance plot set against a background of politics informed by their acquaintance with Russian émigrés living in London. When writing together, the couple often uses the alias "Fabian Bland." The couple's third child, Fabian, is born.

1886 Bland edits the Fabian Society journal, *Today*. His daughter Rosamund is born to Alice Hoatson; Nesbit agrees to raise the child as her own and allows Hoatson to move into the Bland-Nesbit home as a housekeeper. Nesbit has a brief affair with George Bernard Shaw. *Lays and Legends*, Nesbit's collection of poems, is released to critical success. Frances Hodgson Burnett's *Little Lord Fauntleroy* is published.

1892   Nesbit's first long work for children, a book-length narrative poem entitled *The Voyage of Columbus*, is published.

1893   Nesbit publishes two collections of horror stories: *Something Wrong* and *Grim Tales*; the latter includes "Man-size in Marble," one of her most popular tales.

1894   Rudyard Kipling publishes *The Jungle Book*, a collection of animal stories. Robert Louis Stevenson dies.

1895   H. G. Wells publishes *The Time Machine*, his first major work of science fiction.

1896   Nesbit begins to serialize her childhood reminiscences in *The Girl's Own Paper*.

1898   H. G. Wells's *The War of the Worlds* and Kenneth Grahame's *Dream Days* are published.

1899   Nesbit begins her long collaboration with illustrator H. R. Millar when her dragon stories are published in *The Strand Magazine*. She also publishes *Pussy and Doggy Tales*, *The Secret of Kyriels*, an adult Gothic novel, and *The Story of the Treasure Seekers*, the first of the Bastable novels, with illustrations by Gordon Brown and Lewis Baumer. The success of *The Treasure Seekers* allows Nesbit and Bland to move into Well Hall, a spacious manor home. Bland's second child with Alice Hoatson, christened John and nicknamed "The Lamb," is born; Nesbit adopts and raises him.

1900   Nesbit publishes her dragon stories in the collection *The Book of Dragons*. L. Frank Baum publishes *The Wonderful Wizard of Oz*. Beatrix Potter publishes *The Tale of Peter Rabbit*.

1901   *The Wouldbegoods*, another Bastable novel, is published, as is Nesbit's *Nine Unlikely Tales for Children* (later reprinted as *Whereyouwanttogo and Other Unlikely Tales*). Kipling's *Kim* appears.

1902   Nesbit publishes *Five Children and It*, her first fantasy novel. She meets H. G. Wells, an important influence on her fiction and for several years a controversial and outspoken member of the Fabian Society. Nesbit's adult novel *The Red House* and *The Revolt of the Toys, and What Comes of Quarreling* are published. Kipling's *Just So Stories* is released.

1904   *The New Treasure Seekers* (another Bastable novel) and *The Phoenix and the Carpet*, featuring the "five children," are published. J. M. Barrie produces his play *Peter Pan; or The Boy Who Wouldn't Grow Up*.

1905 Frances Hodgson Burnett's *A Little Princess* appears.

1906 *The Railway Children* is published, drawing on Nesbit's childhood at Halstead Hall. *The Story of the Amulet*, the last of the "five children" novels, is also released, as is another adult novel, *The Incomplete Amorist*. Kipling's *Puck of Pook's Hill* appears.

1907 *The Enchanted Castle* is published.

1908 Nesbit publishes her collected political poetry in *Ballads and Lyrics of Socialism, 1883 to 1908*. She introduces a new series with the publication of *The House of Arden*, a children's time-travel romance. Kenneth Grahame's *The Wind in the Willows* is published. London hosts the Olympic Games.

1909 *These Little Ones*, a collection of Nesbit's stories, and *Harding's Luck*, a sequel to *The House of Arden*, are published, as well as two adult novels, *Salome and the Head* (reissued as *The House with No Address*) and *Daphne in Fitzroy Street*, based on her affair with George Bernard Shaw.

1910 Nesbit publishes *The Magic City*, with a character (the Pretenderette) that seems to lampoon a prominent suffragette, Evelyn Sharp, to whom Nesbit writes a letter explaining why she refuses to join the movement.

1911 Nesbit publishes *The Wonderful Garden*, another children's fantasy novel, and *Dormant*, often considered her finest adult novel. Hubert Bland's vision deteriorates, leaving him almost blind and in the care of his wife. Barrie's story about Peter Pan is published as a children's novel titled *Peter and Wendy*, which will later be changed to *Peter Pan*. Frances Hodgson Burnett's *The Secret Garden* appears.

1912 Nesbit publishes *The Magic World*, a collection of stories.

1913 Nesbit publishes *Wet Magic*, a fantastical undersea adventure and her last children's fantasy novel. The book marks the end of her association with illustrator H. R. Millar.

1914 In April, Hubert Bland dies. World War I begins.

1917 Nesbit marries Thomas Tucker, a retired tugboat operator affectionately known as "the Skipper."

1920 A. A. Milne's *Mr. Pym Passes By* is published, as is the first of Hugh Lofting's Dr. Doolittle books.

1921 Nesbit and Tucker leave Well Hall and settle in Jesson St. Mary's near Dymchurch.

1922 Nesbit publishes her last novel, *The Lark*, a romance based on the financial problems of her later years.

1924 Nesbit dies of cancer on May 4 in St. Mary's.

1925 *Five of Us—and Madeline* is published. Rosamund Bland Sharp, Nesbit's adopted daughter, compiles this collection of stories, using material provided by Nesbit's second husband as well as excerpts from Nesbit's memoirs originally published in *The Girl's Own Paper* (1896–1897).

1966 Nesbit's memoirs from *The Girl's Own Paper* are published in book form under the title *Long Ago When I was Young*.

INTRODUCTION

In "The Book of Beasts," the first story in her popular collection *The Book of Dragons* (1900), E. (for Edith) Nesbit tells the tale of a boy who unexpectedly inherits the throne of his country. Like his somewhat eccentric predecessor, the new king is soon drawn to the treasures of the royal library. Ignoring the advice of his counselors, the boy approaches a particularly handsome volume, *The Book of Beasts*, but as he gazes at the beautiful butterfly painted on the front page, the creature begins to flutter its wings and proceeds to fly out the library window. Unfortunately, the same thing occurs with the great dragon who appears on a subsequent page, and soon the beast starts to wreak havoc (though only on Saturdays) throughout the land. After the dragon carries off his rocking horse, the young king sets free a hippogriff from the *The Book of Beasts*, and together the boy and his white-winged companion lure the dragon to the Pebbly Waste, where the fiery creature, now deprived of the shade that keeps it from overheating, wriggles back into the book from which it came. The rocking horse is recovered but asks to live in the hippogriff's page of the book, while the hippogriff, for its efforts, assumes the position of King's Own Rocking Horse.

The release of fantastic creatures into the real world, at once serious and playful, exemplifies the most distinctive feature of Nesbit's fantasies: the ceaseless interplay between the imaginary and the actual, the fluctuation between the magical world that her children enter through their books, games, and adventures, and the limiting conditions of everyday life. Unlike most of her predecessors, who situate the action of their books entirely in an imaginary realm or swiftly transport their protagonists into it, Nesbit's fantasies are perpetually shuffling back and forth between the marvelous and the real, and much of their fascination lies in the interaction and confusion between them. In *Five Children and It* (1902), her first fantasy novel, the children's exercise of imagination comes simply from the opportunity to have their wishes granted, and the results, however amusing to us, are sufficiently troublesome or embarrassing to make them welcome (at least temporarily) the return to the ordinary. In *The Enchanted Castle* (1907), the magic is more elusive and complex, and it leads to a serious meditation on the gift of imagination—its multiform capacity to produce butterflies as well as dragons, and above all its power to redeem and transfigure, as the hippogriff does, the distress, insecurity, and inevitable sorrows of life in this world.

I

The life of Edith Nesbit (1858–1924) spanned the period that is now regarded as the golden age of children's literature in the English-speaking world. The major precondition for this development lies in the emergence of modern industrial society, which produced not only an increasingly literate middle-class population but also a sharp division between home and workplace that effectively created the concept and condition of "childhood" as we now know it. Books for children have a long history, but there is little precedent for the boom in children's fiction that began in the mid-nineteenth century. This new literature appeared in a variety of forms, including, among others, the boys' adventure tale, the family story (a specialty of women writers), and the fantasy novel, which was often cross-written for children and adults. The adventure story, which descends from Defoe's *Robinson Crusoe* (1719) and its many imitators, was pioneered in the mid-nineteenth century by Captain Frederick Marryat (1792–1848), R. M. Ballantyne (1825–1894), and Mayne Reid (1818–1883), and somewhat later by the prolific G. A. Henty (1832–1902), "the boys' own historian," who wrote more than one hundred novels featuring young male heroes caught up in significant historical conflicts. (Nesbit parodies Henty in *Five Children and It*, chapters 6 and 7; see endnote 4.) Among the finest fruits of this genre are the classics by Robert Louis Stevenson (*Treasure Island*, 1883; *Kidnapped*, 1886) and Mark Twain (*The Adventures of Tom Sawyer*, 1876; *Adventures of Huckleberry Finn*, 1884). The family story, which also rose to prominence in this period, is associated primarily with women writers such as Charlotte Yonge (1823–1901), Juliana Horatia Ewing (1841–1885), Mary Louisa Molesworth (1839–1921), and, in America, Louisa May Alcott

(1832–1888), whose *Little Women* (1868) is widely regarded as the first masterpiece of this tradition, which paved the way for later classics such as Nesbit's *The Story of the Treasure Seekers* (1899) and its sequels. In retrospect, perhaps the most remarkable children's genre to emerge in the mid-nineteenth century is the cross-generational fantasy novel. Inspired by the immensely popular fairy tales of the Brothers Grimm (translated 1823–1826) and Hans Christian Andersen (translated in 1846), the fantasy tradition was built on the firm foundation established by three Victorian authors—George MacDonald (1824–1905), Charles Kingsley (1819–1875), and Lewis Carroll (1832–1898)—who produced a series of masterpieces over the course of little more than a decade. These include MacDonald's *Phantastes* (1858), *At the Back of the North Wind* (1871), and *The Princess and the Goblin* (1872); Kingsley's singular classic *The Water-Babies* (1863); and Carroll's *Alice's Adventures in Wonderland* (1865) and *Through the Looking-Glass* (1871). In the first decade of the twentieth century, this tradition produced an especially rich harvest, often in the form of animal fantasies that Rudyard Kipling (1865–1936) popularized in his *Jungle Books* (1894, 1895); Beatrix Potter's *Peter Rabbit* series (begun in 1900); Frank Baum's *The Wizard of Oz* (1900) and its sequels; Kipling's own *Just So Stories* (1902) and *Puck of Pook's Hill* (1906); J. M. Barrie's "Peter Pan" (first staged in 1904); Kenneth Grahame's *The Wind in the Willows* (1908); and Walter de la Mare's *The Three Mulla-Mulgars* (1910). It is no coincidence that in this same brief and remarkable period, which came to an end around World War I, E. Nesbit also produced nearly all of the children's fantasy novels for which she is now remembered.

II

As a writer of children's fiction, Nesbit often drew upon her own early life and her experience as the mother of five children. It is no accident that the absence of one or both parents looms large in her fiction: Her father, a well-known agronomist who ran a small agricultural college in London, died when she was three. For the next few years, his widow managed the college on her own, but when Edith's older sister was diagnosed with tuberculosis, the family began moving from place to place in an ultimately futile effort to find a hospitable climate. Edith herself was dispatched to one unpleasant boarding school after another, but as she recalls in her later memoir, these nomadic years also provided her with a rich quarry of adventures to which she repeatedly returned in her juvenile fiction. (The memoir, "My School-Days," originally a series of vignettes in a children's periodical, was later reprinted under the title Long Ago When I Was Young; see "For Further Reading.")

In 1877 Edith met the dashing, intelligent, and politically active Hubert Bland, and two months after their marriage in 1880 she gave birth to the first of their children. Despite his many gifts, Bland was an uncertain breadwinner, and for many years Edith divided her time between caring for the children and writing (sometimes in collaboration with her husband) to support the family. In 1884 the Blands became founding members of the Fabian Society, the socialist think tank that under the guidance of Sidney Webb, its most outstanding theoretician, and his wife, Beatrice, would play a major role in the formation of progressive social policy over the coming decades. Hubert was not an intellectual on the order of Sidney Webb, but he became a respected newspaper columnist and remained a prominent member of the organization for many years. Edith's position was less well defined, but as an active participant in the society she became acquainted with many prominent artists and intellectuals of the era, including George Bernard Shaw (with whom she had a brief affair in 1886); the exiled Russian philosopher Prince Peter Kropotkin; Annie Besant, the socialist firebrand who went on to lead the influential Theosophical Society; the renowned sexologist Edward Carpenter; and, some years later, H. G. Wells (whose ill-fated adulterous affair with the Blands' daughter complicated his already strained relations with the Fabian leadership and led to his departure from the society). The agenda of the Fabian Society surfaces occasionally in Edith's fiction, especially when she turns her attention to the extreme inequalities of Edwardian society, which were strikingly evident in the dismal conditions of the vast London slums. Nevertheless, scholars have raised questions about the degree and depth of her political commitments. During the height of her fame, she surprised her contemporaries by opposing the drive for women's suffrage (which succeeded by 1918), and the typically good-hearted middle-class children of her most famous novels often amuse themselves by deceiving their bewildered servants.

Similar inconsistencies appear in Nesbit's marriage and in other aspects of her personal life. On the one hand, she was known for her independent spirit. She adopted the trappings of the turn-of-the-century emancipated woman, cutting her hair short, wearing loose-fitting "aesthetic" clothing, and assuming what was then the exclusively male prerogative of smoking cigarettes. She also responded to her husband's incessant womanizing by conducting affairs of her own, including the fling with George Bernard Shaw that she later turned into a romantic novel, *Daphne in Fitzroy Street* (1909). Many men courted the lively, athletic, and by all accounts highly attractive woman, and in later years she would hold court in her large rented home, Well Hall, surrounded by younger male admirers with whom she occasionally became involved. (Noel Coward, whom she met in her old age, called her "the most genuine Bohemian I ever met.")[1]

On the other hand, the volatile and often hot-tempered Edith remained a devoted wife to her philandering husband. She raised two of his children by another woman—her friend Alice Hoatson—as if they were her own, and even allowed Alice to live with the family as a housekeeper. She also acquiesced to Hubert's less palatable political views, including his opposition to women's suffrage, and despite the occasional flare-ups that led Shaw to declare that "no two people were ever married who were better calculated to make the worst of each other," she remained closely tied and dependent upon Hubert until his death in 1914.[2] Three years later she surprised her family and friends by marrying a placid former tugboat operator, known as "the Skipper," and settled into a happy if increasingly penurious old age until her own death in 1924.

Nesbit began publishing poetry in her teens, and for many years her primary aspiration was to develop into a great poet. From the time of her marriage until the end of the century she composed a multitude of verse, essays, short stories, adult novels, and stories for children, often working at top speed to keep the family afloat. Although she acquired a modest reputation as a poet and novelist, very few of these works have survived the test of time. After twenty years of prolific publication, she finally achieved acclaim with the release of her first children's novel, *The Story of the Treasure Seekers: Being the Adven-*

tures of the Bastable Children in Search of a Fortune (1899), a family adventure tale based on stories she had written for various magazines. The book sold well, and she capitalized on its success with a sequel, The Would-begoods: Being the Further Adventures of the Treasure Seekers (1901) and The New Treasure Seekers (1904). At the same time, she wrote her first fantasy novel, Five Children and It (1902), and employed the same set of children in two sequels, The Phoenix and the Carpet (1904) and The Story of the Amulet (1906). By this time her reputation was well established, but more successes would follow. In 1906 she published one of her most enduring family stories, The Railway Children, and the following year The Enchanted Castle, which many regard as her most mature work of fiction. Inspired by the success of H. G. Wells's The Time Machine (1895), she then produced two time-travel romances, The House of Arden (1908) and its sequel, Harding's Luck (1909), which have since lost some of their popular appeal, though a number of readers regard them as her best. A few other notable works appeared in subsequent years—The Magic City (1910), The Wonderful Garden (1911), The Magic World (1912), and Wet Magic (1913)—but in her last decade she wrote comparatively little for children and nothing to match the level of achievement in her decade-long run from The Story of the Treasure Seekers to Harding's Luck.

III

The Story of the Treasure Seekers established the prototype for both the "realistic" family adventures and the "magical" fantasies that Nesbit composed over the next few years. At the outset of these novels, we are introduced to a middle-class family, often in distressed circumstances. Since the parents are either absent or preoccupied, the children are nominally in the care of servants, but usually left to their own devices, they embark on a series of exploits, sometimes designed to rectify the situation at home, at other times simply for the sake of adventure or sheer diversion. In The Treasure Seekers, we meet the six Bastable children (four boys and two girls), whose mother is dead and whose father is struggling with business problems. According to the eldest boy, Oswald, the novel's delightfully bookish and vainglorious narrator, the children seek to restore "the fortunes of the ancient House of Bastable," and they launch their quest by digging for buried treasure in their own garden. The scheme collapses when the roof of their underground tunnel caves in on the hapless Albert-next-door, but thanks to Albert's amiable uncle—the first of several sympathetic adults—the children end up "discovering" a few small coins in their pile of dirt. In successive episodes, the Bastables continue their fortune-hunting by becoming freelance detectives, selling poetry to an amused literary editor, publishing a newspaper (one copy sold), and "kidnapping" Albert-next-door to extract a ransom from his uncle. The consequences of their later exploits are more serious. Finding a newspaper ad for private loans, the children visit the office of their "Generous Benefactor," but complications arise when it turns out that the lender is already their father's creditor. Further embarrassments result from their attempt to secure another benefactor by setting their dog on a rich local aristocrat and pretending to come to his rescue, and from their efforts to market their own wine and Bastable's Certain Cure for Colds. The loose episode structure that emerges from these relatively self-contained adventures is characteristic of Nesbit's early novels, though the interaction between juvenile imagination and adult reality often grows more complex in the later episodes. In one of the final vignettes of *The Treasure Seekers*, the children are imagining the life of a robber when suddenly they see a stranger whom they suspect is the real thing. The stranger, who is actually a friend of their father, pretends that he has been caught in the act, but when another unknown figure appears upon the scene and turns out be a real burglar, the imaginary "robber" borrows the children's toy gun to scare him off. The novel concludes with another reversal of expectations, when the children discover that their seemingly poor and unremarkable Indian Uncle is actually the rich benefactor for whom they've been searching all along. Typical of Nesbit, just as they relinquish their wishes and fantasies in favor of a more realistic point of view, the children discover that the real world may be as enchanted as the world of their dreams. Or as the artfully artless Oswald puts it at the end, "I can't help it if it is like Dickens, because it happens this way. Real life is often something like books."

Nesbit went on to write further adventures of the Bastables, including *The Wouldbegoods*, her greatest financial success, and *The New Treasure Seekers*. She created a new set of protagonists for her next family

adventure novel, The Railway Children (1906), but the design of the
story remains much the same. Once again we find a middle-class
family in straitened circumstances: Recalling the famous Dreyfus affair (still unresolved at the time Nesbit was writing), the father has
been sent to prison, wrongly accused of spying for a foreign power,
while the mother transports the family to a country house and tries
to make ends meet with her writing. The children, initially unaware
of the reason for their father's absence, are drawn to the local railway
line and embark on a series of adventures that lead to unexpected
consequences, ranging from embarrassment over their misguided attempt to raise charity for a poor working-class family to commenda-
tion for their heroic efforts in helping to avert a railway disaster. Their
adventures also place them in contact with a distinguished passenger,
an unnamed "old gentleman" whose intervention, akin to that of the
Indian Uncle in The Treasure Seekers, leads to the exoneration of their father and his return to the family. Although some readers found the
novel excessively sentimental and lamented the loss of the Bastable
clan, The Railway Children has remained a perennial favorite, especially
in Britain, where it has been dramatized repeatedly on film and television.

IV

After completing her first two Bastable novels, Nesbit began a new serial publication, The Psammead (later changed to Five Children and It),
which ran in The Strand Magazine from April to December 1902 with illustrations by her long-term collaborator, H. R. Millar (see endnote
11 to The Enchanted Castle). For this venture she created a new set of siblings—Cyril, Anthea, Robert, Jane, and their infant brother "The
Lamb"—based loosely on her own five children. ("The Lamb," to
whom the book is dedicated, is John Bland, born in 1899, the second child of the affair between Hubert and Alice Hoatson; Edith
raised him as her own, though her other four children were already
in their teens.) The new fictional family (we never learn their surname) is less hard-pressed than the Bastables, but as soon as they arrive at their remote country house, the parents are called away to
attend to other matters, and the children, left in the care of servants,

begin to explore the surrounding area on their own. Nesbit's distinctive mixture of realism and fantasy is apparent from the start. To the children, who have been bottled up in London for two years, the somewhat shabby house seems "a sort of Fairy Palace set down in an Earthly Paradise" (p. 10), and the chimney smoke from the local limekilns makes the valley beneath them glimmer "till they were like an enchanted city out of the *Arabian Nights*" (p. 12). In her casual conversation style, the narrator also gets in on the act. After informing her ostensibly juvenile audience that she will skip over the mundane events—to which adults might respond "How like life!" (p. 12)—she cleverly leads her readers (children and adults alike) into the realm of the marvelous by suggesting that when we think about it, the accepted facts of modern science, such as the roundness of the earth and its rotation around the sun, are no less astonishing than the events she's about to relate, and they require a similar leap beyond the everyday world we can see and feel. Once we accept this demonstration of the marvelous character of the factual, we're ready for the narrator's almost matter-of-fact introduction of the marvelous: "Yet I daresay you believe all that about the earth and the sun, and if so you will find it quite easy to believe that before Anthea and Cyril and the others had been a week in the country they had found a fairy. At least they called it that, because that was what it called itself; and of course it knew best, but it was not at all like any fairy you ever saw or heard of or read about" (p. 13).

The narrator's playful blending of the magical and the real sets the stage for what's to come. As the children begin digging toward Australia in the local gravel-pit, they hear a sound that resolves itself into the words "You let me alone" (p. 16), and out of the sand emerges one of Nesbit's most celebrated inventions—the Psammead, or "Sand-fairy," derived from the Greek *psammos* (sand) and the names *naiad* (water nymph) and *dryad* (wood nymph) of Greek mythology. Like the name itself, this imaginary being, in contrast to the twittering tinkerbells of Victorian fairylands, is a lumpy composite assembled out of the body parts of more familiar creatures: "Its eyes were on long horns like a snail's eyes, and it could move them in and out like telescopes; it had ears like a bat's ears, and its tubby body was shaped like a spider's and covered with thick soft fur; its legs and arms were furry too, and it had hands and feet like a monkey's" (p.

17). (See Millar's illustrations on pp. 6, 58, 76, 111, and 147.) The Psammead's character reveals a similar amalgamation of the real and the marvelous: Grumpy, mercurial, and ever concerned with the hair on its upper left whisker that was once exposed to water, the Psammead is also obliged to fulfill human wishes, though his normal limit is one wish per day, and his magic terminates at sunset. The Psammead's recollection of the prehistoric past, when the shell-filled gravel-pit was still by the seaside and the children of our remotest ancestors asked him for practical things like dinosaur dinners, also combines the ordinary and the magical, awakening the imagination to the presence of a distant past whose traces may still be present in the very ground we stand on.

Nesbit's fantasy novels often hark back to traditional fairy tales, and behind *Five Children and It* lies the well-known tale of "the three wishes," which appears in many versions around the world. Once the children realize that the Psammead will grant their wishes, they consider the implications of one of the variants of the traditional tale—the "black pudding story" (p. 20), in which a man who dislikes his wife's cooking wishes for a helping of black pudding, to which she reacts by wishing the pudding on his nose; he then must use the third and final wish to undo the effects of the second. (Coincidentally, a darker and instantly famous version of the tale, W. W. Jacobs's "The Monkey's Paw," appeared in 1902.) While expressing our desire to transcend the limits of ordinary existence, the fairy tale of "the three wishes" warns us to beware of our own wishes, dreams, and fantasies by revealing the consequences of their literal fulfillment. As Bruno Bettelheim points out, however, the self-canceling circularity of these tales is also reassuring and enhances our willingness to accept the reality of things as they are.[3] In Nesbit's case, the children witness the adverse effects of their wishes and welcome the return to normality at the end of each day, but their recurrent desire to return to the magical, compounded by the sheer excitement of some of their madcap adventures, suggests that the pleasures of the imagination are enticing enough to offset the risks and dangers that its exercise entails.

The children squander their first few wishes on conventional vanities. No sooner does the Psammead fulfill their initial request—to be "as beautiful as the day" (p. 21)—than they long for a return to their flawed natural selves, especially after the Lamb, who fails to rec-

ognize them, starts to cry inconsolably, and the nursemaid Martha, assuming they are strangers, denies them entry into the house. The setting sun rescues the children from their plight, but despite some
precautionary deliberations on the following day, their next wish—
"to be rich beyond the dreams of something or other" (p. 33)—is as
formulaic as their first. It also yields similarly disappointing results
when they discover that the ancient coins with which the Psammead
has filled the gravel-pit are refused by the local villagers, who are sus-
picious enough to summon the police. Nesbit spices up the episode
with the children's supplementary wish that the servants won't notice the Psammead's magic, which leads to mayhem when Martha
appears on the scene and is unable to see the allegedly incriminating
coins with which the children have filled their pockets. Once again,
the dusk brings a return to normal, and when the children wake up
the next morning, their squabbles over the logic of wish-fulfillment
indicates that they've grown somewhat wary of the Psammead and
more discriminating in their wishes.

At the opposite end from these stock desires are the impulsive
wishes that proceed from anger or insecurity. Annoyed that the Lamb
has knocked over his ginger-beer, Robert expresses his anger by
wishing that others would want the child so that "we might get some
peace in our lives" (p. 56). Unfortunately, one of the rules of the
Psammead's magic is that wishes cannot be annulled, and as a result,
from then until sunset the Lamb must be rescued from the affection-
ate clutches of one stranger after another, including the haughty Lady
Chittenden, who otherwise has no love for children. In a similar
episode later on, Cyril blurts out that he wishes the Lamb would
grow up, and consequently the children must spend an entire day
with an insufferable prig who disavows his pet name as "a relic of
foolish and far-off childhood" (p. 152) and insists that his brothers
and sisters address him by one of his baptismal names, Hilary, St.
Maur, or Devereux. (See Millar's illustration on p. 159, which depicts
Martha holding the grown-up Lamb in her arms as if her were an infant, which within her spatial frame of reference he still is.) Also
based on hotheaded desire is the episode in which the children ac-
cost the rather imposing "baker's boy" (p. 128), who is in no mood
to play the victim in a game of bandits, and in the aftermath of the
ensuing skirmish, Robert seeks to avenge his defeat by wishing he

was bigger than his rival. His wish is immediately granted, but the now gargantuan Robert must exercise some restraint in giving the baker's boy his comeuppance; and then, compelled to wait until sundown for the restoration of his normal proportions, he ends up as a sideshow spectacle at the local fair. Each of these incidents portrays the consequences of impetuous desire, but in their common concern with the vulnerability of children, they explore the conflict between the desire to secure the power that presumably comes with adult size and stature, and the grown-up recognition that we bear some responsibility for those who are even less secure than ourselves.

A third class of wishes is associated directly with art and the power of imagination. After the initial wishes for beauty and wealth go awry, the kind and thoughtful Anthea consults the Psammead, and while its only advice is "think before you speak" (p. 77), her wish for wings (that time-honored symbol of creative imagination) results not only in the literal gift of flight but in an experience more "wonderful and more like real magic than any wish the children had had yet" (p. 80). To be sure, when the day is done they are asleep in the turret of a church tower and must be rescued by the local vicar, but in the end the joy of their magical journey seems to outweigh the humiliations of their descent into ordinary reality and the punishment meted out by the angry Martha upon their arrival home. Moreover, as a result of this escapade Martha also meets the gamekeeper of the vicarage; therefore, as the narrator intimates, the magic of this episode may have some enduring effects, though at this point in the novel "that is another story" (p. 100), and we must wait for the final chapter to learn the outcome.

In two later episodes of a similar kind, the books the children read inspire their flights of imagination. In the first instance, the charm of popular "historical romances for the young" (p. 105) produces the transformation of their house into a castle under siege (though the servants, who remain blind to the magic, continue to go about their business as usual). Nesbit seems to enjoy poking at the stilted language of the besiegers, as well as the historical mishmash of their equipment, with shields from the Middle Ages, swords from the Napoleonic era, and tents "of the latest brand" (p. 105). But despite Robert's effort to persuade them that they're merely fictive beings, these storybook soldiers pose a real threat to the "castle," at least as long as daylight lasts, and once the sunset puts an end to the encounter, the children not only breathe a sigh of relief but also find themselves exhilarated by the episode. While engaging in a parody that showcases the absurdity of these historical romances, Nesbit also pays homage to their power to delight and to stimulate the imagination of the juvenile reader.

The last of these literary episodes materializes from a reading of *The Last of the Mohicans*, and it generates considerable suspense as the children wait apprehensively for the Indians—" 'not big ones, you know, but little ones, just about the right size for us to fight' " (p. 161)—to exhibit their legendary stealth and suddenly emerge out of nowhere. Once the savages appear and the children realize that their scalps are really on the line, they make a desperate run for the gravel-pit, but before they can find the Psammead, they are surrounded by their miniature assailants and prepare themselves for the scalping-knife and the flames. Fortunately, the Indians can't find any firewood to burn their enemies, and the peril comes to an end when their chief bewails this "strange unnatural country" and wishes that "we were but in our native forest once more" (p. 171). Like the story of the besieged castle, the comic undercurrent of this episode, which turns on the disparity between the fictive and the real, is offset by the emphasis upon the capacity of imagination to enchant the world that ordinary mortals inhabit. But while the parodic element of the castle episode puts limits on the sense of real danger, Nesbit's transposition of Indian warriors to modern Britain goes further in producing some of the same thrilling emotions that keep us riveted to a well-wrought romance of high adventure.

The heightened intensity of the Indian affair paves the way for the final drama, in which the children eagerly await the return of their parents. But the distinctive magic inherent in the reunion between parents and children is complicated by a final impulsive wish to grace their mother's return with a special gift. When the children hear that Lady Chittenden's valuable jewelry has been stolen, Jane casually wishes that her mother might own such wonderful things. As readers we might well sympathize with the transfer of riches from the child-hating ogress to the loving mother, but the wish turns their mother into a receiver of stolen goods, and the suspicion that wrongly falls on the vicarage gamekeeper threatens to foil Martha's plans for marriage. In desperation the children strike a final deal with the Psammead, who undoes the effects of their folly in exchange for a reprieve from "silly" gift-giving and a promise not to reveal his identity to adults, who might ask for "earnest things" such as "a graduated income-tax, and old-age-pensions and manhood suffrage, and free secondary education, and dull things like that; and get them, and keep them, and the whole world would be turned topsy-turvy" (p. 182). As in the fairy tale of "the three wishes," the Psammead's circular and self-negating magic may help to reconcile us to things as they are, and its final disappearance into the sand represents a return from the enticing world of wishes to the more secure if less enthralling routines of everyday life. But there is more to this story than a lesson on "the vanity of human wishes." At the conclusion of the novel, the return of absent parents, along with the prospective union of Martha and her fiancé, possesses a certain magic of its own. Moreover, Nesbit conveys the sense that as double-edged and dangerous as many of our wishes may be, they also express an enduring impulse to transcend the limited and sometimes painful and unjust conditions of life as it is. And perhaps most of all, the Psammead's magic invites us to engage in flights of imagination that restrictively "realistic" fiction often fails to provide. In this respect, Nesbit carefully balances the moral of "the three wishes" with the seemingly ineradicable desires that give rise not only to traditional fairy tales but also to her own distinctive union of the magical and the mundane.

Nesbit retained the same juvenile ensemble in her two subsequent fantasies, *The Phoenix and the Carpet* and *The Story of the Amulet*. In the first, the scene shifts to London, and the Psammead is replaced by another wishing creature, the Phoenix, the legendary bird known for its beauty and its singular capacity for rebirth from its own ashes. Out of commission for two millennia, Nesbit's high-toned patrician bird returns to life in the family parlor and takes the children on a loosely organized series of romps through London and beyond, all the while exhibiting its somewhat haughty but engagingly comic dignity—proud, poetic, and disdainful of the prosaic character of modern life. The Psammead reappears in *The Story of the Amulet*, but it plays a relatively minor role in the quest for the missing half of a magic charm that has the capacity to confer "our hearts' desire" (p. 281). The clue to the missing half-amulet is buried in the past. The search takes the children on a series of voyages in time, first to a prehistoric village along the Nile (c.6000 B.C.) and then to ancient Babylon at the height of its glory. After that, they voyage to the seafaring civilization of ancient Tyre, the glorious mythical continent of Atlantis just before it sinks into the sea, ancient Britain at the time of Caesar's conquest (55 B.C.), again to ancient Egypt (this time during the reign of the Pharoah), and finally forward in time, first to a utopian London free of the ills of the Edwardian city, and then to the near future, where they encounter their own adult selves. Nesbit has nearly as much fun with overlapping times as she did with overlapping spaces in *Five Children and It*, when, for instance, the Queen of Babylon is transported from her own time to the children's London and is not only appalled by the shabbiness of the modern metropolis but also insists on the return of her jewels from the British Museum. (C. S. Lewis, who admired the novel, recreates this episode in *The Magician's Nephew* [1955], where the much more treacherous Queen Jadis escapes from her own world and stirs up trouble in Edwardian London.)[4] Despite such touches of humor, each of these time-travel adventures invites reflection on the nature of society and the state, and taken together they reflect the increasingly serious mood of Nesbit's later fantasies. So does the joining together of the two halves of the amulet, which produces a vision of a higher domain that transcends the injurious divisions and contradictions of everyday life and allows us to pass "through the perfect charm to the perfect union, which is not of time or space." Nesbit would never abandon the kind of "funny" magic that prevails in *Five Children and It*, but the resolution of *The Story of the Amulet* points to the more "serious" magic that would come to the fore in her next major fantasy, *The Enchanted Castle*.

V

Nesbit's most ambitious work of fiction starts off as most of her previous novels. Once again, we meet a group of middle-class siblings who set forth on a series of adventures. In this instance, we begin with a threesome—Gerald, Kathleen, and Jimmy—who are compelled to remain at school for the holidays in the charge of a young schoolmistress, the good-natured "Mademoiselle." Like the Bastables

and the "five children," these siblings are reasonably well differenti-
ated and inclined to incessant squabbling. Gerald, the oldest and most
resourceful, bears a certain resemblance to Oswald Bastable. Unlike
the latter, he is not the narrator of the novel, but he possesses the
habit of narrating his own actions in a self-conscious literary manner
(annoying to the other children, if amusing to us) that inevitably
grants him pride of place: " 'The young explorers, . . . dazzled at first
by the darkness of the cave, could see nothing. . . . But their dauntless
leader, whose eyes had grown used to the dark while the clumsy
forms of the others were bunging up the entrance, had made a discovery' " (p. 198). Jimmy, by contrast, is the resident skeptic who not
only punctures the pretensions of others but also plays an important
role as the doubting Thomas of this mischievously magical universe.
Kathleen, the middle child, is less well marked, but as with Anthea
and some of Nesbit's other young girls, her common sense and com-
passion offset some of the eccentricities of her male companions and
provide some ballast to the group. Like the "five children" before
them, Nesbit's new team wanders into a magical world, but we soon
discover that in this novel it is often difficult to distinguish the enchanted and the real, and questions of truth and belief play a more
prominent role than in the earlier novels. Over time we also discover
that the plot of this novel, which seems to begin as another loosely
organized sequence of episodes, is more unified and considerably
more complex than its predecessors. Nesbit offers no explicit struc-
tural signposts, but if nothing else, the twelve untitled chapters seem
to fall into two discrete sets of six, and as we shall see, the symme-
tries established by the apparent subdivision of each half of the book
into three two-chapter sets indicates that she took considerable pains
to construct a carefully integrated work of art.

     In the opening section of the novel (chapters 1 and 2), the chil-
dren are resting by the roadside when the chance discovery of a hidden passage transports them into a magical world, or so it seems from
the extraordinary garden that opens before them, with its abundant
statuary and huge stone edifice looming in the distance behind it.
Nesbit draws on classical myth (the Minotaur's labyrinth) and fairy
tale (Sleeping Beauty) to enhance the magical atmosphere: The children enter a maze of hedges and notice a thread that takes them to
the center, where they find the reposing form of "the enchanted

Princess" (p. 208). Jimmy is doubtful—"she's only a little girl dressed up" (p. 208)—but once he wakens her with a kiss, his irrepressible skepticism is sorely tested by her commanding manner—"you're a very unbelieving little boy" (p. 218)—her impressive living quarters, and her display of magic in the treasure chamber, where she makes her jewelry appear and disappear at will. But things begin to change when the girl dons a ring that presumably "makes you invisible" (p. 220). After she asks the children to close their eyes and count, Jimmy debunks her so-called magic (inadvertently we're told) by seeing her lift a secret panel. As it turns out, however, the "Princess" is less distressed by the exposure of her pranks than by the fact that the ring has actually made her invisible. In the true confession that follows, we learn that she is the very ordinary Mabel Prowse, niece of Lord Yalding's housekeeper, and the seemingly enchanted realm into which we and the children have wandered is actually his estate. But if as readers we have shared in the deception and must acknowledge that Jimmy's suspicions have been correct all along, we also join the children in finding ourselves face to face with the new conundrum posed by Mabel's invisibility and the magical ring that confers it. Such oscillations and confusions between imagination and reality are harbingers of things to come.

In the following chapters, reminiscent of the "funny" magic in earlier novels, we follow the children on a set of escapades that proceed from their attempt to exploit the power of invisibility: profiting from a conjuring act at the local fair; assuming the role of detectives, which leads to the sighting of a real burglary; and sowing confusion among the unsuspecting servants. We also learn that wearing the ring produces not only invisibility but also a seemingly random assemblage of other effects, including the indifference of friends and relatives, the suppression of fear, and above all, the capacity to apprehend a higher if still enigmatic dimension of enchantment. In chapter 4, we catch a glimpse of this new dimension when the ring-bearing Gerald enters the Yalding gardens at night and, sensing that he is "in another world" (p. 257), beholds the statues of classical gods and giant dinosaurs awaken into life. The vision is ephemeral and in the short run inconsequential, but it offers the first hint of something that transcends the prosaic magic of earlier episodes; it anticipates the more sustained and momentous vision of the statuary that appears in the fourth chapter of the second half of the novel.

After the fleeting epiphany in the garden, the novel reverts to the type of adventure that preceded it, but things begin to change in chapter 6 with the theatrical pageant—a re-enactment of *Beauty and the Beast*—that brings the first half of the book to an end. The genial Mademoiselle (who seems mysteriously moved by the news that the impoverished Lord Yalding is about to visit his estate) is present to watch the play, but the children enlarge their audience by creating a set of grotesque figures out of sticks, broom handles, pillows, and paper masks. At the end of the pageant's second act, the Beast (Gerald) hands the magical ring to Beauty (Mabel) and announces that it has the power to "give you anything you wish" (p. 301). Unfortunately, when Mabel wishes that the inanimate members of the audience were alive to enhance the applause, the figures suddenly come to life and soon march out the door. On a first reading of the novel, it is difficult to fathom the far-reaching implications of this scene, whose most immediate effect is to launch the pursuit of these animated inanimates (now called the Ugly-Wuglies) in the following chapters. We see that the ring is more mysterious than it seemed, but at this point the apparent transformation into a wishing ring remains an enigma. So does the import of Beauty and the Beast, which at once prefigures the stirring real-life pageant of the final chapter and, as the fairy-tale version of the story of Cupid and Psyche, offers a first taste of the myth that informs the ultimate vision of the novel (see endnote 10).

The encounter with the Ugly-Wuglies (chapters 7 and 8) hovers on the border between comedy and terror. Nesbit never abandons her sense of humor, but in this section of the novel she elicits an element of fear, confusion, and violence that marks a departure from anything we've seen before. At first the Ugly-Wuglies are polite to a fault in their search for "a good hotel" (p. 305), and as creatures of pure surface—clothes without bodies, voices without brains—they seem to represent a world of empty ritual and innocuous cliché. Social satire plays a significant role in this episode, especially after one of the Ugly-Wuglies mutates into a rich London stockbroker. But this aspect of the Uglies is outweighed by the terror they strike in the hearts of the children, who must summon the courage required to face them.

The sudden animation of the inanimate is frightening enough, but once they are corralled into a dark chamber behind the Temple of Flora—the goddess of fertility—these initially docile creatures grow angry and turn into raging furies (who later escape and assault the adult "bailiff" who has helped to confine them). Since the children are aware that these creatures are their own invention, the significance of Flora and her subterranean chamber may lie in the association between fertility and the creative imagination, which is the source of both horrors and delights, the root of vain, violent, and monstrous pursuits as well as the fount of empathy and the enduring ideal of social and cosmic harmony. In this respect, Jimmy's wish (instantly fulfilled) to be as rich as the Ugly-Wugly stockbroker may be regarded as a misuse of imagination, and it suggests that a society which channels its energies into a single-minded obsession with perpetual accumulation becomes at once vapid and vicious, as empty, distorted, and ultimately devoid of imagination as the Ugly-Wuglies themselves.

After this descent into the abyss of distorted imagination, Nesbit quickly prepares us for the visionary ascent of the subsequent section (chapters 9 and 10): "There is a curtain, thin as gossamer, clear as glass, strong as iron, that hangs for ever between the world of magic and the world that seems to us to be real. And when once people have found one of the little weak spots in that curtain which are marked by magic rings, and amulets, and the like, almost anything may happen" (p. 345). In contrast to the playful magic of Mabel's wish to be twelve feet tall, the higher magic begins with a symbolic rebirth (inside the belly of a stone dinosaur) when the kind and sensitive Kathleen is transformed into one of the living statues we first encountered in the middle section of the first half (chapters 3 and 4). Surprisingly free of all fear, she is welcomed by the animate statue of the god Apollo and invited to witness "the beautiful enchantment" (p. 361) of the garden as it comes alive at night. Soon the other children are allowed to join in the "celestial picnic" (p. 370) with the marble Olympians, and Apollo's lyre captivates them with "all the beautiful dreams of all the world . . . and all the lovely thoughts that sometimes hover near, but not so near that you can catch them. . . . and it seemed that the whole world lay like a magic apple in the hand of each listener, and that the whole world was good and beautiful" (pp. 374–375). After the visionary moment fades with the dawn, the children must make their somewhat melancholy journey back to the everyday world. But prior to the end of this section they enter a magnificent hall (later identified as the Hall of Granted Wishes) that is surrounded by arches through which they can discern a multitude of images ranging from "a good hotel" for the Ugly-Wugly—"there are some souls that ask no higher thing of life"—to pictures that reveal "some moment when life had sprung to fire and flower—the best that the soul of man could ask or man's destiny grant" (p. 380). Finally, at the end of the hall the children find the statue of the winged Psyche, symbolically the source of all wishes and imaginings, wearing the magical ring. With ceremonial deference to the goddess, they remove the ring from her hand, and the sensible Kathleen, who is not only aware of the deeper truth that " 'the ring's what you *say* it is' " (p. 347) but also knows when enough is enough for mere mortals, makes the wish that "we were safe in our own beds, undressed, and in our nightgowns, and asleep" (p. 381).

After they return from the visionary world, the children participate in the enchantment of the real world that takes place in the final section of the novel (chapters 11 and 12). We learn that the "bailiff" who assisted with the confinement of the Ugly-Wuglies is actually Lord Yalding himself, and that Mademoiselle is the woman he loves despite the opposition of his relatives, who have deprived him of control over the estate. One by one the obstacles to their marriage are overcome, and at the Temple of Flora we witness a ceremony—reminiscent of the production of *Beauty and the Beast* that concluded the first half of the novel—in which Lord Yalding places the ring on the finger of his ever more radiant bride:

The children have drawn back till they stand close to the lovers. The moonbeam slants more and more; now it touches the far end of the stone, now it draws nearer and nearer to the middle of it, now at last it touches the very heart and centre of that central stone. And then it is as though a spring were touched, a fountain of light released. Everything changes. Or, rather, everything is revealed. There are no more secrets. The plan of the world seems plain, like an easy sum that one writes in big figures on a child's slate. One wonders how one can ever have wondered about anything. Space is not; every place that one has seen or dreamed of is here. Time is not; into this instant is crowded all that one has ever done or dreamed of doing. It is a moment and it is eternity. It is the centre of the universe and it is the universe itself. The eternal light rests on and illuminates the eternal heart of things (p. 409).

As the ceremony continues, all of the statues come alive—ancient creatures both real and imaginary, followed by a vast array of gods and goddesses—and the lovers proceed to the Hall of Granted Wishes (a.k.a. the Hall of Psyche), where the history of the ring is revealed and Mademoiselle makes a final wish "that all the magic this ring has wrought may be undone, and that the ring itself may be no more and no less than a charm to bind thee and me together for evermore" (p. 411). In the ensuing transformation, which echoes Prospero's renunciation of magic at the end of The Tempest, the mystical light dies away, the windows of granted wishes disappear, and the statue of Psyche turns into a mere grave. At the same time, in the spirit of Keats and the Romantics, the very process of demythologizing the myth of Cupid and Psyche reveals its full significance, as the imaginary god and his lover are replaced by a real man and woman who are bound together in a climactic vision of the soul uplifted and transfigured by the power of love. Nesbit concludes the novel on a humorous note, but the return to the more impish manner of her "funny" magic dramatically underscores the turn to the more "serious" magic that gathers force over the second half of the novel. Many readers prefer the vitality of the former to the gravity of the latter, and many of those who admire her later works favor the social critique of The Story of the Amulet, The House of Arden, and Harding's Luck over the Romantic Platonism of The Enchanted Castle. But never again would Nesbit undertake such an ambitious work of children's fiction, and none of her other books possesses either the coherence or the complexity of her architectonic masterpiece.

VI

It is easy to underestimate Nesbit's influence on modern children's fiction, especially in North America, where she has never enjoyed the same level of popularity as she has in the British Isles. Historians continue to debate the degree of her originality, but they seem to agree that however much she was indebted to her Victorian predecessors, Nesbit brought a new and more modern voice to children's fiction, and in certain respect, her distinctive fusion of magic and realism, which cast a spell on later generations of children's authors, endures to this day. According to Colin Manlove, "After Nesbit, children's fantasy was never quite the same again. She showed just how much fun could be made of bringing magic into the ordinary domestic lives of children: And she introduced to children's fantasy the idea of the group of different children, rather than the frequently solitary child of earlier books. Her books demonstrated that fantasy could be wildly inventive and yet follow its own peculiar laws."[5] All of these Nesbit trademarks—the family ensemble, the mixture of the magic and the realism, the rites of passage between worlds—are prominent features of C. S. Lewis's classic cycle *The Chronicles of Narnia* (1950–1956). With good reason Lewis's admirers emphasize the influence of George MacDonald and members of his own literary circle, J. R. R. Tolkien and Charles Williams. But as several Lewis scholars have pointed out, the *Narnia* series is in some ways far more closely related to Nesbit's fiction, which informs the narrative voice, the basic elements of character and plot, and a surprising number of specific details, particularly in *The Magician's Nephew*, which is set in Nesbit's turn-of-the-century London and draws liberally on her works.[6] On the other side of the Atlantic, Lewis's American contemporary, Edward Eager, author of the popular "Half Magic" series (1954–1958), openly identifies Nesbit as the source of his inspiration. At the outset of the first volume, *Half Magic*, a family of four book-loving children forbids oral recitation after suffering through *Evangeline*, but "this summer the rule had changed. This summer the children had found some books by a writer named E. Nesbit, surely the most wonderful books in the world. . . . And now yesterday *The Enchanted Castle* had come in, and they took it out, and Jane, because she could read fastest and loudest, read it out loud all the way home, and when they got home she went on reading, and when their mother came home they hardly said a word to her, and when dinner was served they didn't notice a thing they ate."[7] It is arguable that Nesbit's influence has ebbed since the days of these mid-century testimonials, and that children's fantasy itself has shifted terrain in the last few decades. But Nesbit's imprint is still apparent in some of the genre's most popular practitioners, including Philip Pullman and J. K. Rowling, and even in cinematic productions such as Pixar's *Toy Story* (1995), a direct descendant of *The Magic City* (1910). Admittedly, a century after their appearance her novels seem embedded in a bygone society and reflect some of its now outmoded values. Moreover, as a writer who seems to have one foot planted in Victorian society and the other in the twentieth century, Nesbit has sparked debate over the extent to which she departs from the heavy-handed didacticism of her literary predecessors, and it is often difficult to decide whether she is subverting or affirming the norms of her notably class-conscious and patriarchal society. But what seems to have endured beyond the cultural trappings of her transitional era is the freshness of her narrative voice, the vivacity and playful humor that in the right circumstances might modulate into high seriousness, and, perhaps above all, the perpetual fusion and confusion between the imaginary and the real, the books we read and the lives we live, the magical lure of our wishes, dreams, and desires, and the inevitably limited conditions of existence that they ceaselessly enchant.

Sanford Schwartz teaches English literature at Pennsylvania State University (University Park). He is the author of *The Matrix of Modernism* and various essays on modern literary, cultural, and intellectual history. He is currently writing a book on C. S. Lewis's science fiction trilogy.

Acknowledgments: I wish to thank several friends and colleagues who provided encouragement and indispensable support along the way: Julia Briggs, for clarifying some baffling allusions in these century-old novels; Elizabeth Jenkins, for assistance with the dialects, slang, and semantic subtleties of what I once considered my native tongue; John Poritsky, for direction on recent work in children's literature; and my incomparable research assistant, Jeff Pruchnic, for just about everything.

Notes

1. Quoted in Dorothy Langley Moore, E. Nesbit: A Biography (1933; revised edition, London: Benn, 1967), p. 197.
2. From Shaw's interview with Dorothy Langley Moore, quoted in Julia Briggs, A Woman of Passion: The Life of E. Nesbit, 1858–1924 (London: Hutchinson, 1987), p. xvi.
3. Bruno Bettelheim, The Uses of Enchantment: The Meaning and Importance of Fairy Tales (New York: Alfred A. Knopf, 1976), pp. 71–72.
4. In his autobiography, Surprised by Joy (1955), Lewis recalls his childhood reading of Nesbit's novels: "Much better than either of these [Sir Arthur Conan Doyle's Sir Nigel and Mark Twain's A Connecticut Yankee in King Arthur's Court] was E. Nesbit's trilogy, Five Children and It, The Phoenix and the Wishing Carpet [sic], and The Amulet. The last did most for me. It first opened my eyes to antiquity, the 'dark backward and abysm of time.' I can still reread it with delight." C. S. Lewis, Surprised by Joy: The Shape of My Early Life (San Diego: Harcourt, 1970), p. 14.
5. Colin Manlove, From Alice to Harry Potter: Children's Fantasy in England (Christchurch, New Zealand: Cybereditions, 2003), p. 47.
6. Mervyn Nicholson, "What C. S. Lewis Took from E. Nesbit," Children's Literature Association Quarterly 16 (1991), pp. 16–22.
7. Edward Eager, Half Magic (1954; San Diego: Harcourt, 1999), pp. 4–5.

FIVE CHILDREN AND IT

To John Bland[1]

My Lamb, you are so very small,
You have not learned to read at all.
Yet never a printed book withstands
The urgence of your dimpled hands.
So, though this book is for yourself,
Let mother keep it on the shelf
Till you can read. O days that pass,
That day will come too soon, alas!

CONTENTS

The Psammead

LIST OF ILLUSTRATIONS

CHAPTER I

Beautiful as the Day

The house was three miles from the station, but before the dusty hired fly* had rattled along for five minutes the children began to put their heads out of the carriage window and to say, "Aren't we nearly there?" And every time they passed a house, which was not very often, they all said, "Oh, is this it?" But it never was, till they reached the very top of the hill, just past the chalk-quarry and before you come to the gravel-pit. And then there was a white house with a green garden and an orchard beyond, and mother said, "Here we are!"

"How white the house is," said Robert.

"And look at the roses," said Anthea.

"And the plums," said Jane.

"It is rather decent," Cyril admitted.

The Baby said, "Wanty go walky"; and the fly stopped with a last rattle and jolt.

Everyone got its legs kicked or its feet trodden on in the scramble to get out of the carriage that very minute, but no one seemed to mind. Mother, curiously enough, was in no hurry to get out; and even when she had come down slowly and by the step, and with no jump at all, she seemed to wish to see the boxes carried in, and even to pay the driver, instead of joining in that first glorious rush round the garden and the orchard and the thorny, thistly, briery, brambly wilderness beyond the broken gate and the dry fountain at the side of the house. But the children were wiser, for once. It was not really a pretty house at all; it was quite ordinary, and mother thought it was rather inconvenient, and was quite annoyed at there being no shelves, to speak of, and hardly a cupboard in the place. Father used to say that

---

* Rented one-horse carriage.

That first glorious rush round the garden

the ironwork on the roof and coping was like an architect's nightmare. But the house was deep in the country, with no other house in
sight, and the children had been in London for two years, without so
much as once going to the seaside even for a day by an excursion
train, and so the White House seemed to them a sort of Fairy Palace
set down in an Earthly Paradise. For London is like prison for children, especially if their relations are not rich.

Of course there are the shops and the theatres, and Maskelyne
and Cook's,* and things, but if your people are rather poor you don't
get taken to the theatres, and you can't buy things out of the shops;
and London has none of those nice things that children may play
with without hurting the things or themselves—such as trees and

---

*British magicians John Nevil Maskelyne (1839–1917) and George A. Cooke
(1825–1904) ran a famous theater, the Egyptian Hall, in London. After Cooke's death,
David Devant (1868–1941) became Maskelyne's partner (see *The Enchanted Castle*, p. 221).

sand and woods and waters. And nearly everything in London is the wrong sort of shape—all straight lines and flat streets, instead of being all sorts of odd shapes, like things are in the country. Trees are all different, as you know, and I am sure some tiresome person must have told you that there are no two blades of grass exactly alike. But in streets, where the blades of grass don't grow, everything is like everything else. This is why so many children who live in towns are so extremely naughty. They do not know what is the matter with them, and no more do their fathers and mothers, aunts, uncles, cousins, tutors, governesses, and nurses; but I know. And so do you now. Children in the country are naughty sometimes, too, but that is for quite different reasons.

The children had explored the gardens and the outhouses thoroughly before they were caught and cleaned for tea, and they saw quite well that they were certain to be happy at the White House. They thought so from the first moment, but when they found the back of the house covered with jasmine, all in white flower, and smelling like a bottle of the most expensive scent that is ever given for a birthday present; and when they had seen the lawn, all green and smooth, and quite different from the brown grass in the gardens at Camden Town; and when they had found the stable with a loft over it and some old hay still left, they were almost certain; and when Robert had found the broken swing and tumbled out of it and got a lump on his head the size of an egg, and Cyril had nipped his finger in the door of a hutch that seemed made to keep rabbits in, if you ever had any, they had no longer any doubts whatever.

The best part of it all was that there were no rules about not going to places and not doing things. In London almost everything is labelled "You mustn't touch," and though the label is invisible, it's just as bad, because you know it's there, or if you don't you jolly soon get told.

The White House was on the edge of a hill, with a wood behind it—and the chalk-quarry on one side and the gravel-pit on the other. Down at the bottom of the hill was a level plain, with queer-shaped white buildings where people burnt lime, and a big red brewery and other houses; and when the big chimneys were smoking and the sun was setting, the valley looked as if it was filled with golden mist, and

Cyril had nipped his finger in the door of a hutch

the limekilns and oasthouses* glimmered and glittered till they were like an enchanted city out of the *Arabian Nights*.

Now that I have begun to tell you about the place, I feel that I could go on and make this into a most interesting story about all the ordinary things that the children did—just the kind of things you do yourself, you know—and you would believe every word of it; and when I told about the children's being tiresome, as you are sometimes, your aunts would perhaps write in the margin of the story with a pencil, "How true!" or "How like life!" and you would see it and very likely be annoyed. So I will only tell you the really astonishing things that happened, and you may leave the book about quite

---

* *Limekiln:* kiln in which limestone is heated in order to extract lime; *oasthouse:* building containing an oast, a kiln for drying hops.

safely, for no aunts and uncles either are likely to write "How true!" on the edge of the story. Grown-up people find it very difficult to believe really wonderful things, unless they have what they call proof. But children will believe almost anything, and grown-ups know this. That is why they tell you that the earth is round like an orange, when you can see perfectly well that it is flat and lumpy; and why they say that the earth goes round the sun, when you can see for yourself any day that the sun gets up in the morning and goes to bed at night like a good sun as it is, and the earth knows its place, and lies as still as a mouse. Yet I daresay you believe all that about the earth and the sun, and if so you will find it quite easy to believe that before Anthea and Cyril and the others had been a week in the country they had found a fairy. At least they called it that, because that was what it called itself; and of course it knew best, but it was not at all like any fairy you ever saw or heard of or read about.

It was at the gravel-pits. Father had to go away suddenly on business, and mother had gone away to stay with Granny, who was not very well. They both went in a great hurry, and when they were gone the house seemed dreadfully quiet and empty, and the children wandered from one room to another and looked at the bits of paper and string on the floors left over from the packing, and not yet cleared up, and wished they had something to do. It was Cyril who said:

"I say, let's take our Margate spades and go and dig in the gravel-pits. We can pretend it's seaside."

"Father said it was once," Anthea said; "he says there are shells there thousands of years old."

So they went. Of course they had been to the edge of the gravel-pit and looked over, but they had not gone down into it for fear father should say they mustn't play there, and the same with the chalk-quarry. The gravel-pit is not really dangerous if you don't try to climb down the edges, but go the slow safe way round by the road, as if you were a cart.

Each of the children carried its own spade, and took it in turns to carry the Lamb. He was the baby, and they called him that because "Baa" was the first thing he ever said. They called Anthea "Panther," which seems silly when you read it, but when you say it it sounds a little like her name.

The gravel-pit is very large and wide, with grass growing round the edges at the top, and dry stringy wildflowers, purple and yellow. It is like a giant's wash-hand basin. And there are mounds of gravel, and holes in the sides of the basin where gravel has been taken out, and high up in the steep sides there are the little holes that are the little front doors of the little sand-martins'* little houses.

The children built a castle, of course, but castle-building is rather poor fun when you have no hope of the swishing tide ever coming in to fill up the moat and wash away the drawbridge, and, at the happy last, to wet everybody up to the waist at least.

Cyril wanted to dig out a cave to play smugglers in, but the others thought it might bury them alive, so it ended in all spades going to work to dig a hole through the castle to Australia. These children, you see, believed that the world was round, and that on the other side the little Australian boys and girls were really walking wrong way up, like flies on the ceiling, with their heads hanging down into the air.

The children dug and they dug and they dug, and their hands got sandy and hot and red, and their faces got damp and shiny. The Lamb had tried to eat the sand, and had cried so hard when he found that it was not, as he had supposed, brown sugar, that he was now tired out, and was lying asleep in a warm fat bunch in the middle of the half-finished castle. This left his brothers and sisters free to work really hard, and the hole that was to come out in Australia soon grew so deep that Jane, who was called "Pussy" for short, begged the others to stop.

"Suppose the bottom of the hole gave way suddenly," she said, "and you tumbled out among the little Australians, all the sand would get in their eyes."

"Yes," said Robert; "and they would hate us, and throw stones at us, and not let us see the kangaroos, or opossums, or blue-gums,† or Emu Brand birds,‡ or anything."

Cyril and Anthea knew that Australia was not quite so near as all that, but they agreed to stop using the spades and go on with their

---

* Type of northern swallow that lives in tunnels in clay or sand banks.

† Type of eucalyptus tree native to Australia.

‡ The Australian emu bird provided the logo for "Emu Brand" knitting wool.

hands. This was quite easy, because the sand at the bottom of the hole was very soft and fine and dry, like sea-sand. And there were little shells in it.

"Fancy it having been wet sea here once, all sloppy and shiny," said Jane, "with fishes and conger-eels and coral and mermaids."

"And masts of ships and wrecked Spanish treasure. I wish we could find a gold doubloon,* or something," Cyril said.

"How did the sea get carried away?" Robert asked.

"Not in a pail, silly," said his brother. "Father says the earth got too hot underneath, like you do in bed sometimes, so it just hunched up its shoulders, and the sea had to slip off, like the blankets do off us, and the shoulder was left sticking out, and turned into dry land. Let's go and look for shells; I think that little cave looks likely, and I see something sticking out there like a bit of wrecked ship's anchor, and it's beastly hot in the Australian hole."

The others agreed, but Anthea went on digging. She always liked to finish a thing when she had once begun it. She felt it would be a disgrace to leave that hole without getting through to Australia.

The cave was disappointing, because there were no shells, and the wrecked ship's anchor turned out to be only the broken end of a pickaxe handle, and the cave party were just making up their minds that the sand makes you thirstier when it is not by the seaside, and someone had suggested going home for lemonade, when Anthea suddenly screamed:

"Cyril! Come here! Oh, come quick! It's alive! It'll get away! Quick!"

They all hurried back.

"It's a rat, I shouldn't wonder," said Robert. "Father says they infest old places—and this must be pretty old if the sea was here thousands of years ago."

"Perhaps it is a snake," said Jane, shuddering.

"Let's look," said Cyril, jumping into the hole. "I'm not afraid of snakes. I like them. If it is a snake I'll tame it, and it will follow me everywhere, and I'll let it sleep round my neck at night."

---

* Spanish gold coin; no longer in use.

Anthea suddenly screamed: "It's alive!"

"No, you won't," said Robert firmly. He shared Cyril's bedroom. "But you may if it's a rat."

"Oh, don't be silly!" said Anthea; "it's not a rat, it's much bigger. And it's not a snake. It's got feet; I saw them; and fur! No—not the spade. You'll hurt it! Dig with your hands."

"And let it hurt *me* instead! That's so likely, isn't it?" said Cyril, seizing a spade.

"Oh, don't!" said Anthea. "Squirrel, *don't*. I—it sounds silly, but it said something. It really and truly did."

"What?"

"It said, 'You let me alone.' "

But Cyril merely observed that his sister must have gone off her nut, and he and Robert dug with spades while Anthea sat on the edge of the hole, jumping up and down with hotness and anxiety. They dug carefully, and presently everyone could see that there really was something moving in the bottom of the Australian hole.

Then Anthea cried out, "I'm not afraid. Let me dig," and fell on her knees and began to scratch like a dog does when he has suddenly remembered where it was that he buried his bone.

"Oh, I felt fur," she cried, half laughing and half crying. "I did indeed! I did!" when suddenly a dry husky voice in the sand made them all jump back, and their hearts jumped nearly as fast as they did.

"Let me alone," it said. And now everyone heard the voice and looked at the others to see if they had too.

"But we want to see you," said Robert bravely.

"I wish you'd come out," said Anthea, also taking courage.

"Oh, well—if that's your wish," the voice said, and the sand stirred and spun and scattered, and something brown and furry and fat came rolling out into the hole and the sand fell off it, and it sat there yawning and rubbing the ends of its eyes with its hands.

"I believe I must have dropped asleep," it said, stretching itself.

The children stood round the hole in a ring, looking at the creature they had found. It was worth looking at. Its eyes were on long horns like a snail's eyes, and it could move them in and out like telescopes; it had ears like a bat's ears, and its tubby body was shaped like a spider's and covered with thick soft fur; its legs and arms were furry too, and it had hands and feet like a monkey's.

"What on earth is it?" Jane said. "Shall we take it home?"

The thing turned its long eyes to look at her, and said: "Does she always talk nonsense, or is it only the rubbish on her head that makes her silly?"

It looked scornfully at Jane's hat as it spoke.

"She doesn't mean to be silly," Anthea said gently; "we none of us do, whatever you may think! Don't be frightened; we don't want to hurt you, you know."

"Hurt *me!*" it said. "*Me* frightened? Upon my word! Why, you talk as if I were nobody in particular." All its fur stood out like a cat's when it is going to fight.

"Well," said Anthea, still kindly, "perhaps if we knew who you are in particular we could think of something to say that wouldn't make you cross. Everything we've said so far seems to have. Who are you? And don't get angry! Because really we don't know."

"You don't know?" it said. "Well, I knew the world had changed—

but—well, really—do you mean to tell me seriously you don't know a Psammead* when you see one?"

"A Sammyadd? That's Greek to me."

"So it is to everyone," said the creature sharply. "Well, in plain English, then, a *Sand-fairy*. Don't you know a Sand-fairy when you see one?"

It looked so grieved and hurt that Jane hastened to say, "Of course I see you are, *now*. It's quite plain now one comes to look at you."

"You came to look at me, several sentences ago," it said crossly, beginning to curl up again in the sand.

"Oh—don't go away again! Do talk some more," Robert cried. "I didn't know you were a Sand-fairy, but I knew directly I saw you that you were much the wonderfullest thing I'd ever seen."

The Sand-fairy seemed a shade less disagreeable after this.

"It isn't talking I mind," it said, "as long as you're reasonably civil. But I'm not going to make polite conversation for you. If you talk nicely to me, perhaps I'll answer you, and perhaps I won't. Now say something."

Of course no one could think of anything to say, but at last Robert thought of "How long have you lived here?" and he said it at once.

"Oh, ages—several thousand years," replied the Psammead.

"Tell us all about it. Do."

"It's all in books."

"You aren't!" Jane said. "Oh, tell us everything you can about yourself! We don't know anything about you, and you *are* so nice."

The Sand-fairy smoothed his long rat-like whiskers and smiled between them.

"Do please tell!" said the children all together.

It is wonderful how quickly you get used to things, even the most astonishing. Five minutes before, the children had had no more idea than you that there was such a thing as a sand-fairy in the world, and now they were talking to it as though they had known it all their lives.

It drew its eyes in and said:

---

* Nesbit derived this term for "Sand-fairy" from the Greek *psammos* (sand) and the names *naiad* (water nymph) and *dryad* (wood nymph) of Greek mythology.

"How very sunny it is—quite like old times. Where do you get your Megatheriums from now?"

"What?" said the children all at once. It is very difficult always to remember that "what" is not polite, especially in moments of surprise or agitation.

"Are Pterodactyls plentiful now?" the Sand-fairy went on.

The children were unable to reply.

"What do you have for breakfast?" the Fairy said impatiently, "and who gives it you?"

"Eggs and bacon, and bread-and-milk, and porridge and things. Mother gives it us. What are Mega-what's-its-names and Ptero-what-do-you-call-thems? And does anyone have them for breakfast?"

"Why, almost everyone had Pterodactyl for breakfast in my time! Pterodactyls were something like crocodiles and something like birds—I believe they were very good grilled. You see it was like this: of course there were heaps of sand-fairies then, and in the morning early you went out and hunted for them, and when you'd found one it gave you your wish. People used to send their little boys down to the seashore early in the morning before breakfast to get the day's wishes, and very often the eldest boy in the family would be told to wish for a Megatherium,* ready jointed for cooking. It was as big as an elephant, you see, so there was a good deal of meat on it. And if they wanted fish, the Ichthyosaurus was asked for—he was twenty to forty feet long, so there was plenty of him. And for poultry there was the Plesiosaurus; there were nice pickings on that too. Then the other children could wish for other things. But when people had dinner-parties it was nearly always Megatheriums; and Ichthyosaurus, because his fins were a great delicacy and his tail made soup."

"There must have been heaps and heaps of cold meat left over," said Anthea, who meant to be a good housekeeper some day.

"Oh no," said the Psammead, "that would never have done. Why, of course at sunset what was left over turned into stone. You find the stone bones of the Megatherium and things all over the place even now, they tell me."

---

* Elephant-size sloths that became extinct at the end of the last Ice Age, about 11,000 years ago.

"Who tell you?" asked Cyril; but the Sand-fairy frowned and began to dig very fast with its furry hands.

"Oh, don't go!" they all cried; "tell us more about it when it was Megatheriums for breakfast! Was the world like this then?"

It stopped digging.

"Not a bit," it said; "it was nearly all sand where I lived, and coal grew on trees, and the periwinkles were as big as tea-trays—you find them now; they're turned into stone. We sand-fairies used to live on the seashore, and the children used to come with their little flint-spades and flint-pails and make castles for us to live in. That's thousands of years ago, but I hear that children still build castles on the sand. It's difficult to break yourself of a habit."

"But why did you stop living in the castles?" asked Robert.

"It's a sad story," said the Psammead gloomily. "It was because they would build moats to the castles, and the nasty wet bubbling sea used to come in, and of course as soon as a sand-fairy got wet it caught cold, and generally died. And so there got to be fewer and fewer, and, whenever you found a fairy and had a wish, you used to wish for a Megatherium, and eat twice as much as you wanted, because it might be weeks before you got another wish."

"And did you get wet?" Robert inquired.

The Sand-fairy shuddered. "Only once," it said; "the end of the twelfth hair of my top left whisker—I feel the place still in damp weather. It was only once, but it was quite enough for me. I went away as soon as the sun had dried my poor dear whisker. I scurried away to the back of the beach, and dug myself a house deep in warm dry sand, and there I've been ever since. And the sea changed its lodgings afterwards. And now I'm not going to tell you another thing."

"Just one more, please," said the children. "Can you give wishes now?"

"Of course," said it; "didn't I give you yours a few minutes ago? You said, 'I wish you'd come out,' and I did."

"Oh, please, mayn't we have another?"

"Yes, but be quick about it. I'm tired of you."

I daresay you have often thought what you would do if you had three wishes given you, and have despised the old man and his wife in the black-pudding story,[2] and felt certain that if you had the chance you could think of three really useful wishes without a moment's hesitation. These children had often talked this matter over, but, now the chance had suddenly come to them, they could not make up their minds.

"Quick," said the Sand-fairy crossly. No one could think of anything, only Anthea did manage to remember a private wish of her own and Jane's which they had never told the boys. She knew the boys would not care about it—but still it was better than nothing.

"I wish we were all as beautiful as the day," she said in a great hurry.

The children looked at each other, but each could see that the others were not any better-looking than usual. The Psammead pushed out its long eyes, and seemed to be holding its breath and swelling itself out till it was twice as fat and furry as before. Suddenly it let its breath go in a long sigh.

"I'm really afraid I can't manage it," it said apologetically; "I must be out of practice."

The children were horribly disappointed.

"Oh, *do* try again!" they said.

"Well," said the Sand-fairy, "the fact is, I was keeping back a little strength to give the rest of you your wishes with. If you'll be contented with one wish a day amongst the lot of you I daresay I can screw myself up to it. Do you agree to that?"

"Yes, oh yes!" said Jane and Anthea. The boys nodded. They did not believe the Sand-fairy could do it. You can always make girls believe things much easier than you can boys.

It stretched out its eyes farther than ever, and swelled and swelled and swelled.

"I do hope it won't hurt itself," said Anthea.

"Or crack its skin," Robert said anxiously.

Everyone was very much relieved when the Sand-fairy, after getting so big that it almost filled up the hole in the sand, suddenly let out its breath and went back to its proper size.

"That's all right," it said, panting heavily. "It'll come easier to-morrow."

"Did it hurt much?" asked Anthea.

"Only my poor whisker, thank you," said he, "but you're a kind and thoughtful child. Good day."

It scratched suddenly and fiercely with its hands and feet, and disappeared in the sand. Then the children looked at each other, and each child suddenly found itself alone with three perfect strangers, all radiantly beautiful.

They stood for some moments in perfect silence. Each thought that its brothers and sisters had wandered off, and that these strange children had stolen up unnoticed while it was watching the swelling form of the Sand-fairy. Anthea spoke first—

"Excuse me," she said very politely to Jane, who now had enormous blue eyes and a cloud of russet hair, "but have you seen two little boys and a little girl anywhere about?"

"I was just going to ask you that," said Jane. And then Cyril cried:

"Why, it's you! I know the hole in your pinafore.* You *are* Jane, aren't you? And you're the Panther; I can see your dirty handkerchief that you forgot to change after you'd cut your thumb! Crikey! The wish has come off, after all, I say, am I as handsome as you are?"

"If you're Cyril, I liked you much better as you were before," said Anthea decidedly. "You look like the picture of the young chorister, with your golden hair; you'll die young, I shouldn't wonder. And if that's Robert, he's like an Italian organ-grinder. His hair's all black."

"You two girls are like Christmas cards, then—that's all—silly Christmas cards," said Robert angrily. "And Jane's hair is simply carrots."

It was indeed of that Venetian tint so much admired by artists.

"Well, it's no use finding fault with each other," said Anthea; "let's get the Lamb and lug it home to dinner. The servants will admire us most awfully, you'll see."

Baby was just waking when they got to him, and not one of the children but was relieved to find that he at least was not as beautiful as the day, but just the same as usual.

"I suppose he's too young to have wishes naturally," said Jane. "We shall have to mention him specially next time."

Anthea ran forward and held out her arms.

"Come to own Panther, ducky," she said.

The Baby looked at her disapprovingly, and put a sandy pink thumb in his mouth. Anthea was his favourite sister.

---

* Sleeveless, apron-like garment worn over other clothing.

"Come then," she said.

"G'way long!" said the Baby.

"Come to own Pussy," said Jane.

"Wants my Panty," said the Lamb dismally, and his lip trembled.

"Here, come on, Veteran," said Robert, "come and have a yidey on Yobby's back."

"Yah, narky narky boy," howled the Baby, giving way altogether. Then the children knew the worst. *The Baby did not know them!*

They looked at each other in despair, and it was terrible to each, in this dire emergency, to meet only the beautiful eyes of perfect strangers, instead of the merry, friendly, commonplace, twinkling, jolly little eyes of its own brothers and sisters.

"This is most truly awful," said Cyril when he had tried to lift up the Lamb, and the Lamb had scratched like a cat and bellowed like a bull. "We've got to *make friends* with him! I can't carry him home screaming like that. Fancy having to make friends with our own Baby!—it's too silly."

That, however, was exactly what they had to do. It took over an hour, and the task was not rendered any easier by the fact that the Lamb was by this time as hungry as a lion and as thirsty as a desert.

At last he consented to allow these strangers to carry him home by turns, but as he refused to hold on to such new acquaintances he was a dead weight and most exhausting.

"Thank goodness, we're home!" said Jane, staggering through the iron gate to where Martha, the nursemaid, stood at the front door shading her eyes with her hand and looking out anxiously. "Here! Do take Baby!"

Martha snatched the Baby from her arms.

"Thanks be, *he's* safe back," she said. "Where are the others, and whoever to goodness gracious are all of you?"

"We're *us*, of course," said Robert.

"And who's *us*, when you're at home?" asked Martha scornfully.

"I tell you it's *us*, only we're beautiful as the day," said Cyril. "I'm Cyril, and these are the others, and we're jolly hungry. Let us in, and don't be a silly idiot."

Martha merely dratted Cyril's impudence and tried to shut the door in his face.

The baby did not know them!

"I know we look different, but I'm Anthea, and we're so tired, and it's long past dinner-time."

"Then go home to your dinners, whoever you are; and if our children put you up to this play-acting you can tell them from me they'll catch it, so they know what to expect!" With that she did bang the door. Cyril rang the bell violently. No answer. Presently cook put her head out of a bedroom window and said:

"If you don't take yourselves off, and that precious sharp, I'll go and fetch the police." And she slammed down the window.

"It's no good," said Anthea. "Oh, do, do come away before we get sent to prison!"

The boys said it was nonsense, and the law of England couldn't put you in prison for just being as beautiful as the day, but all the same they followed the others out into the lane.

"We shall be our proper selves after sunset, I suppose," said Jane.

"I don't know," Cyril said sadly; "it mayn't be like that now—things have changed a good deal since Megatherium times."

"Oh," cried Anthea suddenly, "perhaps we shall turn into stone at sunset, like the Megatheriums did, so that there mayn't be any of us left over for the next day."

She began to cry, so did Jane. Even the boys turned pale. No one had the heart to say anything.

It was a horrible afternoon. There was no house near where the children could beg a crust of bread or even a glass of water. They were afraid to go to the village, because they had seen Martha go down there with a basket, and there was a local constable. True, they were all as beautiful as the day, but that is a poor comfort when you are as hungry as a hunter and as thirsty as a sponge.

Three times they tried in vain to get the servants in the White House to let them in and listen to their tale. And then Robert went alone, hoping to be able to climb in at one of the back windows and so open the door to the others. But all the windows were out of reach, and Martha emptied a toilet-jug of cold water over him from a top window, and said:

"Go along with you, you nasty little Eyetalian monkey."

It came at last to their sitting down in a row under the hedge, with their feet in a dry ditch, waiting for sunset, and wondering whether, when the sun did set, they would turn into stone, or only into their own old natural selves; and each of them still felt lonely and among strangers, and tried not to look at the others, for, though their voices were their own, their faces were so radiantly beautiful as to be quite irritating to look at.

"I don't believe we shall turn to stone," said Robert, breaking a long miserable silence, "because the Sand-fairy said he'd give us another wish to-morrow, and he couldn't if we were stone, could he?"

The others said "No," but they weren't at all comforted.

Another silence, longer and more miserable, was broken by Cyril's suddenly saying, "I don't want to frighten you girls, but I believe it's beginning with me already. My foot's quite dead. I'm turning to stone, I know I am, and so will you in a minute."

"Never mind," said Robert kindly, "perhaps you'll be the only

Martha emptied a toilet-jug of cold water over him

stone one, and the rest of us will be all right, and we'll cherish your
statue and hang garlands on it."

But when it turned out that Cyril's foot had only gone to sleep through his sitting too long with it under him, and when it came to life in an agony of pins and needles, the others were quite cross.

"Giving us such a fright for nothing!" said Anthea.

The third and miserablest silence of all was broken by Jane. She said: "If we do come out of this all right, we'll ask the Sammyadd to make it so that the servants don't notice anything different, no matter what wishes we have."

The others only grunted. They were too wretched even to make good resolutions.

At last hunger and fright and crossness and tiredness—four very nasty things—all joined together to bring one nice thing, and that was sleep. The children lay asleep in a row, with their beautiful eyes shut and their beautiful mouths open. Anthea woke first. The sun had set, and the twilight was coming on.

Anthea pinched herself very hard, to make sure, and when she found she could still feel pinching she decided that she was not stone, and then she pinched the others. They, also, were soft.

"Wake up," she said, almost in tears of joy; "it's all right, we're not stone. And oh, Cyril, how nice and ugly you do look, with your old freckles and your brown hair and your little eyes. And so do you all!" she added, so that they might not feel jealous.

When they got home they were very much scolded by Martha, who told them about the strange children.

"A good-looking lot, I must say, but that impudent."

"I know," said Robert, who knew by experience how hopeless it would be to try to explain things to Martha.

"And where on earth have you been all this time, you naughty little things, you?"

"In the lane."

"Why didn't you come home hours ago?"

"We couldn't because of them," said Anthea.

"Who?"

"The children who were as beautiful as the day. They kept us there till after sunset. We couldn't come back till they'd gone. You don't know how we hated them! Oh, do, do give us some supper—we are so hungry."

"Hungry! I should think so," said Martha angrily; "out all day like this. Well, I hope it'll be a lesson to you not to go picking up with strange children—down here after measles, as likely as not! Now mind, if you see them again, don't you speak to them—not one word nor so much as a look—but come straight away and tell me. I'll spoil their beauty for them!"

"If ever we *do* see them again we'll tell you," Anthea said; and Robert, fixing his eyes fondly on the cold beef that was being brought in on a tray by cook, added in heartfelt undertones—

"And we'll take jolly good care we never *do* see them again."

And they never have.

CHAPTER II

GOLDEN GUINEAS

Anthea woke in the morning from a very real sort of dream, in which she was walking in the Zoological Gardens on a pouring wet day without any umbrella. The animals seemed desperately unhappy because of the rain, and were all growling gloomily. When she awoke, both the growling and the rain went on just the same. The growling was the heavy regular breathing of her sister Jane, who had a slight cold and was still asleep. The rain fell in slow drops on to Anthea's face from the wet corner of a bath-towel which her brother Robert was gently squeezing the water out of, to wake her up, as he now explained.

"Oh, drop it!" she said rather crossly; so he did, for he was not a brutal brother, though very ingenious in apple-pie beds,* booby-traps, original methods of awakening sleeping relatives, and the other little accomplishments which make home happy.

"I had such a funny dream," Anthea began.

"So did I," said Jane, wakening suddenly and without warning. "I dreamed we found a Sand-fairy in the gravel-pits, and it said it was a Sammyadd, and we might have a new wish every day, and—"

"But that's what I dreamed," said Robert. "I was just going to tell you—and we had the first wish directly it said so. And I dreamed you girls were donkeys enough to ask for us all to be beautiful as the day, and we jolly well were, and it was perfectly beastly."

"But *can* different people all dream the same thing?" said Anthea, sitting up in bed, "because I dreamed all that as well as about the Zoo, and the rain; and Baby didn't know us in my dream, and the servants shut us out of the house because the radiantness of our beauty was such a complete disguise, and—"

---

* Prank in which bedsheets are doubled up, like an apple turnover, so that a person cannot stretch out her legs under them.

The rain fell in slow drops on to Anthea's face

The voice of the eldest brother sounded from across the landing.

"Come on, Robert," it said, "you'll be late for breakfast again—unless you mean to shirk your bath like you did on Tuesday."

"I say, come here a sec," Robert replied. "I didn't shirk it; I had it after brekker* in father's dressing-room, because ours was emptied away."

Cyril appeared in the doorway, partially clothed.

"Look here," said Anthea, "we've all had such an odd dream. We've all dreamed we found a Sand-fairy."

Her voice died away before Cyril's contemptuous glance. "Dream?" he said, "you little sillies, it's *true*. I tell you it all happened. That's why I'm so keen on being down early. We'll go up there directly after brekker, and have another wish. Only we'll make up our minds, solid, before we go, what it is we do want, and no one must ask for anything unless the others agree first. No more peerless beauties for this child, thank you. Not if I know it!"

The other three dressed, with their mouths open. If all that dream about the Sand-fairy was real, this real dressing seemed very

---

* Breakfast (slang).

like a dream, the girls thought. Jane felt that Cyril was right, but Anthea was not sure, till after they had seen Martha and heard her full and plain reminders about their naughty conduct the day before. Then Anthea was sure. "Because," said she, "servants never dream anything but the things in the *Dream-book*, like snakes and oysters and going to a wedding—that means a funeral, and snakes are a false female friend, and oysters are babies."

"Talking of babies," said Cyril, "where's the Lamb?"

"Martha's going to take him to Rochester* to see her cousins. Mother said she might. She's dressing him now," said Jane, "in his very best coat and hat. Bread-and-butter, please."

"She seems to like taking him too," said Robert in a tone of wonder.

"Servants *do* like taking babies to see their relations," Cyril said. "I've noticed it before—especially in their best things."

"I expect they pretend they're their own babies, and that they're not servants at all, but married to noble dukes of high degree, and they say the babies are the little dukes and duchesses," Jane suggested dreamily, taking more marmalade. "I expect that's what Martha'll say to her cousin. She'll enjoy herself most frightfully."

"She won't enjoy herself most frightfully carrying our infant duke to Rochester," said Robert, "not if she's anything like me—she won't."

"Fancy walking to Rochester with the Lamb on your back! Oh, crikey!" said Cyril in full agreement.

"She's going by carrier," said Jane. "Let's see them off, then we shall have done a polite and kindly act, and we shall be quite sure we've got rid of them for the day."

So they did.

Martha wore her Sunday dress of two shades of purple, so tight in the chest that it made her stoop, and her blue hat with the pink cornflowers and white ribbon. She had a yellow-lace collar with a green bow. And the Lamb had indeed his very best cream-coloured silk coat and hat. It was a smart party that the carrier's cart picked up

---

* Small town in Kent, east of London.

at the Cross Roads. When its white tilt* and red wheels had slowly
vanished in a swirl of chalk-dust—

"And now for the Sammyadd!" said Cyril, and off they went.

As they went they decided on the wish they would ask for. Although they were all in a great hurry they did not try to climb down
the sides of the gravel-pit, but went round by the safe lower road, as
if they had been carts. They had made a ring of stones round the place
where the Sand-fairy had disappeared, so they easily found the spot.
The sun was burning and bright, and the sky was deep blue—without a cloud. The sand was very hot to touch.

"Oh—suppose it was only a dream, after all," Robert said as the
boys uncovered their spades from the sandheap where they had
buried them and began to dig.

"Suppose you were a sensible chap," said Cyril; "one's quite as
likely as the other!"

"Suppose you kept a civil tongue in your head," Robert snapped.

"Suppose we girls take a turn," said Jane, laughing. "You boys
seem to be getting very warm."

"Suppose you don't come shoving your silly oar in," said Robert,
who was now warm indeed.

"We won't," said Anthea quickly. "Robert dear, don't be so
grumpy—we won't say a word, you shall be the one to speak to the
Fairy and tell him what we've decided to wish for. You'll say it much
better than we shall."

"Suppose you drop being a little humbug," said Robert, but not
crossly. "Look out—dig with your hands, now!"

So they did, and presently uncovered the spider-shaped brown
hairy body, long arms and legs, bat's ears and snail's eyes of the Sand-
fairy himself. Everyone drew a deep breath of satisfaction, for now of
course it couldn't have been a dream.

The Psammead sat up and shook the sand out of its fur.

"How's your left whisker this morning?" said Anthea politely.

"Nothing to boast of," said it, "it had rather a restless night. But
thank you for asking."

"I say," said Robert, "do you feel up to giving wishes today, be-

---

* Canopy.

cause we very much want an extra besides the regular one? The extra's a very little one," he added reassuringly.

"Humph!" said the Sand-fairy. (If you read this story aloud, please pronounce "humph" exactly as it is spelt, for that is how he said it.) "Humph! Do you know, until I heard you being disagreeable to each other just over my head, and so loud too, I really quite thought I had dreamed you all. I do have very odd dreams sometimes."

"Do you?" Jane hurried to say, so as to get away from the subject of disagreeableness. "I wish," she added politely, "you'd tell us about your dreams—they must be awfully interesting."

"Is that the day's wish?" said the Sand-fairy, yawning.

Cyril muttered something about "just like a girl," and the rest stood silent. If they said "Yes," then good-bye to the other wishes they had decided to ask for. If they said "No," it would be very rude, and they had all been taught manners, and had learned a little too, which is not at all the same thing. A sigh of relief broke from all lips when the Sand-fairy said:

"If I do I shan't have strength to give you a second wish; not even good tempers, or common sense, or manners, or little things like that."

"We don't want you to put yourself out at all about these things, we can manage them quite well ourselves," said Cyril eagerly; while the others looked guiltily at each other, and wished the Fairy would not keep all on about good tempers, but give them one good rowing if it wanted to, and then have done with it.

"Well," said the Psammead, putting out his long snail's eyes so suddenly that one of them nearly went into the round boy's eyes of Robert, "let's have the little wish first."

"We don't want the servants to notice the gifts you give us."

"Are kind enough to give us," said Anthea in a whisper.

"Are kind enough to give us, I mean," said Robert.

The Fairy swelled himself out a bit, let his breath go, and said—

"I've done that for you—it was quite easy. People don't notice things much, anyway. What's the next wish?"

"We want," said Robert slowly, "to be rich beyond the dreams of something or other."

"Avarice," said Jane.

"So it is," said the Fairy unexpectedly. "But it won't do you much good, that's one comfort," it muttered to itself. "Come—I can't go beyond dreams, you know! How much do you want, and will you have it in gold or notes?"

"Gold, please—and millions of it."

"This gravel-pit full be enough?" said the Fairy in an off-hand manner.

"Oh *yes!*"

"Then get out before I begin, or you'll be buried alive in it."

It made its skinny arms so long, and waved them so frighteningly, that the children ran as hard as they could towards the road by which carts used to come to the gravel-pits. Only Anthea had presence of mind enough to shout a timid "Good-morning, I hope your whisker will be better tomorrow," as she ran.

On the road they turned and looked back, and they had to shut their eyes, and open them very slowly, a little bit at a time, because the sight was too dazzling for their eyes to be able to bear it. It was something like trying to look at the sun at high noon on Midsummer Day.* For the whole of the sand-pit was full, right up to the very top, with new shining gold pieces, and all the little sand-martins' little front doors were covered out of sight. Where the road for the carts wound into the gravel-pit the gold lay in heaps like stones lie by the roadside, and a great bank of shining gold shelved down from where it lay flat and smooth between the tall sides of the gravel-pit. And all the gleaming heap was minted gold. And on the sides and edges of these countless coins the midday sun shone and sparkled, and glowed and gleamed till the quarry looked like the mouth of a smelting furnace, or one of the fairy halls that you see sometimes in the sky at sunset.

The children stood with their mouths open, and no one said a word.

At last Robert stopped and picked up one of the loose coins from the edge of the heap by the cart-road, and looked at it. He looked on both sides. Then he said in a low voice, quite different to his own, "It's not sovereigns."†

---

* June 24, the day on which the summer solstice, the longest day of the year, is traditionally celebrated.

† Gold coins once used in England.

All the gleaming heap was minted gold

"It's gold, anyway," said Cyril. And now they all began to talk at once. They all picked up the golden treasure by handfuls, and let it run through their fingers like water, and the chink it made as it fell was wonderful music. At first they quite forgot to think of spending the money, it was so nice to play with. Jane sat down between two heaps of gold and Robert began to bury her, as you bury your father in sand when you are at the seaside and he has gone to sleep on the beach with the newspaper over his face. But Jane was not half buried before she cried out, "Oh, stop, it's too heavy! It hurts!"

Robert said "Bosh!" and went on.

"Let me out, I tell you," cried Jane, and was taken out, very white, and trembling a little.

"You've no idea what it's like," said she; "it's like stones on you—or like chains."

"Look here," Cyril said, "if this is to do us any good, it's no good our staying gasping at it like this. Let's fill our pockets and go and buy things. Don't you forget, it won't last after sunset. I wish we'd asked the Sammyadd why things don't turn to stone. Perhaps this will. I'll tell you what, there's a pony and cart in the village."

"Do you want to buy that?" asked Jane.

"No, silly—we'll hire it. And then we'll go to Rochester and buy heaps and heaps of things. Look here, let's each take as much as we can carry. But it's not sovereigns. They've got a man's head on one side and a thing like the ace of spades on the other. Fill your pockets with it, I tell you, and come along. You can jaw as we go—if you must jaw."

Cyril sat down and began to fill his pockets.

"You made fun of me for getting father to have nine pockets in my Norfolks,"* said he, "but now you see!"

They did. For when Cyril had filled his nine pockets and his handkerchief and the space between himself and his shirt front with the gold coins, he had to stand up. But he staggered, and had to sit down again in a hurry.

"Throw out some of the cargo," said Robert. "You'll sink the ship, old chap. That comes of nine pockets."

And Cyril had to.

---

* Loose-fitting jackets, sometimes part of a suit with knee breeches.

He staggered, and had to sit down again

Then they set off to walk to the village. It was more than a mile, and the road was very dusty indeed, and the sun seemed to get hotter and hotter, and the gold in their pockets got heavier and heavier.

It was Jane who said, "I don't see how we're to spend it all. There must be thousands of pounds among the lot of us. I'm going to leave some of mine behind this stump in the hedge. And directly we get to the village we'll buy some biscuits; I know it's long past dinner-time." She took out a handful or two of gold and hid it in the hollows of an old hornbeam.* "How round and yellow they are," she said. "Don't you wish they were gingerbread nuts and we were going to eat them?"

* Tree; member of the birch family.

"Well, they're not, and we're not," said Cyril. "Come on!"

But they came on heavily and wearily. Before they reached the village, more than one stump in the hedge concealed its little hoard of hidden treasure. Yet they reached the village with about twelve hundred guineas* in their pockets. But in spite of this inside wealth they looked quite ordinary outside, and no one would have thought they could have more than a half-crown each at the outside. The haze of heat, the blue of the wood smoke, made a sort of dim, misty cloud over the red roofs of the village. The four sat down heavily on the first bench they came to. It happened to be outside the Blue Boar Inn.

It was decided that Cyril should go into the Blue Boar and ask for ginger-beer, because, as Anthea said, "It is not wrong for men to go into public houses, only for children. And Cyril is nearer to being a man than us, because he is the eldest." So he went. The others sat in the sun and waited.

"Oh, hats, how hot it is!" said Robert. "Dogs put their tongues out when they're hot; I wonder if it would cool us at all to put out ours?"

"We might try," Jane said; and they all put their tongues out as far as ever they could go, so that it quite stretched their throats, but it only seemed to make them thirstier than ever, besides annoying everyone who went by. So they took their tongues in again, just as Cyril came back with the ginger-beer.

"I had to pay for it out of my own two-and-seven-pence, though, that I was going to buy rabbits with," he said. "They wouldn't change the gold. And when I pulled out a handful the man just laughed and said it was card-counters.† And I got some sponge-cakes too, out of a glass jar on the bar-counter. And some biscuits with caraways in."

The sponge-cakes were both soft and dry and the biscuits were dry too, and yet soft, which biscuits ought not to be. But the ginger-beer made up for everything.

"It's my turn now to try to buy something with the money," Anthea said; "I'm next eldest. Where is the pony-cart kept?"

It was at The Chequers, and Anthea went in the back way to the

---

* English gold coins worth 21 shillings; not minted since 1813.

† Imitation coins used as stakes in card games.

They all put their tongues out

yard, because they all knew that little girls ought not to go into the bars of public-houses. She came out, as she herself said, "pleased but not proud."

"He'll be ready in a brace of shakes,* he says," she remarked, "and he's to have one sovereign—or whatever it is—to drive us into Rochester and back, besides waiting there till we've got everything we want. I think I managed very well."

---

* Quickly.

"You think yourself jolly clever, I daresay," said Cyril moodily. "How did you do it?"

"I wasn't jolly clever enough to go taking handfuls of money out of my pocket, to make it seem cheap, anyway," she retorted. "I just found a young man doing something to a horse's leg with a sponge and a pail. And I held out one sovereign, and I said, 'Do you know what this is?' He said, 'No,' and he'd call his father. And the old man came, and he said it was a spade guinea; and he said was it my own to do as I liked with, and I said 'Yes'; and I asked about the pony-cart, and I said he could have the guinea if he'd drive us in to Rochester. And his name is S. Crispin. And he said, 'Right oh.'"

It was a new sensation to be driven in a smart ponytrap along pretty country roads; it was very pleasant too (which is not always the case with new sensations), quite apart from the beautiful plans of spending the money which each child made as they went along, silently of course and quite to itself, for they felt it would never have done to let the old innkeeper hear them talk in the affluent sort of way they were thinking. The old man put them down by the bridge at their request.

"If you were going to buy a carriage and horses, where would you go?" asked Cyril, as if he were only asking for the sake of something to say.

"Billy Peasemarsh, at the Saracen's Head," said the old man promptly. "Though all forbid I should recommend any man where it's a question of horses, no more than I'd take anybody else's recommending if I was a-buying one. But if your pa's thinking of a turnout* of any sort, there ain't a straighter man in Rochester, nor a civiller spoken, than Billy, though I says it."

"Thank you," said Cyril. "The Saracen's Head."

And now the children began to see one of the laws of nature turn upside down and stand on its head like an acrobat. Any grown-up persons would tell you that money is hard to get and easy to spend. But the fairy money had been easy to get, and spending it was not only hard, it was almost impossible. The tradespeople of Rochester seemed to shrink, to a tradesperson, from the glittering fairy gold

---

* Carriage with horses, harness, and driver.

("furrin money" they called it, for the most part). To begin with, Anthea, who had had the misfortune to sit on her hat earlier in the day, wished to buy another. She chose a very beautiful one, trimmed with pink roses and the blue breasts of peacocks. It was marked in the window, "Paris Model, three guineas."

"I'm glad," she said, "because, if it says guineas, it means guineas, and not sovereigns, which we haven't got."

But when she took three of the spade guineas in her hand, which was by this time rather dirty owing to her not having put on gloves before going to the gravel-pit, the black-silk young lady in the shop looked very hard at her, and went and whispered something to an older and uglier lady, also in black silk, and then they gave her back the money and said it was not current coin.

"It's good money," said Anthea, "and it's my own."

"I daresay," said the lady, "but it's not the kind of money that's fashionable now, and we don't care about taking it."

"I believe they think we've stolen it," said Anthea, rejoining the others in the street; "if we had gloves they wouldn't think we were so dishonest. It's my hands being so dirty fills their minds with doubts."

So they chose a humble shop, and the girls bought cotton gloves, the kind at sixpence three-farthings, but when they offered a guinea the woman looked at it through her spectacles and said she had no change; so the gloves had to be paid for out of Cyril's two-and-sevenpence that he meant to buy rabbits with, and so had the green imitation crocodile-skin purse at nine-pence-halfpenny which had been bought at the same time. They tried several more shops, the kinds where you buy toys and scent, and silk handkerchiefs and books, and fancy boxes of stationery, and photographs of objects of interest in the vicinity. But nobody cared to change a guinea that day in Rochester, and as they went from shop to shop they got dirtier and dirtier, and their hair got more and more untidy, and Jane slipped and fell down on a part of the road where a water-cart had just gone by. Also they got very hungry, but they found no one would give them anything to eat for their guineas. After trying two pastrycooks in vain, they became so hungry, perhaps from the smell of the cake in the shops, as Cyril suggested, that they formed a plan of campaign in whispers and carried it out in desperation. They marched into a third pastrycook's—Beale his name was—and before the people behind

Mr. Beale snatched the coin and bit it

the counter could interfere each child had seized three new penny buns, clapped the three together between its dirty hands, and taken a big bite out of the triple sandwich. Then they stood at bay, with the twelve buns in their hands and their mouths very full indeed. The shocked pastrycook bounded round the corner.

"Here," said Cyril, speaking as distinctly as he could, and holding out the guinea he got ready before entering the shop, "pay yourself out of that."

Mr. Beale snatched the coin, bit it, and put it in his pocket.

"Off you go," he said, brief and stern like the man in the song.

"But the change?" said Anthea, who, had a saving mind.

"Change!" said the man. "I'll change you! Hout you goes; and you may think yourselves lucky I don't send for the police to find out where you got it!"

In the Castle Gardens the millionaires finished the buns, and though the curranty softness of these were delicious, and acted like a charm in raising the spirits of the party, yet even the stoutest heart quailed at the thought of venturing to sound Mr. Billy Peasemarsh at the Saracen's Head on the subject of a horse and carriage. The boys would have given up the idea, but Jane was always a hopeful child, and Anthea generally an obstinate one, and their earnestness prevailed.

The whole party, by this time indescribably dirty, therefore betook itself to the Saracen's Head. The yard-method of attack having been successful at The Chequers was tried again here. Mr. Peasemarsh was in the yard, and Robert opened the business in these terms—

"They tell me you have a lot of horses and carriages to sell." It had been agreed that Robert should be spokesman, because in books it is always the gentlemen who buy horses, and not ladies, and Cyril had had his go at the Blue Boar.

"They tell you true, young man," said Mr. Peasemarsh. He was a long lean man, with very blue eyes and a tight mouth and narrow lips.

"We should like to buy some, please," said Robert politely.

"I daresay you would."

"Will you show us a few, please? To choose from."

"Who are you a-kiddin of?" inquired Mr. Billy Peasemarsh. "Was you sent here of a message?"

"I tell you," said Robert, "we want to buy some horses and carriages, and a man told us you were straight and civil spoken, but I shouldn't wonder if he was mistaken."

"Upon my sacred!" said Mr. Peasemarsh. "Shall I trot the whole stable out for your Honour's worship to see? Or shall I send round to the Bishop's to see if he's a nag or two to dispose of?"

"Please do," said Robert, "if it's not too much trouble. It would be very kind of you."

Mr. Peasemarsh put his hands in his pockets and laughed, and they did not like the way he did it. Then he shouted "Willum!"

A stooping ostler appeared in a stable door.

"Here, Willum, come and look at this 'ere young dook! Wants to buy the whole stud, lock, stock, and bar'l. And ain't got tuppence* in his pocket to bless hisself with, I'll go bail!"†

---

* Twopence; sum equal to two British pennies.

† I'll guarantee (slang).

Willum's eyes followed his master's pointing thumb with contemptuous interest.

"Do 'e, for sure?" he said.

But Robert spoke, though both the girls were now pulling at his jacket and begging him to "come along." He spoke, and he was very angry; he said:

"I'm not a young duke, and I never pretended to be. And as for tuppence—what do you call this?" And before the others could stop him he had pulled out two fat handfuls of shining guineas, and held them out for Mr. Peasemarsh to look at. He did look. He snatched one up in his finger and thumb. He bit it, and Jane expected him to say, "The best horse in my stables is at your service." But the others knew better. Still it was a blow, even to the most desponding, when he said shortly:

"Willum, shut the yard doors," and Willum grinned and went to shut them.

"Good-afternoon," said Robert hastily; "we shan't buy any of your horses now, whatever you say, and I hope it'll be a lesson to you." He had seen a little side gate open, and was moving towards it as he spoke. But Billy Peasemarsh put himself in the way.

"Not so fast, you young off-scouring!"* he said. "Willum, fetch the pleece."

Willum went. The children stood huddled together like frightened sheep, and Mr. Peasemarsh spoke to them till the pleece arrived. He said many things. Among other things he said:

"Nice lot you are, aren't you, coming tempting honest men with your guineas!"

"They *are* our guineas," said Cyril boldly.

"Oh, of course we don't know all about that, no more we don't—oh no—course not! And dragging little gells into it, too. 'Ere—I'll let the gells go if you'll come along to the pleece quiet."

"We won't be let go," said Jane heroically; "not without the boys. It's our money just as much as theirs, you wicked old man."

"Where'd you get it, then?" said the man, softening slightly, which was not at all what the boys expected when Jane began to call names.

---

* Worthless or contemptible person.

Jane cast a silent glance of agony at the others.

"Lost your tongue, eh? Got it fast enough when it's for calling names with. Come, speak up! Where'd you get it?"

"Out of the gravel-pit," said truthful Jane.

"Next article," said the man.

"I tell you we did," Jane said. "There's a fairy there—all over brown fur—with ears like a bat's and eyes like a snail's, and he gives you a wish a day, and they all come true."

"Touched in the head, eh?" said the man in a low voice, "all the more shame to you boys dragging the poor afflicted child into your sinful burglaries."

"She's not mad; it's true," said Anthea; "there is a fairy. If I ever see him again I'll wish for something for you; at least I would if vengeance wasn't wicked—so there!"

"Lor' lumme,"* said Billy Peasemarsh, "if there ain't another on 'em!"

And now Willum came back with a spiteful grin on his face, and at his back a policeman, with whom Mr. Peasemarsh spoke long in a hoarse earnest whisper.

"I daresay you're right," said the policeman at last. "Anyway, I'll take 'em up on a charge of unlawful possession, pending inquiries. And the magistrate will deal with the case. Send the afflicted ones to a home, as likely as not, and the boys to a reformatory. Now then, come along, youngsters! No use making a fuss. You bring the gells along, Mr. Peasemarsh, sir, and I'll shepherd the boys."

Speechless with rage and horror, the four children were driven along the streets of Rochester. Tears of anger and shame blinded them, so that when Robert ran right into a passer-by he did not recognize her till a well-known voice said, "Well, if ever I did! Oh, Master Robert, whatever have you been a doing of now?" And another voice, quite as well known, said, "Panty; want go own Panty!"

They had run into Martha and the baby!

Martha behaved admirably. She refused to believe a word of the policeman's story, or of Mr. Peasemarsh's either, even when they made Robert turn out his pockets in an archway and show the guineas.

---

* Lord love me (dialect).

They had run into Martha and the baby!

"I don't see nothing," she said. "You've gone out of your senses, you two! There ain't any gold there—only the poor child's hands, all over crock* and dirt, and like the very chimbley.† Oh, that I should ever see the day!"

And the children thought this very noble of Martha, even if rather wicked, till they remembered how the Fairy had promised that the servants should never notice any of the fairy gifts. So of course Martha couldn't see the gold, and so was only speaking the truth, and that was quite right, of course, but not extra noble.

It was getting dusk when they reached the police-station. The policeman told his tale to an inspector, who sat in a large bare room with a thing like a clumsy nursery-fender‡ at one end to put prisoners in. Robert wondered whether it was a cell or a dock.

"Produce the coins, officer," said the inspector.

"Turn out your pockets," said the constable.

Cyril desperately plunged his hands in his pockets, stood still a moment, and then began to laugh—an odd sort of laugh that hurt, and that felt much more like crying. His pockets were empty. So were the pockets of the others. For of course at sunset all the fairy gold had vanished away.

"Turn out your pockets, and stop that noise," said the inspector.

Cyril turned out his pockets, every one of the nine which enriched his Norfolk suit. And every pocket was empty.

"Well!" said the inspector.

"I don't know how they done it—artful little beggars! They walked in front of me the 'ole way, so as for me to keep my eye on them and not to attract a crowd and obstruct the traffic."

"It's very remarkable," said the inspector, frowning.

"If you've quite done a-browbeating of the innocent children," said Martha, "I'll hire a private carriage and we'll drive home to their papa's mansion. You'll hear about this again, young man!—I told you they hadn't got any gold, when you were pretending to see it in their poor helpless hands. It's early in the day for a constable on duty not

---

* Soot.

† Chimney (dialect).

‡ Barrier used in nurseries to restrict children's movements.

He said, "Now then!" to the policeman and Mr. Peasemarsh

to be able to trust his own eyes. As to the other one, the less said the better; he keeps the Saracen's Head, and he knows best what his liquor's like."

"Take them away, for goodness' sake," said the inspector crossly. But as they left the police-station he said, "Now then!" to the policeman and Mr. Peasemarsh, and he said it twenty times as crossly as he had spoken to Martha.

Martha was as good as her word. She took them home in a very grand carriage, because the carrier's cart was gone, and, though she had stood by them so nobly with the police, she was so angry with them as soon as they were alone for "trapseing into Rochester by themselves," that none of them dared to mention the old man with the pony-cart from the village who was waiting for them in Rochester. And so, after one day of boundless wealth, the children found themselves sent to bed in deep disgrace, and only enriched by two pairs of cotton gloves, dirty inside because of the state of the hands they had been put on to cover, an imitation crocodile-skin purse, and twelve penny buns, long since digested.

The thing that troubled them most was the fear that the old gentleman's guinea might have disappeared at sunset with all the rest, so they went down to the village next day to apologize for not meeting him in Rochester, and to see. They found him very friendly. The guinea had not disappeared, and he had bored a hole in it and hung it on his watch-chain. As for the guinea the baker took, the children felt they could not care whether it had vanished or not, which was not perhaps very honest, but on the other hand was not wholly unnatural. But afterwards this preyed on Anthea's mind, and at last she secretly sent twelve stamps by post to "Mr. Beale, Baker, Rochester." Inside she wrote, "To pay for the buns." I hope the guinea did disappear, for that pastrycook was really not at all a nice man, and, besides, penny buns are seven for sixpence in all really respectable shops.

CHAPTER III

BEING WANTED

The morning after the children had been the possessors of boundless wealth, and had been unable to buy anything really useful or enjoyable with it, except two pairs of cotton gloves, twelve penny buns, an imitation crocodile-skin purse, and a ride in a pony-cart, they awoke without any of the enthusiastic happiness which they had felt on the previous day when they remembered how they had had the luck to find a Psammead, or Sand-fairy; and to receive its promise to grant them a new wish every day. For now they had had two wishes, Beauty and Wealth, and neither had exactly made them happy. But the happening of strange things, even if they are not completely pleasant things, is more amusing than those times when nothing happens but meals, and they are not always completely pleasant, especially on the days when it is cold mutton or hash.

There was no chance of talking things over before breakfast, because everyone overslept itself, as it happened, and it needed a vigorous and determined struggle to get dressed so as to be only ten minutes late for breakfast. During this meal some efforts were made to deal with the question of the Psammead in an impartial spirit, but it is very difficult to discuss anything thoroughly and at the same time to attend faithfully to your baby brother's breakfast needs. The Baby was particularly lively that morning. He not only wriggled his body through the bar of his high chair, and hung by his head, choking and purple, but he collared a tablespoon with desperate suddenness, hit Cyril heavily on the head with it, and then cried because it was taken away from him. He put his fat fist in his bread-and-milk, and demanded "nam," which was only allowed for tea. He sang, he put his feet on the table—he clamoured to "go walky." The conversation was something like this:

"Look here—about that Sand-fairy—Look out!—he'll have the milk over."

Milk removed to a safe distance.

"Yes—about that Fairy—No, Lamb dear, give Panther the narky poon."

Then Cyril tried. "Nothing we've had yet has turned out—He nearly had the mustard that time!"

"I wonder whether we'd better wish—Hullo!—you've done it now, my boy!" And, in a flash of glass and pink baby-paws, the bowl of golden carp in the middle of the table rolled on its side, and poured a flood of mixed water and goldfish into the Baby's lap and into the laps of the others.

Everyone was almost as much upset as the goldfish: the Lamb only remaining calm. When the pool on the floor had been mopped up, and the leaping, gasping goldfish had been collected and put back in the water, the Baby was taken away to be entirely redressed by Martha, and most of the others had to change completely. The pinafores and jackets that had been bathed in goldfish-and-water were hung out to dry, and then it turned out that Jane must either mend the dress she had torn the day before or appear all day in her best petticoat. It was white and soft and frilly, and trimmed with lace, and very, very pretty, quite as pretty as a frock, if not more so. Only it was not a frock, and Martha's word was law. She wouldn't let Jane wear her best frock, and she refused to listen for a moment to Robert's suggestion that Jane should wear her best petticoat and call it a dress.

"It's not respectable," she said. And when people say that, it's no use anyone's saying anything. You will find this out for yourselves some day.

So there was nothing for it but for Jane to mend her frock. The hole had been torn the day before when she happened to tumble down in the High Street of Rochester, just where a water-cart had passed on its silvery way. She had grazed her knee, and her stocking was much more than grazed, and her dress was cut by the same stone which had attended to the knee and the stocking. Of course the others were not such sneaks as to abandon a comrade in misfortune, so they all sat on the grass-plot round the sundial, and Jane darned away for dear life. The Lamb was still in the hands of Martha having its clothes changed, so conversation was possible.

Anthea and Robert timidly tried to conceal their inmost thought, which was that the Psammead was not to be trusted; but Cyril said:

"Speak out—say what you've got to say—I hate hinting, and 'don't know,' and sneakish ways like that."

So then Robert said, as in honour bound: "Sneak yourself—Anthea and me weren't so goldfishy as you two were, so we got changed quicker, and we've had time to think it over, and if you ask me—"

"I didn't ask you," said Jane, biting off a needleful of thread as she had always been strictly forbidden to do.

"I don't care who asks or who doesn't," said Robert, "but Anthea and I think the Sammyadd is a spiteful brute. If it can give us our wishes I suppose it can give itself its own, and I feel almost sure it wishes every time that our wishes shan't do us any good. Let's let the tiresome beast alone, and just go and have a jolly good game of forts, on our own, in the chalk-pit."

(You will remember that the happily situated house where these children were spending their holidays lay between a chalk-quarry and a gravel-pit.)

Cyril and Jane were more hopeful—they generally were.

"I don't think the Sammyadd does it on purpose," Cyril said; "and, after all, it was silly to wish for boundless wealth. Fifty pounds in two-shilling pieces would have been much more sensible. And wishing to be beautiful as the day was simply donkeyish. I don't want to be disagreeable, but it was. We must try to find a really useful wish, and wish it."

Jane dropped her work and said:

"I think so too, it's too silly to have a chance like this and not use it. I never heard of anyone else outside a book who had such a chance; there must be simply heaps of things we could wish for that wouldn't turn out Dead Sea fish,* like these two things have. Do let's think hard, and wish something nice, so that we can have a real jolly day—what there is left of it."

---

* Worthless (slang).

Jane darned away again like mad, for time was indeed getting on, and everyone began to talk at once. If you had been there you could not possibly have made head or tail of the talk, but these children were used to talking "by fours,"* as soldiers march, and each of them could say what it had to say quite comfortably, and listen to the agreeable sound of its own voice, and at the same time have three-quarters of two sharp ears to spare for listening to what the others said. That is an easy example in multiplication of vulgar fractions, but, as I daresay you can't do even that, I won't ask you to tell me whether $\frac{3}{4} \times 2 = 1\frac{1}{2}$, but I will ask you to believe me that this was the amount of ear each child was able to lend to the others. Lending ears was common in Roman times,† as we learn from Shakespeare; but I fear I am getting too instructive.

When the frock was darned, the start for the gravel-pit was delayed by Martha's insisting on everybody's washing its hands—which was nonsense, because nobody had been doing anything at all, except Jane, and how can you get dirty doing nothing? That is a difficult question, and I cannot answer it on paper. In real life I could very soon show you—or you me, which is much more likely.

During the conversation in which the six ears were lent (there were four children, so *that* sum comes right), it had been decided that fifty pounds in two-shilling pieces was the right wish to have. And the lucky children, who could have anything in the wide world by just wishing for it, hurriedly started for the gravel-pit to express their wishes to the Psammead. Martha caught them at the gate, and insisted on their taking the Baby with them.

"Not want him indeed! Why, everybody 'ud want him, a duck!‡ with all their hearts they would; and you know you promised your ma to take him out every blessed day," said Martha.

"I know we did," said Robert in gloom, "but I wish the Lamb wasn't quite so young and small. It would be much better fun taking him out."

"He'll mend of his youngness with time," said Martha; "and as

---

* To proceed in lines of four.

† Reference to "Friends, Romans, countrymen, lend me your ears," a line from Shakespeare's *Julius Caesar* (act 3, scene 2).

‡ Term of endearment.

The lucky children hurriedly started for the gravel-pit

for his smallness, I don't think you'd fancy carrying of him any more, however big he was. Besides he can walk a bit, bless his precious fat legs, a ducky! He feels the benefit of the new-laid air, so he does, a pet!"

With this and a kiss, she plumped the Lamb into Anthea's arms, and went back to make new pinafores on the sewing-machine. She was a rapid performer on this instrument.

The Lamb laughed with pleasure, and said, "Walky wif Panty," and rode on Robert's back with yells of joy, and tried to feed Jane with stones, and altogether made himself so agreeable that nobody could long be sorry that he was of the party.

The enthusiastic Jane even suggested that they should devote a week's wishes to assuring the Baby's future, by asking such gifts for him as the good fairies give to Infant Princes in proper fairy-tales, but Anthea soberly reminded her that as the Sand-fairy's wishes only lasted till sunset they could not ensure any benefit to the Baby's later years; and Jane owned that it would be better to wish for fifty pounds in two-shilling pieces, and buy the Lamb a three-pound-fifteen rocking-horse, like those in the Army and Navy Stores list, with part of the money.

It was settled that, as soon as they had wished for the money and got it, they would get Mr. Crispin to drive them into Rochester again, taking Martha with them, if they could not get out of taking her. And they would make a list of the things they really wanted before they started. Full of high hopes and excellent resolutions, they went round the safe slow cart-road to the gravel-pits, and as they went in between the mounds of gravel a sudden thought came to them, and would have turned their ruddy cheeks pale if they had been children in a book. Being real live children, it only made them stop and look at each other with rather blank and silly expressions. For now they remembered that yesterday, when they had asked the Psammead for boundless wealth, and it was getting ready to fill the quarry with the minted gold of bright guineas—millions of them—it had told the children to run along outside the quarry for fear they should be buried alive in the heavy splendid treasure. And they had run. And so it happened that they had not had time to mark the spot where the Psammead was, with a ring of stones, as before. And it was this thought that put such silly expressions on their faces.

"Never mind," said the hopeful Jane, "we'll soon find him."

But this, though easily said, was hard in the doing. They looked and they looked, and though they found their seaside spades, nowhere could they find the Sand-fairy.

At last they had to sit down and rest—not at all because they were weary or disheartened, of course, but because the Lamb insisted on being put down, and you cannot look very carefully after anything you may have happened to lose in the sand if you have an active baby to look after at the same time. Get someone to drop your best knife in the sand next time you go to the seaside, and then take your baby brother with you when you go to look for it, and you will see that I am right.

The Lamb, as Martha had said, was feeling the benefit of the country air, and he was as frisky as a sandhopper.* The elder ones longed to go on talking about the new wishes they would have when

---

* Sand flea.

(or if) they found the Psammead again. But the Lamb wished to enjoy himself.

He watched his opportunity and threw a handful of sand into Anthea's face, and then suddenly burrowed his own head in the sand and waved his fat legs in the air. Then of course the sand got into his eyes, as it had into Anthea's, and he howled.

The thoughtful Robert had brought one solid brown bottle of ginger-beer with him, relying on a thirst that had never yet failed him. This had to be uncorked hurriedly—it was the only wet thing within reach, and it was necessary to wash the sand out of the Lamb's eyes somehow. Of course the ginger hurt horribly, and he howled more than ever. And, amid his anguish of kicking, the bottle was upset and the beautiful ginger-beer frothed out into the sand and was lost for ever.

It was then that Robert, usually a very patient brother, so far forgot himself as to say:

"Anybody would want him, indeed! Only they don't; Martha doesn't, not really, or she'd jolly well keep him with her. He's a little nuisance, that's what he is. It's too bad. I only wish everybody did want him with all their hearts; we might get some peace in our lives."

The Lamb stopped howling now, because Jane had suddenly remembered that there is only one safe way of taking things out of little children's eyes, and that is with your own soft wet tongue. It is quite easy if you love the Baby as much as you ought to.

Then there was a little silence. Robert was not proud of himself for having been so cross, and the others were not proud of him either. You often notice that sort of silence when someone has said something it ought not to—and everyone else holds its tongue and waits for the one who oughtn't to have said it is sorry.

The silence was broken by a sigh—a breath suddenly let out. The children's heads turned as if there had been a string tied to each nose, and someone had pulled all the strings at once.

And everyone saw the Sand-fairy sitting quite close to them, with the expression which it used as a smile on its hairy face.

"Good-morning," it said; "I did that quite easily! Everyone wants him now."

"It doesn't matter," said Robert sulkily, because he knew he had been behaving rather like a pig. "No matter who wants him—there's no one here to—anyhow."

"Ingratitude," said the Psammead, "is a dreadful vice."

"We're not ungrateful," Jane made haste to say, "but we didn't really want that wish. Robert only just said it. Can't you take it back and give us a new one?"

"No—I can't," the Sand-fairy said shortly; "chopping and changing—it's not business. You ought to be careful what you do wish. There was a little boy once, he'd wished for a Plesiosaurus instead of an Ichthyosaurus, because he was too lazy to remember the easy names of everyday things, and his father had been very vexed with him, and had made him go to bed before tea-time, and wouldn't let him go out in the nice flint boat along with the other children—it was the annual school-treat next day—and he came and flung himself down near me on the morning of the treat, and he kicked his little prehistoric legs about and said he wished he was dead. And of course then he was."

"How awful!" said the children all together.

"Only till sunset, of course," the Psammead said; "still it was quite enough for his father and mother. And he caught it when he woke up—I can tell you. He didn't turn to stone—I forget why—but there must have been some reason. They didn't know being dead is only being asleep, and you're bound to wake up somewhere or other, either where you go to sleep or in some better place. You may be sure he caught it, giving them such a turn. Why, he wasn't allowed to taste Megatherium for a month after that. Nothing but oysters and periwinkles, and common things like that."

All the children were quite crushed by this terrible tale. They looked at the Psammead in horror. Suddenly the Lamb perceived that something brown and furry was near him.

"Poof, poof, poofy," he said, and made a grab.

"It's not a pussy," Anthea was beginning, when the Sand-fairy leaped back.

"Oh, my left whisker!" it said; "don't let him touch me. He's wet."

Its fur stood on end with horror—and indeed a good deal of the ginger-beer had been spilt on the blue smock of the Lamb.

The Psammead dug with its hands and feet, and vanished in an instant and a whirl of sand.

"Poof, poof, poofy," he said, and made a grab

The children marked the spot with a ring of stones.

"We may as well get along home," said Robert. "I'll say I'm sorry; but anyway if it's no good it's no harm, and we know where the sandy thing is for tomorrow."

The others were noble. No one reproached Robert at all. Cyril picked up the Lamb, who was now quite himself again, and off they went by the safe cart-road.

The cart-road from the gravel-pits joins the road almost directly.

At the gate into the road the party stopped to shift the Lamb from Cyril's back to Robert's. And as they paused a very smart open carriage came in sight, with a coachman and a groom on the box, and inside the carriage a lady—very grand indeed, with a dress all white lace and red ribbons and a parasol all red and white—and a white fluffy dog on her lap with a red ribbon round its neck. She looked at the children, and particularly at the Baby, and she smiled at him. The children were used to this, for the Lamb was, as all the servants said, a "very taking child." So they waved their hands politely to the lady and expected her to drive on. But she did not. Instead she made the coachman stop. And she beckoned to Cyril, and when he went up to the carriage she said:

"What a dear darling duck of a baby! Oh, I should so like to adopt it! Do you think its mother would mind?"

"She'd mind very much indeed," said Anthea shortly.

"Oh, but I should bring it up in luxury, you know. I am Lady Chittenden. You must have seen my photograph in the illustrated papers. They call me a beauty, you know, but of course that's all nonsense. Anyway——"

She opened the carriage door and jumped out. She had the wonderfullest red high-heeled shoes with silver buckles. "Let me hold him a minute," she said. And she took the Lamb and held him very awkwardly, as if she was not used to babies.

Then suddenly she jumped into the carriage with the Lamb in her arms and slammed the door and said, "Drive on!"

The Lamb roared, the little white dog barked, and the coachman hesitated.

"Drive on, I tell you!" cried the lady; and the coachman did, for, as he said afterwards, it was as much as his place was worth not to.

The four children looked at each other, and then with one accord they rushed after the carriage and held on behind. Down the dusty road went the smart carriage, and after it, at double-quick time, ran the twinkling legs of the Lamb's brothers and sisters.

The Lamb howled louder and louder, but presently his howls changed by slow degree to hiccupy gurgles, and then all was still and they knew he had gone to sleep.

The carriage went on, and the eight feet that twinkled through the dust were growing quite stiff and tired before the carriage stopped at the lodge of a grand park. The children crouched down behind the carriage, and the lady got out. She looked at the Baby as it lay on the carriage seat, and hesitated.

"The darling—I won't disturb it," she said, and went into the lodge to talk to the woman there about a setting of Buff Orpington* eggs that had not turned out well.

The coachman and footman sprang from the box and bent over the sleeping Lamb.

"Fine boy—wish he was mine," said the coachman.

"He wouldn't favour you much," said the groom sourly; "too 'andsome."

---

* Large English chicken.

At double-quick time ran the twinkling legs of the Lamb's brothers and sisters

The coachman pretended not to hear. He said:

"Wonder at her now—I do really! Hates kids. Got none of her own, and can't abide other folkses'."

The children, crouching in the white dust under the carriage, exchanged uncomfortable glances.

"Tell you what," the coachman went on firmly, "blowed if I don't hide the little nipper in the hedge and tell her his brothers took 'im! Then I'll come back for him afterwards."

"No, you don't," said the footman. "I've took to that kid so as never was. If anyone's to have him, it's me—so there!"

Next minute the two were fighting here and there

"Stow your gab!" the coachman rejoined. "You don't want no kids, and, if you did, one kid's the same as another to you. But I'm a married man and a judge of breed. I knows a first-rate yearling when I sees him. I'm a-goin' to 'ave him, an' least said soonest mended."

"I should 'a' thought," said the footman sneeringly, "you'd a'most enough. What with Alfred, an' Albert, an' Louise, an' Victor Stanley, and Helena Beatrice, and another—"

The coachman hit the footman in the chin—the footman hit the coachman in the waistcoat—the next minute the two were fighting here and there, in and out, up and down, and all over everywhere, and the little dog jumped on the box of the carriage and began barking like mad.

Cyril, still crouching in the dust, waddled on bent legs to the side of the carriage farthest from the battlefield. He unfastened the door of the carriage—the two men were far too much occupied with their quarrel to notice anything—took the Lamb in his arms, and, still stooping, carried the sleeping baby a dozen yards along the road to where a stile led into a wood. The others followed, and there among the hazels and young oaks and sweet chestnuts, covered by high strong-scented bracken, they all lay hidden till the angry voices of the men were hushed at the angry voice of the red-and-white lady, and, after a long and anxious search, the carriage at last drove away.

"My only hat!" said Cyril, drawing a deep breath as the sound of wheels at last died away. "Everyone *does* want him now—and no mistake! That Sammyadd has done us again! Tricky brute! For, any sake, let's get the kid safe home."

So they peeped out, and finding on the right hand only lonely white road, and nothing but lonely white road on the left, they took courage, and the road, Anthea carrying the sleeping Lamb.

Adventures dogged their footsteps. A boy with a bundle of faggots on his back dropped his bundle by the roadside and asked to look at the Baby, and then offered to carry him; but Anthea was not to be caught that way twice. They all walked on, but the boy followed, and Cyril and Robert couldn't make him go away till they had more than once invited him to smell their fists. Afterwards a little girl in a blue-and-white checked pinafore actually followed them for a quarter of a mile crying for "the precious Baby," and then she was only got rid of by threats of tying her to a tree in the wood with all their pocket-handkerchiefs. "So that the bears can come and eat you as soon as it gets dark," said Cyril severely. Then she went off crying. It presently seemed wise, to the brothers and sisters of the Baby, who was wanted by everyone, to hide in the hedge whenever they saw anyone coming, and thus they managed to prevent the Lamb from arousing the inconvenient affection of a milkman, a stone-breaker, and a man who drove a cart with a paraffin barrel at the back of it. They were nearly home when the worst thing of all happened. Turning a corner suddenly they came upon two vans, a tent, and a company of gipsies encamped by the side of the road. The vans were hung all round with wicker chairs and cradles, and flower-stands and feather brushes. A lot of ragged children were industriously making dust-pies in the road, two men lay on the grass smoking, and three women were doing the family washing in an old red watering-can with the top broken off.

In a moment all the gipsies, men, women, and children, surrounded Anthea and the Baby.

"Let me hold him, little lady," said one of the gipsy women, who had a mahogany-coloured face and dust-coloured hair; "I won't hurt a hair of his head, the little picture!"

"I'd rather not," said Anthea.

"Let me have him," said the other woman, whose face was also of the hue of mahogany, and her hair jet-black, in greasy curls. "I've nineteen of my own, so I have."

"No," said Anthea bravely, but her heart beat so that it nearly choked her.

Then one of the men pushed forward.

"Swelp me if it ain't!" he cried, "my own long-lost cheild! Have he a strawberry mark on his left ear? No? Then he's my own babby, stolen from me in hinnocent hinfancy. 'And 'im over—and we'll not 'ave the law on yer this time."

He snatched the Baby from Anthea, who turned scarlet and burst into tears of pure rage.

The others were standing quite still; this was much the most terrible thing that had ever happened to them. Even being taken up by the police in Rochester was nothing to this. Cyril was quite white, and his hands trembled a little, but he made a sign to the others to shut up. He was silent a minute, thinking hard. Then he said:

"We don't want to keep him if he's yours. But you see he's used to us. You shall have him if you want him."

"No, no!" cried Anthea—and Cyril glared at her.

"Of course we want him," said the women, trying to get the Baby out of the man's arms. The Lamb howled loudly.

"Oh, he's hurt!" shrieked Anthea; and Cyril, in a savage undertone, bade her "Stow it!"

"You trust to me," he whispered. "Look here," he went on, "he's awfully tiresome with people he doesn't know very well. Suppose we stay here a bit till he gets used to you, and then when it's bedtime I give you my word of honour we'll go away and let you keep him if

He snatched the Baby from Anthea

you want to. And then when we're gone you can decide which of you
is to have him, as you all want him so much."

"That's fair enough," said the man who was holding the Baby,
trying to loosen the red neckerchief which the Lamb had caught hold
of and drawn round his mahogany throat so tight that he could
hardly breathe. The gipsies whispered together, and Cyril took the
chance to whisper too. He said, "Sunset! we'll get away then."

And then his brothers and sisters were filled with wonder and
admiration at his having been so clever as to remember this.

"Oh, do let him come to us!" said Jane. "See we'll sit down here
and take care of him for you till he gets used to you."

"What about dinner?" said Robert suddenly. The others looked at
him with scorn. "Fancy bothering about your beastly dinner when

your br—I mean when the Baby"—Jane whispered hotly. Robert carefully winked at her and went on:

"You won't mind my just running home to get our dinner?" he said to the gipsy; "I can bring it out here in a basket."

His brother and sisters felt themselves very noble, and despised him. They did not know his thoughtful secret intention. But the gipsies did in a minute.

"Oh yes!" they said; "and then fetch the police with a pack of lies about it being your baby instead of ours! D'jever catch a weasel asleep?" they asked.

"If you're hungry you can pick a bit along of us," said the light-haired gipsy woman, not unkindly. "Here, Levi, that blessed kid'll howl all his buttons off. Give him to the little lady, and let's see if they can't get him used to us a bit."

So the Lamb was handed back; but the gipsies crowded so closely that he could not possibly stop howling. Then the man with the red handkerchief said:

"Here, Pharaoh, make up the fire; and you girls see to the pot. Give the kid a chanst." So the gipsies, very much against their will, went off to their work, and the children and the Lamb were left sitting on the grass.

"He'll be all right at sunset," Jane whispered. "But, oh, it is awful! Suppose they are frightfully angry when they come to their senses! They might beat us, or leave us tied to trees, or something."

"No, they won't," Anthea said. ("Oh, my Lamb, don't cry any more, it's all right, Panty's got oo, duckie!") "They aren't unkind people, or they wouldn't be going to give us any dinner."

"Dinner?" said Robert. "I won't touch their nasty dinner. It would choke me!"

The others thought so too then. But when the dinner was ready—it turned out to be supper, and happened between four and five—they were all glad enough to take what they could get. It was boiled rabbit, with onions, and some bird rather like a chicken, but stringier about its legs and with a stronger taste. The Lamb had bread soaked in hot water and brown sugar sprinkled on the top. He liked this very much, and consented to let the two gipsy women feed him with it, as he sat on Anthea's lap. All that long hot afternoon Robert and Cyril and Anthea and Jane had to keep the Lamb amused and happy, while the gipsies looked eagerly on. By the time the shadows grew long and black across the meadows he had really "taken to" the woman with the light hair, and even consented to kiss his hand to the children, and to stand up and bow, with his hand on his chest—"like a gentleman"—to the two men. The whole gipsy camp was in raptures with him, and his brothers and sisters could not help taking some pleasure in showing off his accomplishments to an audience so interested and enthusiastic. But they longed for sunset.

"We're getting into the habit of longing for sunset," Cyril whispered. "How I do wish we could wish something really sensible, that would be of some use, so that we should be quite sorry when sunset came."

The shadows got longer and longer, and at last there were no separate shadows any more, but one soft glowing shadow over everything; for the sun was out of sight—behind the hill—but he had not really set yet. The people who make the laws about lighting bicycle lamps are the people who decide when the sun sets; he has to do it, too, to the minute, or they would know the reason why!

But the gipsies were getting impatient.

"Now, young uns," the red-handkerchief man said, "it's time you were laying of your heads on your pillowses—so it is! The kid's all right and friendly with us now—so you just hand him over and sling that hook o' yours* like you said."

The women and children came crowding round the Lamb, arms were held out, fingers snapped invitingly, friendly faces beaming with admiring smiles; but all failed to tempt the loyal Lamb. He clung with arms and legs to Jane, who happened to be holding him, and uttered the gloomiest roar of the whole day.

"It's no good," the woman said, "hand the little popper† over, miss. We'll soon quiet him."

And still the sun would not set.

"Tell her about how to put him to bed," whispered Cyril; "anything to gain time—and be ready to bolt when the sun really does make up its silly old mind to set."

---

* Leave; clear out (slang).

† Term of endearment for a child.

He consented to let the gipsy women feed him

"Yes, I'll hand him over in just one minute," Anthea began, talking very fast—"but do let me just tell you he has a warm bath every night and cold in the morning, and he has a crockery rabbit to go into the warm bath with him, and little Samuel saying his prayers in white china on a red cushion for the cold bath; and if you let the soap get into his eyes, the Lamb—"

"Lamb kyes," said he—he had stopped roaring to listen.

The woman laughed. "As if I hadn't never bath'd a babby!" she said. "Come—give us a hold of him. Come to 'Melia, my precious."

"G'way, ugsie!" replied the Lamb at once.

"Yes, but," Anthea went on, "about his meals; you really must let me tell you he has an apple or a banana every morning, and bread-and-milk for breakfast, and an egg for his tea sometimes, and—"

"I've brought up ten," said the black-ringleted woman, "besides the others. Come, miss, 'and 'im over—I can't bear it no longer. I just must give him a hug."

"We ain't settled yet whose he's to be, Esther," said one of the men.

"It won't be you, Esther, with seven of 'em at your tail a'ready."

"I ain't so sure of that," said Esther's husband.

"And ain't I nobody, to have a say neither?" said the husband of 'Melia.

Zillah, the girl, said, "An' me? I'm a single girl—and no one but 'im to look after—I ought to have him."

"Hold yer tongue!"

"Shut your mouth!"

"Don't you show me no more of your imperence!"

Everyone was getting very angry. The dark gipsy faces were frowning and anxious-looking. Suddenly a change swept over them, as if some invisible sponge had wiped away these cross and anxious expressions, and left only a blank.

The children saw that the sun really *had* set. But they were afraid to move. And the gipsies were feeling so muddled, because of the invisible sponge that had washed all the feelings of the last few hours out of their hearts, that they could not say a word.

The children hardly dared to breathe. Suppose the gipsies, when they recovered speech, should be furious to think how silly they had been all day?

It was an awkward moment. Suddenly Anthea, greatly daring, held out the Lamb to the red-handkerchief man.

"Here he is!" she said.

The man drew back. "I shouldn't like to deprive you, miss," he said hoarsely.

"Anyone who likes can have my share of him," said the other man.

"After all, I've got enough of my own," said Esther.

"He's a nice little chap, though," said Amelia. She was the only one who now looked affectionately at the whimpering Lamb.

Zillah said, "If I don't think I must have had a touch of the sun. I don't want him."

"Then shall we take him away?" said Anthea.

"Well, suppose you do," said Pharaoh heartily, "and we'll say no more about it!"

And with great haste all the gipsies began to be busy about their tents for the night. All but Amelia. She went with the children as far as the bend in the road—and there she said:

"Let me give him a kiss, miss—I don't know what made us go for to behave so silly. Us gipsies don't steal babies, whatever they may tell you when you're naughty. We've enough of our own, mostly. But I've lost all mine."

She leaned towards the Lamb; and he, looking in her eyes, unexpectedly put up a grubby soft paw and stroked her face.

"Poor, poor!" said the Lamb. And he let the gipsy woman kiss him, and, what is more, he kissed her brown cheek in return—a very nice kiss, as all his kisses are, and not a wet one like some babies give. The gipsy woman moved her finger about on his forehead, as if she had been writing something there, and the same with his chest and his hands and his feet; then she said:

"May he be brave, and have the strong head to think with, and the strong heart to love with, and the strong hands to work with, and the strong feet to travel with, and always come safe home to his own." Then she said something in a strange language no one could understand, and suddenly added:

"Well, I must be saying 'so long'—and glad to have made your acquaintance." And she turned and went back to her home—the tent by the grassy roadside.

The children looked after her till she was out of sight. Then Robert said, "How silly of her! Even sunset didn't put her right. What rot she talked!"

"Well," said Cyril, "if you ask me, I think it was rather decent of her—"

"Decent?" said Anthea; "it was very nice indeed of her. I think she's a dear."

"She's just too frightfully nice for anything," said Jane.

And they went home—very late for tea and unspeakably late for dinner. Martha scolded, of course. But the Lamb was safe.

"I say—it turned out we wanted the Lamb as much as anyone," said Robert, later.

"Of course."

The gipsy woman moved her finger about on his forehead

"But do you feel different about it now the sun's set?"

"No," said all the others together.

"Then it's lasted over sunset with us."

"No, it hasn't," Cyril explained. "The wish didn't do anything to us. We always wanted him with all our hearts when we were our proper selves, only we were all pigs this morning; especially you, Robert." Robert bore this much with a strange calm.

"I certainly *thought* I didn't want him this morning," said he. "Perhaps I was a pig. But everything looked so different when we thought we were going to lose him."

CHAPTER IV

WINGS

The next day was very wet—too wet to go out, and far too wet to think of disturbing a Sand-fairy so sensitive to water that he still, after thousands of years, felt the pain of once having had his left whisker wetted. It was a long day, and it was not till the afternoon that all the children suddenly decided to write letters to their mother. It was Robert who had the misfortune to upset the ink-pot—an unusually deep and full one—straight into that part of Anthea's desk where she had long pretended that an arrangement of gum and cardboard painted with Indian ink was a secret drawer. It was not exactly Robert's fault; it was only his misfortune that he chanced to be lifting the ink across the desk just at the moment when Anthea had got it open, and that that same moment should have been the one chosen by the Lamb to get under the table and break his squeaking bird. There was a sharp convenient wire inside the bird, and of course the Lamb ran the wire into Robert's leg at once; and so, without anyone's meaning to, the secret drawer was flooded with ink. At the same time a stream was poured over Anthea's half-finished letter.

So that her letter was something like this:

Darling Mother,

I hope you are quite well, and I hope Granny is better. The other day we . . .
    Then came a flood of ink, and at the bottom these words in pencil—
    It was not me upset the ink, but it took such a time clearing up, so no more as it is post-time.—From your loving daughter,

                        Anthea.

Robert's letter had not even been begun. He had been drawing a ship on the blotting-paper while he was trying to think of what to say. And of course after the ink was upset he had to help Anthea to clean out her desk, and he promised to make her another secret drawer, better than the other. And she said, "Well, make it now." So it was post-time and his letter wasn't done. And the secret drawer wasn't done either.

Cyril wrote a long letter, very fast, and then went to set a trap for slugs that he had read about in the *Home-made Gardener*, and when it was post-time the letter could not be found, and it never was found. Perhaps the slugs ate it.

Jane's letter was the only one that went. She meant to tell her mother all about the Psammead—in fact they had all meant to do this—but she spent so long thinking how to spell the word that there was no time to tell the story properly, and it is useless to tell a story unless you do tell it properly, so she had to be contented with this—

My dear Mother Dear,

We are all as good as we can, like you told us to, and the Lamb has a little cold, but Martha says it is nothing, only he upset the goldfish into himself yesterday morning. When we were up at the sand-pit the other day we went round by the safe way where carts go, and we found a—

Half an hour went by before Jane felt quite sure that they could none of them spell Psammead. And they could not find it in the dictionary either, though they looked. Then Jane hastily finished her letter.

We found a strange thing, but it is nearly post-time, so no more at present from your little girl,

Jane.

P.S.—If you could have a wish come true, what would you have?

Then the postman was heard blowing his horn, and Robert rushed out in the rain to stop his cart and give him the letter. And that was how it happened that, though all the children meant to tell their mother about the Sand-fairy, somehow or other she never got to know. There were other reasons why she never got to know, but these come later.

The next day Uncle Richard came and took them all to Maidstone in a wagonette—all except the Lamb. Uncle Richard was the very best kind of uncle. He bought them toys at Maidstone. He took them into a shop and let them choose exactly what they wanted, without any restrictions about price, and no nonsense about things being instructive. It is very wise to let children choose exactly what they like, because they are very foolish and inexperienced, and sometimes they will choose a really instructive thing without meaning to. This happened to Robert, who chose, at the last moment, and in a great hurry, a box with pictures on it of winged bulls with men's heads and winged men with eagles' heads. He thought there would be animals inside, the same as on the box. When he got it home it was a Sunday puzzle about ancient Nineveh! The others chose in haste, and were happy at leisure. Cyril had a model engine, and the girls had two dolls, as well as a china tea-set with forget-me-nots on it, to be "between them." The boys' "between them" was bow and arrows.

Then Uncle Richard took them on the beautiful Medway* in a boat, and then they all had tea at a beautiful pastrycook's, and when they reached home it was far too late to have any wishes that day.

They did not tell Uncle Richard anything about the Psammead. I do not know why. And they do not know why. But I daresay you can guess.

The day after Uncle Richard had behaved so handsomely was a very hot day indeed. The people who decide what the weather is to be, and put its orders down for it in the newspapers every morning, said afterwards that it was the hottest day there had been for years. They had ordered it to be "warmer—some showers," and warmer it certainly was. In fact it was so busy being warmer that it had no time to attend to the order about showers, so there weren't any.

Have you ever been up at five o'clock on a fine summer morning? It is very beautiful. The sunlight is pinky and yellowy, and all the grass and trees are covered with dew-diamonds. And all the shadows go the opposite way to the way they do in the evening, which is very interesting and makes you feel as though you were in a new other world.

Anthea awoke at five. She had made herself wake, and I must tell you how it is done, even if it keeps you waiting for the story to go on.

You get into bed at night, and lie down quite flat on your little

---

* Tributary of the River Thames that divides the county of Kent.

back with your hands straight down by your sides. Then you say "I must wake up at five" (or six, or seven, or eight, or nine, or whatever the time is that you want), and as you say it you push your chin down on to your chest and then bang your head back on the pillow. And you do this as many times as there are ones in the time you want to wake up at. (It is quite an easy sum.) Of course everything depends on your really wanting to get up at five (or six, or seven, or eight, or nine); if you don't really want to, it's all of no use. But if you do— well, try it and see. Of course in this, as in doing Latin proses or getting into mischief, practice makes perfect.

Anthea was quite perfect.

At the very moment when she opened her eyes she heard the black-and-gold clock down in the dining-room strike eleven. So she knew it was three minutes to five. The black-and-gold clock always struck wrong, but it was all right when you knew what it meant. It was like a person talking a foreign language. If you know the language it is just as easy to understand as English. And Anthea knew the clock language. She was very sleepy, but she jumped out of bed and put her face and hands into a basin of cold water. This is a fairy charm that prevents your wanting to get back into bed again. Then she dressed, and folded up her night-gown. She did not tumble it together by the sleeves, but folded it by the seams from the hem, and that will show you the kind of well-brought-up little girl she was.

Then she took her shoes in her hand and crept softly down the stairs. She opened the dining-room window and climbed out. It would have been just as easy to go out by the door, but the window was more romantic, and less likely to be noticed by Martha.

"I will always get up at five," she said to herself. "It was quite too awfully pretty for anything."

Her heart was beating very fast, for she was carrying out a plan quite her own. She could not be sure that it was a good plan, but she was quite sure that it would not be any better if she were to tell the others about it. And she had a feeling that, right or wrong, she would rather go through with it alone. She put on her shoes under the iron veranda, on the red-and-yellow shining tiles, and then she ran straight to the sand-pit, and found the Psammead's place, and dug it out; it was very cross indeed.

"It's too bad," it said, fluffing up its fur like pigeons do their

"Thank you," it said, "that's better. What's the wish this morning?"

feathers at Christmas time. "The weather's arctic, and it's the middle of the night."

"I'm so sorry," said Anthea gently, and she took off her white pinafore and covered the Sand-fairy up with it, all but its head, its bat's ears, and its eyes that were like a snail's eyes.

"Thank you," it said, "that's better. What's the wish this morning?"

"I don't know," said she; "that's just it. You see we've been very unlucky, so far. I wanted to talk to you about it. But—would you mind not giving me any wishes till after breakfast? It's so hard to talk to anyone if they jump out at you with wishes you don't really want!"

"You shouldn't say you wish for things if you don't wish for them. In the old days people almost always knew whether it was Megatherium or Ichthyosaurus they really wanted for dinner."

"I'll try not," said Anthea, "but I do wish—"

"Look out!" said the Psammead in a warning voice, and it began to blow itself out.

"Oh, this isn't a magic wish—it's just—I should be so glad if you'd not swell yourself out and nearly burst to give me anything just now. Wait till the others are here."

"Well, well," it said indulgently, but it shivered.

"Would you," asked Anthea kindly—"would you like to come and sit on my lap? You'd be warmer, and I could turn the skirt of my frock up round you. I'd be very careful."

Anthea had never expected that it would, but it did.

"Thank you," it said; "you really are rather thoughtful." It crept on to her lap and snuggled down, and she put her arms round it with a rather frightened gentleness. "Now then!" it said.

"Well then," said Anthea, "everything we have wished has turned out rather horrid. I wish you would advise us. You are so old, you must be very wise."

"I was always generous from a child," said the Sand-fairy. "I've spent the whole of my waking hours in giving. But one thing I won't give—that's advice."

"You see," Anthea went on, "it's such a wonderful thing—such a splendid, glorious chance. It's so good and kind and dear of you to give us our wishes, and it seems such a pity it should all be wasted just because we are too silly to know what to wish for."

Anthea had meant to say that—and she had not wanted to say it before the others. It's one thing to say you're silly, and quite another to say that other people are.

"Child," said the Sand-fairy sleepily, "I can only advise you to think before you speak—"

"But I thought you never gave advice."

"That piece doesn't count," it said. "You'll never take it! Besides, it's not original. It's in all the copybooks."*

"But won't you just say if you think wings would be a silly wish?"

"Wings?" it said. "I should think you might do worse. Only, take care you aren't flying high at sunset. There was a little Ninevite boy I heard of once. He was one of King Sennacherib's sons,† and a traveller brought him a Psammead. He used to keep it in a box of sand

---

* Books in which documents are printed for pupils to imitate.

† Offspring of Sennacherib, king (705–681 B.C.) of the Assyrian Empire, who rebuilt its largest city, Nineveh. He was slain by one, or possibly two, of his sons.

on the palace terrace. It was a dreadful degradation for one of us, of course; still the boy *was* the Assyrian King's son. And one day he wished for wings and got them. But he forgot that they would turn into stone at sunset, and when they did he fell slap on to one of the winged lions at the top of his father's great staircase; and what with his stone wings and the lions' stone wings—well, it's not a pretty story! But I believe the boy enjoyed himself very much till then."

"Tell me," said Anthea, "why don't our wishes turn into stone now? Why do they just vanish?"

"*Autres temps, autres mœurs,*"* said the creature.

"Is that the Ninevite language?" asked Anthea, who had learned no foreign language at school except French.

"What I mean is," the Psammead went on, "that in the old days people wished for good solid everyday gifts—Mammoths and Ptero-dactyls and things—and those could be turned into stone as easy as not. But people wish such high-flying fanciful things nowadays. How are you going to turn being beautiful as the day, or being wanted by everybody, into stone? You see it can't be done. And it would never do to have two rules, so they simply vanish. If being beautiful as the day could be turned into stone it would last an awfully long time, you know—much longer than you would. Just look at the Greek statues. It's just as well as it is. Good-bye. I *am* so sleepy."

It jumped off her lap—dug frantically, and vanished.

Anthea was late for breakfast. It was Robert who quietly poured a spoonful of treacle† down the Lamb's frock, so that he had to be taken away and washed thoroughly directly after breakfast. And it was of course a very naughty thing to do; yet it served two purposes—it delighted the Lamb, who loved above all things to be completely sticky, and it engaged Martha's attention so that the others could slip away to the sand-pit without the Lamb.

They did it, and in the lane Anthea, breathless from the scurry of that slipping, panted out—

"I want to propose we take turns to wish. Only, nobody's to have a wish if the others don't think it's a nice wish. Do you agree?"

---

*Literally, other times, other customs (French); that is, times change, customs change.

† Molasses.

"Who's to have first wish?" asked Robert cautiously.

"Me, if you don't mind," said Anthea apologetically. "And I've thought about it—and it's wings."

There was a silence. The others rather wanted to find fault, but it was hard, because the word "wings" raised a flutter of joyous excitement in every breast.

"Not so dusty," said Cyril generously; and Robert added, "Really, Panther, you're not quite such a fool as you look."

Jane said, "I think it would be perfectly lovely. It's like a bright dream of delirium."

They found the Sand-fairy easily. Anthea said:

"I wish we all had beautiful wings to fly with."

The Sand-fairy blew himself out, and next moment each child felt a funny feeling, half heaviness and half lightness, on its shoulders. The Psammead put its head on one side and turned its snail's eyes from one to the other.

"Not so dusty," it said dreamily. "But really, Robert, you're not quite such an angel as you look." Robert almost blushed.

The wings were very big, and more beautiful than you can possibly imagine—for they were soft and smooth, and every feather lay neatly in its place. And the feathers were of the most lovely mixed changing colours, like the rainbow, or iridescent glass, or the beautiful scum that sometimes floats on water that is not at all nice to drink.

"Oh—but can we fly?" Jane said, standing anxiously first on one foot and then on the other.

"Look out!" said Cyril; "you're treading on my wing."

"Does it hurt?" asked Anthea with interest; but no one answered, for Robert had spread his wings and jumped up, and now he was slowly rising in the air. He looked very awkward in his knickerbocker suit—his boots in particular hung helplessly, and seemed much larger than when he was standing in them. But the others cared but little how he looked—or how they looked, for that matter. For now they all spread out their wings and rose in the air. Of course you all know what flying feels like, because everyone has dreamed about flying, and it seems so beautifully easy—only, you can never remember how you did it; and as a rule you have to do it without wings, in your dreams, which is more clever and uncommon, but not so easy to remember the rule for. Now the four children rose flapping from the ground, and you can't think how good the air felt running against their faces. Their wings were tremendously wide when they were spread out, and they had to fly quite a long way apart so as not to get in each other's way. But little things like this are easily learned.

All the words in the English Dictionary, and in the Greek Lexicon as well, are, I find, of no use at all to tell you exactly what it feels like to be flying, so I will not try. But I will say that to look *down* on the fields and woods, instead of *along* at them, is something like looking at a beautiful live map, where, instead of silly colours on paper, you have real moving sunny woods and green fields laid out one after the other. As Cyril said, and I can't think where he got hold of such a strange expression, "It does you a fair treat!" It was most wonderful and more like real magic than any wish the children had had yet. They flapped and flew and sailed on their great rainbow wings, between green earth and blue sky; and they flew right over Rochester and then swerved round towards Maidstone, and presently they all began to feel extremely hungry. Curiously enough, this happened when they were flying rather low, and just as they were crossing an orchard where some early plums shone red and ripe.

They paused on their wings. I cannot explain to you how this is done, but it is something like treading water when you are swimming, and hawks do it extremely well.

"Yes, I daresay," said Cyril, though no one had spoken. "But stealing is stealing even if you've got wings."

"Do you really think so?" said Jane briskly. "If you've got wings you're a bird, and no one minds birds breaking the commandments. At least, they may *mind*, but the birds always do it, and no one scolds them or sends them to prison."

It was not so easy to perch on a plum-tree as you might think, because the rainbow wings were so *very* large; but somehow they all managed to do it, and the plums were certainly very sweet and juicy.

Fortunately, it was not till they had all had quite as many plums as were good for them that they saw a stout man, who looked exactly as though he owned the plum-trees, come hurrying through the orchard gate with a thick stick, and with one accord they disentangled their wings from the plum-laden branches and began to fly.

The man stopped short, with his mouth open. For he had seen the boughs of his trees moving and twitching, and he had said to

They flew right over Rochester

himself, "Them young varmints—at it again!" And he had come out at once, for the lads of the village had taught him in past seasons that plums want looking after. But when he saw the rainbow wings flutter up out of the plum-tree he felt that he must have gone quite mad, and he did not like the feeling at all. And when Anthea looked down and saw his mouth go slowly open, and stay so, and his face become green and mauve in patches, she called out:

"Don't be frightened," and felt hastily in her pocket for a threepenny-bit with a hole in it, which she had meant to hang on a ribbon round her neck, for luck. She hovered round the unfortunate plum-owner, and said, "We have had some of your plums; we thought it wasn't stealing, but now I am not so sure. So here's some money to pay for them."

She swooped down towards the terror-stricken grower of plums, and slipped the coin into the pocket of his jacket, and in a few flaps she had rejoined the others.

The farmer sat down on the grass, suddenly and heavily.

"Well—I'm blessed!" he said. "This here is what they call delusions, I suppose. But this here three-penny"—he had pulled it out and bitten it—"*that's* real enough. Well, from this day forth I'll be a better man. It's the kind of thing to sober a chap for life, this is. I'm glad it was only wings, though. I'd rather see birds as aren't there, and couldn't be, even if they pretend to talk, than some things as I could name."

He got up slowly and heavily, and went indoors, and he was so nice to his wife that day that she felt quite happy, and said to herself, "Law, whatever have a-come to the man!" and smartened herself up and put a blue ribbon bow at the place where her collar fastened on, and looked so pretty that he was kinder than ever. So perhaps the winged children really did do one good thing that day. If so, it was the only one; for really there is nothing like wings for getting you into trouble. But, on the other hand, if you are in trouble, there is nothing like wings for getting you out of it.

This was the case in the matter of the fierce dog who sprang out at them when they had folded up their wings as small as possible and were going up to a farm door to ask for a crust of bread and cheese, for in spite of the plums they were soon just as hungry as ever again.

Now there is no doubt whatever that, if the four had been ordinary wingless children, that black and fierce dog would have had a good bite out of the brown-stockinged leg of Robert, who was the nearest. But at first growl there was a flutter of wings, and the dog

The farmer sat down on the grass suddenly

was left to strain at his chain and stand on his hind-legs as if he were trying to fly too.

They tried several other farms, but at those where there were no dogs the people were far too frightened to do anything but scream; and at last when it was nearly four o'clock, and their wings were getting miserably stiff and tired, they alighted on a church-tower and held a council of war.

"We can't possibly fly all the way home without dinner or tea," said Robert with desperate decision.

"And nobody will give us any dinner, or even lunch, let alone tea," said Cyril.

"Perhaps the clergyman here might," suggested Anthea. "He must know all about angels—"

"Anybody could see we're not that," said Jane. "Look at Robert's boots and Squirrel's plaid necktie."

"Well," said Cyril firmly, "if the country you're in won't sell provisions, you take them. In wars I mean. I'm quite certain you do. And even in other stories no good brother would allow his little sisters to starve in the midst of plenty."

"Plenty?" repeated Robert hungrily; and the others looked vaguely round the bare leads of the church-tower, and murmured, "In the midst of?"

"Yes," said Cyril impressively. "There is a larder* window at the side of the clergyman's house, and I saw things to eat inside—custard pudding and cold chicken and tongue—and pies—and jam. It's rather a high window—but with wings—"

"How clever of you!" said Jane.

"Not at all," said Cyril modestly; "any born general—Napoleon or the Duke of Marlborough† would have seen it just the same as I did."

"It seems very wrong," said Anthea.

"Nonsense," said Cyril. "What was it Sir Philip Sidney said when the soldier wouldn't stand him a drink?[3] 'My necessity is greater than his.'"

"We'll club our money, though, and leave it to pay for the things, won't we?" Anthea was persuasive, and very nearly in tears, because it is most trying to feel enormously hungry and unspeakably sinful at one and the same time.

"Some of it," was the cautious reply.

---

* Room for storing food.

† John Churchill (1650–1722), celebrated for his victory over France in the Battle of Blenheim (1704).

Everyone now turned out its pockets

Everyone now turned out its pockets on the lead roof of the tower, where visitors for the last hundred and fifty years had cut their own and their sweethearts' initials with penknives in the soft lead. There was five-and-sevenpence-half-penny altogether, and even the upright Anthea admitted that that was too much to pay for four people's dinners. Robert said he thought eighteen pence.

And half-a-crown was finally agreed to be "handsome."

So Anthea wrote on the back of her last term's report, which happened to be in her pocket, and from which she first tore her own name and that of the school, the following letter:

Dear Reverend Clergyman,

> We are very hungry indeed because of having to fly all day, and we think it is not stealing when you are starving to death. We are afraid to ask you for fear you should say "No," because of course you know about angels, but you would not think we were angels. We will only take the nessessities of life, and no pudding or pie, to show you it is not grediness but true starvation that makes us make your larder stand and deliver. But we are not highwaymen by trade.

"Cut it short," said the others with one accord. And Anthea hastily added:

> Our intentions are quite honourable if you only knew. And here is half-a-crown to show we are sinseer and grateful.
> Thank you for your kind hospitality.
>
> From Us Four.

The half-crown was wrapped in this letter, and all the children felt that when the clergyman had read it he would understand everything, as well as anyone could who had not seen the wings.

"Now," said Cyril, "of course there's some risk; we'd better fly straight down the other side of the tower and then flutter low across the churchyard and in through the shrubbery. There doesn't seem to be anyone about. But you never know. The window looks out into the shrubbery. It is embowered in foliage, like a window in a story. I'll go in and get the things. Robert and Anthea can take them as I hand them out through the window; and Jane can keep watch—her eyes

These were the necessaries of life, which Cyril handed out of the larder window

are sharp—and whistle if she sees anyone about. Shut up, Robert! she can whistle quite well enough for that, anyway. It ought not to be a very good whistle—it'll sound more natural and birdlike. Now then—off we go!"

I cannot pretend that stealing is right. I can only say that on this occasion it did not look like stealing to the hungry four, but appeared in the light of a fair and reasonable business transaction. They had never happened to learn that a tongue—hardly cut into—a chicken and a half, a loaf of bread, and a siphon of soda-water cannot be bought in shops for half-a-crown. These were the necessaries of life, which Cyril handed out of the larder window when, quite unobserved and without hindrance or adventure, he had led the others to that happy spot. He felt that to refrain from jam, apple turnovers, cake, and mixed candied peel was a really heroic act—and I agree with him. He was also proud of not taking the custard pudding—and there I think he was wrong—because if he had taken it there would have been a difficulty about returning the dish; no one, however starving, has a right to steal china pie-dishes with little pink flowers on them. The soda-water siphon was different. They could not do without something to drink, and as the maker's name was on it they felt sure it would be returned to him wherever they might leave it. If they had time they would take it back themselves. The man appeared to live in Rochester, which would not be much out of their way home.

Everything was carried up to the top of the tower, and laid down on a sheet of kitchen paper which Cyril had found on the top shelf of the larder. As he unfolded it, Anthea said, "I don't think that's a necessity of life."

"Yes, it is," said he. "We must put the things down somewhere to cut them up; and I heard father say the other day people got diseases from germans in rain-water. Now there must be lots of rain-water here—and when it dries up the germans are left, and they'd get into the things, and we should all die of scarlet fever."

"What are germans?"

"Little waggly things you see with microscopes," said Cyril, with a scientific air. "They give you every illness you can think of. I'm sure the paper was a necessary, just as much as the bread and meat and water. Now then! Oh, my eyes, I am hungry!"

I do not wish to describe the picnic party on the top of the tower. You can imagine well enough what it is like to carve a chicken and a tongue with a knife that has only one blade—and that snapped off short about half-way down. But it was done. Eating with your fingers is greasy and difficult—and paper dishes soon get to look very spotty and horrid. But one thing you can't imagine, and that is how soda-

water behaves when you try to drink it straight out of a siphon—
especially a quite full one. But if imagination will not help you, experience will, and you can easily try it for yourself if you can get a
grown-up to give you the siphon. If you want to have a really thorough experience, put the tube in your mouth and press the handle
very suddenly and very hard. You had better do it when you are
alone—and out of doors is best for this experiment.

However you eat them, tongue and chicken and new bread are
very good things, and no one minds being sprinkled a little with
soda-water on a really fine hot day. So that everyone enjoyed the dinner very much indeed, and everyone ate as much as it possibly could:
first, because it was extremely hungry; and secondly, because, as I
said, tongue and chicken and new bread are very nice.

Now, I daresay you will have noticed that if you have to wait for
your dinner till long after the proper time, and then eat a great deal
more dinner than usual, and sit in the hot sun on the top of a church-
tower—or even anywhere else—you become soon and strangely
sleepy. Now Anthea and Jane and Cyril and Robert were very like you
in many ways, and when they had eaten all they could, and drunk all
there was, they became sleepy, strangely and soon—especially
Anthea, because she had got up so early.

One by one they left off talking and leaned back, and before it
was a quarter of an hour after dinner they had all curled round and
tucked themselves up under their large soft warm wings and were
fast asleep. And the sun was sinking slowly in the west. (I must say it
was in the west, because it is usual in books to say so, for fear care-
less people should think it was setting in the east. In point of fact, it
was not exactly in the west either—but that's near enough.) The sun,
I repeat, was sinking slowly in the west, and the children slept
warmly and happily on—for wings are cosier than eiderdown quilts
to sleep under. The shadow of the church-tower fell across the
churchyard, and across the Vicarage, and across the field beyond; and
presently there were no more shadows, and the sun had set, and the
wings were gone. And still the children slept. But not for long. Twilight is very beautiful, but it is chilly; and you know, however sleepy
you are, you wake up soon enough if your brother or sister happens
to be up first and pulls your blankets off you. The four wingless children shivered and woke. And there they were—on the top of a

The children slept

church-tower in the dusky twilight, with blue stars coming out by ones and twos and tens and twenties over their heads—miles away from home, with three-and-three-half-pence in their pockets, and a doubtful act about the necessities of life to be accounted for if any-one found them with the soda-water siphon.

They looked at each other. Cyril spoke first, picking up the siphon:

"We'd better get along down and get rid of this beastly thing. It's dark enough to leave it on the clergyman's doorstep, I should think. Come on."

There was a little turret at the corner of the tower, and the little turret had a door in it. They had noticed this when they were eating, but had not explored it, as you would have done in their place. Because, of course, when you have wings, and can explore the whole sky, doors seem hardly worth exploring.

Now they turned towards it.

"Of course," said Cyril, "this is the way down."

It was. But the door was locked on the inside!

And the world was growing darker and darker. And they were miles from home. And there was the soda-water siphon.

I shall not tell you whether anyone cried, nor, if so, how many cried, nor who cried. You will be better employed in making up your minds what you would have done if you had been in their place.

CHAPTER V

No Wings

Whether anyone cried or not, there was certainly an interval during which none of the party was quite itself. When they grew calmer, Anthea put her handkerchief in her pocket and her arm round Jane, and said:

"It can't be for more than one night. We can signal with our handkerchiefs in the morning. They'll be dry then. And someone will come up and let us out—"

"And find the siphon," said Cyril gloomily; "and we shall be sent to prison for stealing—"

"You said it wasn't stealing. You said you were sure it wasn't."

"I'm not sure *now*," said Cyril shortly.

"Let's throw the beastly thing slap away among the trees," said Robert, "then no one can do anything to us."

"Oh yes"—Cyril's laugh was not a lighthearted one—"and hit some chap on the head, and be murderers as well as—as the other thing."

"But we can't stay up here all night," said Jane; "and I want my tea."

"You *can't* want your tea," said Robert; "you've only just had your dinner."

"But I *do* want it," she said; "especially when you begin talking about stopping up here all night. Oh, Panther—I want to go home! I want to go home!"

"Hush, hush," Anthea said. "Don't, dear. It'll be all right, somehow. Don't, don't—"

"Let her cry," said Robert desperately; "if she howls loud enough, someone may hear and come and let us out."

"And see the soda-water thing," said Anthea swiftly. "Robert, don't be a brute. Oh, Jane, do try to be a man! It's just the same for all of us."

Jane did try to "be a man"—and reduced her howls to sniffs.

There was a pause. Then Cyril said slowly, "Look here. We must risk that siphon. I'll button it up inside my jacket—perhaps no one will notice it. You others keep well in front of me. There are lights in the clergyman's house. They've not gone to bed yet. We must just yell as loud as ever we can. Now all scream when I say three. Robert, you do the yell like the railway engine, and I'll do the coo-ee like father's. The girls can do as they please. One, two, three!"

A fourfold yell rent the silent peace of the evening, and a maid at one of the Vicarage windows paused with her hand on the blind-cord.

"One, two, three!" Another yell, piercing and complex, startled the owls and starlings to a flutter of feathers in the belfry below. The maid fled from the Vicarage window and ran down the Vicarage stairs and into the Vicarage kitchen, and fainted as soon as she had explained to the manservant and the cook and the cook's cousin that she had seen a ghost. It was quite untrue, of course, but I suppose the girl's nerves were a little upset by the yelling.

"One, two, three!" The Vicar was on his doorstep by this time, and there was no mistaking the yell that greeted him.

"Goodness me," he said to his wife, "my dear, someone's being murdered in the church! Give me my hat and a thick stick, and tell Andrew to come after me. I expect it's the lunatic who stole the tongue."

The children had seen the flash of light when the Vicar opened his front door. They had seen his dark form on the doorstep, and they had paused for breath, and also to see what he would do.

When he turned back for his hat, Cyril said hastily:

"He thinks he only fancied he heard something. You don't half yell! Now! One, two, three!"

It was certainly a whole yell this time, and the Vicar's wife flung her arms round her husband and screamed a feeble echo of it.

"You shan't go!" she said, "not alone. Jessie!"—the maid unfainted and came out of the kitchen—"send Andrew at once. There's a dangerous lunatic in the church, and he must go immediately and catch it."

"I expect he will catch it too," said Jessie to herself as she went through the kitchen door. "Here, Andrew," she said, "there's someone screaming like mad in the church, and the missus says you're to go along and catch it."

"Not alone, I don't," said Andrew in low firm tones. To his master he merely said, "Yes, sir."

"You heard those screams?"

"I did think I noticed a sort of something," said Andrew.

"Well, come on, then," said the Vicar. "My dear, I *must* go!" He pushed her gently into the sitting-room, banged the door, and rushed out, dragging Andrew by the arm.

A volley of yells greeted them. As it died into silence Andrew shouted, "Hullo, you there! Did you call?"

"Yes," shouted four far-away voices.

"They seem to be in the air," said the Vicar. "Very remarkable."

"Where are you?" shouted Andrew: and Cyril replied in his deepest voice, very slow and loud:

"CHURCH! TOWER! TOP!"

"Come down, then!" said Andrew; and the same voice replied:

"CAN'T! DOOR LOCKED!"

"My goodness!" said the Vicar. "Andrew fetch the stable lantern. Perhaps it would be as well to fetch another man from the village."

"With the rest of the gang about, very likely. No, sir; if this 'ere ain't a trap—well, may I never! There's cook's cousin at the back door now. He's a keeper, sir, and used to dealing with vicious characters. And he's got his gun, sir."

"Hullo there!" shouted Cyril from the church-tower; "come up and let us out."

"We're a-coming," said Andrew. "I'm a-going to get a policeman and a gun."

"Andrew, Andrew," said the Vicar, "that's not the truth."

"It's near enough, sir, for the likes of them."

So Andrew fetched the lantern and the cook's cousin; and the Vicar's wife begged them all to be very careful.

They went across the churchyard—it was quite dark now—and as they went they talked. The Vicar was certain a lunatic was on the church-tower—the one who had written the mad letter, and taken the cold tongue and things. Andrew thought it was a "trap"; the cook's cousin alone was calm. "Great cry, little wool,"* said he; "dangerous chaps is quieter." He was not at all afraid. But then he had a gun. That was why he was asked to lead the way up the worn steep dark steps of the church-tower. He did lead the way, with the lantern in one hand and the gun in the other. Andrew went next. He pretended afterwards that this was because he was braver than his master, but really it was because he thought of traps, and he did not like the idea of being behind the others for fear someone should come softly up behind him and catch hold of his legs in the dark. They went on and on, and round and round the little corkscrew staircase—then through the bell-ringers' loft, where the bell-ropes hung with soft furry ends like giant caterpillars—then up another stair into the belfry, where the big quiet bells are—and then on, up a ladder with broad steps—and then up a little stone stair. And at the top of that there was a little door. And the door was bolted on the stair side.

The cook's cousin, who was a gamekeeper, kicked at the door, and said:

"Hullo, you there!"

The children were holding on to each other on the other side of the door, and trembling with anxiousness—and very hoarse with their howls. They could hardly speak, but Cyril managed to reply huskily:

"Hullo, you there!"

"How did you get up there?"

It was no use saying "We flew up," so Cyril said:

"We got up—and then we found the door was locked and we couldn't get down. Let us out—do."

"How many of you are there?" asked the keeper.

"Only four," said Cyril.

"Are you armed?"

"Are we what?"

"I've got my gun handy—so you'd best not try any tricks," said the keeper. "If we open the door, will you promise to come quietly down, and no nonsense?"

"Yes—oh YES!" said all the children together.

---

* Much talk with insignificant results.

The keeper spoke deep-chested words through the keyhole

"Bless me," said the Vicar, "surely that was a female voice?"

"Shall I open the door, sir?" said the keeper. Andrew went down a few steps, "to leave room for the others" he said afterwards.

"Yes," said the Vicar, "open the door. Remember," he said through the keyhole, "we have come to release you. You will keep your promise to refrain from violence?"

"How this bolt do stick," said the keeper; "anyone 'ud think it hadn't been drawed for half a year." As a matter of fact it hadn't.

When all the bolts were drawn, the keeper spoke deep-chested words through the keyhole.

"I don't open," said he, "till you've gone over to the other side of the tower. And if one of you comes at me I fire. Now!"

"We're all over on the other side," said the voices.

The keeper felt pleased with himself, and owned himself a bold man when he threw open that door, and, stepping out into the leads,

flashed the full light of the stable lantern on to the group of desper-
adoes standing against the parapet on the other side of the tower.

He lowered his gun, and he nearly dropped the lantern.

"So help me," he cried, "if they ain't a pack of kiddies!"

The Vicar now advanced.

"How did you come here?" he asked severely. "Tell me at once."

"Oh, take us down," said Jane, catching at his coat, "and we'll tell
you anything you like. You won't believe us, but it doesn't matter. Oh,
take us down!"

The others crowded round him, with the same entreaty. All but
Cyril. He had enough to do with the soda-water siphon, which
would keep slipping down under his jacket. It needed both hands to
keep it steady in its place.

But he said, standing as far out of the lantern light as possible:

"Please do take us down."

So they were taken down. It is no joke to go down a strange
church-tower in the dark, but the keeper helped them—only, Cyril
had to be independent because of the soda-water siphon. It would
keep trying to get away. Half-way down the ladder it all but escaped.
Cyril just caught it by its spout, and as nearly as possible lost his foot-
ing. He was trembling and pale when at last they reached the bottom
of the winding stair and stepped out on to the flags of the church-
porch.

Then suddenly the keeper caught Cyril and Robert each by an
arm.

"You bring along the gells, sir," said he; "you and Andrew can
manage them."

"Let go!" said Cyril, "we aren't running away. We haven't hurt
your old church. Leave go!"

"You just come along," said the keeper; and Cyril dared not op-
pose him with violence, because just then the siphon began to slip
again.

So they were all marched into the Vicarage study, and the Vicar's
wife came rushing in.

"Oh, William, *are* you safe?" she cried.

Robert hastened to allay her anxiety.

"Yes," he said, "he's quite safe. We haven't hurt him at all. And please, we're very late, and they'll be anxious at home. Could you send us home in your carriage?"

"Or perhaps there's a hotel near where we could get a carriage from," said Anthea. "Martha will be very anxious as it is."

The Vicar had sunk into a chair, overcome by emotion and amazement.

Cyril had also sat down, and was leaning forward with his elbows on his knees because of that soda-water siphon.

"But how did you come to be locked up in the church-tower?" asked the Vicar.

"We went up," said Robert slowly, "and we were tired, and we all went to sleep, and when we woke up we found the door was locked, so we yelled."

"I should think you did!" said the Vicar's wife. "Frightening everybody out of their wits like this! You ought to be ashamed of yourselves."

"We *are*," said Jane gently.

"But who locked the door?" asked the Vicar.

"I don't know at all," said Robert, with perfect truth. "Do please send us home."

"Well, really," said the Vicar, "I suppose we'd better. Andrew, put the horse to, and you can take them home."

"Not alone, I don't," said Andrew to himself.

"And," the Vicar went on, "let this be a lesson to you . . ." He went on talking, and the children listened miserably. But the keeper was not listening. He was looking at the unfortunate Cyril. He knew all about poachers of course, so he knew how people look when they're hiding something. The Vicar had just got to the part about trying to grow up to be a blessing to your parents, and not a trouble and a disgrace, when the keeper suddenly said:

"Arst him what he's got there under his jacket"; and Cyril knew that concealment was at an end. So he stood up, and squared his shoulders and tried to look noble, like the boys in books that no one can look in the face of and doubt that they come of brave and noble families and will be faithful to the death, and he pulled out the soda-water siphon and said:

"Well, there you are, then."

There was a silence. Cyril went on—there was nothing else for it:

"Yes, we took this out of your larder, and some chicken and tongue and bread. We were very hungry, and we didn't take the custard or jam. We only took bread and meat and water—and we couldn't help its being the soda kind—just the necessaries of life; and we left half-a-crown to pay for it, and we left a letter. And we're very sorry. And my father will pay a fine or anything you like, but don't send us to prison. Mother would be so vexed. You know what you said about not being a disgrace. Well, don't you go and do it to us—that's all! We're as sorry as we can be. There!"

"However did you get up to the larder window?" said Mrs. Vicar.

"I can't tell you that," said Cyril firmly.

"Is this the whole truth you've been telling me?" asked the clergyman.

"No," answered Jane suddenly; "it's all true, but it's not the whole truth. We can't tell you that. It's no good asking. Oh, do forgive us and take us home!" She ran to the Vicar's wife and threw her arms round her. The Vicar's wife put her arms round Jane, and the keeper whispered behind his hand to the Vicar:

"They're all right, sir—I expect it's a pal they're standing by. Someone put 'em up to it, and they won't peach. Game little kids."

"Tell me," said the Vicar kindly, "are you screening someone else? Had anyone else anything to do with this?"

"Yes," said Anthea, thinking of the Psammead; "but it wasn't their fault."

"Very well, my dears," said the Vicar, "then let's say no more about it. Only just tell us why you wrote such an odd letter."

"I don't know," said Cyril. "You see, Anthea wrote it in such a hurry, and it really didn't seem like stealing then. But afterwards, when we found we couldn't get down off the church-tower, it seemed just exactly like it. We are all very sorry—"

"Say no more about it," said the Vicar's wife; "but another time just think before you take other people's tongues. Now—some cake and milk before you go home?"

When Andrew came to say that the horse was put to, and was he expected to be led alone into the trap that he had plainly seen from the first, he found the children eating cake and drinking milk and laughing at the Vicar's jokes. Jane was sitting on the Vicar's wife's lap.

So you see they got off better than they deserved.

The gamekeeper, who was the cook's cousin, asked leave to drive home with them, and Andrew was only too glad to have someone to protect him from the trap he was so certain of.

When the wagonette reached their own house, between the chalk-quarry and the gravel-pit, the children were very sleepy, but they felt that they and the keeper were friends for life.

Andrew dumped the children down at the iron gate without a word.

"You get along home," said the Vicarage cook's cousin, who was a gamekeeper. "I'll get me home on Shanks' mare."

So Andrew had to drive off alone, which he did not like at all, and it was the keeper that was cousin to the Vicarage cook who went with the children to the door, and, when they had been swept to bed in a whirlwind of reproaches, remained to explain to Martha and the cook and the housemaid exactly what had happened. He explained so well that Martha was quite amiable the next morning.

After that he often used to come over and see Martha, and in the end—but that is another story, as dear Mr. Kipling says.

Martha was obliged to stick to what she had said the night before about keeping the children indoors the next day for a punishment. But she wasn't at all snarky about it, and agreed to let Robert go out for half an hour to get something he particularly wanted.

This, of course, was the day's wish.

Robert rushed to the gravel-pit, found the Psammead, and presently wished for—

But that, too, is another story.

CHAPTER VI

A Castle and no Dinner

The others were to be kept in as a punishment for the misfortunes of the day before. Of course Martha thought it was naughtiness, and not misfortune—so you must not blame her. She only thought she was doing her duty. You know grown-up people often say they do not like to punish you, and that they only do it for your own good, and that it hurts them as much as it hurts you— and this is really very often the truth.

Martha certainly hated having to punish the children quite as much as they hated to be punished. For one thing, she knew what a noise there would be in the house all day. And she had other reasons.

"I declare," she said to the cook, "it seems almost a shame keeping of them indoors this lovely day; but they are that audacious, they'll be walking in with their heads knocked off some of these days, if I don't put my foot down. You make them a cake for tea tomorrow, dear. And we'll have Baby along of us soon as we've got a bit forrard with our work. Then they can have a good romp with them beds. Here's ten o'clock nearly, and no rabbits caught!"

People say that in Kent when they mean "and no work done."

So all the others were kept in, but Robert, as I have said, was allowed to go out for half an hour to get something they all wanted. And that, of course, was the day's wish.

He had no difficulty in finding the Sand-fairy, for the day was already so hot that it had actually, for the first time, come out of its own accord, and it was sitting in a sort of pool of soft sand, stretching itself, and trimming its whiskers, and turning its snail's eyes round and round.

"Ha!" it said when its left eye saw Robert; "I've been looking out for you. Where are the rest of you? Not smashed themselves up with those wings, I hope?"

"No," said Robert; "but the wings got us into a row, just like all the wishes always do. So the others are kept indoors, and I was only let out for half an hour—to get the wish. So please let me wish as quickly as I can."

"Wish away," said the Psammead, twisting itself round in the sand. But Robert couldn't wish away. He forgot all the things he had been thinking about, and nothing would come into his head but little things for himself, like toffee, a foreign stamp album, or a clasp-knife with three blades and a corkscrew. He sat down to think better, but it was no use. He could only think of things the others would not have cared for—such as a football, or a pair of leg-guards, or to be able to lick Simpkins minor* thoroughly when he went back to school.

"Well," said the Psammead at last, "you'd better hurry up with that wish of yours. Time flies."

"I know it does," said Robert. "I can't think what to wish for. I wish you could give one of the others their wish without their having to come here to ask for it. Oh, *don't*!"

But it was too late. The Psammead had blown itself out to about three times its proper size, and now it collapsed like a pricked bubble, and with a deep sigh leaned back against the edge of its sand-pool, quite faint with the effort.

"There!" it said in a weak voice; "it was tremendously hard—but I did it. Run along home, or they're sure to wish for something silly before you get there."

They were—quite sure; Robert felt this, and as he ran home his mind was deeply occupied with the sort of wishes he might find they had wished in his absence. They might wish for rabbits, or white mice, or chocolate, or a fine day tomorrow, or even—and that was most likely—someone might have said, "I do wish to goodness Robert would hurry up." Well, he *was* hurrying up, and so they would have their wish, and the day would be wasted. Then he tried to think what they could wish for—something that would be amusing indoors. That had been his own difficulty from the beginning. So few things are amusing indoors when the sun is shining outside and you mayn't go out, however much you want to.

---

* Term for the younger of two people with the same surname.

Robert was running as fast as he could, but when he turned the corner that ought to have brought him within sight of the architect's nightmare—the ornamental iron-work on the top of the house—he opened his eyes so wide that he had to drop into a walk; for you cannot run with your eyes wide open. Then suddenly he stopped short, for there was no house to be seen. The front-garden railings were gone too, and where the house had stood—Robert rubbed his eyes and looked again. Yes, the others *had* wished—there was no doubt about that—and they must have wished that they lived in a castle; for there the castle stood black and stately, and very tall and broad, with battlements and lancet windows, and eight great towers; and, where the garden and the orchard had been, there were white things dotted like mushrooms. Robert walked slowly on, and as he got nearer he saw that these were tents, and men in armour were walking about among the tents—crowds and crowds of them.

"Oh, crikey!" said Robert fervently. "They *have*! They've wished for a castle, and it's being besieged! It's just like that Sand-fairy! I wish we'd never seen the beastly thing!"

At the little window above the great gateway, across the moat that now lay where the garden had been but half an hour ago, someone was waving something pale dust-coloured. Robert thought it was one of Cyril's handkerchiefs. They had never been white since the day when he had upset the bottle of "Combined Toning and Fixing Solution" into the drawer where they were. Robert waved back, and immediately felt that he had been unwise. For his signal had been seen by the besieging force, and two men in steel-caps were coming towards him. They had high brown boots on their long legs, and they came towards him with such great strides that Robert remembered the shortness of his own legs and did not run away. He knew it would be useless to himself, and he feared it might be irritating to the foe. So he stood still—and the two men seemed quite pleased with him.

"By my halidom," said one, "a brave varlet this!"

Robert felt pleased at being *called* brave, and somehow it made him *feel* brave. He passed over the "varlet." It was the way people talked in historical romances for the young, he knew, and it was evidently not meant for rudeness. He only hoped he would be able to understand what they said to him. He had not always been able quite to follow the conversations in the historical romances for the young.

It had turned into a stately castle

"His garb is strange," said the other. "Some outlandish treachery, belike."

"Say, lad, what brings thee hither?"

Robert knew this meant, "Now then, youngster, what are you up to here, eh?"—so he said:

"If you please, I want to go home."

"Go, then!" said the man in the longest boots; "none hindereth, and nought lets us to follow. Zooks!" he added in a cautious undertone, "I misdoubt me but he beareth tidings to the besieged."

"Where dwellest thou, young knave?" inquired the man with the largest steel-cap.

"Over there," said Robert; and directly he had said it he knew he ought to have said "Yonder!"

"Ha—sayest so?" rejoined the longest boots. "Come hither, boy. This is a matter for our leader."

And to the leader Robert was dragged forthwith—by the reluctant ear.

The leader was the most glorious creature Robert had ever seen. He was exactly like the pictures Robert had so often admired in the historical romances. He had armour, and a helmet, and a horse, and a crest, and feathers, and a shield, and a lance, and a sword. His armour and his weapons were all, I am almost sure, of quite different periods. The shield was thirteenth-century, while the sword was of the pattern used in the Peninsular War.[*] The cuirass was of the time of Charles I,[†] and the helmet dated from the Second Crusade.[‡] The arms on the shield were very grand—three red running lions on a blue ground. The tents were of the latest brand and the whole appearance of camp, army, and leader might have been a shock to some. But Robert was dumb with admiration, and it all seemed to him perfectly correct, because he knew no more of heraldry or archaeology than the gifted artists who usually drew the

---

[*] Major campaign (1808–1814) on the Iberian Peninsula during the Napoleonic Wars.

[†] King of England from 1625 until 1649; he was executed after the defeat of his forces in the English Civil Wars.

[‡] The second (1147–1149) in the series of campaigns to wrest the Holy Land from Muslim control.

Robert was dragged forthwith by the reluctant ear

pictures for the historical romances. The scene was indeed "exactly like a picture." He admired it all so much that he felt braver than ever.

"Come hither, lad," said the glorious leader, when the men in Cromwellian steel-caps* had said a few low eager words. And he took off his helmet, because he could not see properly with it on. He had

---

* Helmets from the era of Oliver Cromwell (1599–1658), who led the Puritan rebellion against Charles I and ruled as lord protector from 1653 until his death.

a kind face, and long fair hair. "Have no fear; thou shalt take no scathe,"* he said.

Robert was glad of that. He wondered what "scathe" was, and if it was nastier than the senna† tea which he had to take sometimes.

"Unfold thy tale without alarm," said the leader kindly. "Whence comest thou, and what is thine intent?"

"My what?" said Robert.

"What seekest thou to accomplish? What is thine errand, that thou wanderest here alone among these rough men-at-arms? Poor child, thy mother's heart aches for thee e'en now, I'll warrant me."

"I don't think so," said Robert; "you see, she doesn't know I'm out."

The leader wiped away a manly tear, exactly as a leader in a historical romance would have done, and said:

"Fear not to speak the truth, my child; thou hast nought to fear from Wulfric de Talbot."

Robert had a wild feeling that this glorious leader of the besieging party—being himself part of a wish—would be able to understand better than Martha, or the gipsies, or the policeman in Rochester, or the clergyman of yesterday, the true tale of the wishes and the Psammead. The only difficulty was that he knew he could never remember enough "quothas" and "beshrew me's," and things like that, to make his talk sound like the talk of a boy in a historical romance. However, he began boldly enough, with a sentence straight out of *Ralph de Courcy; or, The Boy Crusader*.[4] He said:

"Grammercy‡ for thy courtesy, fair sir knight. The fact is, it's like this—and I hope you're not in a hurry, because the story's rather a breather. Father and mother are away, and when we were down playing in the sand-pits we found a Psammead."

"I cry thee mercy! A Sammyadd?" said the knight.

"Yes, a sort of—of fairy, or enchanter—yes, that's it, an enchanter; and he said we could have a wish every day, and we wished first to be beautiful."

---

* Harm.

† Shrub with laxative properties.

‡ Often spelled gramercy; an expression of gratitude (archaic).

The leader wiped away a manly tear

"Thy wish was scarce granted," muttered one of the men-at-arms, looking at Robert, who went on as if he had not heard, though he thought the remark very rude indeed.

"And then we wished for money—treasure, you know; but we couldn't spend it. And yesterday we wished for wings, and we got them, and we had a ripping time to begin with—"

"Thy speech is strange and uncouth," said Sir Wulfric de Talbot. "Repeat thy words—what hadst thou?"

"A ripping—I mean a jolly—no—we were contented with our lot—that's what I mean; only, after that we got into an awful fix."

"What is a fix? A fray, mayhap?"

"No—not a fray. A—a—a tight place."

"A dungeon? Alas for thy youthful fettered limbs!" said the knight, with polite sympathy.

"It wasn't a dungeon. We just—just encountered undeserved misfortunes," Robert explained, "and today we are punished by not being allowed to go out. That's where I live,"—he pointed to the castle. "The others are in there, and they're not allowed to go out. It's all the Psammead's—I mean the enchanter's fault. I wish we'd never seen him."

"He is an enchanter of might?"

"Oh yes—of might and main. Rather!"

"And thou deemest that it is the spells of the enchanter whom thou hast angered that have lent strength to the besieging party," said the gallant leader; "but know thou that Wulfric de Talbot needs no enchanter's aid to lead his followers to victory."

"No, I'm sure you don't," said Robert, with hasty courtesy; "of course not—you wouldn't, you know. But, all the same, it's partly his fault, but we're most to blame. You couldn't have done anything if it hadn't been for us."

"How now, bold boy?" asked Sir Wulfric haughtily. "Thy speech is dark, and eke* scarce courteous. Unravel me this riddle!"

"Oh," said Robert desperately, "of course you don't know it, but you're not *real* at all. You're only here because the others must have been idiots enough to wish for a castle—and when the sun sets you'll just vanish away, and it'll be all right."

The captain and the men-at-arms exchanged glances, at first pitying, and then sterner, as the longest-booted man said, "Beware, noble my lord; the urchin doth but feign madness to escape from our clutches. Shall we not bind him?"

"I'm no more mad than you are," said Robert angrily, "perhaps not so much—only, I was an idiot to think you'd understand anything. Let me go—I haven't done anything to you."

"Whither?" asked the knight, who seemed to have believed all the enchanter story till it came to his own share in it. "Whither wouldst thou wend?"

"Home, of course." Robert pointed to the castle.

"To carry news of succour? Nay!"

"All right then," said Robert, struck by a sudden idea; "then let

---

* Also (archaic).

me go somewhere else." His mind sought eagerly among his memories of the historical romance.

"Sir Wulfric de Talbot," he said slowly, "should think foul scorn to—to keep a chap—I mean one who has done him no hurt—when he wants to cut off quietly—I mean to depart without violence."

"This to my face! Beshrew thee for a knave!" replied Sir Wulfric. But the appeal seemed to have gone home. "Yet thou sayest sooth," he added thoughtfully. "Go where thou wilt," he added nobly, "thou art free. Wulfric de Talbot warreth not with babes, and Jakin here shall bear thee company."

"All right," said Robert wildly. "Jakin will enjoy himself, I think. Come on, Jakin. Sir Wulfric, I salute thee."

He saluted after the modern military manner, and set off running to the sand-pit, Jakin's long boots keeping up easily.

He found the Fairy. He dug it up, he woke it up, he implored it to give him one more wish.

"I've done two today already," it grumbled, "and one was as stiff a bit of work as ever I did."

"Oh, do, do, do, do, *do*!" said Robert, while Jakin looked on with an expression of open-mouthed horror at the strange beast that talked, and gazed with its snail's eyes at him.

"Well, what is it?" snapped the Psammead, with cross sleepiness.

"I wish I was with the others," said Robert. And the Psammead began to swell. Robert never thought of wishing the castle and the siege away. Of course he knew they had all come out of a wish, but swords and daggers and pikes and lances seemed much too real to be wished away. Robert lost consciousness for an instant. When he opened his eyes the others were crowding around him.

"We never heard you come in," they said. "How awfully jolly of you to wish it to give us our wish!"

"Of course we understood that was what you'd done."

"But you ought to have told us. Suppose we'd wished something silly."

"Silly?" said Robert, very crossly indeed. "How much sillier could you have been, I'd like to know? You nearly settled *me*—I can tell you."

Then he told his story, and the others admitted that it certainly had been rough on him. But they praised his courage and cleverness

"Oh, do! do! do! do! do!" said Robert

so much that he presently got back his lost temper, and felt braver than ever, and consented to be captain of the besieged force.

"We haven't done anything yet," said Anthea comfortably; "we waited for you. We're going to shoot at them through these little loopholes with the bow and arrows uncle gave you, and you shall have first shot."

"I don't think I would," said Robert cautiously; "you don't know what they're like near to. They've got *real* bows and arrows—an awful length—and swords and pikes and daggers, and all sorts of sharp things. They're all quite, quite real. It's not just a—a picture, or a vision, or anything; they can hurt us—or kill us even, I shouldn't wonder. I can feel my ear all sore still. Look here—have you explored the castle? Because I think we'd better let them alone as long as they let us alone. I heard that Jakin man say they weren't going to attack till just before sundown. We can be getting ready for the attack. Are there any soldiers in the castle to defend it?"

"We don't know," said Cyril. "You see, directly I'd wished we were in a besieged castle, everything seemed to go upside down, and when it came straight we looked out of the window, and saw the camp and things and you—and of course we kept on looking at everything. Isn't this room jolly? It's as real as real!"

It was. It was square, with stone walls four feet thick, and great beams for ceiling. A low door at the corner led to a flight of steps, up and down. The children went down; they found themselves in a great arched gatehouse—the enormous doors were shut and barred. There was a window in a little room at the bottom of the round turret up which the stair wound, rather larger than the other windows, and looking through it they saw that the drawbridge was up and the portcullis* down; the moat looked very wide and deep. Opposite the great door that led to the moat was another great door, with a little door in it. The children went through this, and found themselves in a big paved courtyard, with the great grey walls of the castle rising dark and heavy on all four sides.

Near the middle of the courtyard stood Martha, moving her right hand backwards and forwards in the air. The cook was stooping down and moving her hands, also in a very curious way. But the oddest and at the same time most terrible thing was the Lamb, who was sitting on nothing, about three feet from the ground, laughing happily.

The children ran towards him. Just as Anthea was reaching out her arms to take him, Martha said crossly, "Let him alone—do, miss, when he is good."

"But what's he *doing?*" said Anthea.

"Doing? Why, a-setting in his high chair as good as gold, a precious, watching me doing of the ironing. Get along with you, do— my iron's cold again."

She went towards the cook, and seemed to poke an invisible fire with an unseen poker—the cook seemed to be putting an unseen dish into an invisible oven.

"Run along with you, do," she said; "I'm behind-hand as it is.

---

* Grate or grille, made of wood or iron and suspended by chains; designed to be low-ered for quick fortification against assault.

You won't get no dinner if you come a-hindering of me like this. Come, off you goes, or I'll pin a dishcloth to some of your tails."

"You're *sure* the Lamb's all right?" asked Jane anxiously.

"Right as ninepence, if you don't come unsettling of him. I thought you'd like to be rid of him for today; but take him, if you want him, for gracious' sake."

"No, no," they said, and hastened away. They would have to defend the castle presently, and the Lamb was safer even suspended in mid-air in an invisible kitchen than in the guardroom of a besieged castle. They went through the first doorway they came to, and sat down helplessly on a wooden bench that ran along the room inside.

"How awful!" said Anthea and Jane together; and Jane added, "I feel as if I was in a mad asylum."

"What does it mean?" Anthea said. "It's creepy; I don't like it. I wish we'd wished for something plain—a rocking-horse, or a donkey, or something."

"It's no use wishing *now*," said Robert bitterly; and Cyril said:

"Do dry up a sec; I want to think."

He buried his face in his hands, and the others looked about them. They were in a long room with an arched roof. There were wooden tables along it, and one across at the end of the room, on a sort of raised platform. The room was very dim and dark. The floor was strewn with dry things like sticks, and they did not smell nice.

Cyril sat up suddenly and said:

"Look here—it's all right. I think it's like this. You know, we wished that the servants shouldn't notice any difference when we got wishes. And nothing happens to the Lamb unless we specially wish it to. So of course they don't notice the castle or anything. But then the castle is on the same place where our house was—is, I mean—and the servants have to go on being in the house, or else they would notice. But you can't have a castle mixed up with our house—and so we can't see the house, because we see the castle; and they can't see the castle, because they go on seeing the house; and so—"

"Oh, *don't!*" said Jane; "you make my head go all swimmy, like being on a roundabout.* It doesn't matter! Only, I hope we shall be

---

* Merry-go-round.

able to see our dinner, that's all—because if it's invisible it'll be un-feelable as well, and then we can't eat it! I *know* it will, because I tried to feel if I could feel the Lamb's chair, and there was nothing under him at all but air. And we can't eat air, and I feel just as if I hadn't had any breakfast for years and years."

"It's no use thinking about it," said Anthea. "Let's go on explor-ing. Perhaps we might find something to eat."

This lighted hope in every breast, and they went on exploring the castle. But though it was the most perfect and delightful castle you can possibly imagine, and furnished in the most complete and beau-tiful manner, neither food nor men-at-arms were to be found in it.

"If only you'd thought of wishing to be besieged in a castle thor-oughly garrisoned and provisioned!" said Jane reproachfully.

"You can't think of everything, you know," said Anthea. "I should think it must be nearly dinner-time by now."

It wasn't; but they hung about watching the strange movements of the servants in the middle of the courtyard, because, of course, they couldn't be sure where the dining-room of the invisible house was. Presently they saw Martha carrying an invisible tray across the courtyard, for it seemed that, by the most fortunate accident, the dining-room of the house and the banqueting-hall of the castle were in the same place. But oh, how their hearts sank when they perceived that the tray was invisible!

They waited in wretched silence while Martha went through the form of carving an unseen leg of mutton and serving invisible greens and potatoes with a spoon that no one could see. When she had left the room, the children looked at the empty table, and then at each other.

"This is worse than anything," said Robert, who had not till now been particularly keen on his dinner.

"I'm not so very hungry," said Anthea, trying to make the best of things, as usual.

Cyril tightened his belt ostentatiously. Jane burst into tears.

CHAPTER VII

A Siege and Bed

The children were sitting in the gloomy banqueting-hall, at the end of one of the long bare wooden tables. There was now no hope. Martha had brought in the dinner, and the dinner was invisible, and unfeelable too; for, when they rubbed their hands along the table, they knew but too well that for them there was nothing there but table.

Suddenly Cyril felt in his pocket.

"Right, oh!" he cried. "Look here! Biscuits."

Rather broken and crumbled, certainly, but still biscuits. Three whole ones, and a generous handful of crumbs and fragments.

"I got them this morning—cook—and I'd quite forgotten," he explained as he divided them with scrupulous fairness into four heaps.

They were eaten in a happy silence, though they tasted a little oddly, because they had been in Cyril's pocket all the morning with a hank* of tarred twine, some green fir-cones, and a ball of cobbler's wax.†

"Yes, but look here, Squirrel," said Robert; "you're so clever at explaining about invisibleness and all that. How is it the biscuits are here, and all the bread and meat and things have disappeared?"

"I don't know," said Cyril after a pause, "unless it's because we had them. Nothing about us has changed. Everything's in my pocket all right."

"Then if we had the mutton it would be real," said Robert. "Oh, don't I wish we could find it!"

---

* Loop or coil.

† Resinous substance used to strengthen the thread that is used to sew shoes or to bind whips, ropes, and other goods.

"But we can't find it. I suppose it isn't ours till we've got it in our mouths."

"Or in our pockets," said Jane, thinking of the biscuits.

"Who puts mutton in their pockets, goose-girl?" said Cyril. "But I know—at any rate, I'll try it!"

He leaned over the table with his face about an inch from it, and kept opening and shutting his mouth as if he were taking bites out of air.

"It's no good," said Robert in deep dejection. "You'll only— Hullo!"

Cyril stood up with a grin of triumph, holding a square piece of bread in his mouth. It was quite real. Everyone saw it. It is true that, directly he bit a piece off, the rest vanished; but it was all right, because he knew he had it in his hand though he could neither see nor feel it. He took another bite from the air between his fingers, and it turned into bread as he bit. The next moment all the others were following his example, and opening and shutting their mouths an inch or so from the bare-looking table. Robert captured a slice of mutton, and—but I think I will draw a veil over the rest of this painful scene. It is enough to say that they all had enough mutton, and that when Martha came to change the plates she said she had never seen such a mess in all her born days.

The pudding was, fortunately, a plain suet roly-poly,* and in answer to Martha's questions the children all with one accord said that they would not have treacle on it—nor jam, nor sugar—"Just plain, please," they said. Martha said, "Well, I never—what next, I wonder!" and went away.

Then ensued another scene on which I will not dwell, for nobody looks nice picking up slices of suet pudding from the table in its mouth, like a dog.

The great thing, after all, was that they had had dinner; and now everyone felt more courage to prepare for the attack that was to be delivered before sunset. Robert, as captain, insisted on climbing to the top of one of the towers to reconnoitre, so up they all went. And now they could see all round the castle, and could see, too, that be-

---

* Baked or boiled pudding made of a sheet of pastry covered with jam and rolled up.

yond the moat, on every side, the tents of the besieging party were
pitched. Rather uncomfortable shivers ran down the children's backs
as they saw that all the men were very busy cleaning or sharpening
their arms, re-stringing their bows, and polishing their shields. A
large party came along the road, with horses dragging along the great
trunk of a tree; and Cyril felt quite pale, because he knew this was for
a battering-ram.

"What a good thing we've got a moat," he said; "and what a
good thing the drawbridge is up—I should never have known how
to work it."

"Of course it would be up in a besieged castle."

"You'd think there ought to have been soldiers in it, wouldn't
you?" said Robert.

"You see you don't know how long it's been besieged," said Cyril
darkly; "perhaps most of the brave defenders were killed quite early
in the siege and all the provisions eaten, and now there are only a few
intrepid survivors—that's us, and we are going to defend it to the
death."

"How do you begin—defending to the death, I mean?" asked
Anthea.

"We ought to be heavily armed—and then shoot at them when
they advance to the attack."

"They used to pour boiling lead down on besiegers when they
got too close," said Anthea. "Father showed me the holes on purpose
for pouring it down through at Bodiam Castle.* And there are holes
like it in the gate-tower here."

"I think I'm glad it's only a game; it is only a game, isn't it?" said
Jane.

But no one answered.

The children found plenty of strange weapons in the castle, and
if they were armed at all it was soon plain that they would be, as Cyril
said, "armed heavily"—for these swords and lances and crossbows
were far too weighty even for Cyril's manly strength; and as for the
longbows, none of the children could even begin to bend them. The
daggers were better; but Jane hoped that the besiegers would not
come close enough for daggers to be of any use.

---

* Castle in East Sussex built by an English knight in 1385.

"Never mind, we can hurl them like javelins," said Cyril, "or drop them on people's heads. I say—there are lots of stones on the other side of the courtyard. If we took some of those up? Just to drop on their heads if they were to try swimming the moat."

So a heap of stones grew apace, up in the room above the gate; and another heap, a shiny spiky dangerous-looking heap, of daggers and knives.

As Anthea was crossing the courtyard for more stones, a sudden and valuable idea came to her. She went to Martha and said, "May we have just biscuits for tea? We're going to play at besieged castles, and we'd like the biscuits to provision the garrison. Put mine in my pocket, please, my hands are so dirty. And I'll tell the others to fetch theirs."

This was indeed a happy thought, for now with four generous handfuls of air, which turned to biscuit as Martha crammed it into their pockets, the garrison was well provisioned till sundown.

They brought up some iron pots of cold water to pour on the besiegers instead of hot lead, with which the castle did not seem to be provided.

The afternoon passed with wonderful quickness. It was very exciting; but none of them, except Robert, could feel all the time that this was real deadly dangerous work. To the others, who had only seen the camp and the besiegers from a distance, the whole thing seemed half a game of make-believe, and half a splendidly distinct and perfectly safe dream. But it was only now and then that Robert could feel this.

When it seemed to be tea-time the biscuits were eaten with water from the deep well in the courtyard, drunk out of horns. Cyril insisted on putting by eight of the biscuits, in case anyone should feel faint in stress of battle.

Just as he was putting away the reserve biscuits in a sort of little stone cupboard without a door, a sudden sound made him drop three. It was the loud fierce cry of a trumpet.

"You see it is real," said Robert, "and they are going to attack."

All rushed to the narrow windows.

"Yes," said Robert, "they're all coming out of their tents and moving about like ants. There's that Jakin dancing about where the bridge joins on. I wish he could see me put my tongue out at him! Yah!"

The others were far too pale to wish to put their tongues out at anybody. They looked at Robert with surprised respect. Anthea said:

"You really *are* brave, Robert."

"Rot!" Cyril's pallor turned to redness now, all in a minute. "He's been getting ready to be brave all the afternoon. And I wasn't ready, that's all. I shall be braver than he is in half a jiffy."

"Oh dear!" said Jane, "what does it matter which of you is the bravest? I think Cyril was a perfect silly to wish for a castle, and I don't want to play."

"It *isn't*"—Robert was beginning sternly, but Anthea interrupted—

"Oh yes, you do," she said coaxingly; "it's a very nice game, really, because they can't possibly get in, and if they do the women and children are always spared by civilized armies."

"But are you quite, quite sure they *are* civilized?" asked Jane, panting. "They seem to be such a long time ago."

"Of course they are." Anthea pointed cheerfully through the narrow window. "Why, look at the little flags on their lances, how bright they are—and how fine the leader is! Look, that's him—isn't it, Robert?—on the grey horse."

Jane consented to look, and the scene was almost too pretty to be alarming. The green turf, the white tents, the flash of pennoned lances, the gleam of armour, and the bright colours of scarf and tunic—it was just like a splendid coloured picture. The trumpets were sounding, and when the trumpets stopped for breath the children could hear the cling-clang of armour and the murmur of voices.

A trumpeter came forward to the edge of the moat, which now seemed very much narrower than at first, and blew the longest and loudest blast they had yet heard. When the blaring noise had died away, a man who was with the trumpeter shouted:

"What ho, within there!" and his voice came plainly to the garrison in the gate-house.

"Hullo there!" Robert bellowed back at once.

"In the name of our Lord the King, and of our good lord and trusty leader Sir Wulfric de Talbot, we summon this castle to surrender—on pain of fire and sword and no quarter. Do ye surrender?"

"No," bawled Robert, "of course we don't! Never, Never, NEVER!"

The man answered back:

"Then your fate be on your own heads."

"Cheer," said Robert in a fierce whisper. "Cheer to show them we aren't afraid, and rattle the daggers to make more noise. One, two, three! Hip, hip, hooray! Again—Hip, hip, hooray! One more—Hip, hip, hooray!" The cheers were rather high and weak, but the rattle of the daggers lent them strength and depth.

There was another shout from the camp across the moat—and then the beleaguered fortress felt that the attack had indeed begun.

It was getting rather dark in the room above the great gate, and Jane took a very little courage as she remembered that sunset couldn't be far off now.

"The moat is dreadfully thin," said Anthea.

"But they can't get into the castle even if they do swim over," said Robert. And as he spoke he heard feet on the stair outside—heavy feet and the clank of steel. No one breathed for a moment. The steel and the feet went on up the turret stairs. Then Robert sprang softly to the door. He pulled off his shoes.

"Wait here," he whispered, and stole quickly and softly after the boots and the spur-clank. He peeped into the upper room. The man was there—and it was Jakin, all dripping with moat-water, and he was fiddling about with the machinery which Robert felt sure worked the drawbridge. Robert banged the door suddenly, and turned the great key in the lock, just as Jakin sprang to the inside of the door. Then he tore downstairs and into the little turret at the foot of the tower where the biggest window was.

"We ought to have defended this!" he cried to the others as they followed him. He was just in time. Another man had swum over, and his fingers were on the window-ledge. Robert never knew how the man had managed to climb up out of the water. But he saw the clinging fingers, and hit them as hard as he could with an iron bar that he caught up from the floor. The man fell with a plop-plash into the moat-water. In another moment Robert was outside the little room, had banged its door and was shooting home the enormous bolts, and calling to Cyril to lend a hand.

Then they stood in the arched gate-house, breathing hard and looking at each other.

The man fell with a plop-plash into the moat-water

Jane's mouth was open.

"Cheer up, Jenny," said Robert—"it won't last much longer."

There was a creaking above, and something rattled and shook. The pavement they stood on seemed to tremble. Then a crash told them that the drawbridge had been lowered to its place.

"That's that beast Jakin," said Robert. "There's still the portcullis; I'm almost certain that's worked from lower down."

And now the drawbridge rang and echoed hollowly to the hoofs of horses and the tramp of armed men.

"Up—quick!" cried Robert. "Let's drop things on them."

Even the girls were feeling almost brave now. They followed Robert quickly, and under his directions began to drop stones out through the long narrow windows. There was a confused noise below, and some groans.

"Oh dear!" said Anthea, putting down the stone she was just going to drop out. "I'm afraid we've hurt somebody!"

Robert caught up the stone in a fury.

"I should just hope we *had!*" he said; "I'd give something for a jolly good boiling kettle of lead. Surrender, indeed!"

And now came more tramping, and a pause, and then the thundering thump of the battering-ram. And the little room was almost quite dark.

"We've held it," cried Robert, "we *won't* surrender! The sun *must* set in a minute. Here—they're all jawing underneath again. Pity there's no time to get more stones! Here, pour that water down on them. It's no good, of course, but they'll hate it."

"Oh dear!" said Jane; "don't you think we'd better surrender?"

"Never!" said Robert; "we'll have a parley if you like, but we'll never surrender. Oh, I'll be a soldier when I grow up—you just see if I don't. I won't go into the Civil Service, whatever anyone says."

"Let's wave a handkerchief and ask for a parley," Jane pleaded. "I don't believe the sun's going to set tonight at all."

"Give them the water first—the brutes!" said the bloodthirsty Robert. So Anthea tilted the pot over the nearest lead-hole, and poured. They heard a splash below, but no one below seemed to have felt it. And again the ram battered the great door. Anthea paused.

"How idiotic," said Robert, lying flat on the floor and putting one eye to the lead hole. "Of course the holes go straight down into the gate-

Anthea tilted the pot over the nearest lead-hole

house—that's for when the enemy has got past the door and the portcullis, and almost all is lost. Here, hand me the pot." He crawled on to the three-cornered window-ledge in the middle of the wall, and, taking the pot from Anthea, poured the water out through the arrow-slit.

And as he began to pour, the noise of the battering-ram and the trampling of the foe and the shouts of "Surrender!" and "De Talbot for ever!" all suddenly stopped and went out like the snuff of a candle; the little dark room seemed to whirl round and turn topsy-turvy, and when the children came to themselves there they were safe and sound, in the big front bedroom of their own house—the house with the ornamental nightmare iron-top to the roof.

They all crowded to the window and looked out. The moat and the tents and the besieging force were all gone—and there was the garden with its tangle of dahlias and marigolds and asters and late roses, and the spiky iron railings and the quiet white road.

Everyone drew a deep breath.

"And that's all right!" said Robert. "I told you so! And, I say, we didn't surrender, did we?"

"Aren't you glad now I wished for a castle?" asked Cyril.

"I think I am *now*," said Anthea slowly. "But I wouldn't wish for it again, I think, Squirrel dear!"

"Oh, it was simply splendid!" said Jane unexpectedly. "I wasn't frightened a bit."

"Oh, I say!" Cyril was beginning, but Anthea stopped him.

"Look here," she said, "it's just come into my head. This is the very first thing we've wished for that hasn't got us into a row. And there hasn't been the least little scrap of a row about this. Nobody's raging downstairs, we're safe and sound, we've had an awfully jolly day—at least, not jolly exactly, but you know what I mean. And we know now how brave Robert is—and Cyril too, of course," she added hastily, "and Jane as well. And we haven't got into a row with a single grown up."

The door was opened suddenly and fiercely.

"You ought to be ashamed of yourselves," said the voice of Martha, and they could tell by her voice that she was very angry indeed. "I thought you couldn't last through the day without getting up to some doggery! A person can't take a breath of air on the front doorstep but you must be emptying the wash-hand jug on to their heads! Off you go to bed, the lot of you, and try to get up better children in the morning. Now then—don't let me have to tell you twice. If I find any of you not in bed in ten minutes I'll let you know it, that's all! A new cap, and everything!"

She flounced out amid a disregarded chorus of regrets and apologies. The children were very sorry, but really it was not their faults. You can't help it if you are pouring water on a besieging foe, and your castle suddenly changes into your house—and everything changes with it except the water, and that happens to fall on somebody else's clean cap.

"I don't know why the water didn't change into nothing, though," said Cyril.

"Why should it?" asked Robert. "Water's water all the world over."

"I expect the castle well was the same as ours in the stable-yard," said Jane. And that was really the case.

"I thought we couldn't get through a wish-day without a row," said Cyril; "it was much too good to be true. Come on, Bobs, my military hero. If we lick into bed sharp she won't be so frumious, and perhaps she'll bring us up some supper. I'm jolly hungry! Good-night, kids."

"Good-night. I hope the castle won't come creeping back in the night," said Jane.

"Of course it won't," said Anthea briskly, "but Martha will—not in the night, but in a minute. Here, turn round, I'll get that knot out of your pinafore strings."

"Wouldn't it have been degrading for Sir Wulfric de Talbot," said Jane dreamily, "if he could have known that half the besieged garrison wore pinafores?"

"And the other half knickerbockers. Yes—frightfully. Do stand still—you're only tightening the knot," said Anthea.

CHAPTER VIII

BIGGER THAN THE BAKER'S BOY

L ook here," said Cyril. "I've got an idea."

"Does it hurt much?" said Robert sympathetically.

"Don't be a jackape! I'm not humbugging."

"Shut up, Bobs!" said Anthea.

"Silence for the Squirrel's oration," said Robert.

Cyril balanced himself on the edge of the water-butt in the back-yard, where they all happened to be, and spoke.

"Friends, Romans, countrymen—and women—we found a Sammyadd. We have had wishes. We've had wings, and being beautiful as the day—ugh!—that was pretty jolly beastly if you like—and wealth and castles, and that rotten gipsy business with the Lamb. But we're no forrader.* We haven't really got anything worth having for our wishes."

"We've had things happening," said Robert; "that's always something."

"It's not enough, unless they're the right things," said Cyril firmly. "Now I've been thinking—"

"Not really?" whispered Robert.

"In the silent what's-its-names of the night. It's like suddenly being asked something out of history—the date of the Conquest or something; you know it all right all the time, but when you're asked it all goes out of your head. Ladies and gentlemen, you know jolly well that when we're all rotting about in the usual way heaps of things keep cropping up, and then real earnest wishes come into the heads of the beholder—"

"Hear, hear!" said Robert.

"—of the beholder, however stupid he is," Cyril went on. "Why,

_____

* Further ahead.

even Robert might happen to think of a really useful wish if he didn't injure his poor little brains trying so hard to think.—Shut up, Bobs, I tell you!—You'll have the whole show over."

A struggle on the edge of a water-butt is exciting, but damp. When it was over, and the boys were partially dried, Anthea said:

"It really was you began it, Bobs. Now honour is satisfied, do let Squirrel go on. We're wasting the whole morning."

"Well then," said Cyril, still wringing the water out of the tails of his jacket, "I'll call it pax* if Bobs will."

"Pax then," said Robert sulkily. "But I've got a lump as big as a cricket ball over my eye."

Anthea patiently offered a dust-coloured handkerchief, and Robert bathed his wounds in silence. "Now, Squirrel," she said.

"Well then—let's just play bandits, or forts, or soldiers, or any of the old games. We're dead sure to think of something if we try not to. You always do."

The others consented. Bandits was hastily chosen for the game. "It's as good as anything else," said Jane gloomily. It must be owned that Robert was at first but a half-hearted bandit, but when Anthea had borrowed from Martha the red-spotted handkerchief in which the keeper had brought her mushrooms that morning, and had tied up Robert's head with it so that he could be the wounded hero who had saved the bandit captain's life the day before, he cheered up wonderfully. All were soon armed. Bows and arrows slung on the back look well; and umbrellas and cricket stumps stuck through the belt give a fine impression of the wearer's being armed to the teeth. The white cotton hats that men wear in the country nowadays have a very brigandish effect when a few turkey's feathers are stuck in them. The Lamb's mail-cart was covered with a red-and-blue checked table-cloth, and made an admirable baggage-wagon. The Lamb asleep inside it was not at all in the way. So the banditti set out along the road that led to the sand-pit.

"We ought to be near the Sammyadd," said Cyril, "in case we think of anything suddenly."

It is all very well to make up your minds to play bandits—or

---

* Peace (Latin).

chess, or ping-pong, or any other agreeable game—but it is not easy to do it with spirit when all the wonderful wishes you can think of, or can't think of, are waiting for you round the corner. The game was dragging a little, and some of the bandits were beginning to feel that the others were disagreeable things, and were saying so candidly, when the baker's boy came along the road with loaves in a basket. The opportunity was not one to be lost.

"Stand and deliver!" cried Cyril.

"Your money or your life!" said Robert.

And they stood on each side of the baker's boy. Unfortunately, he did not seem to enter into the spirit of the thing at all. He was a baker's boy of an unusually large size. He merely said:

"Chuck it now,* d'ye hear!" and pushed the bandits aside most disrespectfully.

Then Robert lassoed him with Jane's skipping-rope, and instead of going round his shoulders, as Robert intended, it went round his feet and tripped him up. The basket was upset, the beautiful new loaves went bumping and bouncing all over the dusty chalky road. The girls ran to pick them up, and all in a moment Robert and the baker's boy were fighting it out, man to man, with Cyril to see fair play, and the skipping-rope twisting round their legs like an interested snake that wished to be a peacemaker. It did not succeed; indeed the way the boxwood handles sprang up and hit the fighters on the shins and ankles was not at all peace-making. I know this is the second fight—or contest—in this chapter, but I can't help it. It was that sort of day. You know yourself there are days when rows seem to keep on happening, quite without your meaning them to. If I were a writer of tales of adventure such as those which used to appear in *The Boys of England* when I was young, of course I should be able to describe the fight, but I cannot do it. I never can see what happens during a fight, even when it is only dogs. Also, if I had been one of these *Boys of England*† writers, Robert would have got the best of it. But I am like George Washington—I cannot tell a lie, even about a cherry-tree, much less about a fight, and I cannot conceal from you that Robert was badly beaten, for the second time that day. The baker's boy

---

*Cut it out (slang).

† Popular weekly magazine launched by Edwin J. Brett in 1866.

He also pulled Robert's hair

blacked his other eye, and, being ignorant of the first rules of fair play and gentlemanly behaviour, he also pulled Robert's hair, and kicked him on the knee. Robert always used to say he could have licked the butcher if it hadn't been for the girls. But I am not sure. Anyway, what happened was this, and very painful it was to self-respecting boys.

Cyril was just tearing off his coat so as to help his brother in proper style, when Jane threw her arms round his legs and began to cry and ask him not to go and be beaten too. That "too" was very nice for Robert, as you can imagine—but it was nothing to what he felt when Anthea rushed in between him and the baker's boy, and caught that unfair and degraded fighter round the waist, imploring him not to fight any more.

"Oh, don't hurt my brother any more!" she said in floods of tears. "He didn't mean it—it's only play. And I'm sure he's very sorry."

You see how unfair this was to Robert. Because, if the baker's boy had had any right and chivalrous instincts, and had yielded to Anthea's pleading and accepted her despicable apology, Robert could not, in honour, have done anything to him at a future time. But

Robert's fears, if he had any, were soon dispelled. Chivalry was a stranger to the breast of the baker's boy. He pushed Anthea away very roughly, and he chased Robert with kicks and unpleasant conversation right down the road to the sand-pit, and there, with one last kick, he landed him in a heap of sand.

"I'll larn you, you young varmint!" he said, and went off to pick up his loaves and go about his business. Cyril, impeded by Jane, could do nothing without hurting her, for she clung round his legs with the strength of despair. The baker's boy went off red and damp about the face; abusive to the last, he called them a pack of silly idiots, and disappeared round the corner. Then Jane's grasp loosened. Cyril turned away in silent dignity to follow Robert, and the girls followed him, weeping without restraint.

It was not a happy party that flung itself down in the sand beside the sobbing Robert. For Robert was sobbing—mostly with rage. Though of course I know that a really heroic boy is always dry-eyed after a fight. But then he always wins, which had not been the case with Robert.

Cyril was angry with Jane; Robert was furious with Anthea; the girls were miserable; and not one of the four was pleased with the baker's boy. There was, as French writers say, "a silence full of emotion."

Then Robert dug his toes and his hands into the sand and wriggled in his rage. "He'd better wait till I'm grown up—the cowardly brute! Beast!—I hate him! But I'll pay him out. Just because he's bigger than me."

"You began," said Jane incautiously.

"I know I did, silly—but I was only rotting—and he kicked me—look here—"

Robert tore down a stocking and showed a purple bruise touched up with red.

"I only wish I was bigger than him, that's all."

He dug his fingers in the sand, and sprang up, for his hand had touched something furry. It was the Psammead, of course—"On the look-out to make sillies of them as usual," as Cyril remarked later. And of course the next moment Robert's wish was granted, and he was bigger than the baker's boy. Oh, but much, much bigger. He was bigger than the big policeman who used to be at the crossing at the

Mansion House* years ago—the one who was so kind in helping old ladies over the crossing—and he was the biggest man I have ever seen, as well as the kindest. No one had a foot-rule in its pocket, so Robert could not be measured—but he was taller than your father would be if he stood on your mother's head, which I am sure he would never be unkind enough to do. He must have been ten or eleven feet high, and as broad as a boy of that height ought to be, his Norfolk suit had fortunately grown too, and now he stood up in it—with one of his enormous stockings turned down to show the gigantic bruise on his vast leg. Immense tears of fury still stood on his flushed giant face. He looked so surprised, and he was so large to be wearing an Eton collar,† that the others could not help laughing.

"The Sammyadd's done us again," said Cyril.

"Not us—*me*," said Robert. "If you'd got any decent feeling you'd try to make it make you the same size. You've no idea how silly it feels," he added thoughtlessly.

"And I don't want to; I can jolly well see how silly it looks," Cyril was beginning; but Anthea said:

"Oh, *don't*! I don't know what's the matter with you boys today. Look here, Squirrel, let's play fair. It is hateful for poor old Bobs, all alone up there. Let's ask the Sammyadd for another wish, and, if it will, I do really think we ought to be made the same size."

The others agreed, but not gaily; but when they found the Psammead, it wouldn't.

"Not I," it said crossly, rubbing its face with its feet. "He's a rude violent boy, and it'll do him good to be the wrong size for a bit. What did he want to come digging me out with his nasty wet hands for? He nearly touched me! He's a perfect savage. A boy of the Stone Age would have had more sense."

Robert's hands had indeed been wet—with tears.

"Go away and leave me in peace, do," the Psammead went on. "I can't think why you don't wish for something sensible—something to eat or drink, or good manners, or good tempers. Go along with you, do!"

---

* Official residence of London's lord mayor.

† Broad, stiff white collar worn over a jacket's lapels.

"The Sammyadd's done us again," said Cyril

It almost snarled as it shook its whiskers, and turned a sulky brown back on them. The most hopeful felt that further parley was vain.

They turned again to the colossal Robert.

"Whatever shall we do?" they said; and they all said it.

"First," said Robert grimly, "I'm going to reason with that baker's boy. I shall catch him at the end of the road."

"Don't hit a chap littler than yourself, old man," said Cyril.

"Do I look like hitting him?" said Robert scornfully. "Why, I should kill him. But I'll give him something to remember. Wait till I pull up my stocking." He pulled up his stocking, which was as large as a small bolstercase,* and strode off. His strides were six or seven feet long, so that it was quite easy for him to be at the bottom of the hill, ready to meet the baker's boy when he came down swinging the empty basket to meet his master's cart, which had been leaving bread at the cottages along the road.

Robert crouched behind a haystack in the farmyard, that is at the corner, and when he heard the boy come whistling along, he jumped out at him and caught him by the collar.

"Now," he said, and his voice was about four times its usual size, just as his body was four times its, "I'm going to teach you to kick boys smaller than you."

He lifted up the baker's boy and set him on the top of the haystack, which was about sixteen feet from the ground, and then he sat down on the roof of the cowshed and told the baker's boy exactly what he thought of him. I don't think the boy heard it all—he was in a sort of trance of terror. When Robert had said everything he could think of, and some things twice over, he shook the boy and said:

"And now get down the best way you can," and left him.

I don't know how the baker's boy got down, but I do know that he missed the cart, and got into the very hottest of hot water when he turned up at last at the bakehouse. I am sorry for him, but, after all, it was quite right that he should be taught that English boys mustn't use their feet when they fight, but their fists. Of course the water he got into only became hotter when he tried to tell his master about the boy he had licked and the giant as high as a church, because no one could possibly believe such a tale as that. Next day the tale was believed—but that was too late to be of any use to the baker's boy.

When Robert rejoined the others he found them in the garden. Anthea had thoughtfully asked Martha to let them have dinner out there—because the dining-room was rather small, and it would have been so awkward to have a brother the size of Robert in there. The Lamb, who had slept peacefully during the whole stormy morning,

---

* Cloth covering for a long, narrow pillow.

He lifted up the baker's boy and set him on top of the haystack

was now found to be sneezing, and Martha said he had a cold and would be better indoors.

"And really it's just as well," said Cyril, "for I don't believe he'd ever have stopped screaming if he'd once seen you the awful size you are!"

Robert was indeed what a draper would call an "out-size" in boys. He found himself able to step right over the iron gate in the front garden.

Martha brought out the dinner—it was cold veal and baked potatoes, with sago pudding and stewed plums to follow.

She of course did not notice that Robert was anything but the usual size, and she gave him as much meat and potatoes as usual and no more. You have no idea how small your usual helping of dinner looks when you are many times your proper size. Robert groaned, and asked for more bread. But Martha would not go on giving more bread for ever. She was in a hurry, because the keeper intended to call on his way to Benenhurst Fair, and she wished to be dressed smartly before he came.

"I wish *we* were going to the Fair," said Robert.

"You can't go anywhere that size," said Cyril.

"Why not?" said Robert. "They have giants at fairs, much bigger ones than me."

"Not much, they don't," Cyril was beginning, when Jane screamed "Oh!" with such loud suddenness that they all thumped her on the back and asked whether she had swallowed a plum-stone.*

"No," she said, breathless from being thumped, "it's—it's not a plum-stone. It's an idea. Let's take Robert to the Fair, and get them to give us money for showing him! Then we really *shall* get something out of the old Sammyadd at last!"

"Take me, indeed!" said Robert indignantly. "Much more likely me take you!"

And so it turned out. The idea appealed irresistibly to everyone but Robert, and even he was brought round by Anthea's suggestion that he should have a double share of any money they might make. There was a little old pony-trap in the coach-house—the kind that is called a governess-cart. It seemed desirable to get to the Fair as quickly as possible, so Robert—who could now take enormous steps and so go very fast indeed—consented to wheel the others in this. It was as easy to him now as wheeling the Lamb in the mail-cart had been in the morning. The Lamb's cold prevented his being of the party.

It was a strange sensation being wheeled in a pony-carriage by a giant. Everyone enjoyed the journey except Robert and the few people they passed on the way. These mostly went into what looked like some kind of standing-up fits by the roadside, as Anthea said. Just

---

* Pit of a plum.

It was a strange sensation being wheeled in a pony-carriage by a giant

outside Benenhurst, Robert hid in a barn, and the others went on to the Fair.

There were some swings, and a hooting tooting blaring merry-go-round, and a shooting-gallery and coconut shies.* Resisting an impulse to win a coconut—or at least to attempt the enterprise—Cyril went up to the woman who was loading little guns before the array of glass bottles on strings against a sheet of canvas.

"Here you are, little gentleman!" she said. "Penny a shot!"

"No, thank you," said Cyril, "we are here on business, not on pleasure. Who's the master?"

"The what?"

---

* Sideshow at a fair; contestants throw a ball to try to knock a coconut off its stand.

"The master—the head—the boss of the show."

"Over there," she said, pointing to a stout man in a dirty linen jacket who was sleeping in the sun; "but I don't advise you to wake him sudden. His temper's contrary, especially these hot days. Better have a shot while you're waiting."

"It's rather important," said Cyril. "It'll be very profitable to him. I think he'll be sorry if we take it away."

"Oh, if it's money in his pocket," said the woman. "No kid now? What is it?"

"It's a giant."

"You *are* kidding?"

"Come along and see," said Anthea.

The woman looked doubtfully at them, then she called to a ragged little girl in striped stockings and a dingy white petticoat that came below her brown frock, and leaving her in charge of the "shooting-gallery" she turned to Anthea and said, "Well, hurry up! But if you *are* kidding, you'd best say so. I'm as mild as milk myself, but my Bill he's a fair terror and—"

Anthea led the way to the barn. "It really *is* a giant," she said. "He's a giant little boy—in Norfolks like my brother's there. And we didn't bring him up to the Fair because people do stare so, and they seem to go into kind of standing-up fits when they see him. And we thought perhaps you'd like to show him and get pennies; and if you like to pay us something, you can—only, it'll have to be rather a lot, because we promised him he should have a double share of whatever we made."

The woman murmured something indistinct, of which the children could only hear the words, "Swelp me!"* "balmy," and "crumpet,"† which conveyed no definite idea to their minds.

She had taken Anthea's hand, and was holding it very firmly; and Anthea could not help wondering what would happen if Robert should have wandered off or turned his proper size during the interval. But she knew that the Psammead's gifts really did last till sunset, however inconvenient their lasting might be; and she did not think,

---

* So help me! (dialect).

† Reference to the slang expression "balmy in the crumpet" (wrong in the head or crazy).

somehow, that Robert would care to go out alone while he was that size.

When they reached the barn and Cyril called "Robert!" there was a stir among the loose hay, and Robert began to come out. His hand and arm came first—then a foot and leg. When the woman saw the hand she said "My!" but when she saw the foot she said "Upon my civvy!"* and when, by slow and heavy degrees, the whole of Robert's enormous bulk was at last completely disclosed, she drew a long breath and began to say many things, compared with which "balmy" and "crumpet" seemed quite ordinary. She dropped into understandable English at last.

"What'll you take for him?" she said excitedly. "Anything in reason. We'd have a special van built—leastways, I know where there's a second-hand one would do up handsome—what a baby elephant had, as died. What'll you take? He's soft, ain't he? Them giants mostly is—but I never see—no, never! What'll you take? Down on the nail. We'll treat him like a king, and give him first-rate grub and a doss† fit for a bloomin' dook. He must be dotty or he wouldn't need you kids to cart him about. What'll you take for him?"

"They won't take anything," said Robert sternly. "I'm no more soft than you are—not so much, I shouldn't wonder. I'll come and be a show for today if you'll give me"—he hesitated at the enormous price he was about to ask—"if you'll give me fifteen shillings."

"Done," said the woman, so quickly that Robert felt he had been unfair to himself, and wished he had asked thirty. "Come on now—and see my Bill—and we'll fix a price for the season. I dessay you might get as much as two quid‡ a week reg'lar. Come on—and make yourself as small as you can, for gracious sake!"

This was not very small, and a crowd gathered quickly, so that it was at the head of an enthusiastic procession that Robert entered the trampled meadow where the Fair was held, and passed over the stubbly yellow dusty grass to the door of the biggest tent. He crept in, and the woman went to call her Bill. He was the big sleeping man, and

---

* Upon my word of honor! (slang).

† Bed (slang).

‡ Two pounds (slang).

he did not seem at all pleased at being awakened. Cyril, watching through a slit in the tent, saw him scowl and shake a heavy fist and a sleepy head. Then the woman went on speaking very fast. Cyril heard "Strewth,"* and "biggest draw you ever, so help me!" and he began to share Robert's feeling that fifteen shillings was indeed far too little. Bill slouched up to the tent and entered. When he beheld the magnificent proportions of Robert he said but little—"Strike me pink!" were the only words the children could afterwards remember—but he produced fifteen shillings, mainly in six-pences and coppers,† and handed it to Robert.

"We'll fix up about what you're to draw when the show's over tonight," he said with hoarse heartiness. "Lor' love a duck!‡ you'll be that happy with us you'll never want to leave us. Can you do a song now—or a bit of a breakdown?"§

"Not today," said Robert, rejecting the idea of trying to sing "As once in May," a favourite of his mother's, and the only song he could think of at the moment.

"Get Levi and clear them bloomin' photos out. Clear the tent. Stick up a curtain or suthink," the man went on. "Lor', what a pity we ain't got no tights his size! But we'll have 'em before the week's out. Young man, your fortune's made. It's a good thing you came to me, and not to some chaps as I could tell you on. I've known blokes as beat their giants, and starved 'em too; so I'll tell you straight, you're in luck this day if you never was afore. 'Cos I'm a lamb, I am— and I don't deceive you."

"I'm not afraid of anyone's beating *me*," said Robert, looking down on the "lamb." Robert was crouched on his knees, because the tent was not big enough for him to stand upright in, but even in that position he could still look down on most people. "But I'm awfully hungry—I wish you'd get me something to eat."

"Here, 'Becca," said the hoarse Bill. "Get him some grub—the best you've got, mind!" Another whisper followed, of which the children only heard, "Down in black and white—first thing tomorrow."

---

* An oath—short for "God's truth" (slang).

† Small change (slang).

‡ Exclamation of surprise (slang).

§ Riotous dance.

Then the woman went to get the food—it was only bread and cheese when it came, but it was delightful to the large and empty Robert; and the man went to post sentinels round the tent, to give the alarm if Robert should attempt to escape with his fifteen shillings.

"As if we weren't honest," said Anthea indignantly when the meaning of the sentinels dawned on her.

Then began a very strange and wonderful afternoon.

Bill was a man who knew his business. In a very little while, the photographic views, the spy-glasses you look at them through, so that they really seem rather real, and the lights you see them by, were all packed away. A curtain—it was an old red-and-black carpet really—was run across the tent. Robert was concealed behind, and Bill was standing on a trestle-table outside the tent making a speech. It was rather a good speech. It began by saying that the giant it was his privilege to introduce to the public that day was the eldest son of the Emperor of San Francisco, compelled through an unfortunate love affair with the Duchess of the Fiji Islands to leave his own country and take refuge in England—the land of liberty—where freedom was the right of every man, no matter how big he was. It ended by the announcement that the first twenty who came to the tent door should see the giant for threepence apiece. "After that," said Bill, "the price is riz, and I don't undertake to say what it won't be riz to. So now's yer time."

A young man squiring his sweetheart on her afternoon out was the first to come forward. For that occasion his was the princely attitude—no expense spared—money no object. His girl wished to see the giant? Well, she should see the giant, even though seeing the giant cost threepence each and the other entertainments were all penny ones.

The flap of the tent was raised—the couple entered. Next moment a wild shriek from the girl thrilled through all present. Bill slapped his leg. "That's done the trick!" he whispered to 'Becca. It was indeed a splendid advertisement of the charms of Robert. When the girl came out she was pale and trembling, and a crowd was round the tent.

"What was it like?" asked a bailiff.

"Oh!—horrid!—you wouldn't believe," she said. "It's as big as a

When the girl came out she was pale and trembling

barn, and that fierce. It froze the blood in my bones. I wouldn't ha' missed seeing it for anything."

The fierceness was only caused by Robert's trying not to laugh. But the desire to do that soon left him, and before sunset he was more inclined to cry than to laugh, and more inclined to sleep than either. For, by ones and twos and threes, people kept coming in all the afternoon, and Robert had to shake hands with those who wished it, and allow himself to be punched and pulled and patted and thumped, so that people might make sure he was really real.

The other children sat on a bench and watched and waited, and were very bored indeed. It seemed to them that this was the hardest way of earning money that could have been invented. And only fifteen shillings! Bill had taken four times that already, for the news of the giant had spread, and tradespeople in carts, and gentlepeople in carriages, came from far and near. One gentleman with an eyeglass, and a very large yellow rose in his buttonhole, offered Robert, in an obliging whisper, ten pounds a week to appear at the Crystal Palace.[5] Robert had to say "No."

"I can't," he said regretfully. "It's no use promising what you can't do."

"Ah, poor fellow, bound for a term of years, I suppose! Well, here's my card; when your time's up come to me."

"I will—if I'm the same size then," said Robert truthfully.

"If you grow a bit, so much the better," said the gentleman.

When he had gone, Robert beckoned Cyril and said:

"Tell them I must and will have an easy. And I want my tea."

Tea was provided, and a paper hastily pinned on the tent. It said:

CLOSED FOR HALF AN HOUR
WHILE THE GIANT GETS HIS TEA

Then there was a hurried council.

"How am I to get away?" said Robert. "I've been thinking about it all the afternoon."

"Why, walk out when the sun sets and you're your right size. They can't do anything to us."

Robert opened his eyes. "Why, they'd nearly kill us," he said, "when they saw me get my right size. No, we must think of some other way. We must be alone when the sun sets."

"I know," said Cyril briskly, and he went to the door, outside which Bill was smoking a clay pipe and talking in a low voice to 'Becca. Cyril heard him say—"Good as havin' a fortune left you."

"When your time's up come to me"

"Look here," said Cyril, "you can let people come in again in a minute. He's nearly finished his tea. But he must be left alone when the sun sets. He's very queer at that time of day, and if he's worried I won't answer for the consequences."

"Why—what comes over him?" asked Bill.

"I don't know; it's—it's a sort of a *change*," said Cyril candidly. "He isn't at all like himself—you'd hardly know him. He's very queer indeed. Someone'll get hurt if he's not alone about sunset." This was true.

"He'll pull round for the evening, I s'pose?"

"Oh yes—half an hour after sunset he'll be quite himself again."

"Best humour him," said the woman.

And so, at what Cyril judged was about half an hour before sunset, the tent was again closed "whilst the giant gets his supper."

The crowd was very merry about the giant's meals and their coming so close together.

"Well, he can pick a bit," Bill owned. "You see he has to eat hearty, being the size he is."

Inside the tent the four children breathlessly arranged a plan of retreat.

"You go now," said Cyril to the girls, "and get along home as fast as you can. Oh, never mind the beastly pony-cart; we'll get that to-morrow. Robert and I are dressed the same. We'll manage somehow, like Sydney Carton[6] did. Only, you girls must get out, or it's all no go. We can run, but you can't—whatever you may think. No, Jane, it's no good Robert going out and knocking people down. The police would follow him till he turned his proper size, and then arrest him like a shot. Go you must! If you don't, I'll never speak to you again. It was you got us into this mess really, hanging round people's legs the way you did this morning. Go, I tell you!"

And Jane and Anthea went.

"We're going home," they said to Bill. "We're leaving the giant with you. Be kind to him." And that, as Anthea said afterwards, was very deceitful, but what were they to do?

When they had gone, Cyril went to Bill.

"Look here," he said, "he wants some ears of corn—there's some in the next field but one. I'll just run and get it. Oh, and he says can't you loop up the tent at the back a bit? He says he's stifling for a breath of air. I'll see no one peeps in at him. I'll cover him up, and he can take a nap while I go for the corn. He will have it—there's no holding him when he gets like this."

The giant was made comfortable with a heap of sacks and an old tarpaulin. The curtain was looped up, and the brothers were left alone. They matured their plan in whispers. Outside, the merry-go-round blared out its comic tunes, screaming now and then to attract public notice.

Half a minute after the sun had set, a boy in a Norfolk suit came out past Bill.

"I'm off for the corn," he said, and mingled quickly with the crowd.

At the same instant a boy came out of the back of the tent past 'Becca, posted there as sentinel.

"I'm off after the corn," said this boy also. And he, too, moved away quietly and was lost in the crowd. The front-door boy was Cyril; the back-door was Robert—now, since sunset, once more his proper size. They walked quickly through the field, and along the road, where Robert caught Cyril up. Then they ran. They were home as soon as the girls were, for it was a long way, and they ran most of it. It was indeed a very long way, as they found when they had to go and drag the pony-trap home next morning, with no enormous Robert to wheel them in it as if it were a mail-cart, and they were babies and he was their gigantic nursemaid.

I cannot possibly tell you what Bill and 'Becca said when they found that the giant had gone. For one thing, I do not know.

CHAPTER IX

GROWN UP

Cyril had once pointed out that ordinary life is full of occasions on which a wish would be most useful. And this thought filled his mind when he happened to wake early on the morning after the morning after Robert had wished to be bigger than the baker's boy, and had been it. The day that lay between these two days had been occupied entirely by getting the governess-cart home from Benenhurst.

Cyril dressed hastily; he did not take a bath, because tin baths are so noisy, and he had no wish to rouse Robert, and he slipped off alone, as Anthea had once done, and ran through the dewy morning to the sand-pit. He dug up the Psammead very carefully and kindly, and began the conversation by asking it whether it still felt any ill effects from the contact with the tears of Robert the day before yesterday. The Psammead was in a good temper. It replied politely.

"And now, what can I do for you?" it said. "I suppose you've come here so early to ask for something for yourself, something your brothers and sisters aren't to know about, eh? Now, do be persuaded for your own good! Ask for a good fat Megatherium and have done with it."

"Thank you—not today, I think," said Cyril cautiously. "What I really wanted to say was—you know how you're always wishing for things when you're playing at anything?"

"I seldom play," said the Psammead coldly.

"Well, you know what I mean," Cyril went on impatiently. "What I want to say is: won't you let us have our wish just when we think of it, and just where we happen to be? So that we don't have to come and disturb you again," added the crafty Cyril.

"It'll only end in your wishing for something you don't really want, like you did about the castle," said the Psammead, stretching its

Ask for a good fat Megatherium and have done with it

brown arms and yawning. "It's always the same since people left off eating really wholesome things. However, have it your own way. Good-bye."

"Good-bye," said Cyril politely.

"I'll tell you what," said the Psammead suddenly, shooting out its long snail's eyes—"I'm getting tired of you—all of you. You have no more sense than so many oysters. Go along with you!"

And Cyril went.

"What an awful long time babies *stay* babies," said Cyril after the Lamb had taken his watch out of his pocket while he wasn't noticing, and with coos and clucks of naughty rapture had opened the case and used the whole thing as a garden spade, and when even immersion in a wash-hand basin had failed to wash the mould from the works and make the watch go again. Cyril had said several things in the heat of the moment; but now he was calmer, and had even consented to carry the Lamb part of the way to the woods. Cyril had persuaded the others to agree to his plan, and not to wish for anything more till they really did wish it. Meantime it seemed good to go to the woods for nuts, and on the mossy grass under a sweet chestnut-tree the five were sitting. The Lamb was pulling up the moss by fat handfuls, and Cyril was gloomily contemplating the ruins of his watch.

"He does grow," said Anthea. "Doesn't oo, precious?"

"I suppose he'll be grown up some day"

"Me grow," said the Lamb cheerfully—"me grow big boy, have guns an' mouses—an'—an' . . ." Imagination or vocabulary gave out here. But anyway it was the longest speech the Lamb had ever made, and it charmed everyone, even Cyril, who tumbled the Lamb over and rolled him in the moss to the music of delighted squeals.

"I suppose he'll be grown up some day," Anthea was saying, dreamily looking up at the blue of the sky that showed between the long straight chestnut-leaves. But at that moment the Lamb, struggling gaily with Cyril, thrust a stoutly-shod little foot against his brother's chest; there was a crack!—the innocent Lamb had broken the glass of father's second-best Waterbury watch,* which Cyril had borrowed without leave.

---

* Inexpensive watch made by the Waterbury Watch Company in Connecticut.

"Grow up some day!" said Cyril bitterly, plumping the Lamb down on the grass. "I daresay he will—when nobody wants him to. I wish to goodness he would—"

"Oh, take care!" cried Anthea in an agony of apprehension. But it was too late—like music to a song her words and Cyril's came out together—

Anthea—"Oh, take care!"

Cyril—"Grow up now!"

The faithful Psammead was true to its promise, and there, before the horrified eyes of its brothers and sisters, the Lamb suddenly and violently grew up. It was the most terrible moment. The change was not so sudden as the wish-changes usually were. The Baby's face changed first. It grew thinner and larger, lines came in the forehead, the eyes grew more deep-set and darker in colour, the mouth grew longer and thinner; most terrible of all, a little dark moustache appeared on the lip of one who was still—except as to the face—a two-year-old baby in a linen smock and white open-work socks.*

"Oh, I wish it wouldn't! Oh, I wish it wouldn't! You boys might wish as well!" They all wished hard, for the sight was enough to dismay the most heartless. They all wished so hard, indeed, that they felt quite giddy and almost lost consciousness; but the wishing was quite vain, for, when the wood ceased to whirl round, their dazzled eyes were riveted at once by the spectacle of a very proper-looking young man in flannels and a straw hat—a young man who wore the same little black moustache which just before they had actually seen growing upon the Baby's lip. This, then, was the Lamb—grown up! Their own Lamb! It was a terrible moment. The grown-up Lamb moved gracefully across the moss and settled himself against the trunk of the sweet chestnut. He tilted the straw hat over his eyes. He was evidently weary. He was going to sleep. The Lamb—the original little tiresome beloved Lamb often went to sleep at odd times and in unexpected places. Was this new Lamb in the grey flannel suit and the pale green necktie like the other Lamb? or had his mind grown up together with his body?

That was the question which the others, in a hurried council

---

* Socks made with decorative openings.

This, then, was the Lamb—grown up!

held among the yellowing bracken a few yards from the sleeper, de-
bated eagerly.

"Whichever it is, it'll be just as awful," said Anthea. "If his inside senses are grown up too, he won't stand our looking after him;
and if he's still a baby inside of him how on earth are we to get him

to do anything? And it'll be getting on for dinner-time in a minute—"

"And we haven't got any nuts," said Jane.

"Oh, bother nuts!" said Robert; "but dinner's different—I didn't have half enough dinner yesterday. Couldn't we tie him to the tree and go home to our dinners and come back afterwards?"

"A fat lot of dinner we should get if we went back without the Lamb!" said Cyril in scornful misery. "And it'll be just the same if we go back with him in the state he is now. Yes, I know it's my doing; don't rub it in! I know I'm a beast, and not fit to live; you can take that for settled, and say no more about it. The question is, what are we going to do?"

"Let's wake him up, and take him into Rochester or Maidstone and get some grub at a pastrycook's," said Robert hopefully.

"Take him?" repeated Cyril. "Yes—do! It's all my fault—I don't deny that—but you'll find you've got your work cut out for you if you try to take that young man anywhere. The Lamb always was spoilt, but now he's grown up he's a demon—simply. I can see it. Look at his mouth."

"Well then," said Robert, "let's wake him up and see what *he'll* do. Perhaps *he'll* take us to Maidstone and stand Sam. He ought to have a hat of money in the pockets of those extra-special bags. We must have dinner, anyway."

They drew lots with little bits of bracken. It fell to Jane's lot to waken the grown-up Lamb.

She did it gently by tickling his nose with a twig of wild honeysuckle. He said "Bother the flies!" twice, and then opened his eyes.

"Hullo, kiddies!" he said in a languid tone, "still here? What's the giddy hour? You'll be late for your grub!"

"I know we shall," said Robert bitterly.

"Then cut along home," said the grown-up Lamb.

"What about your grub, though?" asked Jane.

"Oh, how far is it to the station, do you think? I've a sort of notion that I'll run up to town and have some lunch at the club."

Blank misery fell like a pall on the four others. The Lamb—alone—unattended—would go to town and have lunch at a club! Perhaps he would also have tea there. Perhaps sunset would come upon him amid the dazzling luxury of club-land, and a helpless cross sleepy baby would find itself alone amid unsympathetic waiters, and would wail miserably for "Panty" from the depths of a club armchair! The picture moved Anthea almost to tears.

"Oh no, Lamb ducky, you mustn't do that!" she cried incautiously.

The grown-up Lamb frowned. "My dear Anthea," he said, "how often am I to tell you that my name is Hilary or St. Maur or Devereux?—any of my baptismal names are free to my little brothers and sisters, but not 'Lamb'—a relic of foolish and far-off childhood."

This was awful. He was their elder brother now, was he? Well, of course he was, if he was grown up—since they weren't. Thus, in whispers, Anthea and Robert.

But the almost daily adventures resulting from the Psammead wishes were making the children wise beyond their years.

"Dear Hilary," said Anthea, and the others choked at the name, "you know father didn't wish you to go to London. He wouldn't like us to be left alone without you to take care of us. Oh, deceitful beast that I am!" she added to herself.

"Look here," said Cyril, "if you're our elder brother, why not behave as such and take us over to Maidstone and give us a jolly good blow-out, and we'll go on the river afterwards?"

"I'm infinitely obliged to you," said the Lamb courteously, "but I should prefer solitude. Go home to your lunch—I mean your dinner. Perhaps I may look in about tea-time—or I may not be home till after you are in your beds."

Their beds! Speaking glances flashed between the wretched four. Much bed there would be for them if they went home without the Lamb.

"We promised mother not to lose sight of you if we took you out," Jane said before the others could stop her.

"Look here, Jane," said the grown-up Lamb, putting his hands in his pockets and looking down at her, "little girls should be seen and not heard. You kids must learn not to make yourselves a nuisance. Run along home now—and perhaps, if you're good, I'll give you each a penny tomorrow."

"Look here," said Cyril, in the best "man to man" tone at his command, "where are you going, old man? You might let Bobs and me come with you—even if you don't want the girls."

"You kids must learn not to make yourselves a nuisance"

This was really rather noble of Cyril, for he never did care much about being seen in public with the Lamb, who of course after sunset would be a baby again.

The "man to man" tone succeeded.

"I shall just run over to Maidstone on my bike," said the new Lamb airily, fingering the little black moustache. "I can lunch at The Crown—and perhaps I'll have a pull on the river; but I can't take you

There, sure enough, stood a bicycle

all on the machine—now, can I? Run along home, like good children."

The position was desperate. Robert exchanged a despairing look with Cyril. Anthea detached a pin from her waistband, a pin whose withdrawal left a gaping chasm between skirt and bodice, and handed it furtively to Robert—with a grimace of the darkest and deepest meaning. Robert slipped away to the road. There, sure enough, stood a bicycle—a beautiful new free-wheel. Of course Robert understood at once that if the Lamb was grown up he must have a bicycle. This had always been one of Robert's own reasons for wishing to be grown up. He hastily began to use the pin—eleven punctures in the back tyre, seven in the front. He would have made the total twenty-two but for the rustling of the yellow hazel-leaves, which warned him of the approach of the others. He hastily leaned a hand on each wheel, and was rewarded by the "whish" of what was left of the air escaping from eighteen neat pin-holes.

"Your bike's run down," said Robert, wondering how he could so soon have learned to deceive.

"So it is," said Cyril.

"It's a puncture," said Anthea, stooping down, and standing up again with a thorn which she had got ready for the purpose. "Look here."

The grown-up Lamb (or Hilary, as I suppose one must now call him) fixed his pump and blew up the tyre. The punctured state of it was soon evident.

"I suppose there's a cottage somewhere near—where one could get a pail of water?" said the Lamb.

There was; and when the number of punctures had been made manifest, it was felt to be a special blessing that the cottage provided "teas for cyclists." It provided an odd sort of tea-and-hammy meal for the Lamb and his brothers. This was paid for out of the fifteen shillings which had been earned by Robert when he was a giant—for the Lamb, it appeared, had unfortunately no money about him. This was a great disappointment for the others; but it is a thing that will happen, even to the most grown-up of us. However, Robert had enough to eat, and that was something. Quietly but persistently the miserable four took it in turns to try to persuade the Lamb (or St. Maur) to spend the rest of the day in the woods. There was not very much of the day left by the time he had mended the eighteenth puncture. He looked up from the completed work with a sigh of relief, and suddenly put his tie straight.

"There's a lady coming," he said briskly—"for goodness' sake, get out of the way. Go home—hide—vanish somehow! I can't be seen with a pack of dirty kids." His brothers and sisters were indeed rather dirty, because, earlier in the day, the Lamb, in his infant state, had sprinkled a good deal of garden soil over them. The grown-up Lamb's voice was so tyrant-like, as Jane said afterwards, that they actually retreated to the back garden, and left him with his little moustache and his flannel suit to meet alone the young lady, who now came up the front garden wheeling a bicycle.

The woman of the house came out, and the young lady spoke to her—the Lamb raised his hat as she passed him—and the children could not hear what she said, though they were craning round the corner by the pig-pail and listening with all their ears. They felt it to be "perfectly fair," as Robert said, "with that wretched Lamb in that condition."

When the Lamb spoke in a languid voice heavy with politeness, they heard well enough.

"A puncture?" he was saying. "Can I not be of any assistance? If you could allow me—?"

There was a stifled explosion of laughter behind the pig-pail— the grown-up Lamb (otherwise Devereux) turned the tail of an angry eye in its direction.

"You're very kind," said the lady, looking at the Lamb. She looked rather shy, but, as the boys put it, there didn't seem to be any non-sense about her.

"But oh," whispered Cyril behind the pig-pail, "I should have thought he'd had enough bicycle-mending for one day—and if she only knew that really and truly he's only a whiny-piny, silly little baby!"

"He's not," Anthea murmured angrily. "He's a dear—if people only let him alone. It's our own precious Lamb still, whatever silly id-iots may turn him into—isn't he, Pussy?"

Jane doubtfully supposed so.

Now, the Lamb—whom I must try to remember to call St. Maur—was examining the lady's bicycle and talking to her with a very grown-up manner indeed. No one could possibly have sup-posed, to see and hear him, that only that very morning he had been a chubby child of two years breaking other people's Waterbury watches. Devereux (as he ought to be called for the future) took out a gold watch when he had mended the lady's bicycle, and all the on-lookers behind the pig-pail said "Oh!"—because it seemed so unfair that the Baby, who had only that morning destroyed two cheap but honest watches, should now, in the grown-upness Cyril's folly had raised him to, have a real gold watch—with a chain and seals!

Hilary (as I will now term him) withered his brothers and sisters with a glance, and then said to the lady—with whom he seemed to be quite friendly:

"If you will allow me, I will ride with you as far as the Cross Roads; it is getting late, and there are tramps about."

No one will ever know what answer the young lady intended to give to this gallant offer, for, directly Anthea heard it made, she rushed out, knocking against the pig-pail, which overflowed in a tur-bid stream, and caught the Lamb (I suppose I ought to say Hilary) by the arm. The others followed, and in an instant the four dirty children were visible, beyond disguise.

"Don't let him," said Anthea; "he's not fit to go with anyone"

"Don't let him," said Anthea to the lady, and she spoke with intense earnestness; "he's not fit to go with anyone!"

"Go away, little girl!" said St. Maur (as we will now call him) in a terrible voice. "Go home at once!"

"You'd much better not have anything to do with him," the now reckless Anthea went on. "He doesn't know who he is. He's something very different from what you think he is."

"What do you mean?" asked the lady not unnaturally, while Devereux (as I must term the grown-up Lamb) tried vainly to push Anthea away. The others backed her up, and she stood solid as a rock.

"You just let him go with you," said Anthea, "you'll soon see what I mean! How would you like to suddenly see a poor little helpless baby spinning along downhill beside you with its feet up on a bicycle it had lost control of?"

The lady had turned rather pale.

"Who are these very dirty children?" she asked the grown-up Lamb (sometimes called St. Maur in these pages).

"I don't know," he lied miserably.

"Oh, Lamb! how *can* you?" cried Jane—"when you know perfectly well you're our own little baby brother that we're so fond of. We're his big brothers and sisters," she explained, turning to the lady, who with trembling hands was now turning her bicycle towards the gate, "and we've got to take care of him. And we must get him home before sunset, or I don't know whatever will become of us. You see, he's sort of under a spell—enchanted—you know what I mean!"

Again and again the Lamb (Devereux, I mean) had tried to stop Jane's eloquence, but Robert and Cyril held him, one by each leg, and no proper explanation was possible. The lady rode hastily away, and electrified her relatives at dinner by telling them of her escape from a family of dangerous lunatics. "The little girl's eyes were simply those of a maniac. I can't think how she came to be at large," she said.

When her bicycle had whizzed away down the road, Cyril spoke gravely.

"Hilary, old chap," he said, "you must have had a sunstroke or something. And the things you've been saying to that lady! Why, if we were to tell you the things you've said when you are yourself again, say tomorrow morning, you wouldn't even understand them—let alone believe them! You trust to me, old chap, and come home now, and if you're not yourself in the morning we'll ask the milkman to ask the doctor to come."

The poor grown-up Lamb (St. Maur was really one of his Christian names) seemed now too bewildered to resist.

"Since you seem all to be as mad as the whole worshipful company of hatters," he said bitterly, "I suppose I *had* better take you home. But you're not to suppose I shall pass this over. I shall have something to say to you all tomorrow morning."

"Yes, you will, my Lamb," said Anthea under her breath, "but it won't be at all the sort of thing you think it's going to be."

In her heart she could hear the pretty, soft little loving voice of the baby Lamb—so different from the affected tones of the dreadful grown-up Lamb (one of whose names was Devereux)—saying, "Me love Panty—wants to come to own Panty."

"Oh, let's get home, for goodness' sake," she said. "You shall say

The grown-up Lamb struggled furiously

whatever you like in the morning—if you can," she added in a whisper.

It was a gloomy party that went home through the soft evening. During Anthea's remarks Robert had again made play with the pin and the bicycle tyre and the Lamb (whom they had to call St. Maur or Devereux or Hilary) seemed really at last to have had his fill of bicycle-mending. So the machine was wheeled.

The sun was just on the point of setting when they arrived at the

White House. The four elder children would have liked to linger in the lane till the complete sunsetting turned the grown-up Lamb (whose Christian names I will not further weary you by repeating) into their own dear tiresome baby brother. But he, in his grown-upness, insisted on going on, and thus he was met in the front garden by Martha.

Now you remember that, as a special favour, the Psammead had arranged that the servants in the house should never notice any change brought about by the wishes of the children. Therefore Martha merely saw the usual party, with the baby Lamb, about whom she had been desperately anxious all the afternoon, trotting beside Anthea on fat baby legs, while the children, of course, still saw the grown-up Lamb (never mind what names he was christened by), and Martha rushed at him and caught him in her arms, exclaiming:

"Come to his own Martha, then—a precious poppet!"

The grown-up Lamb (whose names shall now be buried in oblivion) struggled furiously. An expression of intense horror and annoyance was seen on his face. But Martha was stronger than he. She lifted him up and carried him into the house. None of the children will ever forget that picture. The neat grey-flannel-suited grown-up young man with the green tie and the little black moustache—fortunately, he was slightly built, and not tall—struggling in the sturdy arms of Martha, who bore him away helpless, imploring him, as she went, to be a good boy now, and come and have his nice bremmilk! Fortunately, the sun set as they reached the doorstep, the bicycle disappeared, and Martha was seen to carry into the house the real live darling sleepy two-year-old Lamb. The grown-up Lamb (nameless henceforth) was gone for ever.

"For ever," said Cyril, "because, as soon as ever the Lamb's old enough to be bullied, we must jolly well begin to bully him, for his own sake—so that he mayn't grow up like *that*."

"You shan't bully him," said Anthea stoutly; "not if I can stop it."

"We must tame him by kindness," said Jane.

"You see," said Robert, "if he grows up in the usual way, there'll be plenty of time to correct him as he goes along. The awful thing today was his growing up so suddenly. There was no time to improve him at all."

"He doesn't want any improving," said Anthea as the voice of the Lamb came cooing through the open door, just as she had heard it in her heart that afternoon:

"Me loves Panty—wants to come to own Panty!"

CHAPTER X

SCALPS

Probably the day would have been a greater success if Cyril had not been reading *The Last of the Mohicans*.* The story was running in his head at breakfast, and as he took his third cup of tea he said dreamily, "I wish there were Red Indians in England—not big ones, you know, but little ones, just about the right size for us to fight."

Everyone disagreed with him at the time, and no one attached any importance to the incident. But when they went down to the sand-pit to ask for a hundred pounds in two-shilling pieces with Queen Victoria's head on, to prevent mistakes—which they had always felt to be a really reasonable wish that must turn out well—they found out that they had done it again! For the Psammead, which was very cross and sleepy, said:

"Oh, don't bother me. You've had your wish."

"I didn't know it," said Cyril.

"Don't you remember yesterday?" said the Sand-fairy, still more disagreeably. "You asked me to let you have your wishes wherever you happened to be, and you wished this morning, and you've got it."

"Oh, have we?" said Robert. "What is it?"

"So you've forgotten?" said the Psammead, beginning to burrow. "Never mind; you'll know soon enough. And I wish you joy of it! A nice thing you've let yourselves in for!"

"We always do, somehow," said Jane sadly.

And now the odd thing was that no one could remember anyone's having wished for anything that morning. The wish about the Red Indians had not stuck in anyone's head. It was a most anxious

---

* Famous novel, published in 1826, by James Fenimore Cooper (1789–1851).

morning. Everyone was trying to remember what had been wished for, and no one could, and everyone kept expecting something awful to happen every minute. It was most agitating; they knew, from what the Psammead had said, that they must have wished for something more than usually undesirable, and they spent several hours in most agonizing uncertainty. It was not till nearly dinner-time that Jane tumbled over *The Last of the Mohicans*—which had, of course, been left face downwards on the floor—and when Anthea had picked her and the book up she suddenly said, "I know!" and sat down flat on the carpet.

"Oh, Pussy, how awful! It was Indians he wished for—Cyril—at breakfast, don't you remember? He said, "I wish there were Red Indians in England,"—and now there are, and they're going about scalping people all over the country, like as not."

"Perhaps they're only in Northumberland* and Durham,"† said Jane soothingly. It was almost impossible to believe that it could really hurt people much to be scalped so far away as that.

"Don't you believe it!" said Anthea. "The Sammyadd said we'd let ourselves in for a nice thing. That means they'll come *here*. And suppose they scalped the Lamb!"

"Perhaps the scalping would come right again at sunset," said Jane; but she did not speak so hopefully as usual.

"Not it!" said Anthea. "The things that grow out of the wishes don't go. Look at the fifteen shillings! Pussy, I'm going to break something, and you must let me have every penny of money you've got. The Indians will come *here*, don't you see? That spiteful Psammead as good as said so. You see what my plan is? Come on!"

Jane did not see at all. But she followed her sister meekly into their mother's bedroom.

Anthea lifted down the heavy water-jug—it had a pattern of storks and long grasses on it, which Anthea never forgot. She carried it into the dressing-room, and carefully emptied the water out of it into the bath. Then she took the jug back into the bedroom and dropped it on the floor. You know how a jug always breaks if you happen to drop it by accident. If you happen to drop it on purpose, it is

---

quite different. Anthea dropped that jug three times, and it was as unbroken as ever. So at last she had to take her father's boot-tree and break the jug with that in cold blood. It was heartless work.

Next she broke open the missionary-box with the poker. Jane told her that it was wrong, of course, but Anthea shut her lips very tight and then said:

"Don't be silly—it's a matter of life and death."

There was not very much in the missionary-box—only seven-and-fourpence—but the girls between them had nearly four shillings. This made over eleven shillings, as you will easily see.

Anthea tied up the money in a corner of her pocket-handkerchief. "Come on, Jane!" she said, and ran down to the farm. She knew that the farmer was going into Rochester that afternoon. In fact it had been arranged that he was to take the four children with him. They had planned this in the happy hour when they believed that they were going to get that hundred pounds, in two-shilling pieces, out of the Psammead. They had arranged to pay the farmer two shillings each for the ride. Now Anthea hastily explained to him that they could not go, but would he take Martha and the Baby instead? He agreed, but he was not pleased to get only half-a-crown instead of eight shillings.

Then the girls ran home again. Anthea was agitated, but not flurried. When she came to think it over afterwards, she could not help seeing that she had acted with the most far-seeing promptitude, just like a born general. She fetched a little box from her corner drawer, and went to find Martha, who was laying the cloth and not in the best of tempers.

"Look here," said Anthea. "I've broken the toilet jug in mother's room."

"Just like you—always up to some mischief," said Martha, dumping down a salt-cellar with a bang.

"Don't be cross, Martha dear," said Anthea. "I've got enough money to pay for a new one—if only you'll be a dear and go and buy it for us. Your cousins keep a china-shop, don't they? And I would like you to get it today, in case mother comes home tomorrow. You know she said she might, perhaps."

"But you're all going into town yourselves," said Martha.

"We can't afford to, if we get the new jug," said Anthea; "but we'll pay for you to go, if you'll take the Lamb. And I say, Martha, look here—I'll give you my Liberty box, if you'll go. Look, it's most awfully pretty—all inlaid with real silver and ivory and ebony like King Solomon's temple."

"I see," said Martha; "no, I don't want your box, miss. What you want is to get the precious Lamb off your hands for the afternoon. Don't you go for to think I don't see through you!"

This was so true that Anthea longed to deny it at once. Martha had no business to know so much. But she held her tongue.

Martha set down the bread with a bang that made it jump off its trencher.

"I *do* want the jug got," said Anthea softly. "You will go, won't you?"

"Well, just for this once, I don't mind; but mind you don't get into none of your outrageous mischief while I'm gone—that's all!"

"He's going earlier than he thought," said Anthea eagerly. "You'd better hurry and get dressed. Do put on that lovely purple frock, Martha, and the hat with the pink cornflowers, and the yellow-lace collar. Jane'll finish laying the cloth, and I'll wash the Lamb and get him ready."

As she washed the unwilling Lamb, and hurried him into his best clothes, Anthea peeped out of the window from time to time; so far all was well—she could see no Red Indians. When with a rush and a scurry and some deepening of the damask of Martha's complexion she and the Lamb had been got off, Anthea drew a deep breath.

"He's safe!" she said, and, to Jane's horror, flung herself down on the floor and burst into floods of tears. Jane did not understand at all how a person could be so brave and like a general, and then suddenly give way and go flat like an air-balloon when you prick it. It is better not to go flat, of course, but you will observe that Anthea did not give way till her aim was accomplished. She had got the dear Lamb out of danger—she felt certain the Red Indians would be round the White House or nowhere—the farmer's cart would not come back till after sunset, so she could afford to cry a little. It was partly with joy that she cried, because she had done what she meant to do. She cried for about three minutes, while Jane hugged her miserably and said at five-second intervals, "Don't cry, Panther dear!"

Then she jumped up, rubbed her eyes hard with the corner of

her pinafore, so that they kept red for the rest of the day, and started to tell the boys. But just at that moment cook rang the dinner-bell, and nothing could be said till they had all been helped to minced beef. Then cook left the room, and Anthea told her tale. But it is a mistake to tell a thrilling tale when people are eating minced beef and boiled potatoes. There seemed somehow to be something about the food that made the idea of Red Indians seem flat and unbelievable. The boys actually laughed, and called Anthea a little silly.

"Why," said Cyril, "I'm almost sure it was before I said that, that Jane said she wished it would be a fine day."

"It wasn't," said Jane briefly.

"Why, if it was Indians," Cyril went on—"salt, please, and mustard—I must have something to make this mush go down—if it was Indians, they'd have been infesting the place long before this—you know they would. I believe it's the fine day."

"Then why did the Sammyadd say we'd let ourselves in for a nice thing?" asked Anthea. She was feeling very cross. She knew she had acted with nobility and discretion, and after that it was very hard to be called a little silly, especially when she had the weight of a burglared missionary-box and about seven-and-fourpence, mostly in coppers, lying like lead upon her conscience.

There was a silence, during which cook took away the mincy plates and brought in the treacle-pudding. As soon as she had retired, Cyril began again.

"Of course I don't mean to say," he admitted, "that it wasn't a good thing to get Martha and the Lamb out of the light for the afternoon; but as for Red Indians—why, you know jolly well the wishes always come that very minute. If there was going to be Red Indians, they'd be here now."

"I expect they are," said Anthea; "they're lurking amid the undergrowth, for anything you know. I do think you're most beastly unkind."

"Indians almost always *do* lurk, really, though, don't they?" put in Jane, anxious for peace.

"No, they don't," said Cyril tartly. "And I'm not unkind, I'm only truthful. And I say it was utter rot breaking the water-jug; and as for the missionary-box, I believe it's a treason-crime, and I shouldn't wonder if you could be hanged for it, if any of us was to split—"

"Shut up, can't you?" said Robert; but Cyril couldn't. You see, he felt in his heart that if there *should* be Indians they would be entirely his own fault, so he did not wish to believe in them. And trying not to believe things when in your heart you are almost sure they are true, is as bad for the temper as anything I know.

"It's simply idiotic," he said, "talking about Indians, when you can see for yourselves that it's Jane who's got her wish. Look what a fine day it is—*OH*—"

He had turned towards the window to point out the fineness of the day—the others turned too—and a frozen silence caught at Cyril, and none of the others felt at all like breaking it. For there, peering round the corner of the window, among the red leaves of the Virginia creeper, was a face—a brown face, with a long nose and a tight mouth and very bright eyes. And the face was painted in coloured patches. It had long black hair, and in the hair were feathers!

Every child's mouth in the room opened, and stayed open. The treacle-pudding was growing white and cold on their plates. No one could move.

Suddenly the feathered head was cautiously withdrawn, and the spell was broken. I am sorry to say that Anthea's first words were very like a girl.

"There, now!" she said. "I told you so!"

Treacle-pudding had now definitely ceased to charm. Hastily wrapping their portions in a *Spectator** of the week before the week before last, they hid them behind the crinkled-paper stove-ornament, and fled upstairs to reconnoitre and to hold a hurried council.

"Pax," said Cyril handsomely when they reached their mother's bedroom. "Panther, I'm sorry if I was a brute."

"All right," said Anthea, "but you see now!"

No further trace of Indians, however, could be discerned from the windows.

"Well," said Robert, "what are we to do?"

"The only thing I can think of," said Anthea, who was now generally admitted to be the heroine of the day, "is—if we dressed up as like Indians as we can, and looked out of the windows, or even went

---

* Weekly magazine established in 1828.

out. They might think we were the powerful leaders of a large neighbouring tribe, and—and not do anything to us, you know, for fear of awful vengeance."

"But Eliza, and the cook?" said Jane.

"You forget—they can't notice anything," said Robert. "They wouldn't notice anything out of the way, even if they were scalped or roasted at a slow fire."

"But would they come right at sunset?"

"Of course. You can't be really scalped or burned to death without noticing it, and you'd be sure to notice it next day, even if it escaped your attention at the time," said Cyril. "I think Anthea's right, but we shall want a most awful lot of feathers."

"I'll go down to the hen-house," said Robert. "There's one of the turkeys in there—it's not very well. I could cut its feathers without it minding much. It's very bad—doesn't seem to care what happens to it. Get me the cutting-out scissors."

Earnest reconnoitring convinced them all that no Indians were in the poultry-yard. Robert went. In five minutes he came back—pale, but with many feathers.

"Look here," he said, "this is jolly serious. I cut off the feathers, and when I turned to come out there was an Indian squinting at me from under the old hen-coop. I just brandished the feathers and yelled, and got away before he could get the coop off the top of himself. Panther, get the coloured blankets off our beds, and look slippy, can't you?"

It is wonderful how like an Indian you can make yourselves with blankets and feathers and coloured scarves. Of course none of the children happened to have long black hair, but there was a lot of black calico that had been got to cover school-books with. They cut strips of this into a sort of fine fringe, and fastened it round their heads with the amber-coloured ribbons off the girls' Sunday dresses. Then they stuck turkeys' feathers in the ribbons. The calico looked very like long black hair, especially when the strips began to curl up a bit.

"But our faces," said Anthea, "they're not at all the right colour. We're all rather pale, and I'm sure I don't know why, but Cyril is the colour of putty."

"I'm not," said Cyril.

"The real Indians outside seem to be brownish," said Robert

hastily. "I think we ought to be really *red*—it's sort of superior to have a red skin, if you are one."

The red ochre cook used for the kitchen bricks seemed to be about the reddest thing in the house. The children mixed some in a saucer with milk, as they had seen cook do for the kitchen floor. Then they carefully painted each other's faces and hands with it, till they were quite as red as any Red Indian need be—if not redder.

They knew at once that they must look very terrible when they met Eliza in the passage, and she screamed aloud. This unsolicited testimonial pleased them very much. Hastily telling her not to be a goose, and that it was only a game, the four blanketed, feathered, really and truly Redskins went boldly out to meet the foe. I say boldly. That is because I wish to be polite. At any rate, they went.

Along the hedge dividing the wilderness from the garden was a row of dark heads, all highly feathered.

"It's our only chance," whispered Anthea. "Much better than to wait for their blood-freezing attack. We must pretend like mad. Like that game of cards where you pretend you've got aces when you haven't. Fluffing they call it, I think. Now then. Whoop!"

With four wild war-whoops—or as near them as English children could be expected to go without any previous practice—they rushed through the gate and struck four warlike attitudes in face of the line of Red Indians. These were all about the same height, and that height was Cyril's.

"I hope to goodness they can talk English," said Cyril through his attitude.

Anthea knew they could, though she never knew how she came to know it. She had a white towel tied to a walking-stick. This was a flag of truce, and she waved it, in the hope that the Indians would know what it was. Apparently they did—for one who was browner than the others stepped forward.

"Ye seek a pow-wow?" he said in excellent English. "I am Golden Eagle, of the mighty tribe of Rock-dwellers."

"And I," said Anthea, with a sudden inspiration, "am the Black Panther—chief of the—the—the Mazawattee tribe. My brothers—I don't mean—yes, I do—the tribe—I mean the Mazawattees—are in ambush below the brow of yonder hill."

"And what mighty warriors be these?" asked Golden Eagle, turning to the others.

Cyril said he was the great chief Squirrel, of the Moning Congo tribe, and, seeing that Jane was sucking her thumb and could evidently think of no name for herself, he added, "This great warrior is Wild Cat—Pussy Ferox we call it in this land—leader of the vast Phiteezi tribe."

"And thou, valorous Redskin?" Golden Eagle inquired suddenly of Robert, who, taken unawares, could only reply that he was Bobs, leader of the Cape Mounted Police.

"And now," said Black Panther, "our tribes, if we just whistle them up, will far outnumber your puny forces; so resistance is useless. Return, therefore, to your own land, O brother, and smoke pipes of peace in your wampums with your squaws and your medicinemen, and dress yourselves in the gayest wigwams, and eat happily of the juicy fresh-caught moccasins."

"You've got it all wrong," murmured Cyril angrily. But Golden Eagle only looked inquiringly at her.

"Thy customs are other than ours, O Black Panther," he said. "Bring up thy tribe, that we may hold pow-wow in state before them, as becomes great chiefs."

"We'll bring them up right enough," said Anthea, "with their bows and arrows, and tomahawks, and scalping-knives, and everything you can think of, if you don't look sharp and go."

She spoke bravely enough, but the hearts of all the children were beating furiously, and their breath came in shorter and shorter gasps. For the little real Red Indians were closing up round them—coming nearer and nearer with angry murmurs—so that they were the centre of a crowd of dark, cruel faces.

"It's no go," whispered Robert. "I knew it wouldn't be. We must make a bolt for the Psammead. It might help us. If it doesn't—well, I suppose we shall come alive again at sunset. I wonder if scalping hurts as much as they say."

"I'll wave the flag again," said Anthea. "If they stand back, we'll run for it."

She waved the towel, and the chief commanded his followers to stand back. Then, charging wildly at the place where the line of Indians was thinnest, the four children started to run. Their first rush knocked down some half-dozen Indians, over whose blanketed bodies the children leaped, and made straight for the sand-pit. This was no time for the safe easy way by which carts go down—right over the edge of the sand-pit they went, among the yellow and pale purple flowers and dried grasses, past the little sand-martins' little front doors, skipping, clinging, bounding, stumbling, sprawling, and finally rolling.

Yellow Eagle and his followers came up with them just at the very spot where they had seen the Psammead that morning.

Breathless and beaten, the wretched children now awaited their fate. Sharp knives and axes gleamed round them, but worse than these was the cruel light in the eyes of Golden Eagle and his followers.

"Ye have lied to us, O Black Panther of the Mazawattees—and thou, too, Squirrel of the Moning Congos. These also, Pussy Ferox of the Phiteezi, and Bobs of the Cape Mounted Police—these also have lied to us, if not with their tongue, yet by their silence. Ye have lied under the cover of the Truce-flag of the Pale-face. Ye have no followers. Your tribes are far away—following the hunting trail. What shall be their doom?" he concluded, turning with a bitter smile to the other Red Indians.

"Build we the fire!" shouted his followers; and at once a dozen ready volunteers started to look for fuel. The four children, each held between two strong little Indians, cast despairing glances round them. Oh, if they could only see the Psammead!

"Do you mean to scalp us first and then roast us?" asked Anthea desperately.

"Of course!" Redskin opened his eyes at her. "It's always done."

The Indians had formed a ring round the children, and now sat on the ground gazing at their captives. There was a threatening silence.

Then slowly, by twos and threes, the Indians who had gone to look for firewood came back, and they came back empty-handed. They had not been able to find a single stick of wood, for a fire! No one ever can, as a matter of fact, in that part of Kent.

The children drew a deep breath of relief, but it ended in a moan of terror. For bright knives were being brandished all about them. Next moment each child was seized by an Indian; each closed its eyes and tried not to scream. They waited for the sharp agony of the knife. It did not come. Next moment they were released, and fell in a trembling heap. Their heads did not hurt at all. They only felt strangely cool! Wild war-whoops rang in their ears. When they ventured to open their eyes they saw four of their foes dancing round them with wild leaps and screams, and each of the four brandished in his hand a scalp of long flowing black hair. They put their hands to their heads—their own scalps were safe! The poor untutored savages had indeed scalped the children. But they had only, so to speak, scalped them of the black calico ringlets!

The children fell into each other's arms, sobbing and laughing.

"Their scalps are ours," chanted the chief; "ill-rooted were their ill-fated hairs! They came off in the hands of the victors—without struggle, without resistance, they yielded their scalps to the conquering Rock-dwellers! Oh, how little a thing is a scalp so lightly won!"

"They'll take our real ones in a minute; you see if they don't," said Robert, trying to rub some of the red ochre off his face and hands on to his hair.

"Cheated of our just and fiery revenge are we," the chant went on—"but there are other torments than the scalping-knife and the flames. Yet is the slow fire the correct thing. O strange unnatural country, wherein a man may find no wood to burn his enemy!—Ah, for the boundless forests of my native land, where the great trees for thousands of miles grow but to furnish firewood wherewithal to burn our foes. Ah, would we were but in our native forest once more!"

Suddenly, like a flash of lightning, the golden gravel shone all round the four children instead of the dusky figures. For every single Indian had vanished on the instant at their leader's word. The Psammead must have been there all the time. And it had given the Indian chief his wish.

Martha brought home a jug with a pattern of storks and long grasses on it. Also she brought back all Anthea's money.

"My cousin, she give me the jug for luck; she said it was an odd one what the basin of had got smashed."

"Oh, Martha, you are a dear!" sighed Anthea, throwing her arms round her.

"Yes," giggled Martha, "you'd better make the most of me while you've got me. I shall give your ma notice directly minute she comes back."

"Oh, Martha, we haven't been so *very* horrid to you, have we?" asked Anthea, aghast.

"Oh, it ain't that, miss." Martha giggled more than ever. "I'm a-goin' to be married. It's Beale the game-keeper. He's been a-proposin' to me off and on ever since you come home from the clergyman's where you got locked up on the church-tower. And today I said the word an' made him a happy man."

Anthea put the seven-and-fourpence back in the missionary-box, and pasted paper over the place where the poker had broken it. She was very glad to be able to do this, and she does not know to this day whether breaking open a missionary-box is or is not a hanging matter.

CHAPTER XI (AND LAST)

THE LAST WISH

Of course you, who see above that this is the eleventh (and last) chapter, know very well that the day of which this chapter tells must be the last on which Cyril, Anthea, Robert, and Jane will have a chance of getting anything out of the Psammead, or Sand-fairy.

But the children themselves did not know this. They were full of rosy visions, and, whereas on other days they had often found it extremely difficult to think of anything really nice to wish for, their brains were now full of the most beautiful and sensible ideas. "This," as Jane remarked afterwards, "is always the way." Everyone was up extra early that morning, and these plans were hopefully discussed in the garden before breakfast. The old idea of one hundred pounds in modern florins* was still first favourite, but there were others that ran it close—the chief of these being the "pony each" idea. This had a great advantage. You could wish for a pony each during the morning, ride it all day, have it vanish at sunset, and wish it back again next day. Which would be an economy of litter and stabling. But at breakfast two things happened. First, there was a letter from mother. Granny was better, and mother and father hoped to be home that very afternoon. A cheer arose. And of course this news at once scattered all the before-breakfast wish-ideas. For everyone saw quite plainly that the wish for the day must be something to please mother and not to please themselves.

"I wonder what she would like," pondered Cyril.

"She'd like us all to be good," said Jane primly.

"Yes—but that's so dull for us," Cyril rejoined; "and, besides, I should hope we could be that without sand-fairies to help us. No; it

---

* English coin worth 2 shillings; first minted in 1849.

must be something splendid, that we couldn't possibly get without wishing for."

"Look out," said Anthea in a warning voice; "don't forget yesterday. Remember, we get our wishes now just wherever we happen to be when we say 'I wish.' Don't let's let ourselves in for anything silly—today of all days."

"All right," said Cyril. "You needn't jaw."

Just then Martha came in with a jug full of hot water for the teapot—and a face full of importance for the children.

"A blessing we're all alive to eat our breakfasses!" she said darkly.

"Why, whatever's happened?" everybody asked.

"Oh, nothing," said Martha, "only it seems nobody's safe from being murdered in their beds nowadays."

"Why," said Jane as an agreeable thrill of horror ran down her back and legs and out at her toes, "has anyone been murdered in their beds?"

"Well—not exactly," said Martha; "but they might just as well. There's been burglars over at Peasmarsh Place—Beale's just told me—and they've took every single one of Lady Chittenden's diamonds and jewels and things, and she's a-goin' out of one fainting fit into another, with hardly time to say 'Oh, my diamonds!' in between. And Lord Chittenden's away in London."

"Lady Chittenden," said Anthea; "we've seen her. She wears a red-and-white dress, and she has no children of her own and can't abide other folkses'."

"That's her," said Martha. "Well, she's put all her trust in riches, and you see how she's served. They say the diamonds and things was worth thousands of thousands of pounds. There was a necklace and a river—whatever that is—and no end of bracelets; and a tarrer and ever so many rings. But there, I mustn't stand talking and all the place to clean down afore your ma comes home."

"I don't see why she should ever have had such lots of diamonds," said Anthea when Martha had flounced off. "She was rather a nasty lady, I thought. And mother hasn't any diamonds, and hardly any jewels—the topaz necklace, and the sapphire ring daddy gave her when they were engaged, and the garnet star, and the little pearl brooch with great-grandpapa's hair in it—that's about all."

"When I'm grown up I'll buy mother no end of diamonds," said

Robert, "if she wants them. I shall make so much money exploring in Africa I shan't know what to do with it."

"Wouldn't it be jolly," said Jane dreamily, "if mother could find all those lovely things, necklaces and rivers of diamonds and tarrers?"

"Ti—*aras*," said Cyril.

"Ti—aras, then—and rings and everything in her room when she came home? I wish she would."

The others gazed at her in horror.

"Well, she *will*," said Robert; "you've wished, my good Jane—and our only chance now is to find the Psammead, and if it's in a good temper it *may* take back the wish and give us another. If not—well—goodness knows what we're in for!—the police, of course, and—Don't cry, silly! We'll stand by you. Father says we need never be afraid if we don't do anything wrong and always speak the truth."

But Cyril and Anthea exchanged gloomy glances. They remembered how convincing the truth about the Psammead had been once before when told to the police.

It was a day of misfortunes. Of course the Psammead could not be found. Nor the jewels, though every one of the children searched their mother's room again and again.

"Of course," Robert said, "*we* couldn't find them. It'll be mother who'll do that. Perhaps she'll think they've been in the house for years and years, and never know they are the stolen ones at all."

"Oh yes!" Cyril was very scornful; "then mother will be a receiver of stolen goods, and you know jolly well what *that's* worse than."

Another and exhaustive search of the sand-pit failed to reveal the Psammead, so the children went back to the house slowly and sadly.

"I don't care," said Anthea stoutly, "we'll tell mother the truth, and she'll give back the jewels—and make everything all right."

"Do you think so?" said Cyril slowly. "Do you think she'll believe us? Could anyone believe about a Sammyadd unless they'd seen it? She'll think we're pretending. Or else she'll think we're raving mad, and then we shall be sent to Bedlam.* How would you like it?"—he turned suddenly on the miserable Jane—"how would you like it, to

---

* Popular name for the Hospital of St. Mary of Bethlehem, England's oldest psychiatric hospital.

be shut up in an iron cage with bars and padded walls, and nothing to do but stick straws in your hair all day, and listen to the howlings and ravings of the other maniacs? Make up your minds to it, all of you. It's no use telling mother."

"But it's true," said Jane.

"Of course it is, but it's not true enough for grown-up people to believe it," said Anthea. "Cyril's right. Let's put flowers in all the vases, and try not to think about diamonds. After all, everything has come right in the end all the other times."

So they filled all the pots they could find with flowers—asters and zinnias, and loose-leaved late red roses from the wall of the stable-yard, till the house was a perfect bower.

And almost as soon as dinner was cleared away mother arrived, and was clasped in eight loving arms. It was very difficult indeed not to tell her all about the Psammead at once, because they had got into the habit of telling her everything. But they did succeed in not telling her.

Mother, on her side, had plenty to tell them—about Granny, and Granny's pigeons, and Auntie Emma's lame tame donkey. She was very delighted with the flowery-boweryness of the house; and everything seemed so natural and pleasant, now that she was home again, that the children almost thought they must have dreamed the Psammead.

But, when mother moved towards the stairs to go up to her bedroom and take off her bonnet, the eight arms clung round her just as if she only had two children, one the Lamb and the other an octopus.

"Don't go up, mummy darling," said Anthea; "let me take your things up for you."

"Or I will," said Cyril.

"We want you to come and look at the rose-tree," said Robert.

"Oh, don't go up!" said Jane helplessly.

"Nonsense, dears," said mother briskly, "I'm not such an old woman yet that I can't take my bonnet off in the proper place. Besides, I must wash these black hands of mine."

So up she went, and the children, following her, exchanged glances of gloomy foreboding.

Mother took off her bonnet—it was a very pretty hat, really, with white roses on it—and when she had taken it off she went to the dressing-table to do her pretty hair.

On the table between the ring-stand and the pincushion lay a green leather case. Mother opened it.

"Oh, how lovely!" she cried. It was a ring, a large pearl with shining many-lighted diamonds set round it. "Wherever did this come from?" mother asked, trying it on her wedding finger, which it fitted beautifully. "However did it come here?"

"I don't know," said each of the children truthfully.

"Father must have told Martha to put it here," mother said. "I'll run down and ask her."

"Let me look at it," said Anthea, who knew Martha would not be able to see the ring. But when Martha was asked, of course she denied putting the ring there, and so did Eliza and cook.

Mother came back to her bedroom, very much interested and pleased about the ring. But, when she opened the dressing-table drawer and found a long case containing an almost priceless diamond necklace, she was more interested still, though not so pleased. In the wardrobe, when she went to put away her "bonnet," she found a tiara and several brooches, and the rest of the jewellery turned up in various parts of the room during the next half-hour. The children looked more and more uncomfortable, and now Jane began to sniff.

Mother looked at her gravely.

"Jane," she said, "I am sure you know something about this. Now think before you speak, and tell me the truth."

"We found a Fairy," said Jane obediently.

"No nonsense, please," said her mother sharply.

"Don't be silly, Jane," Cyril interrupted. Then he went on desperately. "Look here, mother, we've never seen the things before, but Lady Chittenden at Peasmarsh Place lost all her jewellery by wicked burglars last night. Could this possibly be it?"

All drew a deep breath. They were saved.

"But how could they have put it here? And why should they?" asked mother, not unreasonably. "Surely it would have been easier and safer to make off with it?"

"Suppose," said Cyril, "they thought it better to wait for—for sunset—nightfall, I mean, before they went off with it. No one but us knew that you were coming back today."

"I must send for the police at once," said mother distractedly. "Oh, how I wish daddy were here!"

"Wouldn't it be better to wait till he *does* come?" asked Robert, knowing that his father would not be home before sunset.

"No, no; I can't wait a minute with all this on my mind," cried mother. "All this" was the heap of jewel-cases on the bed. They put them all in the wardrobe, and mother locked it. Then mother called Martha.

"Martha," she said, "has any stranger been into my room since I've been away? Now, answer me truthfully."

"No, mum," answered Martha; "leastways, what I mean to say—" She stopped.

"Come," said her mistress kindly; "I see someone has. You must tell me at once. Don't be frightened. I'm sure you haven't done anything wrong."

Martha burst into heavy sobs.

"I was a-goin' to give you warning this very day, mum, to leave at the end of my month, so I was—on account of me being going to make a respectable young man happy. A gamekeeper he is by trade, mum—and I wouldn't deceive you—of the name of Beale. And it's as true as I stand here, it was your coming home in such a hurry, and no warning given, out of the kindness of his heart it was, as he says, 'Martha, my beauty,' he says—which I ain't, and never was, but you know how them men will go on—'I can't see you a-toiling and a-moiling and not lend a 'elping 'and; which mine is a strong arm and it's yours, Martha, my dear,' says he. And so he helped me a-cleanin' of the windows—but outside, mum, the whole time, and me in; if I never say another breathing word it's the gospel truth."

"Were you with him the whole time?" asked her mistress.

"Him outside and me in, I was," said Martha; "except for fetching up a fresh pail and the leather that that slut of a Eliza 'd hidden away behind the mangle."*

"That will do," said the children's mother. "I am not pleased with you, Martha, but you have spoken the truth, and that counts for something."

---

* Machine for drying clothes.

When Martha had gone, the children clung round their mother.

"Oh, mummy darling," cried Anthea, "it isn't Beale's fault, it isn't really! He's a great dear; he is, truly and honourably, and as honest as the day. Don't let the police take him, mummy! Oh, don't, don't, don't!"

It was truly awful. Here was an innocent man accused of robbery through that silly wish of Jane's, and it was absolutely useless to tell the truth. All longed to, but they thought of the straws in the hair and the shrieks of the other frantic maniacs, and they could not do it.

"Is there a cart hereabouts?" asked mother feverishly. "A trap of any sort? I must drive into Rochester and tell the police at once."

All the children sobbed, "There's a cart at the farm, but, oh, don't go!—Don't go!—Oh, don't go!—wait till daddy comes home!"

Mother took not the faintest notice. When she had set her mind on a thing she always went straight through with it; she was rather like Anthea in this respect.

"Look here, Cyril," she said, sticking on her hat with long sharp violet-headed pins, "I leave you in charge. Stay in the dressing-room. You can pretend to be swimming boats in the bath, or something. Say I gave you leave. But stay there, with the landing door open; I've locked the other. And don't let anyone go into my room. Remember, no one knows the jewels are there except me, and all of you, and the wicked thieves who put them there. Robert, you stay in the garden and watch the windows. If anyone tries to get in you must run and tell the two farm men that I'll send up to wait in the kitchen. I'll tell them there are dangerous characters about—that's true enough. Now, remember, I trust you both. But I don't think they'll try it till after dark, so you're quite safe. Good-bye, darlings."

And she locked her bedroom door and went off with the key in her pocket.

The children could not help admiring the dashing and decided way in which she had acted. They thought how useful she would have been in organizing escape from some of the tight places in which they had found themselves of late in consequence of their ill-timed wishes.

"She's a born general," said Cyril—"but I don't know what's going to happen to us. Even if the girls were to hunt for that beastly Sammyadd and find it, and get it to take the jewels away again, mother would only think we hadn't looked out properly and let the burglars sneak in and nick them—or else the police will think *we've* got them—or else that she's been fooling them. Oh, it's a pretty decent average ghastly mess this time, and no mistake!"

He savagely made a paper boat and began to float it in the bath, as he had been told to do.

Robert went into the garden and sat down on the worn yellow grass, with his miserable head between his helpless hands.

Anthea and Jane whispered together in the passage downstairs, where the coconut matting* was—with the hole in it that you always caught your foot in if you were not careful. Martha's voice could be heard in the kitchen—grumbling loud and long.

"It's simply quite too dreadfully awful," said Anthea. "How do you know all the diamonds are there, too? If they aren't, the police will think mother and father have got them, and that they've only given up some of them for a kind of desperate blind. And they'll be put in prison, and we shall be branded outcasts, the children of felons. And it won't be at all nice for father and mother either," she added, by a candid afterthought.

"But what can we *do*?" asked Jane.

"Nothing—at least we might look for the Psammead again. It's a very, *very* hot day. He may have come out to warm that whisker of his."

"He won't give us any more beastly wishes today," said Jane flatly. "He gets crosser and crosser every time we see him. I believe he hates having to give wishes."

Anthea had been shaking her head gloomily—now she stopped shaking it so suddenly that it really looked as though she were pricking up her ears.

"What is it?" asked Jane. "Oh, have you thought of something?"

"Our one chance," cried Anthea dramatically; "the last lone-lorn forlorn hope. Come on."

At a brisk trot she led the way to the sand-pit. Oh, joy!—there was the Psammead, basking in a golden sandy hollow and preening its whiskers happily in the glowing afternoon sun. The moment it saw them it whisked round and began to burrow—it evidently preferred

---

* Floor covering made from the fiber of coconut husks.

its own company to theirs. But Anthea was too quick for it. She caught it by its furry shoulders gently but firmly, and held it.

"Here—none of that!" said the Psammead. "Leave go of me, will you?"

But Anthea held him fast.

"Dear kind darling Sammyadd," she said breathlessly.

"Oh yes—it's all very well," it said; "you want another wish, I expect. But I can't keep on slaving from morning till night giving people their wishes. I must have some time to myself."

"Do you hate giving wishes?" asked Anthea gently, and her voice trembled with excitement.

"Of course I do," it said. "Leave go of me or I'll bite!—I really will—I mean it. Oh, well, if you choose to risk it."

Anthea risked it and held on.

"Look here," she said, "don't bite me—listen to reason. If you'll only do what we want today, we'll never ask you for another wish as long as we live."

The Psammead was much moved.

"I'd do anything," it said in a tearful voice. "I'd almost burst myself to give you one wish after another, as long as I held out, if you'd only never, never ask me to do it after today. If you knew how I hate to blow myself out with other people's wishes, and how frightened I am always that I shall strain a muscle or something. And then to wake up every morning and know you've got to do it. You don't know what it is—you don't know what it is, you don't!" Its voice cracked with emotion, and the last "don't" was a squeak.

Anthea set it down gently on the sand.

"It's all over now," she said soothingly. "We promise faithfully never to ask for another wish after today."

"Well, go ahead," said the Psammead; "let's get it over."

"How many can you do?"

"I don't know—as long as I can hold out."

"Well, first, I wish Lady Chittenden may find she's never lost her jewels."

The Psammead blew itself out, collapsed, and said, "Done."

"I wish," said Anthea more slowly, "mother mayn't get to the police."

"Done," said the creature after the proper interval.

"I wish," said Jane suddenly, "mother could forget all about the diamonds."

"Done," said the Psammead; but its voice was weaker.

"Wouldn't you like to rest a little?" asked Anthea considerately.

"Yes, please," said the Psammead; "and, before we go further, will you wish something for me?"

"Can't you do wishes for yourself?"

"Of course not," it said; "we were always expected to give each other our wishes—not that we had any to speak of in the good old Megatherium days. Just wish, will you, that you may never be able, any of you, to tell anyone a word about *Me*."

"Why?" asked Jane.

"Why, don't you see, if you told grown-ups I should have no peace of my life. They'd get hold of me, and they wouldn't wish silly things like you do, but real earnest things; and the scientific people would hit on some way of making things last after sunset, as likely as not; and they'd ask for a graduated income-tax, and old-age-pensions and manhood suffrage, and free secondary education, and dull things like that; and get them, and keep them, and the whole world would be turned topsy-turvy. Do wish it! Quick!"

Anthea repeated the Psammead's wish, and it blew itself out to a larger size than they had yet seen it attain.

"And now," it said as it collapsed, "can I do anything more for you?"

"Just one thing; and I think that clears everything up, doesn't it, Jane? I wish Martha to forget about the diamond ring, and mother to forget about the keeper cleaning the windows."

"It's like the 'Brass Bottle,' " said Jane.[7]

"Yes, I'm glad we read that or I should never have thought of it."

"Now," said the Psammead faintly, "I'm almost worn out. Is there anything else?"

"No; only thank you kindly for all you've done for us, and I hope you'll have a good long sleep, and I hope we shall see you again some day."

"Is that a wish?" it said in a weak voice.

"Yes, please," said the two girls together.

Then for the last time in this story they saw the Psammead blow itself out and collapse suddenly. It nodded to them, blinked its long snail's eyes, burrowed, and disappeared, scratching fiercely to the last, and the sand closed over it.

"I hope we've done right?" said Jane.

"I'm sure we have," said Anthea. "Come on home and tell the boys."

Anthea found Cyril glooming over his paper boats, and told him. Jane told Robert. The two tales were only just ended when mother walked in, hot and dusty. She explained that as she was being driven into Rochester to buy the girls' autumn school-dresses the axle had broken, and but for the narrowness of the lane and the high soft hedges she would have been thrown out. As it was, she was not hurt, but she had had to walk home. "And oh, my dearest dear chicks," she said, "I am simply dying for a cup of tea! Do run and see if the kettle boils!"

"So you see it's all right," Jane whispered. "She doesn't remember."

"No more does Martha," said Anthea, who had been to ask after the state of the kettle.

As the servants sat at their tea, Beale the gamekeeper dropped in. He brought the welcome news that Lady Chittenden's diamonds had not been lost at all. Lord Chittenden had taken them to be re-set and cleaned, and the maid who knew about it had gone for a holiday. So that was all right.

"I wonder if we ever shall see the Psammead again," said Jane wistfully as they walked in the garden, while mother was putting the Lamb to bed.

"I'm sure we shall," said Cyril, "if you really wished it."

"We've promised never to ask it for another wish," said Anthea.

"I never want to," said Robert earnestly.

They did see it again, of course, but not in this story. And it was not in a sand-pit either, but in a very, very, very different place. It was in a— But I must say no more.

EXPLICIT

THE ENCHANTED CASTLE

The hall in which the children found themselves

Peggy, you came from the heath and moor,
And you brought their airs through my open door;
You brought the blossom of youth to blow
In the Latin Quarter of Soho.

For the sake of that magic I send you here
A tale of enchantments, Peggy dear,
—A bit of my work, and a bit of my heart . . .
The bit that you left when we had to part.

Royalty Chambers, Soho, W.
25 September 1907

LIST OF ILLUSTRATIONS

CHAPTER I

There were three of them—Jerry, Jimmy, and Kathleen. Of course, Jerry's name was Gerald, and not Jeremiah, whatever you may think; and Jimmy's name was James; and Kathleen was never called by her name at all, but Cathy, or Catty, or Puss Cat, when her brothers were pleased with her, and Scratch Cat when they were not pleased. And they were at school in a little town in the West of England—the boys at one school, of course, and the girl at another, because the sensible habit of having boys and girls at the same school is not yet as common as I hope it will be some day. They used to see each other on Saturdays and Sundays at the house of a kind maiden lady; but it was one of those houses where it is impossible to play. You know the kind of house, don't you? There is a sort of a something about that kind of house that makes you hardly able even to talk to each other when you are left alone, and playing seems unnatural and affected. So they looked forward to the holidays, when they should all go home and be together all day long, in a house where playing was natural and conversation possible, and where the Hampshire forests and fields were full of interesting things to do and see. Their Cousin Betty was to be there too, and there were plans. Betty's school broke up before theirs, and so she got to the Hampshire* home first, and the moment she got there she began to have measles, so that my three couldn't go home at all. You may imagine their feelings. The thought of seven weeks at Miss Hervey's was not to be borne, and all three wrote home and said so. This astonished their parents very much, because they had always thought it was so nice for the children to have dear Miss Hervey's to go to. However, they were "jolly decent about it," as Jerry said, and after a lot of letters and telegrams, it was arranged that the boys should go and stay at Kathleen's school, where there were now no girls left and no mistresses except the French one.

---

* County on the southern coast of England.

"It'll be better than being at Miss Hervey's," said Kathleen, when the boys came round to ask Mademoiselle when it would be convenient for them to come; "and, besides, our school's not half so ugly as yours. We do have tablecloths on the tables and curtains at the windows, and yours is all deal boards, and desks, and inkiness."

When they had gone to pack their boxes Kathleen made all the rooms as pretty as she could with flowers in jam jars—marigolds chiefly, because there was nothing much else in the back garden. There were geraniums in the front garden, and calceolarias and lobelias; of course, the children were not allowed to pick these.

"We ought to have some sort of play to keep us going through the holidays," said Kathleen, when tea was over, and she had unpacked and arranged the boys' clothes in the painted chests of drawers, feeling very grown-up and careful as she neatly laid the different sorts of clothes in tidy little heaps in the drawers. "Suppose we write a book."

"You couldn't," said Jimmy.

"I didn't mean me, of course," said Kathleen, a little injured; "I meant us."

"Too much fag,"* said Gerald briefly.

"If we wrote a book," Kathleen persisted, "about what the insides of schools really *are* like, people would read it and say how clever we were."

"More likely expel us," said Gerald. "No; we'll have an out-of-doors game—bandits, or something like that. It wouldn't be bad if we could get a cave and keep stores in it, and have our meals there."

"There aren't any caves," said Jimmy, who was fond of contradicting everyone. "And, besides, your precious Mam'selle won't let us go out alone, as likely as not."

"Oh, we'll see about that," said Gerald. "I'll go and talk to her like a father."

"Like that?" Kathleen pointed the thumb of scorn at him, and he looked in the glass.

"To brush his hair and his clothes and to wash his face and hands

---

* Hard work (slang).

was to our hero but the work of a moment," said Gerald, and went to suit the action to the word.

It was a very sleek boy, brown and thin and interesting-looking, that knocked at the door of the parlour where Mademoiselle sat reading a yellow-covered book and wishing vain wishes. Gerald could always make himself look interesting at a moment's notice, a very useful accomplishment in dealing with strange grown-ups. It was done by opening his grey eyes rather wide, allowing the corners of his mouth to droop, and assuming a gentle, pleading expression, resembling that of the late little Lord Fauntleroy—who must, by the way, be quite old now, and an awful prig.[1]

"Entrez!" said Mademoiselle, in shrill French accents. So he entered.

"Eh bien?"* she said rather impatiently.

"I hope I am not disturbing you," said Gerald, in whose mouth, it seemed, butter would not have melted.

"But no," she said, somewhat softened. "What is it that you desire?"

"I thought I ought to come and say how do you do," said Gerald, "because of you being the lady of the house."

He held out the newly-washed hand, still damp and red. She took it.

"You are a very polite little boy," she said.

"Not at all," said Gerald, more polite than ever. "I am so sorry for you. It must be dreadful to have us to look after in the holidays."

"But not at all," said Mademoiselle in her turn. "I am sure you will be very good childrens."

Gerald's look assured her that he and the others would be as near angels as children could be without ceasing to be human.

"We'll try," he said earnestly.

"Can one do anything for you?" asked the French governess kindly.

"Oh, no, thank you," said Gerald. "We don't want to give you any trouble at all. And I was thinking it would be less trouble for you if we were to go out into the woods all day tomorrow and take our

---

* Well? (French).

"Little deceiver!" she said

dinner with us—something cold, you know—so as not to be a trouble to the cook."

"You are very considerate," said Mademoiselle coldly. Then Gerald's eyes smiled; they had a trick of doing this when his lips were quite serious. Mademoiselle caught the twinkle, and she laughed and Gerald laughed too.

"Little deceiver!" she said. "Why not say at once you want to be free of *surveillance*, how you say—overwatching—without pretending it is me you wish to please?"

"You have to be careful with grown-ups," said Gerald, "but it isn't all pretence either. We *don't* want to trouble you—and we don't want you to—"

"To trouble you. Eh bien! Your parents, they permit these days at woods?"

"Oh, yes," said Gerald truthfully.

"Then I will not be more a dragon than the parents. I will forewarn the cook. Are you content?"

"Rather!" said Gerald. "Mademoiselle, you are a dear."

"A deer?" she repeated—"a stag?"

"No, a—a *chérie*,"* said Gerald—"a regular A1 *chérie*. And you shan't repent it. Is there anything we can do for you—wind your wool, or find your spectacles, or—?"

"He thinks me a grandmother!" said Mademoiselle, laughing more than ever. "Go then, and be not more naughty than you must."

"Well, what luck?" the others asked.

"It's all right," said Gerald indifferently. "I told you it would be. The ingenuous youth won the regard of the foreign governess, who in her youth had been the beauty of her humble village."

"I don't believe she ever was. She's too stern," said Kathleen.

"Ah!" said Gerald, "that's only because you don't know how to manage her. She wasn't stern with *me*."

"I say, what a humbug you are though, aren't you?" said Jimmy.

"No, I'm a dip—what's-its-name? Something like an ambassador. Dipsoplomatist—that's what I am. Anyhow, we've got our day, and if we don't find a cave in it my name's not Jack Robinson."

Mademoiselle, less stern than Kathleen had ever seen her, presided at supper, which was bread and treacle spread several hours before, and now harder and drier than any other food you can think of. Gerald was very polite in handing her butter and cheese, and pressing her to taste the bread and treacle.

"Bah! it is like sand in the mouth—of a dryness! Is it possible this pleases you?"

"No," said Gerald, "it is not possible, but it is not polite for boys to make remarks about their food!"

---

*Dear (French).

She laughed, but there was no more dried bread and treacle for supper after that.

"How *do* you do it?" Kathleen whispered admiringly as they said good night.

"Oh, it's quite easy when you've once got a grown-up to see what you're after. You'll see, I shall drive her with a rein of darning cotton after this."

Next morning Gerald got up early and gathered a little bunch of pink carnations from a plant which he found hidden among the marigolds. He tied it up with black cotton and laid it on Mademoiselle's plate. She smiled and looked quite handsome as she stuck the flowers in her belt.

"Do you think it's quite decent," Jimmy asked later—"sort of bribing people to let you do as you like with flowers and things and passing them the salt?"

"It's not that," said Kathleen suddenly. "I know what Gerald means, only I never think of the things in time myself. You see, if you want grown-ups to be nice to you the least you can do is to be nice to them and think of little things to please them. I never think of any myself. Jerry does; that's why all the old ladies like him. It's not bribery. It's a sort of honesty—like paying for things."

"Well, anyway," said Jimmy, putting away the moral question, "we've got a ripping day for the woods."

They had.

The wide High Street, even at the busy morning hour almost as quiet as a dream-street, lay bathed in sunshine; the leaves shone fresh from last night's rain, but the road was dry, and in the sunshine the very dust of it sparkled like diamonds. The beautiful old houses, standing stout and strong, looked as though they were basking in the sunshine and enjoying it.

"But *are* there any woods?" asked Kathleen as they passed the market-place.

"It doesn't much matter about woods," said Gerald dreamily, "we're sure to find *something*. One of the chaps told me his father said when he was a boy there used to be a little cave under the bank in a lane near the Salisbury Road; but he said there was an enchanted castle there too, so perhaps the cave isn't true either."

"If we were to get horns," said Kathleen, "and to blow them very hard all the way, we might find a magic castle."

"If you've got the money to throw away on horns . . ." said Jimmy contemptuously.

"Well, I have, as it happens, so there!" said Kathleen. And the horns were bought in a tiny shop with a bulging window full of a tangle of toys and sweets and cucumbers and sour apples.

And the quiet square at the end of the town where the church is, and the houses of the most respectable people, echoed to the sound of horns blown long and loud. But none of the houses turned into enchanted castles.

So they went along the Salisbury Road, which was very hot and dusty, so they agreed to drink one of the bottles of ginger-beer.

"We might as well carry the ginger-beer inside us as inside the bottle," said Jimmy, "and we can hide the bottle and call for it as we come back."

Presently they came to a place where the road, as Gerald said, went two ways at once.

"That looks like adventures," said Kathleen; and they took the right-hand road, and the next time they took a turning it was a left-hand one, so as to be quite fair, Jimmy said, and then a right-hand one and then a left, and so on, till they were completely lost.

"Completely," said Kathleen; "how jolly!"

And now trees arched overhead, and the banks of the road were high and bushy. The adventurers had long since ceased to blow their horns. It was too tiring to go on doing that, when there was no one to be annoyed by it.

"Oh, kriky!" observed Jimmy suddenly, "let's sit down a bit and have some of our dinner. We might call it lunch, you know," he added persuasively.

So they sat down in the hedge and ate the ripe red gooseberries that were to have been their dessert.

And as they sat and rested and wished that their boots did not feel so full of feet, Gerald leaned back against the bushes, and the bushes gave way so that he almost fell over backward. Something had yielded to the pressure of his back, and there was the sound of something heavy that fell.

"Oh, Jimminy!" he remarked, recovering himself suddenly;

"there's something hollow in there—the stone I was leaning against simply *went*!"

"I wish it was a cave," said Jimmy; "but of course it isn't."

"If we blow the horns perhaps it will be," said Kathleen, and hastily blew her own.

Gerald reached his hand through the bushes. "I can't feel anything but air," he said; "it's just a hole full of emptiness." The other two pulled back the bushes. There certainly was a hole in the bank. "I'm going to go in," observed Gerald.

"Oh, don't!" said his sister. "I wish you wouldn't. Suppose there were snakes!"

"Not likely," said Gerald, but he leaned forward and struck a match. "It *is* a cave!" he cried, and put his knee on the mossy stone he had been sitting on, scrambled over it, and disappeared.

A breathless pause followed.

"You all right?" asked Jimmy.

"Yes; come on. You'd better come feet first—there's a bit of a drop."

"I'll go next," said Kathleen, and went—feet first, as advised. The feet waved wildly in the air.

"Look out!" said Gerald in the dark; "you'll have my eye out. Put your feet *down*, girl, not up. It's no use trying to fly here—there's no room."

He helped her by pulling her feet forcibly down and then lifting her under the arms. She felt rustling dry leaves under her boots, and stood ready to receive Jimmy, who came in head first, like one diving into an unknown sea.

"It *is* a cave," said Kathleen.

"The young explorers," explained Gerald, blocking up the hole of entrance with his shoulders, "dazzled at first by the darkness of the cave, could see nothing."

"Darkness doesn't dazzle," said Jimmy.

"I wish we'd got a candle," said Kathleen.

"Yes, it does," Gerald contradicted—"could see nothing. But their dauntless leader, whose eyes had grown used to the dark while the clumsy forms of the others were bunging up the entrance, had made a discovery."

"Oh, what!" Both the others were used to Gerald's way of telling

Jimmy came in head first

a story while he acted it, but they did sometimes wish that he didn't talk quite so long and so like a book in moments of excitement.

"He did not reveal the dread secret to his faithful followers till one and all had given him their word of honour to be calm."

"We'll be calm all right," said Jimmy impatiently.

"Well, then," said Gerald, ceasing suddenly to be a book and becoming a boy, "there's a light over there—look behind you!"

They looked. And there was. A faint greyness on the brown walls of the cave, and a brighter greyness cut off sharply by a dark line, showed that round a turning or angle of the cave there was daylight.

"Attention!" said Gerald; at least, that was what he meant, though what he said was " 'Shun!" as becomes the son of a soldier. The others mechanically obeyed.

"You will remain at attention till I give the word 'Slow march!' on which you will advance cautiously in open order, following your hero leader, taking care not to tread on the dead and wounded."

"I wish you wouldn't!" said Kathleen.

"There aren't any," said Jimmy, feeling for her hand in the dark; "he only means, take care not to tumble over stones and things."

Here he found her hand, and she screamed.

"It's only me," said Jimmy. "I thought you'd like me to hold it. But you're just like a girl."

Their eyes had now begun to get accustomed to the darkness, and all could see that they were in a rough stone cave, that went straight on for about three or four yards and then turned sharply to the right.

"Death or victory!" remarked Gerald. "Now, then—Slow march!"

He advanced carefully, picking his way among the loose earth and stones that were the floor of the cave. "A sail, a sail!" he cried, as he turned the corner.

"How splendid!" Kathleen drew a long breath as she came out into the sunshine.

"I don't see any sail," said Jimmy, following.

The narrow passage ended in a round arch all fringed with ferns and creepers. They passed through the arch into a deep, narrow gully whose banks were of stones, moss-covered; and in the crannies grew more ferns and long grasses. Trees growing on the top of the bank arched across, and the sunlight came through in changing patches of brightness, turning the gully to a roofed corridor of goldy-green. The path, which was of greeny-grey flagstones where heaps of leaves had drifted, sloped steeply down, and at the end of it was another round arch, quite dark inside, above which rose rocks and grass and bushes.

"It's like the outside of a railway tunnel," said James.

"It's the entrance to the enchanted castle," said Kathleen. "Let's blow the horns."

"Dry up!" said Gerald. "The bold Captain, reproving the silly chatter of his subordinates—"

"It's the entrance to the enchanted castle"

"I like that!" said Jimmy, indignant.

"I thought you would," resumed Gerald—"of his subordinates, bade them advance with caution and in silence, because after all there might be somebody about, and the other arch might be an ice-house* or something dangerous."

"What?" asked Kathleen anxiously.

"Bears, perhaps," said Gerald briefly.

"There aren't any bears without bars—in England, anyway," said Jimmy. "They call bears bars in America," he added absently.

"Quick march!" was Gerald's only reply.

And they marched. Under the drifted damp leaves the path was firm and stony to their shuffling feet. At the dark arch they stopped.

"There are steps down," said Jimmy.

"It *is* an ice-house," said Gerald.

"Don't let's," said Kathleen.

"Our hero," said Gerald, "who nothing could dismay, raised the faltering hopes of his abject minions by saying that he was jolly well going on, and they could do as they liked about it."

"If you call names," said Jimmy, "you can go on by yourself." He added, "So there!"

"It's part of the game, silly," explained Gerald kindly. "You can be Captain tomorrow, so you'd better hold your jaw now, and begin to think about what names you'll call us when it's your turn."

Very slowly and carefully they went down the steps. A vaulted stone arched over their heads. Gerald struck a match when the last step was found to have no edge, and to be, in fact, the beginning of a passage, turning to the left.

"This," said Jimmy, "will take us back into the road."

"Or under it," said Gerald. "We've come down eleven steps."

They went on, following their leader, who went very slowly for fear, as he explained, of steps. The passage was very dark.

"I don't half like it!" whispered Jimmy.

Then came a glimmer of daylight that grew and grew, and presently ended in another arch that looked out over a scene so like a picture out of a book about Italy that everyone's breath was taken

---

* Partly or wholly underground structure used to store ice.

away, and they simply walked forward silent and staring. A short avenue of cypresses led, widening as it went, to a marble terrace that lay broad and white in the sunlight. The children, blinking, leaned their arms on the broad, flat balustrade and gazed. Immediately below them was a lake—just like a lake in "The Beauties of Italy"—a lake with swans and an island and weeping willows; beyond it were green slopes dotted with groves of trees, and amid the trees gleamed the white limbs of statues. Against a little hill to the left was a round white building with pillars, and to the right a waterfall came tumbling down among mossy stones to splash into the lake. Steps fed from the terrace to the water, and other steps to the green lawns beside it. Away across the grassy slopes deer were feeding, and in the distance where the groves of trees thickened into what looked almost a forest were enormous shapes of grey stone, like nothing that the children had ever seen before.

"That chap at school—" said Gerald.

"It *is* an enchanted castle," said Kathleen.

"I don't see any castle," said Jimmy.

"What do you call that, then?" Gerald pointed to where, beyond a belt of lime-trees, white towers and turrets broke the blue of the sky.

"There doesn't seem to be anyone about," said Kathleen, "and yet it's all so tidy. I believe it is magic."

"Magic mowing machines," Jimmy suggested.

"If we were in a book it would be an enchanted castle—certain to be," said Kathleen.

"It *is* an enchanted castle," said Gerald in hollow tones.

"But there aren't any." Jimmy was quite positive.

"How do you know? Do you think there's nothing in the world but what *you've* seen?" His scorn was crushing.

"I think magic went out when people began to have steam-engines," Jimmy insisted, "and newspapers, and telephones and wireless telegraphing."

"Wireless is rather like magic when you come to think of it," said Gerald.

"Oh, *that* sort!" Jimmy's contempt was deep.

"Perhaps there's given up being magic because people didn't believe in it any more," said Kathleen.

"This is an enchanted garden"

"Well, don't let's spoil the show with any silly old not believing,"
said Gerald with decision. "I'm going to believe in magic as hard as
I can. This is an enchanted garden, and that's an enchanted castle, and
I'm jolly well going to explore. The dauntless knight then led the way,
leaving his ignorant squires to follow or not, just as they jolly well
chose." He rolled off the balustrade and strode firmly down towards
the lawn, his boots making, as they went, a clatter full of determina-
tion.

The others followed. There never was such a garden—out of a
picture or a fairy-tale. They passed quite close by the deer, who only

raised their pretty heads to look, and did not seem startled at all. And after a long stretch of turf they passed under the heaped-up heavy masses of lime-trees and came into a rose-garden, bordered with thick, close-cut yew hedges, and lying red and pink and green and white in the sun, like a giant's many-coloured, highly-scented pocket-handkerchief.

"I know we shall meet a gardener in a minute, and he'll ask what we're doing here. And then what will you say?" Kathleen asked with her nose in a rose.

"I shall say we have lost our way, and it will be quite true," said Gerald.

But they did not meet a gardener or anybody else, and the feeling of magic got thicker and thicker, till they were almost afraid of the sound of their feet in the great silent place. Beyond the rose garden was a yew hedge with an arch cut in it, and it was the beginning of a maze like the one in Hampton Court.[2]

"Now," said Gerald, "you mark my words. In the middle of this maze we shall find the secret enchantment. Draw your swords, my merry men all, and hark forward tallyho in the utmost silence."

Which they did.

It was very hot in the maze, between the close yew hedges, and the way to the maze's heart was hidden well. Again and again they found themselves at the black yew arch that opened on the rose garden, and they were all glad that they had brought large, clean pocket-handkerchiefs with them.

It was when they found themselves there for the fourth time that Jimmy suddenly cried, "Oh, I wish—" and then stopped short very suddenly. "Oh!" he added in quite a different voice, "where's the dinner?" And then in a stricken silence they all remembered that the basket with the dinner had been left at the entrance of the cave. Their thoughts dwelt fondly on the slices of cold mutton, the six tomatoes, the bread and butter, the screwed-up paper of salt, the apple turnovers, and the little thick glass that one drank the ginger-beer out of.

"Let's go back," said Jimmy, "now this minute, and get our things and have our dinner."

"Let's have one more try at the maze. I hate giving things up," said Gerald.

"I *am* so hungry!" said Jimmy.

"Why didn't you say so before?" asked Gerald bitterly.

"I wasn't before."

"Then you can't be now. You don't get hungry all in a minute. What's that?"

"That" was a gleam of red that lay at the foot of the yew hedge—a thin little line, that you would hardly have noticed unless you had been staring in a fixed and angry way at the roots of the hedge.

It was a thread of cotton. Gerald picked it up. One end of it was tied to a thimble with holes in it, and the other—

"There *is* no other end," said Gerald, with firm triumph. "It's a clue—that's what it is. What price cold mutton now? I've always felt something magic would happen some day, and now it has."

"I expect the gardener put it there," said Jimmy.

"With a Princess's silver thimble on it? Look! there's a crown on the thimble."

There was.

"Come," said Gerald in low, urgent tones, "if you are adventurers *be* adventurers; and anyhow, I expect someone has gone along the road and bagged the mutton hours ago."

He walked forward, winding the red thread round his fingers as he went. And it *was* a clue, and it led them right into the middle of the maze. And in the very middle of the maze they came upon the wonder.

The red clue led them up two stone steps to a round grass plot. There was a sun-dial in the middle, and all round against the yew hedge a low, wide marble seat. The red clue ran straight across the grass and by the sun-dial, and ended in a small brown hand with jewelled rings on every finger. The hand was, naturally, attached to an arm, and that had many bracelets on it, sparkling with red and blue and green stones. The arm wore a sleeve of pink and gold brocaded silk, faded a little here and there but still extremely imposing, and the sleeve was part of a dress, which was worn by a lady who lay on the stone seat asleep in the sun. The rosy gold dress fell open over an embroidered petticoat of a soft green colour. There was old yellow lace the colour of scalded cream, and a thin white veil spangled with silver stars covered the face.

The red clue ran straight across the grass

"It's the enchanted Princess," said Gerald, now really impressed. "I told you so."

"It's the Sleeping Beauty," said Kathleen. "It is—look how old-fashioned her clothes are, like the pictures of Marie Antoinette's ladies in the history book. She has slept for a hundred years. Oh, Gerald, you're the eldest; you must be the Prince, and we never knew it."

"She isn't really a Princess," said Jimmy. But the others laughed at him, partly because his saying things like that was enough to spoil any game, and partly because they really were not at all sure that it was not a Princess who lay there as still as the sunshine. Every stage of the adventure—the cave, the wonderful gardens, the maze, the clue, had deepened the feeling of magic, till now Kathleen and Gerald were almost completely bewitched.

"Lift the veil up, Jerry," said Kathleen in a whisper; "if she isn't beautiful we shall know she can't be the Princess."

"Lift it yourself," said Gerald.

"I expect you're forbidden to touch the figures," said Jimmy.

"It's not wax, silly," said his brother.

"No," said his sister, "wax wouldn't be much good in this sun. And, besides, you can see her breathing. It's the Princess right enough." She very gently lifted the edge of the veil and turned it back. The Princess's face was small and white between long plaits of black hair. Her nose was straight and her brows finely traced. There were a few freckles on cheekbones and nose.

"No wonder," whispered Kathleen, "sleeping all these years in all this sun!" Her mouth was not a rosebud. But all the same—

"Isn't she lovely!" Kathleen murmured.

"Not so dusty,"* Gerald was understood to reply.

"Now, Jerry," said Kathleen firmly, "you're the eldest."

"Of course I am," said Gerald uneasily.

"Well, you've got to wake the Princess."

"She's not a Princess," said Jimmy, with his hands in the pockets of his knickerbockers; "she's only a little girl dressed up."

"But she's in long dresses," urged Kathleen.

---

* Not so bad (slang).

"Yes, but look what a little way down her frock her feet come. She wouldn't be any taller than Jerry if she was to stand up."

"Now then," urged Kathleen. "Jerry, don't be silly. You've got to do it."

"Do what?" asked Gerald, kicking his left boot with his right.

"Why, kiss her awake, of course."

"Not me!" was Gerald's unhesitating rejoinder.

"Well, someone's got to."

"She'd go for me as likely as not the minute she woke up," said Gerald anxiously.

"I'd do it like a shot," said Kathleen, "but I don't suppose it 'ud make any difference me kissing her."

She did it; and it didn't. The Princess still lay in deep slumber.

"Then you must, Jimmy. I dare say you'll do. Jump back quickly before she can hit you."

"She won't hit him, he's such a little chap," said Gerald.

"Little yourself!" said Jimmy. "I don't mind kissing her. I'm not a coward, like Some People. Only if I do, I'm going to be the dauntless leader for the rest of the day."

"No, look here—hold on!" cried Gerald, "perhaps I'd better—" But, in the meantime, Jimmy had planted a loud, cheerful-sounding kiss on the Princess's pale cheek, and now the three stood breathless, awaiting the result.

And the result was that the Princess opened large, dark eyes, stretched out her arms, yawned a little, covering her mouth with a small brown hand, and said, quite plainly and distinctly, and without any room at all for mistake:

"Then the hundred years are over? How the yew hedges have grown! Which of you is my Prince that aroused me from my deep sleep of so many long years?"

"I did," said Jimmy fearlessly, for she did not look as though she were going to slap anyone.

"My noble preserver!" said the Princess, and held out her hand. Jimmy shook it vigorously.

"But I say," said he, "you aren't really a Princess, are you?"

"Of course I am," she answered; "who else could I be? Look at my crown!" She pulled aside the spangled veil, and showed beneath

The three stood breathless, awaiting the result

it a coronet of what even Jimmy could not help seeing to be diamonds.

"But—" said Jimmy.

"Why," she said, opening her eyes very wide, you must have known about my being here, or you'd never have come. How did you get past the dragons?"

Gerald ignored the question. "I say," he said, "do you really believe in magic, and all that?"

"I ought to," she said, "if anybody does. Look, here's the place where I pricked my finger with the spindle." She showed a little scar on her wrist.

"Then this really is an enchanted castle?"

"Of course it is," said the Princess. "How stupid you are!" She stood up, and her pink brocaded dress lay in bright waves about her feet.

"I said her dress would be too long," said Jimmy.

"It was the right length when I went to sleep," said the Princess; "it must have grown in the hundred years."

"I don't believe you're a Princess at all," said Jimmy; "at least—"

"Don't bother about believing it, if you don't like," said the Princess. "It doesn't so much matter what you believe as what I am." She turned to the others.

"Let's go back to the castle," she said, "and I'll show you all my lovely jewels and things. Wouldn't you like that?"

"Yes," said Gerald with very plain hesitation. "But—"

"But what?" The Princess's tone was impatient.

"But we're most awfully hungry."

"Oh, so am I!" cried the Princess.

"We've had nothing to eat since breakfast."

"And it's three now," said the Princess, looking at the sun-dial. "Why, you've had nothing to eat for hours and hours and hours. But think of me! I haven't had anything to eat for a hundred years. Come along to the castle."

"The mice will have eaten everything," said Jimmy sadly. He saw now that she really *was* a Princess.

"Not they," cried the Princess joyously. "You forget everything's enchanted here. Time simply stood still for a hundred years. Come along, and one of you must carry my train, or I shan't be able to move now it's grown such a frightful length."

CHAPTER II

When you are young so many things are difficult to be- lieve, and yet the dullest people will tell you that they are true—such things, for instance, as that the earth goes round the sun, and that it is not flat but round. But the things that seem really likely, like fairy-tales and magic, are, so say the grown- ups, not true at all. Yet they are so easy to believe, especially when you see them happening. And, as I am always telling you, the most won- derful things happen to all sorts of people, only you never hear about them because the people think that no one will believe their stories, and so they don't tell them to any one except me. And they tell me, because they know that I can believe anything.

When Jimmy had awakened the Sleeping Princess, and she had invited the three children to go with her to her palace and get some- thing to eat, they all knew quite surely that they had come into a place of magic happenings. And they walked in a slow procession along the grass towards the castle. The Princess went first, and Kathleen carried her shining train; then came Jimmy, and Gerald came last. They were all quite sure that they had walked right into the middle of a fairy- tale, and they were the more ready to believe it because they were so tired and hungry. They were, in fact, so hungry and tired that they hardly noticed where they were going, or observed the beauties of the formal gardens through which the pink-silk Princess was leading them. They were in a sort of dream, from which they only partially awakened to find themselves in a big hall, with suits of armour and old flags round the walls, the skins of beasts on the floor, and heavy oak tables and benches ranged along it.

The Princess entered, slow and stately, but once inside she twitched her sheeny* train out of Jimmy's hand and turned to the three.

"You just wait here a minute," she said, "and mind you don't talk

_____

* Shiny.

while I'm away. This castle is crammed with magic, and I don't know what will happen if you talk." And with that, picking up the thick goldy-pink folds under her arms, she ran out, as Jimmy said afterwards, "most unprincesslike," showing as she ran black stockings and black strap shoes.

Jimmy wanted very much to say that he didn't believe anything would happen, only he was afraid something would happen if he did, so he merely made a face and put out his tongue. The others pretended not to see this, which was much more crushing than anything they could have said. So they sat in silence, and Gerald ground the heel of his boot upon the marble floor. Then the Princess came back, very slowly and kicking her long skirts in front of her at every step. She could not hold them up now because of the tray she carried.

It was not a silver tray, as you might have expected, but an oblong tin one. She set it down noisily on the end of the long table and breathed a sigh of relief.

"Oh! it *was* heavy," she said. I don't know what fairy feast the children's fancy had been busy with. Anyhow, this was nothing like it. The heavy tray held a loaf of bread, a lump of cheese, and a brown jug of water. The rest of its heaviness was just plates and mugs and knives.

"Come along," said the Princess hospitably. "I couldn't find anything but bread and cheese—but it doesn't matter, because everything's magic here, and unless you have some dreadful secret fault the bread and cheese will turn into anything you like. What *would* you like?" she asked Kathleen.

"Roast chicken," said Kathleen, without hesitation.

The pinky Princess cut a slice of bread and laid it on a dish.

"There you are," she said, "roast chicken. Shall I carve it, or will you?"

"You, please," said Kathleen, and received a piece of dry bread on a plate.

"Green peas?" asked the Princess, cut a piece of cheese and laid it beside the bread.

Kathleen began to eat the bread, cutting it up with knife and fork as you would eat chicken. It was no use owning that she didn't see any chicken and peas, or anything but cheese and dry bread, because that would be owning that she had some dreadful secret fault.

"It's a game, isn't it?" asked Jimmy

"If I have, it is a secret, even from me," she told herself.

The others asked for roast beef and cabbage—and got it, she supposed, though to her it only looked like dry bread and Dutch cheese.

"I do wonder what my dreadful secret fault is," she thought, as the Princess remarked that, as for her, she could fancy a slice of roast peacock. "This one," she added, lifting a second mouthful of dry bread on her fork, "is quite delicious."

"It's a game, isn't it?" asked Jimmy suddenly.

"What's a game?" asked the Princess, frowning.

"Pretending it's beef—the bread and cheese, I mean."

"A game? But it is beef. Look at it," said the Princess, opening her eyes very wide.

"Yes, of course," said Jimmy feebly. "I was only joking."

Bread and cheese is not perhaps so good as roast beef or chicken or peacock (I'm not sure about the peacock. I never tasted peacock, did you?); but bread and cheese is, at any rate, very much better than nothing when you have gone on having nothing since breakfast (gooseberries and ginger-beer hardly count) and it is long past your proper dinner-time. Everyone ate and drank and felt much better.

"Now," said the Princess, brushing the breadcrumbs off her green silk lap, "if you're sure you won't have any more meat you can come and see my treasures. Sure you won't take the least bit more chicken? No? Then follow me."

She got up and they followed her down the long hall to the end where the great stone stairs ran up at each side and joined in a broad flight leading to the gallery above. Under the stairs was a hanging of tapestry.

"Beneath this arras," said the Princess, "is the door leading to my private apartments." She held the tapestry up with both hands, for it was heavy, and showed a little door that had been hidden by it.

"The key," she said, "hangs above."

And so it did, on a large rusty nail.

"Put it in," said the Princess, "and turn it."

Gerald did so, and the great key creaked and grated in the lock.

"Now push," she said; "push hard, all of you."

They pushed hard, all of them. The door gave way, and they fell over each other into the dark space beyond.

The Princess dropped the curtain and came after them, closing the door behind her.

"Look out!" she said; "look out! there are two steps down."

"Thank you," said Gerald, rubbing his knee at the bottom of the steps. "We found that out for ourselves."

"I'm sorry," said the Princess, "but you can't have hurt yourselves much. Go straight on. There aren't any more steps."

They went straight on—in the dark.

"When you come to the door just turn the handle and go in. Then stand still till I find the matches. I know where they are."

"Did they have matches a hundred years ago?" asked Jimmy.

"I meant the tinder-box," said the Princess quickly. "We always called it the matches. Don't you? Here, let me go first."

She did, and when they had reached the door she was waiting for them with a candle in her hand. She thrust it on Gerald.

"Hold it steady," she said, and undid the shutters of a long window, so that first a yellow streak and then a blazing great oblong of light flashed at them and the room was full of sunshine.

She was waiting for them with a candle in her hand

"It makes the candle look quite silly," said Jimmy.

"So it does," said the Princess, and blew out the candle. Then she took the key from the outside of the door, put it in the inside keyhole, and turned it.

The room they were in was small and high. Its domed ceiling was of deep blue with gold stars painted on it. The walls were of wood, panelled and carved, and there was no furniture in it whatever.

"This," said the Princess, "is my treasure chamber."

"But where," asked Kathleen politely, "*are* the treasures?"

"Don't you see them?" asked the Princess.

"No, we don't," said Jimmy bluntly. "You don't come that bread-and-cheese game with me—not twice over, you don't!"

"If you *really* don't see them," said the Princess, "I suppose I shall have to say the charm. Shut your eyes, please. And give me your word of honour you won't look till I tell you, and that you'll never tell anyone what you've seen."

Their words of honour were something that the children would rather not have given just then, but they gave them all the same, and shut their eyes tight.

"Wiggadil yougadoo begadee leegadeeve nowgadow?" said the Princess rapidly; and they heard the swish of her silk train moving across the room. Then there was a creaking, rustling noise.

"She's locking us in!" cried Jimmy.

"Your word of honour," gasped Gerald.

"Oh, do be quick!" moaned Kathleen.

"You may look," said the voice of the Princess. And they looked. The room was not the same room, yet—yes, the starry-vaulted blue ceiling was there, and below it half a dozen feet of the dark panelling, but below that the walls of the room blazed and sparkled with white and blue and red and green and gold and silver. Shelves ran round the room, and on them were gold cups and silver dishes, and platters and goblets set with gems, ornaments of gold and silver, tiaras of diamonds, necklaces of rubies, strings of emeralds and pearls, all set out in unimaginable splendour against a background of faded blue velvet. It was like the Crown jewels that you see when your kind uncle takes you to the Tower,* only there seemed to be far more jewels than you or anyone else has ever seen together at the Tower or anywhere else.

The three children remained breathless, open-mouthed, staring at the sparkling splendours all about them, while the Princess stood, her arm stretched out in a gesture of command, and a proud smile on her lips.

"My word!" said Gerald, in a low whisper. But no one spoke out loud. They waited as if spellbound for the Princess to speak.

She spoke.

---

* Tower of London, where the Crown Jewels are housed.

"What price bread-and-cheese games now?" she asked triumphantly. "Can I do magic, or can't I?"

"You can; oh, you can!" said Kathleen.

"May we—may we *touch*?" asked Gerald.

"All that's mine is yours," said the Princess, with a generous wave of her brown hand, and added quickly, "Only, of course, you mustn't take anything away with you."

"We're not thieves!" said Jimmy. The others were already turning over the wonderful things on the blue velvet shelves.

"Perhaps not," said the Princess, "but you're a very unbelieving little boy. You think I can't see inside you, but I can. I know what you've been thinking."

"What?" asked Jimmy.

"Oh, you know well enough," said the Princess. "You're thinking about the bread and cheese that I changed into beef, and about your secret fault. I say, let's all dress up and you be princes and princesses too."

"To crown our hero," said Gerald, lifting a gold crown with a cross on the top, "was the work of a moment." He put the crown on his head, and added a collar of SS* and a zone of sparkling emeralds, which would not quite meet round his middle. He turned from fixing it by an ingenious adaptation of his belt to find the others already decked with diadems, necklaces, and rings.

"How splendid you look!" said the Princess, "and how I wish your clothes were prettier. What ugly clothes people wear nowadays! A hundred years ago—"

Kathleen stood quite still with a diamond bracelet raised in her hand.

"I say," she said. "The King and Queen?"

"*What* King and Queen?" asked the Princess.

"Your father and mother, your sorrowing parents," said Kathleen. "They'll have waked up by now. Won't they be wanting to see you, after a hundred years, you know?"

"Oh—ah—yes," said the Princess slowly. "I embraced my rejoicing parents when I got the bread and cheese. They're having their din-

---

* Decorative gold necklace, traditionally restricted to certain government officials, composed of a string of small emblems shaped like the letter S.

Looking at herself in the little silver-framed mirror

ner. They won't expect me yet. Here," she added, hastily putting a ruby bracelet on Kathleen's arm, "see how splendid that is!"

Kathleen would have been quite content to go on all day trying on different jewels and looking at herself in the little silver-framed mirror that the Princess took from one of the shelves, but the boys were soon weary of this amusement.

"Look here," said Gerald, "if you're sure your father and mother won't want you, let's go out and have a jolly good game of something. You could play besieged castles awfully well in that maze— unless you can do any more magic tricks."

"You forget," said the Princess, "I'm grown up. I don't play games. And I don't like to do too much magic at a time, it's so tiring. Besides, it'll take us ever so long to put all these things back in their proper places."

It did. The children would have laid the jewels just anywhere; but the Princess showed them that every necklace, or ring, or bracelet had its own home on the velvet—a slight hollowing in the shelf beneath, so that each stone fitted into its own little nest.

As Kathleen was fitting the last shining ornament into its proper place, she saw that part of the shelf near it held, not bright jewels, but rings and brooches and chains, as well as queer things that she did not know the names of, and all were of dull metal and odd shapes.

"What's all this rubbish?" she asked.

"Rubbish, indeed!" said the Princess. "Why those are all magic things! This bracelet—anyone who wears it has got to speak the truth. This chain makes you as strong as ten men; if you wear this spur your horse will go a mile a minute; or if you're walking it's the same as seven-league boots."*

"What does this brooch do?" asked Kathleen, reaching out her hand. The princess caught her by the wrist.

"You mustn't touch," she said; "if anyone but me touches them all the magic goes out at once and never comes back. That brooch will give you any wish you like."

"And this ring?" Jimmy pointed.

"Oh, that makes you invisible."

"What's this?" asked Gerald, showing a curious buckle.

"Oh, that undoes the effect of all the other charms."

"Do you mean really?" Jimmy asked. "You're not just kidding?"

"Kidding indeed!" repeated the Princess scornfully. "I should have thought I'd shown you enough magic to prevent you speaking to a Princess like that!"

"I say," said Gerald, visibly excited. "You might show us how some of the things act. Couldn't you give us each a wish?"

The Princess did not at once answer. And the minds of the three played with granted wishes—brilliant yet thoroughly reasonable— the kind of wish that never seems to occur to people in fairy-tales when they suddenly get a chance to have their three wishes granted.

"No," said the Princess suddenly, "no; I can't give wishes to you,

---

* In the French fairy tale Le Petit Poucet ("Little Tom Thumb"), by Charles Perrault (1628–1703), the young hero deceives an ogre and steals a pair of magic boots that allow the wearer to cover 7 leagues (about 3 miles) in one stride.

it only gives me wishes. But I'll let you see the ring make *me* invisible. Only you must shut your eyes while I do it."

They shut them.

"Count fifty," said the Princess, "and then you may look. And then you must shut them again, and count fifty, and I'll reappear."

Gerald counted, aloud. Through the counting one could hear a creaking, rustling sound.

"Forty-seven, forty-eight, forty-nine, fifty!" said Gerald, and they opened their eyes.

They were alone in the room. The jewels had vanished and so had the Princess.

"She's gone out by the door, of course," said Jimmy, but the door was locked.

"That *is* magic," said Kathleen breathlessly.

"Maskelyne and Devant* can do *that* trick," said Jimmy. "And I want my tea."

"Your tea!" Gerald's tone was full of contempt. "The lovely Princess," he went on, "reappear'd as soon as our hero had finished counting fifty. One, two, three, four—"

Gerald and Kathleen had both closed their eyes. But somehow Jimmy hadn't. He didn't mean to cheat, he just forgot. And as Gerald's count reached twenty he saw a panel under the window open slowly.

"Her," he said to himself. "I *knew* it was a trick!" and at once shut his eyes, like an honourable little boy.

On the word "fifty" six eyes opened. And the panel was closed and there was no Princess.

"She hasn't pulled it off this time," said Gerald.

"Perhaps you'd better count again," said Kathleen.

"I believe there's a cupboard under the window," said Jimmy, "and she's hidden in it. Secret panel, you know."

"You looked! that's cheating," said the voice of the Princess so close to his ear that he quite jumped.

"I didn't cheat."

"Where on earth—What ever—" said all three together. For still there was no Princess to be seen.

---

* Famous stage magicians (see footnote on p. 10 to *Five Children and It*).

"Come back visible, Princess dear," said Kathleen. "Shall we shut our eyes and count again?"

"Don't be silly!" said the voice of the Princess, and it sounded very cross.

"We're *not* silly," said Jimmy, and his voice was cross too. "Why can't you come back and have done with it? You know you're only hiding."

"Don't!" said Kathleen gently. "She is invisible, you know."

"So should I be if I got into the cupboard," said Jimmy.

"Oh yes," said the sneering tone of the Princess, "you think yourselves very clever, I dare say. But I don't mind. We'll play that you *can't* see me, if you like."

"Well, but we *can't*," said Gerald. "It's no use getting in a wax. If you're hiding, as Jimmy says, you'd better come out. If you've really turned invisible, you'd better make yourself visible again."

"Do you really mean," asked a voice quite changed, but still the Princess's, "that you *can't* see me?"

"Can't you *see* we can't?" asked Jimmy rather unreasonably.

The sun was blazing in at the window; the eight-sided room was very hot, and everyone was getting cross.

"You can't *see* me?" There was the sound of a sob in the voice of the invisible Princess.

"*No*, I tell you," said Jimmy, "and I want my tea—and—"

What he was saying was broken off short, as one might break a stick of sealing wax. And then in the golden afternoon a really quite horrid thing happened: Jimmy suddenly leaned backwards, then forwards, his eyes opened wide and his mouth too. Backward and forward he went, very quickly and abruptly, then stood still.

"Oh, he's in a fit! Oh, Jimmy, dear Jimmy!" cried Kathleen, hurrying to him. "What is it, dear, what is it?"

"It's *not* a fit," gasped Jimmy angrily. "She shook me."

"Yes," said the voice of the Princess, "and I'll shake him again if he keeps on saying he can't see me."

"You'd better shake *me*," said Gerald angrily. "I'm nearer your own size."

And instantly she did. But not for long. The moment Gerald felt hands on his shoulders he put up his own and caught those other hands by the wrists. And there he was, holding wrists that he couldn't

Backward and forward he went

see. It was a dreadful sensation. An invisible kick made him wince, but he held tight to the wrists.

"Cathy," he cried, "come and hold her legs; she's kicking me."

"Where?" cried Kathleen, anxious to help. "I don't *see* any legs."

"This is her hands I've got," cried Gerald. "She is invisible right enough. Get hold of this hand, and then you can feel your way down to her legs."

Kathleen did so. I wish I could make you understand how very, very uncomfortable and frightening it is to feel, in broad daylight, hands and arms that you can't see.

"I *won't* have you hold my legs," said the invisible Princess, struggling violently.

"What are you so cross about?" Gerald was quite calm. "You said you'd be invisible and you *are*."

"I'm not."

"You are really. Look in the glass."

"I'm not; I can't be."

"Look in the glass," Gerald repeated, quite unmoved.

"Let go, then," she said.

Gerald did, and the moment he had done so he found it impossible to believe that he really had been holding invisible hands.

"You're just pretending not to see me," said the Princess anxiously, "aren't you? Do say you are. You've had your joke with me. Don't keep it up. I don't like it."

"On our sacred word of honour," said Gerald, "you're still invisible."

There was a silence. Then, "Come," said the Princess. "I'll let you out, and you can go. I'm tired of playing with you."

They followed her voice to the door, and through it, and along the little passage into the hall. No one said anything. Everyone felt very uncomfortable.

"Let's get out of this," whispered Jimmy as they got to the end of the hall.

But the voice of the Princess said: "Come out this way; it's quicker. I think you're perfectly hateful. I'm sorry I ever played with you. Mother always told me not to play with strange children."

A door abruptly opened, though no hand was seen to touch it. "Come through, can't you!" said the voice of the Princess.

It was a little ante-room, with long, narrow mirrors between its long, narrow windows.

"Good-bye," said Gerald. "Thanks for giving us such a jolly time. Let's part friends," he added, holding out his hand.

An unseen hand was slowly put in his, which closed on it, vice-like.

"Now," he said, "you've jolly well got to look in the glass and own that we're not liars."

He led the invisible Princess to one of the mirrors, and held her in front of it by the shoulders.

"Now," he said, "you just look for yourself."

There was a silence, and then a cry of despair rang through the room.

"Oh—oh—oh! I *am* invisible. Whatever shall I do?"

"Take the ring off," said Kathleen, suddenly practical.

Another silence.

"I can't!" cried the Princess. "It won't come off. But it can't be the ring; rings don't make you invisible."

"You said this one did," said Kathleen, "and it has."

"But it *can't*," said the Princess. "I was only playing at magic. I just hid in the secret cupboard—it was only a game. Oh, whatever *shall* I do?"

"A game?" said Gerald slowly; "but you *can* do magic—the invisible jewels, and you made them come visible."

"Oh, it's only a secret spring and the panelling slides up. Oh, what am I to do?"

Kathleen moved towards the voice and gropingly got her arms round a pink-silk waist that she couldn't see. Invisible arms clasped her, a hot invisible cheek was laid against hers, and warm invisible tears lay wet between the two faces.

"Don't cry, dear," said Kathleen; "let me go and tell the King and Queen."

"The—?"

"Your royal father and mother."

"Oh, *don't* mock me!" said the poor Princess. "You *know* that was only a game, too, like—"

"Like the bread and cheese," said Jimmy triumphantly. "I knew *that* was!"

"But your dress and being asleep in the maze, and—"

"Oh, I dressed up for fun, because everyone's away at the fair, and I put the clue just to make it all more real. I was playing at Fair Rosamond first, and then I heard you talking in the maze,[3] and I thought what fun; and now I'm invisible, and I shall never come right again, never—I know I shan't! It serves me right for lying, but I didn't really think you'd believe it—not more than half, that is," she added hastily, trying to be truthful.

"But if you're not the Princess, who *are* you?" asked Kathleen, still embracing the unseen.

"I'm—my aunt lives here," said the invisible Princess. "She may be home any time. Oh, what shall I do?"

"Perhaps she knows some charm—"

"Oh, nonsense!" said the voice sharply; "she doesn't believe in charms. She *would* be so vexed. Oh, I daren't let her see me like this!" she added wildly. "And all of you here, too. She'd be so dreadfully cross."

The beautiful magic castle that the children had believed in now felt as though it were tumbling about their ears. All that was left was the invisibleness of the Princess. But that, you will own, was a good deal.

"I just said it," moaned the voice, "and it came true. I wish I'd never played at magic—I wish I'd never played at anything at all."

"Oh, don't say that," Gerald said kindly. "Let's go out into the garden, near the lake, where it's cool, and we'll hold a solemn council. You'll like that, won't you?"

"Oh!" cried Kathleen suddenly, "the buckle; that makes magic come undone!"

"It doesn't *really*," murmured the voice that seemed to speak without lips. "I only just *said* that."

"You only 'just said' about the ring," said Gerald. "Anyhow, let's try."

"Not *you*—*me*," said the voice. "You go down to the Temple of Flora, by the lake. I'll go back to the jewel-room by myself. Aunt might see you."

"She won't see *you*," said Jimmy.

"Don't rub it in," said Gerald. "Where *is* the Temple of Flora?"

"That's the way," the voice said; "down those steps and along the winding path through the shrubbery. You can't miss it. It's white marble, with a statue goddess inside."

The three children went down to the white marble Temple of Flora that stood close against the side of the little hill, and sat down in its shadowy inside. It had arches all round except against the hill behind the statue, and it was cool and restful.

They had not been there five minutes before the feet of a runner sounded loud on the gravel. A shadow, very black and distinct, fell on the white marble floor.

"Your shadow's not invisible, anyhow," said Jimmy.

"Your shadow's not invisible, anyhow"

"Oh, bother my shadow!" the voice of the Princess replied. "We left the key inside the door, and it's shut itself with the wind, and it's a spring lock!"

There was a heartfelt pause.

Then Gerald said, in his most business-like manner:

"Sit down, Princess, and we'll have a thorough good palaver about it."

"I shouldn't wonder," said Jimmy, "if we was to wake up and find it was dreams."

"No such luck," said the voice.

"Well," said Gerald, "first of all, what's your name, and if you're not a Princess, who are you?"

"I'm—I'm," said a voice broken with sobs, "I'm the—house-keeper's—niece—at—the—castle—and my name's Mabel Prowse."

"That's exactly what I thought," said Jimmy, without a shadow of truth, because how could he? The others were silent. It was a moment full of agitation and confused ideas.

"Well, any how," said Gerald, "you belong here."

"Yes," said the voice, and it came from the floor, as though its owner had flung herself down in the madness of despair. "Oh yes, I belong here right enough, but what's the use of belonging anywhere if you're invisible?"

CHAPTER III

Those of my readers who have gone about much with an invisible companion will not need to be told how awkward the whole business is. For one thing, however much you may have been convinced that your companion is invisible, you will, I feel sure, have found yourself every now and then saying, "This must be a dream!" or "I know I shall wake up in half a sec!" And this was the case with Gerald, Kathleen, and Jimmy as they sat in the white marble Temple of Flora, looking out through its arches at the sunshiny park and listening to the voice of the enchanted Princess, who really was not a Princess at all, but just the housekeeper's niece, Mabel Prowse; though, as Jimmy said, "she was enchanted, right enough."

"It's no use talking," she said again and again, and the voice came from an empty-looking space between two pillars; "I never believed anything would happen, and now it has."

"Well," said Gerald kindly, "can we do anything for you? Because, if not, I think we ought to be going."

"Yes," said Jimmy; "I do want my tea!"

"Tea!" said the unseen Mabel scornfully. "Do you mean to say you'd go off to your teas and leave me after getting me into this mess?"

"Well, of all the unfair Princesses I ever met!" Gerald began. But Kathleen interrupted.

"Oh, don't rag her," she said. "Think how horrid it must be to be invisible!"

"I don't think," said the hidden Mabel, "that my aunt likes me very much as it is. She wouldn't let me go to the fair because I'd forgotten to put back some old trumpery* shoe that Queen Elizabeth† wore—I got it out from the glass case to try it on."

"Did it fit?" asked Kathleen, with interest.

---

* Tawdry (archaic).

† Elizabeth I (1533–1603), the venerated British monarch who was also known for her stately self-display.

"Not it—much too small," said Mabel. "I don't believe it ever fitted anyone."

"I do want my tea!" said Jimmy.

"I do really think perhaps we ought to go," said Gerald. "You see, it isn't as if we could do anything for you."

"You'll have to tell your aunt," said Kathleen kindly.

"No, no, no!" moaned Mabel invisibly; "take me with you. I'll leave her a note to say I've run away to sea."

"Girls don't run away to sea."

"They might," said the stone floor between the pillars, "as stowaways, if nobody wanted a cabin boy—cabin girl, I mean."

"I'm sure you oughtn't," said Kathleen firmly.

"Well, what *am* I to do?"

"Really," said Gerald, "I don't know what the girl *can* do. Let her come home with us and have—"

"Tea—oh, yes," said Jimmy, jumping up.

"And have a good council."

"After tea," said Jimmy.

"But her aunt'll find she's gone."

"So she would if I stayed."

"Oh, come on," said Jimmy.

"But the aunt'll think something's happened to her."

"So it has."

"And she'll tell the police, and they'll look everywhere for me."

"They'll never find you," said Gerald. "Talk of impenetrable disguises!"

"I'm sure," said Mabel, "aunt would much rather never see me again than see me like this. She'd never get over it; it might kill her—she has spasms as it is. I'll write to her, and we'll put it in the big letter-box at the gate as we go out. Has anyone got a bit of pencil and a scrap of paper?"

Gerald had a note-book, with leaves of the shiny kind which you have to write on, not with a blacklead pencil, but with an ivory thing with a point of real lead. And it won't write on any other paper except the kind that is in the book, and this is often very annoying when you are in a hurry. Then was seen the strange spectacle of a little ivory stick, with a leaden point, standing up at an odd, impossible-looking slant, and moving along all by itself as ordinary pencils do when you are writing with them.

"May we look over?" asked Kathleen.

There was no answer. The pencil went on writing.

"Mayn't we look over?" Kathleen said again.

"Of course you may!" said the voice near the paper. "I nodded, didn't I? Oh, I forgot, my nodding's invisible too."

The pencil was forming round, clear letters on the page torn out of the note-book. This is what it wrote:—

"*Dear Aunt,—*

"*I am afraid you will not see me again for some time. A lady in a motor-car has adopted me, and we are going straight to the coast and then in a ship. It is useless to try to follow me. Farewell, and may you be happy. I hope you enjoyed the fair.*

"*Mabel.*"

"But that's all lies," said Jimmy bluntly.

"No, it isn't; it's fancy," said Mabel. "If I said I've become invisible, she'd think that was a lie, anyhow."

"Oh, come along," said Jimmy; "you can quarrel just as well walking."

Gerald folded up the note as a lady in India had taught him to do years before, and Mabel led them by another and very much nearer way out of the park. And the walk home was a great deal shorter, too, than the walk out had been.

The sky had clouded over while they were in the Temple of Flora, and the first spots of rain fell as they got back to the house, very late indeed for tea.

Mademoiselle was looking out of the window, and came herself to open the door.

"But it is that you are in lateness, in lateness!" she cried. "You have had a misfortune—no? All goes well?"

"We are very sorry indeed," said Gerald. "It took us longer to get home than we expected. I do hope you haven't been anxious. I have been thinking about you most of the way home."

The bread and butter waving about in the air

"Go, then," said the French lady, smiling; "you shall have them in the same time—the tea and the supper."

Which they did.

"How *could* you say you were thinking about her all the time?" said a voice just by Gerald's ear, when Mademoiselle had left them alone with the bread and butter and milk and baked apples. "It was just as much a lie as me being adopted by a motor lady."

"No, it wasn't," said Gerald, through bread and butter. "I *was* thinking about whether she'd be in a wax or not. So there!"

There were only three plates, but Jimmy let Mabel have his, and shared with Kathleen. It was rather horrid to see the bread and butter waving about in the air, and bite after bite disappearing from it apparently by no human agency; and the spoon rising with apple in it and returning to the plate empty. Even the tip of the spoon disappeared as long as it was in Mabel's unseen mouth; so that at times it looked as though its bowl had been broken off.

Everyone was very hungry, and more bread and butter had to be fetched. Cook grumbled when the plate was filled for the third time.

"I tell you what," said Jimmy; "I did want my tea."

"I tell you what," said Gerald; "it'll be jolly difficult to give Mabel any breakfast. Mademoiselle will be here then. She'd have a fit if she saw bits of forks with bacon on them vanishing, and then the forks coming back out of vanishment, and the bacon lost for ever."

"We shall have to buy things to eat and feed our poor captive in secret," said Kathleen.

"Our money won't last long," said Jimmy, in gloom. "Have you got any money?"

He turned to where a mug of milk was suspended in the air without visible means of support.

"I've not got much money," was the reply from near the milk, "but I've got heaps of ideas."

"We must talk about everything in the morning," said Kathleen. "We must just say good night to Mademoiselle, and then you shall sleep in my bed, Mabel. I'll lend you one of my nightgowns."

"I'll get my own tomorrow," said Mabel cheerfully.

"You'll go back to get things?"

"Why not? Nobody can see me. I think I begin to see all sorts of amusing things coming along. It's not half bad being invisible."

It was extremely odd, Kathleen thought, to see the Princess's clothes coming out of nothing. First the gauzy veil appeared hanging in the air. Then the sparkling coronet suddenly showed on the top of the chest of drawers. Then a sleeve of the pinky gown showed, then another, and then the whole gown lay on the floor in a glistening ring as the unseen legs of Mabel stepped out of it. For each article of clothing became visible as Mabel took it off. The nightgown, lifted from the bed, disappeared a bit at a time.

"Get into bed," said Kathleen, rather nervously.

The bed creaked and a hollow appeared in the pillow. Kathleen put out the gas and got into bed; all this magic had been rather upsetting, and she was just the least bit frightened, but in the dark she found it was not so bad. Mabel's arms went round her neck the moment she got into bed, and the two little girls kissed in the kind darkness, where the visible and the invisible could meet on equal terms.

"Good night," said Mabel. "You're a darling, Cathy; you've been most awfully good to me, and I shan't forget it. I didn't like to say so before the boys, because I know boys think you're a muff* if you're grateful. But I *am*. Good night."

Kathleen lay awake for some time. She was just getting sleepy when she remembered that the maid who would call them in the morning would see those wonderful Princess clothes.

"I'll have to get up and hide them," she said. "What a bother!"

And as she lay thinking what a bother it was she happened to fall asleep, and when she woke again it was bright morning, and Eliza was standing in front of the chair where Mabel's clothes lay, gazing at the pink Princess-frock that lay on the top of her heap and saying, "Law!"†

"Oh, don't touch, *please!*" Kathleen leaped out of bed as Eliza was reaching out her hand.

"Where on earth did you get hold of that?"

"We're going to use it for acting," said Kathleen, on the desperate inspiration of the moment. "It's lent me for that."

"You might show *me*, miss," suggested Eliza.

"Oh, please not!" said Kathleen, standing in front of the chair in her nightgown. "You shall see us act when we are dressed up. There! And you won't tell anyone, will you?"

"Not if you're a good little girl," said Eliza. "But you be sure to let me see when you *do* dress up. But where—"

Here a bell rang and Eliza had to go, for it was the postman, and she particularly wanted to see him.

"And now," said Kathleen, pulling on her first stocking, "we shall have to *do* the acting. Everything seems very difficult."

"Acting isn't," said Mabel; and an unsupported stocking waved in the air and quickly vanished. "I shall love it."

"You forget," said Kathleen gently, "invisible actresses can't take part in plays unless they're magic ones."

"Oh," cried a voice from under a petticoat that hung in the air, "I've got *such* an idea!"

"Tell it us after breakfast," said Kathleen, as the water in the basin began to splash about and to drip from nowhere back into itself.

---

* Fool (slang).

† Exclamation of surprise (slang).

"And oh! I do wish you hadn't written such whoppers to your aunt. I'm sure we oughtn't to tell lies for anything."

"What's the use of telling the truth if nobody believes you?" came from among the splashes.

"I don't know," said Kathleen, "but I'm sure we ought to tell the truth."

"You can, if you like," said a voice from the folds of a towel that waved lonely in front of the wash-hand stand.

"All right. We will, then, first thing after brek*—your brek, I mean. You'll have to wait up here till we can collar something and bring it up to you. Mind you dodge Eliza when she comes to make the bed."

The invisible Mabel found this a fairly amusing game; she further enlivened it by twitching out the corners of tucked-up sheets and blankets when Eliza wasn't looking.

"Drat the clothes!" said Eliza; "anyone 'ud think the things was bewitched."

She looked about for the wonderful Princess clothes she had glimpsed earlier in the morning. But Kathleen had hidden them in a perfectly safe place—under the mattress, which she knew Eliza never turned.

Eliza hastily brushed up from the floor those bits of fluff which come from goodness knows where in the best regulated houses. Mabel, very hungry and exasperated at the long absence of the others at their breakfast, could not forbear to whisper suddenly in Eliza's ear:

"Always sweep under the mats."

The maid started and turned pale. "I must be going silly," she murmured; "though it's just what mother always used to say. Hope I ain't going dotty, like Aunt Emily. Wonderful what you can fancy, ain't it?"

She took up the hearth-rug all the same, swept under it, and under the fender. So thorough was she, and so pale, that Kathleen, entering with a chunk of bread raided by Gerald from the pantry window, exclaimed:

---

* Breakfast (slang).

"Not done yet. I say, Eliza, you do look ill! What's the matter?"

"I thought I'd give the room a good turn-out," said Eliza, still very pale.

"Nothing's happened to upset you?" Kathleen asked. She had her own private fears.

"Nothing—only my fancy, miss," said Eliza. "I always was fanciful from a child—dreaming of the pearly gates and them little angels with nothing on only their heads and wings—so cheap to dress, I always think, compared with children."

When she was got rid of, Mabel ate the bread and drank water from the tooth-mug.

"I'm afraid it tastes of cherry tooth-paste rather," said Kathleen apologetically.

"It doesn't matter," a voice replied from the tilted mug; "it's more interesting than water. I should think red wine in ballads was rather like this."

"We've got leave for the day again," said Kathleen, when the last bit of bread had vanished, "and Gerald feels like I do about lies. So we're going to tell your aunt where you really are."

"She won't believe you."

"That doesn't matter, if we speak the truth," said Kathleen primly.

"I expect you'll be sorry for it," said Mabel; "but come on—and, I say, do be careful not to shut me in the door as you go out. You nearly did just now."

In the blazing sunlight that flooded the High Street four shadows to three children seemed dangerously noticeable. A butcher's boy looked far too earnestly at the extra shadow, and his big, liver-coloured lurcher snuffed at the legs of that shadow's mistress and whined uncomfortably.

"Get behind me," said Kathleen; "then our two shadows will look like one."

But Mabel's shadow, very visible, fell on Kathleen's back, and the ostler* of the Davenant Arms looked up to see what big bird had cast that big shadow.

A woman driving a cart with chickens and ducks in it called out:

---

* Innkeeper or stableman at an inn.

"Halloa, missy, ain't you blacked yer back, neither!"

"Halloa, missy, ain't you blacked yer back, neither! What you been leaning up against?"

Everyone was glad when they got out of the town.

Speaking the truth to Mabel's aunt did not turn out at all as anyone—even Mabel—expected. The aunt was discovered reading a pink novelette at the window of the housekeeper's room, which, framed in clematis and green creepers, looked out on a nice little courtyard to which Mabel led the party.

"Excuse me," said Gerald, "but I believe you've lost your niece?"

"Not lost, my boy," said the aunt, who was spare and tall, with a drab fringe and a very genteel voice.

"We could tell you something about her," said Gerald.

"Now," replied the aunt, in a warning voice, "no complaints, please. My niece has gone, and I am sure no one thinks less than I do of her little pranks. If she's played any tricks on you it's only her light-hearted way. Go away, children, I'm busy."

"Did you get her note?" asked Kathleen.

The aunt showed rather more interest than before, but she still kept her finger in the novelette.

"Oh," she said, "so you witnessed her departure? Did she seem glad to go?"

"Quite," said Gerald truthfully.

"Then I can only be glad that she is provided for," said the aunt. "I dare say you were surprised. These romantic adventures do occur in our family. Lord Yalding selected me out of eleven applicants for the post of housekeeper here. I've not the slightest doubt the child was changed at birth and her rich relatives have claimed her."

"But aren't you going to do anything—tell the police, or—"

"Shish!" said Mabel.

"I won't shish," said Jimmy. "Your Mabel's invisible—that's all it is. She's just beside me now."

"I detest untruthfulness," said the aunt severely, "in all its forms. Will you kindly take that little boy away? I am quite satisfied about Mabel."

"Well," said Gerald, "you *are* an aunt and no mistake! But what will Mabel's father and mother say?"

"Mabel's father and mother are dead," said the aunt calmly, and a little sob sounded close to Gerald's ear.

"All right," he said, "we'll be off. But don't you go saying we didn't tell you the truth, that's all."

"You have told me nothing," said the aunt, "none of you, except that little boy, who has told me a silly falsehood."

"We meant well," said Gerald gently. "You don't mind our having come through the grounds, do you? We're very careful not to touch anything."

"No visitors are allowed," said the aunt, glancing down at her novel rather impatiently.

"Ah! but you wouldn't count us visitors," said Gerald in his best manner. "We're friends of Mabel's. Our father's Colonel of the ——th."

"Indeed!" said the aunt.

"And our aunt's Lady Sandling, so you can be sure we wouldn't hurt anything on the estate."

"I'm sure you wouldn't hurt a fly," said the aunt absently. "Good-bye. Be good children."

And on this they got away quickly.

"Why," said Gerald, when they were outside the little court, "your aunt's as mad as a hatter. Fancy not caring what becomes of you, and fancy believing that rot about the motor lady!"

"I knew she'd believe it when I wrote it," said Mabel modestly. "She's not mad, only she's always reading novelettes. I read the books in the big library. Oh, it's such a jolly room—such a queer smell, like boots, and old leather books sort of powdery at the edges. I'll take you there some day. Now your consciences are all right about my aunt, I'll tell you my great idea. Let's get down to the Temple of Flora. I'm glad you got aunt's permission for the grounds. It would be so awkward for you to have to be always dodging behind bushes when one of the gardeners came along."

"Yes," said Gerald modestly, "I thought of that."

The day was as bright as yesterday had been, and from the white marble temple the Italian-looking landscape looked more than ever like a steel engraving coloured by hand, or an oleographic* imitation of one of Turner's pictures.

When the three children were comfortably settled on the steps that led up to the white statue, the voice of the fourth child said sadly: "I'm not ungrateful, but I'm rather hungry. And you can't be always taking things for me through your larder window. If you like, I'll go back and live in the castle. It's supposed to be haunted. I suppose I could haunt it as well as anyone else. I am a sort of ghost now, you know. I will if you like."

"Oh no," said Kathleen kindly; "you must stay with us."

"But about food. I'm not ungrateful, really I'm not, but breakfast is breakfast, and bread's only bread."

---

* Type of colored lithograph finished to resemble an oil painting.

"If you could get the ring off, you could go back."

"Yes," said Mabel's voice, "but you see, I can't. I tried again last night in bed, and again this morning. And it's like stealing, taking things out of your larder—even if it's only bread."

"Yes, it is," said Gerald, who had carried out this bold enterprise.

"Well, now, what we must do is to earn some money."

Jimmy remarked that this was all very well. But Gerald and Kathleen listened attentively.

"What I mean to say," the voice went on, "I'm really sure it's all for the best, me being invisible. We shall have adventures—you see if we don't."

" 'Adventures,' said the bold buccaneer, 'are not always profitable.' " It was Gerald who murmured this.

"This one will be, anyhow, you see. Only you mustn't all go. Look here, if Jerry could make himself look common—"

"That ought to be easy," said Jimmy. And Kathleen told him not to be so jolly disagreeable.

"I'm not," said Jimmy, "only—"

"Only he has an inside feeling that this Mabel of yours is going to get us into trouble," put in Gerald. "Like La Belle Dame Sans Merci, and he does not want to be found in future ages alone and palely loitering in the middle of sedge and things."[4]

"I won't get you into trouble, indeed I won't," said the voice. "Why, we're a band of brothers for life, after the way you stood by me yesterday. What I mean is—Gerald can go to the fair and do conjuring."

"He doesn't know any," said Kathleen.

"I should do it really," said Mabel, "but Jerry could look like doing it. Move things without touching them and all that. But it wouldn't do for all three of you to go. The more there are of children, the younger they look, I think, and the more people wonder what they're doing all alone by themselves."

"The accomplished conjurer deemed these the words of wisdom," said Gerald; and answered the dismal "Well, but what about us?" of his brother and sister by suggesting that they should mingle unsuspected with the crowd. "But don't let on that you know me," he said; "and try to look as if you belonged to some of the grown-ups at the fair. If you don't, as likely as not you'll have the kind policemen taking the little lost children by the hand and leading them home to their stricken relations—French governess, I mean."

"Let's go now," said the voice that they never could get quite used to hearing, coming out of different parts of the air as Mabel moved from one place to another. So they went.

The fair was held on a waste bit of land, about half a mile from the castle gates. When they got near enough to hear the steam-organ of the merry-go-round, Gerald suggested that as he had ninepence he should go ahead and get something to eat, the amount spent to be paid back out of any money they might make by conjuring. The others waited in the shadows of a deep-banked lane, and he came back, quite soon, though long after they had begun to say what a long time he had been gone. He brought some Barcelona nuts, red-streaked apples, small sweet yellow pears, pale pasty gingerbread, a whole quarter of a pound of peppermint bullseyes, and two bottles of ginger-beer.

"It's what they call an investment," he said, when Kathleen said something about extravagance. "We shall all need special nourishing to keep our strength up, especially the bold conjurer."

They ate and drank. It was a very beautiful meal, and the far-off music of the steam-organ added the last touch of festivity to the scene. The boys were never tired of seeing Mabel eat, or rather of seeing the strange, magic-looking vanishment of food which was all that showed of Mabel's eating. They were entranced by the spectacle, and pressed on her more than her just share of the feast, just for the pleasure of seeing it disappear.

"My aunt!" said Gerald, again and again; "that ought to knock 'em!"

It did.

Jimmy and Kathleen had the start of the others, and when they got to the fair they mingled with the crowd, and were as unsuspected as possible.

They stood near a large lady who was watching the coconut shies, and presently saw a strange figure with its hands in its pockets strolling across the trampled yellowy grass among the bits of drifting paper and the sticks and straws that always litter the ground of an English fair. It was Gerald, but at first they hardly knew him. He had taken off his tie, and round his head, arranged like a turban, was the crimson school-scarf that had supported his white flannels. The tie, one supposed, had taken on the duties of the handkerchief. And his face and hands were a bright black, like very nicely polished stoves!

Everyone turned to look at him.

"He's just like a conjurer!" whispered Jimmy. "I don't suppose it'll ever come off, do you?"

They followed him at a distance, and when he went close to the door of a small tent, against whose door-post a long-faced melancholy woman was lounging, they stopped and tried to look as though they belonged to a farmer who strove to send up a number by banging with a big mallet on a wooden block.

Gerald went up to the woman.

"Taken much?" he asked, and was told, but not harshly, to go away with his impudence.

"I'm in business myself," said Gerald, "I'm a conjurer, from India."

"Not you!" said the woman; "you ain't no conjurer. Why, the backs of yer ears is all white."

"Are they?" said Gerald. "How clever of you to see that!" He rubbed them with his hands. "That better?"

"That's all right. What's your little game?"

"Conjuring, really and truly," said Gerald. "There's smaller boys than me put on to it in India. Look here, I owe you one for telling me about my ears. If you like to run the show for me I'll go shares. Let me have your tent to perform in, and you do the patter at the door."

"Lor' love you! I can't do no patter. And you're getting at me. Let's see you do a bit of conjuring, since you're so clever an' all."

"Right you are," said Gerald firmly. "You see this apple? Well, I'll make it move slowly through the air, and then when I say 'Go!' it'll vanish."

"Yes—into your mouth! Get away with your nonsense."

"You're too clever to be so unbelieving," said Gerald. "Look here!"

He held out one of the little apples, and the woman saw it move slowly and unsupported along the air.

"Now—*go*!" cried Gerald, to the apple, and it went. "How's that?" he asked, in tones of triumph.

The woman was glowing with excitement, and her eyes shone.

"You're getting at me"

"The best I ever see!" she whispered. "I'm on, mate, if you know any more tricks like that."

"Heaps," said Gerald confidently; "hold out your hand." The woman held it out; and from nowhere, as it seemed, the apple appeared and was laid on her hand. The apple was rather damp.

She looked at it a moment, and then whispered: "Come on! there's to be no one in it but just us two. But not in the tent. You take a pitch here, 'longside the tent. It's worth twice the money in the open air."

"But people won't pay if they can see it all for nothing."

"Not for the first turn, but they will after—you see. And you'll have to do the patter."

"Will you lend me your shawl?" Gerald asked. She unpinned it—it was a red and black plaid—and he spread it on the ground as he had seen Indian conjurers do, and seated himself cross-legged behind it.

"I mustn't have anyone behind me, that's all," he said; and the woman hastily screened off a little enclosure for him by hanging old sacks to two of the guy-ropes of the tent. "Now I'm ready," he said. The woman got a drum from the inside of the tent and beat it. Quite soon a little crowd had collected.

"Ladies and gentlemen," said Gerald, "I come from India, and I can do a conjuring entertainment the like of which you've never seen. When I see two shillings on the shawl I'll begin."

"I dare say you will!" said a bystander; and there were several short, disagreeable laughs.

"Of course," said Gerald, "if you can't afford two shillings between you"—there were about thirty people in the crowd by now—"I say no more."

Two or three pennies fell on the shawl, then a few more, then the fall of copper ceased.

"Ninepence," said Gerald. "Well, I've got a generous nature. You'll get such a ninepennyworth as you've never had before. I don't wish to deceive you—I have an accomplice, but my accomplice is invisible."

The crowd snorted.

"By the aid of that accomplice," Gerald went on, "I will read any letter that any of you may have in your pocket. If one of you will just step over the rope and stand beside me, my invisible accomplice will read that letter over his shoulder."

A man stepped forward, a ruddy-faced, horsy-looking person. He pulled a letter from his pocket and stood plain in the sight of all, in a place where everyone saw that no one could see over his shoulder.

"Now!" said Gerald. There was a moment's pause. Then from quite the other side of the enclosure came a faint, faraway, sing-song voice. It said:

" 'Sir,—Yours of the fifteenth duly to hand. With regard to the mortgage on your land, we regret our inability—' "

"Stow it!" cried the man, turning threateningly on Gerald.

"Stow it!" cried the man

He stepped out of the enclosure explaining that there was nothing of that sort in his letter; but nobody believed him, and a buzz of interested chatter began in the crowd, ceasing abruptly when Gerald began to speak.

"Now," said he, laying the nine pennies down on the shawl, "you keep your eyes on those pennies, and one by one you'll see them disappear."

And of course they did. Then one by one they were laid down again by the invisible hand of Mabel. The crowd clapped loudly. "Bravo!" "That's something like!" "Show us another!" cried the people in the front rank. And those behind pushed forward.

"Now," said Gerald, "you've seen what I can do, but I don't do any more till I see five shillings on this carpet."

And in two minutes seven-and-threepence lay there and Gerald did a little more conjuring.

When the people in front didn't want to give any more money, Gerald asked them to stand back and let the others have a look in. I wish I had time to tell you of all the tricks he did—the grass round his enclosure was absolutely trampled off by the feet of the people who thronged to look at him. There is really hardly any limit to the wonders you can do if you have an invisible accomplice. All sorts of things were made to move about, apparently by themselves, and even to vanish—into the folds of Mabel's clothing. The woman stood by, looking more and more pleasant as she saw the money come tumbling in, and beating her shabby drum every time Gerald stopped conjuring.

The news of the conjurer had spread all over the fair. The crowd was frantic with admiration. The man who ran the coconut shies begged Gerald to throw in his lot with him; the owner of the rifle gallery offered him free board and lodging and go shares; and a brisk, broad lady, in stiff black silk and a violet bonnet, tried to engage him for the forthcoming Bazaar for Reformed Bandsmen.

And all this time the others mingled with the crowd—quite unobserved, for who could have eyes for anyone but Gerald? It was getting quite late, long past tea-time, and Gerald, who was getting very tired indeed, and was quite satisfied with his share of the money, was racking his brains for a way to get out of it.

"How are we to hook it?" he murmured, as Mabel made his cap disappear from his head by the simple process of taking it off and putting it in her pocket. "They'll never let us get away. I didn't think of that before."

"Let me think!" whispered Mabel; and next moment she said, close to his ear: "Divide the money, and give her something for the shawl. Put the money on it and say . . ." She told him what to say.

Gerald's pitch was in the shade of the tent; otherwise, of course, everyone would have seen the shadow of the invisible Mabel as she moved about making things vanish.

Gerald told the woman to divide the money, which she did honestly enough.

"Now," he said, while the impatient crowd pressed closer and closer, "I'll give you five bob for your shawl."

"Seven-and-six," said the woman mechanically.

"Righto!" said Gerald, putting his heavy share of the money in his trouser pocket.

"This shawl will now disappear," he said, picking it up. He handed it to Mabel, who put it on; and, of course, it disappeared. A roar of applause went up from the audience.

"Now," he said, "I come to the last trick of all. I shall take three steps backwards and vanish." He took three steps backwards, Mabel wrapped the invisible shawl round him, and—he did not vanish. The shawl, being invisible, did not conceal him in the least.

"Yah!" cried a boy's voice in the crowd. "Look at 'im! 'E knows 'e can't do it."

"I wish I could put you in my pocket," said Mabel. The crowd was crowding closer. At any moment they might touch Mabel, and then anything might happen—simply anything. Gerald took hold of his hair with both hands, as his way was when he was anxious or discouraged. Mabel, in invisibility, wrung her hands, as people are said to do in books; that is, she clasped them and squeezed very tight.

"Oh!" she whispered suddenly, "it's loose. I can get it off."

"Not—"

"Yes—the ring."

"Come on, young master. Give us summat for our money," a farm labourer shouted.

"I will," said Gerald. "This time I really will vanish. Slip round into the tent," he whispered to Mabel. "Push the ring under the canvas. Then slip out at the back and join the others. When I see you with them I'll disappear. Go slow, and I'll catch you up."

"It's me," said a pale and obvious Mabel in the ear of Kathleen. "He's got the ring; come on, before the crowd begins to scatter."

As they went out of the gate they heard a roar of surprise and annoyance rise from the crowd, and knew that this time Gerald really *had* disappeared.

They had gone a mile before they heard footsteps on the road, and looked back. No one was to be seen.

Next moment Gerald's voice spoke out of clear, empty-looking space.

"Halloa!" it said gloomily.

"How horrid!" cried Mabel; "you did make me jump! Take the ring off; it makes me feel quite creepy, you being nothing but a voice."

"So did you us," said Jimmy.

"Don't take it off yet," said Kathleen, who was really rather thoughtful for her age, "because you're still blackleaded,* I suppose, and you might be recognized, and eloped with by gipsies, so that you should go on doing conjuring for ever and ever."

"I should take it off," said Jimmy; "it's no use going about invisible, and people seeing us with Mabel and saying we've eloped with her."

"Yes," said Mabel impatiently, "that would be simply silly. And, besides, I want my ring."

"It's not yours any more than ours, anyhow," said Jimmy.

"Yes, it is," said Mabel.

"Oh, stow it!" said the weary voice of Gerald beside her. "What's the use of jawing?"

"I want the ring," said Mabel, rather mulishly.

"Want"—the words came out of the still evening air—"want must be your master. You can't have the ring. I *can't get it off!*"

---

* Covered in black polish derived from graphite.

CHAPTER IV

The difficulty was not only that Gerald had got the ring on and couldn't get it off, and was therefore invisible, but that Mabel, who had been invisible and therefore possible to be smuggled into the house, was now plain to be seen and impossible for smuggling purposes.

The children would have not only to account for the apparent absence of one of themselves, but for the obvious presence of a perfect stranger.

"I can't go back to aunt. I can't and I won't," said Mabel firmly, "not if I was visible twenty times over."

"She'd smell a rat if you did," Gerald owned—"about the motor-car, I mean, and the adopting lady. And what we're to say to Mademoiselle about you—!" He tugged at the ring.

"Suppose you told the truth," said Mabel meaningly.

"She wouldn't believe it," said Cathy; "or, if she did, she'd go stark, staring, raving mad."

"No," said Gerald's voice, "we daren't *tell* her. But she's really rather decent. Let's ask her to let you stay the night because it's too late for you to get home."

"That's all right," said Jimmy, "but what about you?"

"I shall go to bed," said Gerald, "with a bad headache. Oh, *that's* not a lie! I've got one right enough. It's the sun, I think. I know black-lead attracts the concentration of the sun."

"More likely the pears and the gingerbread," said Jimmy unkindly. "Well, let's get along. I wish it was me was invisible. I'd do something different from going to bed with a silly headache, I know that."

"What would you do?" asked the voice of Gerald just behind him.

"Do keep in one place, you silly cuckoo!" said Jimmy. "You make me feel all jumpy." He had indeed jumped rather violently. "Here, walk between Cathy and me."

"What would you do?" repeated Gerald, from that apparently unoccupied position.

"I'd be a burglar," said Jimmy.

Cathy and Mabel in one breath reminded him how wrong burgling was, and Jimmy replied:

"Well, then—a detective."

"There's got to be something to detect before you can begin detectiving," said Mabel.

"Detectives don't always detect things," said Jimmy, very truly. "If I couldn't be any other kind I'd be a baffled detective. You could be one all right, and have no end of larks just the same. Why don't you do it?"

"It's exactly what I *am* going to do," said Gerald. "We'll go round by the police-station and see what they've got in the way of crimes."

They did, and read the notices on the board outside. Two dogs had been lost, a purse, and a portfolio of papers "of no value to any but the owner." Also Houghton Grange had been broken into and a quantity of silver plate stolen. "Twenty pounds reward offered for any information that may lead to the recovery of the missing property."

"That burglary's my lay,"* said Gerald; "I'll detect that. Here comes Johnson," he added; "he's going off duty. Ask him about it. The fell detective, being invisible, was unable to pump the constable, but the young brother of our hero made the inquiries in quite a creditable manner. Be creditable, Jimmy."

Jimmy hailed the constable.

"Halloa, Johnson!" he said.

And Johnson replied: "Halloa, young shaver!"†

"Shaver yourself!" said Jimmy, but without malice.

"What are you doing this time of night?" the constable asked jocosely. "All the dicky birds is gone to their little nesteses."

"We've been to the fair," said Kathleen. "There was a conjurer there. I wish you could have seen him."

"Heard about him," said Johnson; "all fake, you know. The quickness of the 'and deceives the hi."

---

* Occupation.
† Little fellow (slang).

"What's that?" the policeman asked quickly

Such is fame. Gerald, standing in the shadow, jingled the loose money in his pocket to console himself.

"What's that?" the policeman asked quickly.

"Our money jingling," said Jimmy, with perfect truth.

"It's well to be some people," Johnson remarked; "wish I'd got my pockets full to jingle with."

"Well, why haven't you?" asked Mabel. "Why don't you get that twenty pounds reward?"

"I'll tell you why I don't. Because in this 'ere realm of liberty, and Britannia ruling the waves, you ain't allowed to arrest a chap on suspicion, even if you know puffickly well who done the job."

"What a shame!" said Jimmy warmly. "And who do you think did it?"

"I don't think—I know." Johnson's voice was ponderous as his boots. "It's a man what's known to the police on account of a heap o' crimes he's done, but we never can't bring it 'ome to 'im, nor yet get sufficient evidence to convict."

"Well," said Jimmy, "when I've left school I'll come to you and be apprenticed, and be a detective. Just now I think we'd better get home and detect our supper. Good night!"

They watched the policeman's broad form disappear through the swing door of the police-station; and as it settled itself into quiet again the voice of Gerald was heard complaining bitterly.

"You've no more brains than a halfpenny bun," he said; "no details about how and when the silver was taken."

"But he told us he knew," Jimmy urged.

"Yes, that's all you've got out of him. A silly policeman's silly idea. Go home and detect your precious supper! It's all you're fit for."

"What'll you do about supper?" Mabel asked.

"Buns!" said Gerald, "halfpenny buns. They'll make me think of my dear little brother and sister. Perhaps you've got enough sense to buy buns? I can't go into a shop in this state."

"Don't you be so disagreeable," said Mabel with spirit. "We did our best. If I were Cathy you should whistle for your nasty buns."

"If you were Cathy the gallant young detective would have left home long ago. Better the cabin of a tramp steamer than the best family mansion that's got a brawling sister in it," said Gerald. "You're a bit of an outsider at present, my gentle maiden. Jimmy and Cathy know well enough when their bold leader is chaffing and when he isn't."

"Not when we can't see your face we don't," said Cathy, in tones of relief. "I really thought you were in a flaring wax, and so did Jimmy, didn't you?"

"Oh, rot!" said Gerald. "Come on! This way to the bun shop."

They went. And it was while Cathy and Jimmy were in the shop and the others were gazing through the glass at the jam tarts and Swiss rolls and Victoria sandwiches and Bath buns under the spread yellow muslin in the window, that Gerald discoursed in Mabel's ear of the plans and hopes of one entering on a detective career.

"I shall keep my eyes open tonight, I can tell you," he began. "I shall keep my eyes skinned, and no jolly error. The invisible detective may not only find out about the purse and the silver, but detect some crime that isn't even done yet. And I shall hang about until I see some suspicious-looking characters leave the town, and follow them furtively and catch them red-handed, with their hands full of priceless jewels, and hand them over."

"Oh!" cried Mabel, so sharply and suddenly that Gerald was roused from his dream to express sympathy.

"Pain?" he said quite kindly. "It's the apples—they were rather hard."

"Oh, it's not that," said Mabel very earnestly. "Oh, how awful! I never thought of that before."

"Never thought of *what*?" Gerald asked impatiently.

"The window."

"What window?"

"The panelled-room window. At home, you know—at the castle. That settles it—I *must* go home. We left it open and the shutters as well, and all the jewels and things there. Auntie'll never go in; she never does. That settles it; I *must* go home—now—this minute."

Here the others issued from the shop, bun-bearing, and the situation was hastily explained to them.

"So you see I must go," Mabel ended.

And Kathleen agreed that she must.

But Jimmy said he didn't see what good it would do. "Because the key's inside the door, anyhow."

"She will be cross," said Mabel sadly. "She'll have to get the gardeners to get a ladder and—"

"Hooray!" said Gerald. "Here's me! Nobler and more secret than gardeners or ladders was the invisible Jerry. I'll climb in at the window—it's all ivy, I know I could—and shut the window and the shutters all sereno,* put the key back on the nail, and slip out unperceived the back way, threading my way through the maze of unconscious retainers. There'll be plenty of time. I don't suppose burglars begin their fell work until the night is far advanced."

---

* All serene (slang)—that is, "so everyone's happy."

"I must *go* home—now—this minute"

"Won't you be afraid?" Mabel asked. "Will it be safe—suppose you were caught?"

"As houses.* I can't be," Gerald answered, and wondered that the question came from Mabel and not from Kathleen, who was usually inclined to fuss a little annoyingly about the danger and folly of adventures.

But all Kathleen said was, "Well, good-bye; we'll come and see you tomorrow, Mabel. The floral temple at half-past ten. I hope you won't get into an awful row about the motor-car lady."

"Let's detect our supper now," said Jimmy.

---

* From "safe as houses," a saying that refers to the stability of the real estate market.

"All right," said Gerald a little bitterly. It is hard to enter on an adventure like this and to find the sympathetic interest of years suddenly cut off at the meter, as it were. Gerald felt that he ought, at a time like this, to have been the centre of interest. And he wasn't. They could actually talk about supper. Well, let them. He didn't care! He spoke with sharp sternness: "Leave the pantry window undone for me to get in by when I've done my detecting. Come on, Mabel." He caught her hand. "Bags I the buns, though," he added, by a happy afterthought, and snatching the bag, pressed it on Mabel, and the sound of four boots echoed on the pavement of the High Street as the outlines of the running Mabel grew small with distance.

Mademoiselle was in the drawing-room. She was sitting by the window in the waning light reading letters.

"Ah, *vous voici!*"* she said unintelligibly. "You are again late; and my little Gerald, where is he?"

This was an awful moment. Jimmy's detective scheme had not included any answer to this inevitable question. The silence was unbroken till Jimmy spoke.

"He *said* he was going to bed because he had a headache." And this, of course, was true.

"This poor Gerald!" said Mademoiselle. "Is it that I should mount him some supper?"

"He never eats anything when he's got one of his headaches," Kathleen said. And this also was the truth.

Jimmy and Kathleen went to bed, wholly untroubled by anxiety about their brother, and Mademoiselle pulled out the bundle of letters and read them amid the ruins of the simple supper.

"It is ripping being out late like this," said Gerald through the soft summer dusk.

"Yes," said Mabel, a solitary-looking figure plodding along the high-road. "I do hope auntie won't be *very* furious."

"Have another bun," suggested Gerald kindly, and a sociable munching followed.

---

* Here you are (French).

It was the aunt herself who opened to a very pale and trembling Mabel the door which is appointed for the entrances and exits of the domestic staff at Yalding Towers. She looked over Mabel's head first, as if she expected to see someone taller. Then a very small voice said:

"Aunt!"

The aunt started back, then made a step towards Mabel.

"You naughty, naughty girl!" she cried angrily; "how could you give me such a fright? I've a good mind to keep you in bed for a week for this, miss. Oh, Mabel, thank Heaven you're safe!" And with that the aunt's arms went round Mabel and Mabel's round the aunt in such a hug as they had never met in before.

"But you didn't seem to care a bit this morning," said Mabel, when she had realized that her aunt really had been anxious, really was glad to have her safe home again.

"How do you know?"

"I was there listening. Don't be angry, auntie."

"I feel as if I could never be angry with you again, now I've got you safe," said the aunt surprisingly.

"But how was it?" Mabel asked.

"My dear," said the aunt impressively, "I've been in a sort of trance. I think I must be going to be ill. I've always been fond of you, but I didn't want to spoil you. But yesterday, about half-past three, I was talking about you to Mr. Lewson, at the fair, and quite suddenly I felt as if you didn't matter at all. And I felt the same when I got your letter and when those children came. And today in the middle of tea I suddenly woke up and realized that you were gone. It was awful. I think I must be going to be ill. Oh, Mabel, why did you do it?"

"It was—a joke," said Mabel feebly. And then the two went in and the door was shut.

"That's most uncommon odd," said Gerald, outside; "looks like more magic to me. I don't feel as if we'd got to the bottom of this yet, by any manner of means. There's more about this castle than meets the eye."

There certainly was. For this castle happened to be—but it would not be fair to Gerald to tell you more about it than he knew on that night when he went alone and invisible through the shadowy great grounds of it to look for the open window of the panelled room. He knew that night no more than I have told you; but as he went along the dewy lawns and through the groups of shrubs and trees, where pools lay like giant looking-glasses reflecting the quiet stars, and the white limbs of statues gleamed against a background of shadow, he began to feel—well, not excited, not surprised, not anxious, but— different.

The incident of the invisible Princess had surprised, the incident of the conjuring had excited, and the sudden decision to be a detective had brought its own anxieties; but all these happenings, though wonderful and unusual, had seemed to be, after all, inside the circle of possible things—wonderful as the chemical experiments are where two liquids poured together make fire, surprising as legerdemain,* thrilling as a juggler's display, but nothing more. Only now a new feeling came to him as he walked through those gardens; by day those gardens were like dreams, at night they were like visions. He could not see his feet as he walked, but he saw the movement of the dewy grass-blades that his feet displaced. And he had that extraordinary feeling so difficult to describe, and yet so real and so unforgettable—the feeling that he was in another world, that had covered up and hidden the old world as a carpet covers a floor. The floor was there all right, underneath, but what he walked on was the carpet that covered it—and that carpet was drenched in magic, as the turf was drenched in dew.

The feeling was very wonderful; perhaps you will feel it some day. There are still some places in the world where it can be felt, but they grow fewer every year.

The enchantment of the garden held him.

"I'll not go in yet," he told himself; "it's too early. And perhaps I shall never be here at night again. I suppose it is the night that makes everything look so different."

Something white moved under a weeping willow; white hands parted the long, rustling leaves. A white figure came out, a creature with horns and goat's legs and the head and arms of a boy. And Gerald was not afraid. That was the most wonderful thing of all, though he would never have owned it. The white thing stretched its limbs, rolled on the grass, righted itself and frisked away across the lawn.

---

* Sleight of hand; a conjuring trick.

Still something white gleamed under the willow; three steps nearer and Gerald saw that it was the pedestal of a statue—empty.

"They come alive," he said; and another white shape came out of the Temple of Flora and disappeared in the laurels. "The statues come alive."

There was a crunching of the little stones in the gravel of the drive. Something enormously long and darkly grey came crawling towards him, slowly, heavily. The moon came out just in time to show its shape. It was one of those great lizards that you see at the Crystal Palace,* made in stone, of the same awful size which they were millions of years ago when they were masters of the world, before Man was.

"It can't see me," said Gerald. "I am not afraid. It's come to life, too."

As it writhed past him he reached out a hand and touched the side of its gigantic tail. It was of stone. It had not "come alive," as he had fancied, but *was* alive in its stone. It turned, however, at the touch; but Gerald also had turned, and was running with all his speed towards the house. Because at that stony touch Fear had come into the garden and almost caught him. It was Fear that he ran from, and not the moving stone beast.

He stood panting under the fifth window; when he had climbed to the window-ledge by the twisted ivy that clung to the wall, he looked back over the grey slope—there was a splashing at the fish-pool that had mirrored the stars—the shape of the great stone beast was wallowing in the shallows among the lily-pads.

Once inside the room, Gerald turned for another look. The fish-pond lay still and dark, reflecting the moon. Through a gap in the drooping willow the moonlight fell on a statue that stood calm and motionless on its pedestal. Everything was in its place now in the garden. Nothing moved or stirred.

"How extraordinarily rum!" said Gerald. "I shouldn't have thought you *could* go to sleep walking through a garden and dream—like that."

He shut the window, lit a match, and closed the shutters. Another

---

* Built for the Great Exhibition of 1851; see endnote 5 to *Five Children and It*.

The moving stone beast

match showed him the door. He turned the key, went out, locked the door again, hung the key on its usual nail, and crept to the end of the passage. Here he waited, safe in his invisibility, till the dazzle of the matches should have gone from his eyes, and he be once more able to find his way by the moonlight that fell in bright patches on the floor through the barred, unshuttered windows of the hall.

"Wonder where the kitchen is," said Gerald. He had quite forgotten that he was a detective. He was only anxious to get home and tell the others about that extraordinarily odd dream that he had had in the gardens. "I suppose it doesn't matter what doors I open. I'm invisible all right still, I suppose? Yes; can't see my hand before my face." He held up a hand for the purpose. "Here goes!"

He opened many doors, wandered into long rooms with furniture dressed in brown holland covers* that looked white in that strange light, rooms with chandeliers hanging in big bags from the high ceilings, rooms whose walls were alive with pictures, rooms whose walls were deadened with rows on rows of old books, state bedrooms in whose great plumed four-posters Queen Elizabeth had no doubt slept. (That Queen, by the way, must have been very little at home, for she seems to have slept in every old house in England.) But he could not find the kitchen. At last a door opened on stone steps that went up—there was a narrow stone passage—steps that went down—a door with a light under it. It was, somehow, difficult to put out one's hand to that door and open it.

"Nonsense!" Gerald told himself, "don't be an ass! Are you invisible, or aren't you?"

Then he opened the door, and someone inside said something in a sudden rough growl.

Gerald stood back, flattened against the wall, as a man sprang to the doorway and flashed a lantern into the passage.

"All right," said the man, with almost a sob of relief. "It was only the door swung open, it's that heavy—that's all."

"Blow the door!" said another growling voice; "blessed if I didn't think it was a fair cop that time."

They closed the door again. Gerald did not mind. In fact, he rather preferred that it should be so. He didn't like the look of those men. There was an air of threat about them. In their presence even invisibility seemed too thin a disguise. And Gerald had seen as much as he wanted to see. He had seen that he had been right about the gang.

---

* Unbleached linen fabric originally from Holland.

The men were taking silver out of two great chests

By wonderful luck—beginner's luck, a card-player would have told him—he had discovered a burglary on the very first night of his detective career. The men were taking silver out of two great chests, wrapping it in rags, and packing it in baize* sacks. The door of the room was of iron six inches thick. It was, in fact, the strong-room, and these men had picked the lock. The tools they had done it with lay on the floor, on a neat cloth roll, such as wood-carvers keep their chisels in.

---

* Coarse woolen cloth.

"Hurry up!" Gerald heard. "You needn't take all night over it."

The silver rattled slightly. "You're a rattling of them trays like bloomin' castanets," said the gruffest voice. Gerald turned and went away, very carefully and very quickly. And it is a most curious thing that, though he couldn't find the way to the servants' wing when he had nothing else to think of, yet now, with his mind full, so to speak, of silver forks and silver cups, and the question of who might be coming after him down those twisting passages, he went straight as an arrow to the door that led from the hall to the place he wanted to get to.

As he went the happenings took words in his mind.

"The fortunate detective," he told himself, "having succeeded beyond his wildest dreams, himself left the spot in search of assistance."

But what assistance? There were, no doubt, men in the house, also the aunt; but he could not warn them. He was too hopelessly invisible to carry any weight with strangers. The assistance of Mabel would not be of much value. The police? Before they could be got— and the getting of them presented difficulties—the burglars would have cleared away with their sacks of silver.

Gerald stopped and thought hard; he held his head with both hands to do it. You know the way—the same as you sometimes do for simple equations or the dates of the battles of the Civil War.

Then with pencil, note-book, a window-ledge, and all the cleverness he could find at the moment, he wrote:

"You know the room where the silver is. Burglars are burgling it, the thick door is picked. Send a man for police. I will follow the burglars if they get away ere police arrive on the spot."

He hesitated a moment, and ended—

"From a Friend—this is not a sell."

This letter, tied tightly round a stone by means of a shoelace, thundered through the window of the room where Mabel and her aunt, in the ardour of reunion, were enjoying a supper of unusual charm—stewed plums, cream, spongecakes, custard in cups, and cold bread-and-butter pudding.

Gerald, in hungry invisibility, looked wistfully at the supper before he threw the stone. He waited till the shrieks had died away, saw the stone picked up, the warning letter read.

"Nonsense!" said the aunt, growing calmer. "How wicked! Of course it's a hoax."

"Oh! do send for the police, like he says," wailed Mabel.

"Like who says?" snapped the aunt.

"Whoever it is," Mabel moaned.

"Send for the police at once," said Gerald, outside, in the manliest voice he could find. "You'll only blame yourself if you don't. I can't do any more for you."

"I—I'll set the dogs on you!" cried the aunt.

"Oh, auntie, don't!" Mabel was dancing with agitation. "It's true—I know it's true. Do—do wake Bates!"

"I don't believe a word of it," said the aunt. No more did Bates when, owing to Mabel's persistent worryings, he was awakened. But when he had seen the paper, and had to choose whether he'd go to the strong-room and see that there really wasn't anything to believe or go for the police on his bicycle, he chose the latter course.

When the police arrived the strong-room door stood ajar, and the silver, or as much of it as the three men could carry, was gone.

Gerald's note-book and pencil came into play again later on that night. It was five in the morning before he crept into bed, tired out and cold as a stone.

"Master Gerald!"—it was Eliza's voice in his ears—"it's seven o'clock and another fine day, and there's been another burglary—My cats alive!" she screamed, as she drew up the blind and turned towards the bed; "look at his bed, all crocked* with black, and him not there! Oh, Jimminy!" It was a scream this time. Kathleen came running from her room; Jimmy sat up in his bed and rubbed his eyes.

"Whatever is it?" Kathleen cried.

"I dunno when I 'ad such a turn." Eliza sat down heavily on a box as she spoke. "First thing his bed all empty and black as the chimley† back, and him not in it, and then when I looks again he is in it all the time. I must be going silly. I thought as much when I heard

---

* Soiled (slang).

† Chimney (dialect).

them haunting angel voices yesterday morning. But I'll tell Mam'selle of you, my lad, with your tricks, you may rely on that. Blacking yourself all over and crocking up your clean sheets and pillow-cases. It's going back of beyond, this is."

"Look here," said Gerald slowly; "I'm going to tell you something."

Eliza simply snorted, and that was rude of her; but then, she had had a shock and had not got over it.

"Can you keep a secret?" asked Gerald, very earnest through the grey of his partly rubbed-off blacklead.

"Yes," said Eliza.

"Then keep it and I'll give you two bob."

"But what was you going to tell me?"

"That. About the two bob and the secret. And you keep your mouth shut."

"I didn't ought to take it," said Eliza, holding out her hand eagerly. "Now you get up, and mind you wash all the corners, Master Gerald."

"Oh, I'm so glad you're safe," said Kathleen, when Eliza had gone.

"You didn't seem to care much last night," said Gerald coldly.

"I can't think how I let you go. I didn't care last night. But when I woke this morning and remembered!"

"There, that'll do—it'll come off on you," said Gerald through the reckless hugging of his sister.

"How did you get visible?" Jimmy asked.

"It just happened when she called me—the ring came off."

"Tell us all about everything," said Kathleen.

"Not yet," said Gerald mysteriously.

"Where's the ring?" Jimmy asked after breakfast. "I want to have a try now."

"I—I forgot it," said Gerald; "I expect it's in the bed somewhere."

But it wasn't. Eliza had made the bed.

"I'll swear there ain't no ring there," she said. "I should 'a' seen it if there had 'a' been."

CHAPTER V

Search and research proving vain," said Gerald, when every corner of the bedroom had been turned out and the ring had not been found, "the noble detective hero of our tale remarked that he would have other fish to fry in half a jiff, and if the rest of you want to hear about last night . . ."

"Let's keep it till we get to Mabel," said Kathleen heroically.

"The assignation was ten-thirty, wasn't it? Why shouldn't Gerald gas as we go along? I don't suppose anything very much happened, anyhow." This, of course, was Jimmy.

"That shows," remarked Gerald sweetly, "how much you know. The melancholy Mabel will await the tryst without success, as far as this one is concerned. 'Fish, fish, other fish—other fish I fry!'" he warbled to the tune of "Cherry Ripe,"[5] till Kathleen could have pinched him.

Jimmy turned coldly away, remarking, "When you've quite done."

But Gerald went on singing—

> "'Where the lips of Johnson smile,
> There's the land of Cherry Isle.
> Other fish, other fish,
> Fish I fry.
> Stately Johnson, come and buy!'"

"How can you," asked Kathleen, "be so aggravating?"

"I don't know," said Gerald, returning to prose. "Want of sleep or intoxication—of success, I mean. Come where no one can hear us.

> "Oh, come to some island where no one can hear,
> And beware of the keyhole that's glued to an ear,"

he whispered, opened the door suddenly, and there, sure enough, was Eliza, stooping without. She flicked feebly at the wainscot with a duster, but concealment was vain.

"You know what listeners never hear," said Jimmy severely.

"I didn't, then—so there!" said Eliza, whose listening ears were crimson. So they passed out, and up the High Street, to sit on the churchyard wall and dangle their legs. And all the way Gerald's lips were shut into a thin, obstinate line.

"Now," said Kathleen. "Oh, Jerry, don't be a goat! I'm simply dying to hear what happened."

"That's better," said Gerald, and he told his story. As he told it some of the white mystery and magic of the moonlit gardens got into his voice and his words, so that when he told of the statues that came alive, and the great beast that was alive through all its stone, Kathleen thrilled responsive, clutching his arm, and even Jimmy ceased to kick the wall with his boot heels, and listened open-mouthed.

Then came the thrilling tale of the burglars, and the warning letter flung into the peaceful company of Mabel, her aunt, and the bread-and-butter pudding. Gerald told the story with the greatest enjoyment and such fullness of detail that the church clock chimed half-past eleven as he said, "Having done all that human agency could do, and further help being despaired of, our gallant young detective—Hullo, there's Mabel!"

There was. The tail-board of a cart shed her almost at their feet.

"I couldn't wait any longer," she explained, "when you didn't come. And I got a lift. Has anything more happened? The burglars had gone when Bates got to the strong-room."

"You don't mean to say all that wheeze is *real*?" Jimmy asked.

"Of course it's real," said Kathleen. "Go on, Jerry. He's just got to where he threw the stone into your bread-and-butter pudding, Mabel. Go on."

Mabel climbed on to the wall. "You've got visible again quicker than I did," she said.

Gerald nodded and resumed:

"Our story must be told in as few words as possible, owing to the fish-frying taking place at twelve, and it's past the half-hour now. Having left his missive to do its warning work, Gerald de Sherlock Holmes sped back, wrapped in invisibility, to the spot where by the light of their dark-lanterns the burglars were still—still burgling with the utmost punctuality and despatch. I didn't see any sense in running into danger, so I just waited outside the passage where the steps are—you know?"

Mabel nodded.

"Presently they came out, very cautiously, of course, and looked about them. They didn't see me—so deeming themselves unobserved they passed in silent Indian file along the passage—one of the sacks of silver grazed my front part—and out into the night."

"But which way?"

"Through the little looking-glass room where you looked at yourself when you were invisible. The hero followed swiftly on his invisible tennis-shoes. The three miscreants instantly sought the shelter of the groves and passed stealthily among the rhododendrons and across the park, and"—his voice dropped and he looked straight before him at the pinky convolvulus netting a heap of stones beyond the white dust of the road—"the stone things that come alive, they kept looking out from between bushes and under trees—and I saw them all right, but they didn't see me. They saw the burglars though, right enough; but the burglars couldn't see them. Rum, wasn't it?"

"The stone things?" Mabel had to have them explained to her.

"I never saw them come alive," she said, "and I've been in the gardens in the evening as often as often."

"I saw them," said Gerald stiffly.

"I know, I know," Mabel hastened to put herself right with him; "what I mean to say is I shouldn't wonder if they're only visible when you're invisible—the liveness of them, I mean, not the stoniness."

Gerald understood, and I'm sure I hope you do.

"I shouldn't wonder if you're right," he said. "The castle garden's enchanted right enough; but what I should like to know is *how* and why. I say, come on, I've got to catch Johnson before twelve. We'll walk as far as the market and then we'll have to run for it."

"But go on with the adventure," said Mabel. "You can talk as we go. Oh, do—it is so awfully thrilling!"

This pleased Gerald, of course.

"Well, I just followed, you know, like in a dream, and they got out the cavy way—you know, where we got in—and I jolly well thought I'd lost them; I had to wait till they'd moved off down the road so that they shouldn't hear me rattling the stones, and I had to tear to catch them up. I took my shoes off—I expect my stockings are done for. And I followed and followed and followed and they went through the place where the poor people live, and right down to the river. And—I say, we must run for it."

So the story stopped and the running began.

Johnson in his own back-yard washing

They caught Johnson in his own back-yard washing at a bench against his own back-door.

"Look here, Johnson," Gerald said, "what'll you give me if I put you up to winning that fifty pounds reward?"

"Halves," said Johnson promptly, "and a clout 'long-side your head if you was coming any of your nonsense over me."

"It's not nonsense," said Gerald very impressively. "If you'll let us in I'll tell you all about it. And when you've caught the burglars and got the swag* back you just give me a quid† for luck. I won't ask for more."

---

* Stolen goods.

† Money; a pound (slang).

"Come along in, then," said Johnson, "if the young ladies'll excuse the towel. But I bet you *do* want something more off of me. Else why not claim the reward yourself?"

"Great is the wisdom of Johnson—he speaks winged words." The children were all in the cottage now, and the door was shut. "I want you never to let on who told you. Let them think it was your own unaided pluck and far-sightedness."

"Sit you down," said Johnson, "and if you're kidding you'd best send the little gells home afore I begin on you."

"I am not kidding," replied Gerald loftily, "never less. And anyone but a policeman would see why I don't want anyone to know it was me. I found it out at dead of night, in a place where I wasn't supposed to be; and there'd be a beastly row if they found out at home about me being out nearly all night. Now do you see, my bright-eyed daisy?"

Johnson was now too interested, as Jimmy said afterwards, to mind what silly names he was called. He said he did see—and asked to see more.

"Well, don't you ask any questions, then. I'll tell you all it's good for you to know. Last night about eleven I was at Yalding Towers. No—it doesn't matter how I got there or what I got there for—and there was a window open and I got in, and there was a light. And it was in the strong-room, and there were three men, putting silver in a bag."

"Was it you give the warning, and they sent for the police?" Johnson was leaning eagerly forward, a hand on each knee.

"Yes, that was me. You can let them think it was you, if you like. You were off duty, weren't you?"

"I was," said Johnson, "in the arms of Murphy—"*

"Well, the police didn't come quick enough. But I was there—a lonely detective. And I followed them."

"You did?"

"And I saw them hide the booty and I know the other stuff from Houghton's Court's in the same place, and I heard them arrange about when to take it away."

"Come and show me where," said Johnson, jumping up so quickly that his Windsor arm-chair fell over backwards, with a crack, on the red-brick floor.

---

* That is, in the arms of Morpheus; in other words, asleep.

"Not so," said Gerald calmly; "if you go near the spot before the appointed time you'll find the silver, but you'll never catch the thieves."

"You're right there." The policeman picked up his chair and sat down in it again. "Well?"

"Well, there's to be a motor to meet them in the lane beyond the boat-house by Sadler's Rents at one o'clock tonight. They'll get the things out at half-past twelve and take them along in a boat. So now's your chance to fill your pockets with chink* and cover yourself with honour and glory."

"So help me!"—Johnson was pensive and doubtful still—"so help me! you *couldn't* have made all this up out of your head."

"Oh yes, I could. But I didn't. Now look here. It's the chance of your lifetime, Johnson! A quid for me, and a still tongue for you, and the job's done. Do you agree?"

"Oh, I agree right enough," said Johnson. "I *agree*. But if you're coming any of your larks—"

"Can't you *see* he isn't?" Kathleen put in impatiently. "He's not a liar—we none of us are."

"If you're not on, say so," said Gerald, "and I'll find another policeman with more sense."

"I could split about you being out all night," said Johnson.

"But you wouldn't be so ungentlemanly," said Mabel brightly. "Don't you be so unbelieving, when we're trying to do you a good turn."

"If I were you," Gerald advised, "I'd go to the place where the silver is, with two other men. You could make a nice little ambush in the wood-yard—it's close there. And I'd have two or three more men up trees in the lane to wait for the motor-car."

"You ought to have been in the force, you ought," said Johnson admiringly; "but s'pose it *was* a hoax!"

"Well, then you'd have made an ass of yourself—I don't suppose it ud be the first time," said Jimmy.

"Are you on?" said Gerald in haste. "Hold your jaw, Jimmy, you idiot!"

---

* Coins (slang).

"*Yes*," said Johnson.

"Then when you're on duty you go down to the wood-yard, and the place where you see me blow my nose is the place. The sacks are tied with string to the posts under the water. You just stalk by in your dignified beauty and make a note of the spot. That's where glory waits you, and when Fame elates you and you're a sergeant, please remember me."

Johnson said he was blessed. He said it more than once, and then remarked that he was on, and added that he must be off that instant minute.

Johnson's cottage lies just out of the town beyond the blacksmith's forge and the children had come to it through the wood. They went back the same way, and then down through the town, and through its narrow, unsavoury streets to the towing-path by the timber yard. Here they ran along the trunks of the big trees, peeped into the saw-pit, and—the men were away at dinner and this was a favourite play place of every boy within miles—made themselves a see-saw with a fresh cut, sweet-smelling pine plank and an elm-root.

"What a ripping place!" said Mabel, breathless on the see-saw's end. "I believe I like this better than pretending games or even magic."

"So do I," said Jimmy. "Jerry, don't keep sniffing so—you'll have no nose left."

"I can't help it," Gerald answered; "I daren't use my hankey for fear Johnson's on the lookout somewhere unseen. I wish I'd thought of some other signal." Sniff! "No, nor I shouldn't want to now if I hadn't got not to. That's what's so rum. The moment I got down here and remembered what I'd said about the signal I began to have a cold—and—Thank goodness! here he is."

The children, with a fine air of unconcern, abandoned the see-saw.

"Follow my leader!" Gerald cried, and ran along a barked oak trunk, the others following. In and out and round about ran the file of children, over heaps of logs, under the jutting ends of piled planks, and just as the policeman's heavy boots trod the towing-path Gerald halted at the end of a little landing-stage of rotten boards, with a rickety handrail, cried "Pax!" and blew his nose with loud fervour.

"Morning," he said immediately.

Gerald halted at the end of a little landing-stage

"Morning," said Johnson. "Got a cold, ain't you?"

"Ah! I shouldn't have a cold if I'd got boots like yours," returned Gerald admiringly. "Look at them. Anyone ud know your fairy foot-step a mile off. How do you ever get near enough to anyone to arrest them?" He skipped off the landing-stage, whispered as he passed Johnson, "Courage, promptitude, and dispatch. That's the place," and was off again, the active leader of an active procession.

"We've brought a friend home to dinner," said Kathleen, when Eliza opened the door. "Where's Mademoiselle?"

"Gone to see Yalding Towers. Today's show day, you know. An' just you hurry over your dinners. It's my afternoon out, and my gentle-man friend don't like it if he's kept waiting."

"All right, we'll eat like lightning," Gerald promised. "Set another place, there's an angel."

They kept their word. The dinner—it was minced veal and pota-toes and rice-pudding, perhaps the dullest food in the world—was over in a quarter of an hour.

"And now," said Mabel, when Eliza and a jug of hot water had disappeared up the stairs together, "where's the ring? I ought to put it back."

"I haven't had a turn yet," said Jimmy. "When we find it Cathy and I ought to have turns same as you and Gerald did."

"When you find it—?" Mabel's pale face turned paler between her dark locks.

"I'm very sorry—we're all very sorry," began Kathleen, and then the story of the losing had to be told.

"You couldn't have looked properly," Mabel protested. "It can't have vanished."

"You don't know what it can do—no more do we. It's no use getting your quills up, fair lady. Perhaps vanishing itself is just what it does do. You see, it came off my hand in the bed. We looked every-where."

"Would you mind if I looked?" Mabel's eyes implored her little hostess. "You see, if it's lost it's my fault. It's almost the same as steal-ing. That Johnson would say it was just the same. I know he would."

"Let's all look again," said Cathy, jumping up. "We *were* rather in a hurry this morning."

So they looked, and they looked. In the bed, under the bed, under the carpet, under the furniture. They shook the curtains, they explored the corners, and found dust and flue, but no ring. They looked, and they looked. Everywhere they looked. Jimmy even looked fixedly at the ceiling, as though he thought the ring might have bounced up there and stuck. But it hadn't.

"Then," said Mabel at last, "your housemaid must have stolen it. That's all. I shall tell her I think so."

And she would have done it too, but at that moment the front door banged and they knew that Eliza had gone forth in all the glory of her best things to meet her "gentleman friend."

"It's no use"—Mabel was almost in tears; "look here—will you leave me alone? Perhaps you others looking distracts me. And I'll go over every inch of the room by myself."

"Respecting the emotion of their guest, the kindly charcoal-burners withdrew," said Gerald. And they closed the door softly from the outside on Mabel and her search.

They waited for her, of course—politeness demanded it, and besides, they had to stay at home to let Mademoiselle in; though it was a dazzling day, and Jimmy had just remembered that Gerald's pockets were full of the money earned at the fair, and that nothing had yet been bought with that money, except a few buns in which he had had no share. And of course they waited impatiently.

It seemed about an hour, and was really quite ten minutes, before they heard the bedroom door open and Mabel's feet on the stairs.

"She hasn't found it," Gerald said.

"How do you know?" Jimmy asked.

"The way she walks," said Gerald. You can, in fact, almost always tell whether the thing has been found that people have gone to look for by the sound of their feet as they return. Mabel's feet said "No go" as plain as they could speak. And her face confirmed the cheerless news.

A sudden and violent knocking at the back door prevented anyone from having to be polite about how sorry they were, or fanciful about being sure the ring would turn up soon.

All the servants except Eliza were away on their holidays, so the children went together to open the door, because, as Gerald said, if it was the baker they could buy a cake from him and eat it for dessert. "That kind of dinner sort of *needs* dessert," he said.

But it was not the baker. When they opened the door they saw in the paved court where the pump is, and the dust-bin, and the water-butt,* a young man, with his hat very much on one side, his mouth open under his fair bristly moustache, and his eyes as nearly round as human eyes can be. He wore a suit of a bright mustard colour, a blue necktie, and a goldish watch-chain across his waistcoat. His body was thrown back and his right arm stretched out towards the door, and

---

* Rain barrel.

his expression was that of a person who is being dragged somewhere against his will. He looked so strange that Kathleen tried to shut the door in his face, murmuring, "Escaped insane." But the door would not close. There was something in the way.

"Leave go of me!" said the young man.

"Ho yus! I'll leave go of you!" It was the voice of Eliza—but no Eliza could be seen.

"Who's got hold of you?" asked Kathleen.

"*She* has, miss," replied the unhappy stranger.

"Who's she?" asked Kathleen, to gain time, as she afterwards explained, for she now knew well enough that what was keeping the door open was Eliza's unseen foot.

"My fyongsay, miss. At least it sounds like her voice, and it feels like her bones, but something's come over me, miss, an' I can't see her."

"That's what he keeps on saying," said Eliza's voice. " 'E's my gentleman friend; is 'e gone dotty, or is it me?"

"Both, I shouldn't wonder," said Jimmy.

"Now," said Eliza, "you call yourself a man; you look me in the face and say you can't see me."

"Well—I can't," said the wretched gentleman friend.

"If I'd stolen a ring," said Gerald, looking at the sky, "I should go indoors and be quiet, not stand at the back door and make an exhibition of myself."

"Not much exhibition about her," whispered Jimmy; "good old ring!"

"I haven't stolen *anything*," said the gentleman friend. "Here, you leave me be. It's my eyes has gone wrong. Leave go of me, d'ye hear?"

Suddenly his hand dropped and he staggered back against the water-butt. Eliza had "left go" of him. She pushed past the children, shoving them aside with her invisible elbows. Gerald caught her by the arm with one hand, felt for her ear with the other, and whispered, "You stand still and don't say a word. If you do—well, what's to stop me from sending for the police?"

Eliza did not know what there was to stop him. So she did as she was told, and stood invisible and silent, save for a sort of blowing, snorting noise peculiar to her when she was out of breath.

The mustard-coloured young man had recovered his balance,

He staggered back against the water-butt

and stood looking at the children with eyes, if possible, rounder than before.

"What is it?" he gasped feebly. "What's up? What's it all about?"

"If you don't know, I'm afraid we can't tell you," said Gerald politely.

"Have I been talking very strange-like?" he asked, taking off his hat and passing his hand over his forehead.

"Very," said Mabel.

"I hope I haven't said anything that wasn't good manners," he said anxiously.

"Not at all," said Kathleen. "You only said your fiancée had hold of your hand, and that you couldn't see her."

"No more I can."

"No more can we," said Mabel.

"But I couldn't have dreamed it, and then come along here making a penny show of myself like this, could I?"

"You know best," said Gerald courteously.

"But," the mustard-coloured victim almost screamed, "do you mean to tell me . . ."

"I don't mean to tell you anything," said Gerald quite truly, "but I'll give you a bit of advice. You go home and lie down a bit and put a wet rag on your head. You'll be all right tomorrow."

"But I haven't—"

"I should," said Mabel; "the sun's very hot, you know."

"I feel all right now," he said, "but—well, I can only say I'm sorry, that's all I can say. I've never been taken like this before, miss. I'm not subject to it—don't you think that. But I could have sworn Eliza—Ain't she gone out to meet me?"

"Eliza's indoors," said Mabel. "She can't come out to meet anybody today."

"You won't tell her about me carrying on this way, will you, miss? It might set her against me if she thought I was liable to fits, which I never was from a child."

"We won't tell Eliza anything about you."

"And you'll overlook the liberty?"

"Of course. We know you couldn't help it," said Kathleen. "You go home and lie down. I'm sure you must need it. Good afternoon."

"Good afternoon, I'm sure, miss," he said dreamily. "All the same I can feel the print of her finger-bones on my hand while I'm saying it. And you won't let it get round to my boss—my employer I mean? Fits of all sorts are against a man in any trade."

"No, no, no, it's all right—good-bye," said everyone. And a silence fell as he went slowly round the water-butt and the green yard-gate shut behind him. The silence was broken by Eliza.

"Give me up!" she said. "Give me up to break my heart in a prison cell!"

There was a sudden splash, and a round wet drop lay on the doorstep.

"Thunder shower," said Jimmy; but it was a tear from Eliza.

"Give me up," she went on, "give me up"—splash "but don't let me be took here in the town where I'm known and respected"—splash. "I'll walk ten miles to be took by a strange police—not Johnson as keeps company with my own cousin"—splash. "But I do thank you for one thing. You didn't tell Elf as I'd stolen the ring. And I didn't"—splash—"I only sort of borrowed it, it being my day out, and my gentleman friend such a toff,* like you can see for yourselves."

The children had watched, spellbound, the interesting tears that became visible as they rolled off the invisible nose of the miserable Eliza. Now Gerald roused himself, and spoke.

"It's no use your talking," he said. "We can't see you!"

"That's what *he* said," said Eliza's voice, "but—"

"You can't see yourself," Gerald went on. "Where's your hand?"

Eliza, no doubt, tried to see it, and of course failed; for instantly, with a shriek that might have brought the police if there had been any about, she went into a violent fit of hysterics. The children did what they could, everything that they had read of in books as suitable to such occasions, but it is extremely difficult to do the right thing with an invisible housemaid in strong hysterics and her best clothes. That was why the best hat was found, later on, to be completely ruined, and why the best blue dress was never quite itself again. And as they were burning bits of the feather dusting-brush as nearly under Eliza's nose as they could guess, a sudden spurt of flame and a horrible smell, as the flame died between the quick hands of Gerald, showed but too plainly that Eliza's feather boa had tried to help.

It did help. Eliza "came to" with a deep sob and said, "Don't burn me real ostrich stole; I'm better now."

They helped her up and she sat down on the bottom step, and the children explained to her very carefully and quite kindly that she really was invisible, and that if you steal—or even borrow—rings you can never be sure what will happen to you.

"But 'ave I got to go on stopping like this," she moaned, when they had fetched the little mahogany looking-glass from its nail over

---

* Such a swell (slang).

the kitchen sink, and convinced her that she was really invisible, "for ever and ever? An' we was to a bin married come Easter. No one won't marry a gell as 'e can't see. It ain't likely."

"No, not for ever and ever," said Mabel kindly, "but you've got to go through with it—like measles. I expect you'll be all right tomorrow."

"Tonight, I think," said Gerald.

"We'll help you all we can, and not tell anyone," said Kathleen.

"Not even the police," said Jimmy.

"Now let's get Mademoiselle's tea ready," said Gerald.

"And ours," said Jimmy.

"No," said Gerald, "we'll have our tea out. We'll have a picnic and we'll take Eliza. I'll go out and get the cakes."

"I shan't eat no cake, Master Jerry," said Eliza's voice, "so don't you think it. You'd see it going down inside my chest. It wouldn't be what I should call nice of me to have cake showing through me in the open air. Oh, it's a dreadful judgement—just for a borrow!"

They reassured her, set the tea, deputed Kathleen to let in Mademoiselle—who came home tired and a little sad, it seemed—waited for her and Gerald and the cakes, and started off for Yalding Towers.

"Picnic parties aren't allowed," said Mabel.

"Ours will be," said Gerald briefly. "Now, Eliza, you catch on to Kathleen's arm and I'll walk behind to conceal your shadow. My aunt! take your hat off; it makes your shadow look like I don't know what. People will think we're the county lunatic asylum turned loose."

It was then that the hat, becoming visible in Kathleen's hand, showed how little of the sprinkled water had gone where it was meant to go—on Eliza's face.

"Me best 'at," said Eliza, and there was a silence with sniffs in it.

"Look here," said Mabel, "you cheer up. Just you think this is all a dream. It's just the kind of thing you might dream if your conscience had got pains in it about the ring."

"But will I wake up again?"

"Oh yes, you'll wake up again. Now we're going to bandage your eyes and take you through a very small door, and don't you resist, or we'll bring a policeman into the dream like a shot."

I have not time to describe Eliza's entrance into the cave. She went head first: the girls propelled and the boys received her. If Gerald had not thought of tying her hands someone would certainly have been scratched. As it was Mabel's hand was scraped between the cold rock and a passionate boot-heel. Nor will I tell you all that she said as they led her along the fern-bordered gully and through the arch into the wonderland of Italian scenery. She had but little language left when they removed her bandage under a weeping willow where a statue of Diana,* bow in hand, stood poised on one toe, a most unsuitable attitude for archery, I have always thought.

"Now," said Gerald, "it's all over—nothing but niceness now and cake and things."

"It's time we did have our tea," said Jimmy. And it was.

Eliza, once convinced that her chest, though invisible, was not transparent, and that her companions could not by looking through it count how many buns she had eaten, made an excellent meal. So did the others. If you want really to enjoy your tea, have minced veal and potatoes and rice-pudding for dinner, with several hours of excitement to follow, and take your tea late.

The soft, cool green and grey of the garden were changing—the green grew golden, the shadows black, and the lake where the swans were mirrored upside down, under the Temple of Phoebus,† was bathed in rosy light from the little fluffy clouds that lay opposite the sunset.

"It is pretty," said Eliza, "just like a picture-postcard, ain't it?—the tuppenny kind."

"I ought to be getting home," said Mabel.

"I can't go home like this. I'd stay and be a savage and live in that white hut if it had any walls and doors," said Eliza.

"She means the Temple of Dionysus,"‡ said Mabel, pointing to it.

The sun set suddenly behind the line of black fir-trees on the top of the slope, and the white temple, that had been pink, turned grey.

"It would be a very nice place to live in even as it is," said Kathleen.

"Draughty," said Eliza, "and law, what a lot of steps to clean!

---

* Roman goddess of the hunt and the moon.

† Byname for Apollo, the Greek sun god associated with song and wisdom.

‡ Greek god of wine and patron of agriculture and the theater.

What they make houses for without no walls to 'em? Who'd live in—"
She broke off, stared, and added: "What's that?"

"What?"

"That white thing coming down the steps. Why, it's a young man in statooary."

"The statues do come alive here, after sunset," said Gerald in very matter-of-fact tones.

"I see they do." Eliza did not seem at all surprised or alarmed. "There's another of 'em. Look at them little wings to his feet like pigeons."

"I expect that's Mercury,"* said Gerald.

"It's 'Hermes'† under the statue that's got wings on its feet," said Mabel, "but—"

"I don't see any statues," said Jimmy. "What are you punching me for?"

"Don't you see?" Gerald whispered; but he need not have been so troubled, for all Eliza's attention was with her wandering eyes that followed hither and thither the quick movements of unseen statues. "Don't you see? The statues come alive when the sun goes down— and you can't see them unless you're invisible—and I—if you *do* see them you're not frightened—unless you *touch* them."

"Let's get her to touch one and see," said Jimmy.

" 'E's lep' into the water," said Eliza in a rapt voice. "My, can't he swim neither! And the one with the pigeons' wings is flying all over the lake having larks with 'im. I do call that pretty. It's like cupids as you see on wedding-cakes. And here's another of 'em, a little chap with long ears and a baby deer galloping alongside! An' look at the lady with the baby, throwing it up and catching it like as if it was a ball. I wonder she ain't afraid. But it's pretty to see 'em."

The broad park lay stretched before the children in growing greyness and a stillness that deepened. Amid the thickening shadows they could see the statues gleam white and motionless. But Eliza saw other things. She watched in silence presently, and they watched

---

* Roman god of commerce and the messenger of the gods.

† Greek equivalent of Mercury.

" 'E's lep' into the water"

silently, and the evening fell like a veil that grew heavier and blacker. And it was night. And the moon came up above the trees.

"Oh," cried Eliza suddenly, "here's the dear little boy with the deer—he's coming right for me, bless his heart!"

Next moment she was screaming, and her screams grew fainter and there was the sound of swift boots on gravel.

"Come on!" cried Gerald; "she touched it, and then she was frightened. Just like I was. Run! she'll send everyone in the town mad if she gets there like that. Just a voice and boots! Run! Run!"

They ran. But Eliza had the start of them. Also when she ran on the grass they could not hear her footsteps and had to wait for the sound of leather on far-away gravel. Also she was driven by fear, and fear drives fast.

She went, it seemed, the nearest way, invisibly through the waxing moonlight, seeing she only knew what amid the glades and groves.

"I'll stop here; see you tomorrow," gasped Mabel, as the loud pursuers followed Eliza's clatter across the terrace. "She's gone through the stable yard."

"The back way," Gerald panted as they turned the corner of their own street, and he and Jimmy swung in past the water-butt.

An unseen but agitated presence seemed to be fumbling with the locked back-door. The church clock struck the half-hour.

"Half-past nine," Gerald had just breath to say. "Pull at the ring. Perhaps it'll come off now."

He spoke to the bare doorstep. But it was Eliza, dishevelled, breathless, her hair coming down, her collar crooked, her dress twisted and disordered, who suddenly held out a hand—a hand that they could see; and in the hand, plainly visible in the moonlight, the dark circle of the magic ring.

"'Alf a mo!"* said Eliza's gentleman friend next morning. He was waiting for her when she opened the door with pail and hearthstone in her hand. "Sorry you couldn't come out yesterday."

"So'm I." Eliza swept the wet flannel along the top step. "What did you do?"

"I 'ad a bit of a headache," said the gentleman friend. "I laid down most of the afternoon. What were you up to?"

"Oh, nothing pertickler," said Eliza.

---

* Half a moment (dialect).

It was Eliza, dishevelled, breathless

"Then it was all a dream," she said, when he was gone; "but it'll be a lesson to me not to meddle with anybody's old ring again in a hurry."

"So they didn't tell 'er about me behaving like I did," said he as he went—"sun, I suppose—like our Army in India. I hope I ain't going to be liable to it, that's all!"

CHAPTER VI

Johnson was the hero of the hour. It was he who had tracked the burglars, laid his plans, and recovered the lost silver. He had not thrown the stone—public opinion decided that Mabel and her aunt must have been mistaken in supposing that there was a stone at all. But he did not deny the warning letter. It was Gerald who went out after breakfast to buy the newspaper, and who read aloud to the others the two columns of fiction which were the *Liddlesby Observer's* report of the facts. As he read every mouth opened wider and wider, and when he ceased with "this gifted fellow-townsman with detective instincts which out-rival those of Messrs. Lecoq and Holmes,* and whose promotion is now assured," there was quite a blank silence.

"Well," said Jimmy, breaking it, "he doesn't stick it on neither, does he?"

"I feel," said Kathleen, "as if it was our fault—as if it was us had told all these whoppers; because if it hadn't been for you they couldn't have, Jerry. How could he say all that?"

"Well," said Gerald, trying to be fair, "you know, after all, the chap had to say something. I'm glad I—" He stopped abruptly.

"You're glad you what?"

"No matter," said he, with an air of putting away affairs of state. "Now, what are we going to do today? The faithful Mabel approaches; she will want her ring. And you and Jimmy want it too. Oh, I know. Mademoiselle hasn't had any attention paid to her for more days than our hero likes to confess."

"I wish you wouldn't always call yourself 'our hero,' " said Jimmy; "you aren't mine, anyhow."

"You're both of you mine," said Kathleen hastily.

---

* Monsieur Lecoq, the detective created by Émile Gaboriau (c.1832–1873); the character preceded by several decades his more famous counterpart, Sherlock Holmes, the creation of Sir Arthur Conan Doyle (1859–1930).

"Good little girl." Gerald smiled annoyingly. "Keep baby brother in a good temper till Nursie comes back."

"You're not going out without us?" Kathleen asked in haste.

> " 'I haste away,
>   'Tis market day,' "

sang Gerald,

> " 'And in the market there
>   Buy roses for my fair."

If you want to come too, get your boots on, and look slippy about it."

"I don't want to come," said Jimmy, and sniffed.

Kathleen turned a despairing look on Gerald.

"Oh, James, James," said Gerald sadly, "how difficult you make it for me to forget that you're my little brother! If ever I treat you like one of the other chaps, and rot you like I should Turner or Moberley or any of my pals—well, this is what comes of it."

"You don't call them your baby brothers," said Jimmy, and truly.

"No; and I'll take precious good care I don't call you it again. Come on, my hero and heroine. The devoted Mesrour is your salaaming slave.*

The three met Mabel opportunely at the corner of the square where every Friday the stalls and the awnings and the green umbrellas were pitched, and poultry, pork, pottery, vegetables, drapery, sweets, toys, tools, mirrors, and all sorts of other interesting merchandise were spread out on trestle tables, piled on carts whose horses were stabled and whose shafts were held in place by piled wooden cases, or laid out, as in the case of crockery and hardware, on the bare flagstones of the market-place.

The sun was shining with great goodwill, and, as Mabel remarked, "all Nature looked smiling and gay." There were a few

---

* Slave who performs a low bow accompanied by the placement of his right palm on his forehead. In The Arabian Nights, Mesrour is a henchman of the Khalif Haroun er Reshid.

bunches of flowers among the vegetables, and the children hesitated, balanced in choice.

"Mignonette is sweet," said Mabel.

"Roses are roses," said Kathleen.

"Carnations are tuppence," said Jimmy; and Gerald, sniffing among the bunches of tightly-tied tea-roses, agreed that this settled it.

So the carnations were bought, a bunch of yellow ones, like sulphur, a bunch of white ones like clotted cream, and a bunch of red ones like the cheeks of the doll that Kathleen never played with. They took the carnations home, and Kathleen's green hair-ribbon came in beautifully for tying them up, which was hastily done on the doorstep.

Then discreetly Gerald knocked at the door of the drawing-room, where Mademoiselle seemed to sit all day.

"Entrez!" came her voice; and Gerald entered. She was not reading, as usual, but bent over a sketch-book; on the table was an open colour-box of un-English appearance, and a box of that slate-coloured liquid so familiar alike to the greatest artist in watercolours and to the humblest child with a sixpenny paint-box.

"With all of our loves," said Gerald, laying the flowers down suddenly before her.

"But it is that you are a dear child. For this it must that I embrace you—no?" And before Gerald could explain that he was too old, she kissed him with little quick French pecks on the two cheeks.

"Are you painting?" he asked hurriedly, to hide his annoyance at being treated like a baby.

"I achieve a sketch of yesterday," she answered; and before he had time to wonder what yesterday would look like in a picture she showed him a beautiful and exact sketch of Yalding Towers.

"Oh, I say—ripping!" was the critic's comment. "I say, mayn't the others come and see?" The others came, including Mabel, who stood awkwardly behind the rest, and looked over Jimmy's shoulder.

"I say, you are clever," said Gerald respectfully.

"To what good to have the talent, when one must pass one's life at teaching the infants?" said Mademoiselle.

"It must be fairly beastly," Gerald owned.

She kissed him with little quick French pecks

"You, too, see the design?" Mademoiselle asked Mabel, adding: "A friend from the town, yes?"

"How do you do?" said Mabel politely. "No, I'm not from the town. I live at Yalding Towers."

The name seemed to impress Mademoiselle very much. Gerald anxiously hoped in his own mind that she was not a snob.

"Yalding Towers," she repeated, "but this is very extraordinary. Is it possible that you are then of the family of Lord Yalding?"

"He hasn't any family," said Mabel; "he's not married."

"I would say are you—how you say?—cousin—sister—niece?"

"No," said Mabel, flushing hotly, "I'm nothing grand at all. I'm Lord Yalding's housekeeper's niece."

"But you know Lord Yalding, is it not?"

"No," said Mabel, "I've never seen him."

"He comes then never to his château?"

"Not since I've lived there. But he's coming next week."

"Why lives he not there?" Mademoiselle asked.

"Auntie says he's too poor," said Mabel, and proceeded to tell the tale as she had heard it in the housekeeper's room: how Lord Yalding's uncle had left all the money he could leave away from Lord Yalding to Lord Yalding's second cousin, and poor Lord Yalding had only just enough to keep the old place in repair, and to live very quietly indeed somewhere else, but not enough to keep the house open or to live there; and how he couldn't sell the house because it was "in tale."*

"What is it then—in tail?" asked Mademoiselle.

"In a tale that the lawyers write out," said Mabel, proud of her knowledge and flattered by the deep interest of the French governess; "and when once they've put your house in one of their tales you can't sell it or give it away, but you have to leave it to your son, even if you don't want to."

"But how his uncle could he be so cruel—to leave him the château and no money?" Mademoiselle asked; and Kathleen and Jimmy stood amazed at the sudden keenness of her interest in what seemed to them the dullest story.

"Oh, I can tell you that too," said Mabel. "Lord Yalding wanted to marry a lady his uncle didn't want him to, a barmaid or a ballet lady or something, and he wouldn't give her up, and his uncle said, 'Well then,' and left everything to the cousin."

"And you say he is not married."

"No—the lady went into a convent; I expect she's bricked-up alive by now."

"Bricked—?"

"In a wall, you know," said Mabel, pointing explainingly at the pink and gilt roses of the wall-paper, "shut up to kill them. That's what they do to you in convents."

"Not at all," said Mademoiselle; "in convents are very kind good women; there is but one thing in convents that is detestable—the

---

* Mable means "entail"; the property has an assigned line of inheritance and can be sold or bequeathed only to a specified class of heirs.

locks on the doors. Sometimes people cannot get out, especially when they are very young and their relations have placed them there for their welfare and happiness. But brick—how you say it?—enwalling ladies to kill them. No—it does itself never. And this Lord—he did not then seek his lady?"

"Oh, yes—he sought her right enough," Mabel assured her; "but there are millions of convents, you know, and he had no idea where to look, and they sent back his letters from the post-office, and—"

"Ciel!"* cried Mademoiselle, "but it seems that one knows all in the housekeeper's saloon."

"Pretty well all," said Mabel simply.

"And you think he will find her? No?"

"Oh, he'll find her all right," said Mabel, "when he's old and broken down, you know—and dying; and then a gentle sister of charity will soothe his pillow, and just when he's dying she'll reveal herself and say: 'My own lost love!' and his face will light up with a wonderful joy and he'll expire with her beloved name on his parched lips."

Mademoiselle's was the silence of sheer astonishment. "You do the prophecy, it appears?" she said at last.

"Oh no," said Mabel, "I got that out of a book. I can tell you lots more fatal love stories any time you like."

The French governess gave a little jump, as though she had suddenly remembered something.

"It is nearly dinner-time," she said. "Your friend—Mabelle, yes—will be your convivial, and in her honour we will make a little feast. My beautiful flowers—put them to the water, Kathleen. I run to buy the cakes. Wash the hands, all, and be ready when I return."

Smiling and nodding to the children, she left them, and ran up the stairs.

"Just as if she was young," said Kathleen.

"She is young," said Mabel. "Heaps of ladies have offers of marriage when they're no younger than her. I've seen lots of weddings too, with much older brides. And why didn't you tell me she was so beautiful?"

---

* Heavens! (French).

"Is she?" asked Kathleen.

"Of course she is; and what a darling to think of cakes for me, and calling me a convivial!"

"Look here," said Gerald, "I call this jolly decent of her. You know, governesses never have more than the meanest pittance, just enough to sustain life, and here she is spending her little all on us. Supposing we just don't go out today, but play with her instead. I expect she's most awfully bored really."

"Would she really like it?" Kathleen wondered. "Aunt Emily says grown-ups never really like playing. They do it to please us."

"They little know," Gerald answered, "how often we do it to please them."

"We've got to do that dressing-up with the Princess clothes anyhow—we said we would," said Kathleen. "Let's treat her to that."

"Rather near tea-time," urged Jimmy, "so that there'll be a fortunate interruption and the play won't go on for ever."

"I suppose all the things are safe?" Mabel asked.

"Quite. I told you where I put them. Come on, Jimmy; let's help lay the table. We'll get Eliza to put out the best china."

They went.

"It was lucky," said Gerald, struck by a sudden thought, "that the burglars didn't go for the diamonds in the treasure-chamber."

"They couldn't," said Mabel almost in a whisper; "they didn't know about them. I don't believe anybody knows about them, except me—and you, and you're sworn to secrecy." This, you will remember, had been done almost at the beginning. "I know aunt doesn't know. I just found out the spring by accident. Lord Yalding's kept the secret well."

"I wish I'd got a secret like that to keep," said Gerald.

"If the burglars *do* know," said Mabel, "it'll all come out at the trial. Lawyers make you tell everything you know at trials, and a lot of lies besides."

"There won't be any trial," said Gerald, kicking the leg of the piano thoughtfully.

"No trial?"

"It said in the paper," Gerald went on slowly, " 'The miscreants must have received warning from a confederate, for the admirable preparations to arrest them as they returned for their ill-gotten plunder were unavailing. But the police have a clue.' "

"What a pity!" said Mabel.

"You needn't worry—they haven't got any old clue," said Gerald, still attentive to the piano leg.

"I didn't mean the clue; I meant the confederate."

"It's a pity you think he's a pity, because he was *me*," said Gerald, standing up and leaving the piano leg alone. He looked straight before him, as the boy on the burning deck may have looked.

"I couldn't help it," he said. "I know you'll think I'm a criminal, but I couldn't do it. I don't know how detectives can. I went over a prison once, with father; and after I'd given the tip to Johnson I remembered that, and I just couldn't. I know I'm a beast, and not worthy to be a British citizen."

"I think it was rather nice of you," said Mabel kindly. "How did you warn them?"

"I just shoved a paper under the man's door—the one that I knew where he lived—to tell him to lie low."

"Oh! do tell me—what did you put on it exactly?" Mabel warmed to this new interest.

"It said: 'The police know all except your names. Be virtuous and you are safe. But if there's any more burgling I shall split and you may rely on that from a friend.' I know it was wrong, but I couldn't help it. Don't tell the others. They wouldn't understand why I did it. I don't understand it myself."

"I do," said Mabel: "it's because you've got a kind and noble heart."

"Kind fiddlestick, my good child!" said Gerald, suddenly losing the burning boy expression and becoming in a flash entirely himself. "Cut along and wash your hands; you're as black as ink."

"So are you," said Mabel, "and I'm not. It's dye with me. Auntie was dyeing a blouse this morning. It told you how in *Home Drivel*—and she's as black as ink too, and the blouse is all streaky. Pity the ring won't make just parts of you invisible—the dirt, for instance."

"Perhaps," Gerald said unexpectedly, "it won't make even all of you invisible again."

"Why not? You haven't been doing anything to it—have you?" Mabel sharply asked.

"No; but didn't you notice you were invisible twenty-one hours,

I was fourteen hours invisible, and Eliza only seven—that's seven less each time. And now we've come to—"

"How frightfully good you are at sums!" said Mabel, awe-struck.

"You see, it's got seven hours less each time, and seven from seven is nought; it's got to be something different this time. And then afterwards—it can't be minus seven, because I don't see how—unless it made you more visible—thicker, you know."

"Don't!" said Mabel; "you make my head go round."

"And there's another odd thing," Gerald went on; "when you're invisible your relations don't love you. Look at your aunt, and Cathy never turning a hair at me going burgling. We haven't got to the bottom of that ring yet. Crikey! here's Mademoiselle with the cakes. Run, bold bandits—wash for your lives!"

They ran.

It was not cakes only; it was plums and grapes and jam tarts and soda-water and raspberry vinegar, and chocolates in pretty boxes and "pure, thick, rich" cream in brown jugs, also a big bunch of roses. Mademoiselle was strangely merry, for a governess. She served out the cakes and tarts with a liberal hand, made wreaths of the flowers for all their heads—she was not eating much herself—drank the health of Mabel, as the guest of the day, in the beautiful pink drink that comes from mixing raspberry vinegar and soda-water, and actually persuaded Jimmy to wear his wreath, on the ground that the Greek gods as well as the goddesses always wore wreaths at a feast.

There never was such a feast provided by any French governess since French governesses began. There were jokes and stories and laughter. Jimmy showed all those tricks with forks and corks and matches and apples which are so deservedly popular. Mademoiselle told them stories of her own schooldays when she was "a quite little girl with two tight tresses—so," and when they could not understand the tresses, called for paper and pencil and drew the loveliest little picture of herself when she was a child with two short fat pig-tails sticking out from her head like knitting-needles from a ball of dark worsted. Then she drew pictures of everything they asked for, till Mabel pulled Gerald's jacket and whispered: "The acting!"

"Draw us the front of a theatre," said Gerald tactfully, "a French theatre."

"They are the same thing as the English theatres," Mademoiselle told him.

"Do you like acting—the theatre, I mean?"

"But yes—I love it."

"All right," said Gerald briefly. "We'll act a play for you—now—this afternoon if you like."

"Eliza will be washing up," Cathy whispered, "and she was promised to see it."

"Or this evening," said Gerald "and please, Mademoiselle, may Eliza come in and look on?"

"But certainly," said Mademoiselle; "amuse yourselves well, my children."

"But it's *you*," said Mabel suddenly, "that we want to amuse. Because we love you very much—don't we, all of you?"

"Yes," the chorus came unhesitatingly. Though the others would never have thought of saying such a thing on their own account. Yet, as Mabel said it, they found to their surprise that it was true.

"Tiens!"* said Mademoiselle, "you love the old French governess? Impossible," and she spoke rather indistinctly.

"You're not old," said Mabel; "at least not so very," she added brightly, "and you're as lovely as a Princess."

"Go then, flatteress!" said Mademoiselle, laughing; and Mabel went. The others were already half-way up the stairs.

Mademoiselle sat in the drawing-room as usual, and it was a good thing that she was not engaged in serious study, for it seemed that the door opened and shut almost ceaselessly all throughout the afternoon. Might they have the embroidered antimacassars and the sofa cushions? Might they have the clothes-line out of the wash-house? Eliza said they mightn't, but might they? Might they have the sheepskin hearthrugs? Might they have tea in the garden, because they had almost got the stage ready in the dining-room, and Eliza wanted to set tea? Could Mademoiselle lend them any coloured clothes—scarves or dressing-gowns, or anything bright? Yes, Mademoiselle could, and did—silk things, surprisingly lovely for a governess to have. Had Mademoiselle any rouge? They had always heard

* So! (French).

Down came the loveliest blue-black hair

that French ladies—No. Mademoiselle hadn't—and to judge by the colour of her face, Mademoiselle didn't need it. Did Mademoiselle think the chemist sold rouge—or had she any false hair to spare? At this challenge Mademoiselle's pale fingers pulled out a dozen hair-pins, and down came the loveliest blue-black hair, hanging to her knees in straight, heavy lines.

"No, you terrible infants," she cried. "I have not the false hair, nor the rouge. And my teeth—you want them also, without doubt?"

She showed them in a laugh.

"I said you were a Princess," said Mabel, "and now I know. You're Rapunzel. Do always wear your hair like that! May we have the peacock fans, please, off the mantelpiece, and the things that loop back the curtains, and all the handkerchiefs you've got?"

Mademoiselle denied them nothing. They had the fans and the handkerchiefs and some large sheets of expensive drawing-paper out of the school cupboard, and Mademoiselle's best sable paint-brush and her paint-box.

"Who would have thought," murmured Gerald, pensively sucking the brush and gazing at the paper mask he had just painted, "that she was such a brick in disguise? I wonder why crimson lake always tastes just like Liebig's Extract."*

Everything was pleasant that day somehow. There are some days like that, you know, when everything goes well from the very beginning; all the things you want are in their places, nobody misunderstands you, and all that you do turns out admirably. How different from those other days which we all know too well, when your shoelace breaks, your comb is mislaid, your brush spins on its back on the floor and lands under the bed where you can't get at it—you drop the soap, your buttons come off, an eyelash gets into your eye, you have used your last clean handkerchief, your collar is frayed at the edge and cuts your neck, and at the very last moment your suspender breaks, and there is no string. On such a day as this you are naturally late for breakfast, and everyone thinks you did it on purpose. And the day goes on and on, getting worse and worse—you mislay your exercise-book, you drop your arithmetic in the mud, your pencil breaks, and when you open your knife to sharpen the pencil you split your nail. On such a day you jam your thumb in doors, and muddle the messages you are sent on by grown-ups. You upset your tea, and your bread-and-butter won't hold together for a moment. And when at last you get to bed—usually in disgrace—it is no comfort at all to you to know that not a single bit of it is your own fault.

This day was not one of those days, as you will have noticed. Even the tea in the garden—there was a bricked bit by a rockery that

---

* Concentrated liquid extract of beef, marketed by German chemist Justus von Liebig (1803–1873) as an inexpensive source of meat nutrients.

made a steady floor for the tea-table—was most delightful, though the thoughts of four out of the five were busy with the coming play, and the fifth had thoughts of her own that had had nothing to do with tea or acting.

Then there was an interval of slamming doors, interesting silences, feet that flew up and down stairs.

It was still good daylight when the dinner-bell rang—the signal had been agreed upon at tea-time, and carefully explained to Eliza. Mademoiselle laid down her book and passed out of the sunset-yellowed hall into the faint yellow gaslight of the dining-room. The giggling Eliza held the door open before her, and followed her in. The shutters had been closed—streaks of daylight showed above and below them. The green-and-black tablecloths of the school dining-tables were supported on the clothes-line from the backyard. The line sagged in a graceful curve, but it answered its purpose of supporting the curtains which concealed that part of the room which was the stage.

Rows of chairs had been placed across the other end of the room—all the chairs in the house, as it seemed—and Mademoiselle started violently when she saw that fully half a dozen of these chairs were occupied. And by the queerest people, too: an old woman with a poke bonnet* tied under her chin with a red handkerchief, a lady in a large straw hat wreathed in flowers and the oddest hands that stuck out over the chair in front of her, several men with strange, clumsy figures, and all with hats on.

"But," whispered Mademoiselle, through the chinks of the table-cloths, "you have then invited other friends? You should have asked me, my children."

Laughter and something like a "hurrah" answered her from behind the folds of the curtaining tablecloths.

"All right, Mademoiselle Rapunzel," cried Mabel; "turn the gas up. It's only part of the entertainment."

Eliza, still giggling, pushed through the lines of chairs, knocking off the hat of one of the visitors as she did so, and turned up the three incandescent burners.

---

* Bonnet with a projecting brim.

Fully half a dozen of these chairs were occupied

Mademoiselle looked at the figure seated nearest to her, stooped to look more closely, half laughed, quite screamed, and sat down suddenly.

"Oh!" she cried, "they are not alive!"

Eliza, with a much louder scream, had found out the same thing and announced it differently. "They ain't got no insides," said she. The seven members of the audience seated among the wilderness of chairs had, indeed, no insides to speak of. Their bodies were bolsters and rolled-up blankets, their spines were broom-handles, and their arm and leg bones were hockey sticks and umbrellas. Their shoulders were the wooden crosspieces that Mademoiselle used for keeping her jackets in shape; their hands were gloves stuffed out with handkerchiefs; and their faces were the paper masks painted in the afternoon by the untutored brush of Gerald, tied on to the round heads made of the ends of stuffed bolster-cases. The faces were really rather dreadful. Gerald had done his best, but even after his best had been done you would hardly have known they were faces, some of them, if they hadn't been in the positions which faces usually occupy, between the collar and the hat. Their eyebrows were furious with lamp-black frowns—their eyes the size, and almost the shape, of five-shilling pieces, and on their lips and cheeks had been spent much crimson lake and nearly the whole of a half-pan of vermilion.

"You have made yourself an auditors, yes? Bravo!" cried Mademoiselle, recovering herself and beginning to clap. And to the sound of that clapping the curtain went up—or, rather, apart. A voice said, in a breathless, choked way, "Beauty and the Beast," and the stage was revealed.

It was a real stage too—the dining-tables pushed close together and covered with pink-and-white counterpanes. It was a little unsteady and creaky to walk on, but very imposing to look at. The scene was simple, but convincing. A big sheet of cardboard, bent square, with slits cut in it and a candle behind, represented, quite transparently, the domestic hearth; a round hat-tin of Eliza's, supported on a stool with a night-light under it, could not have been mistaken, save by wilful malice, for anything but a copper. A waste-paper basket with two or three school dusters and an overcoat in it, and a pair of blue pyjamas over the back of a chair, put the finishing touch to the scene. It did not need the announcement from the wings, "The laundry at Beauty's home." It was so plainly a laundry and nothing else.

In the wings: "They look just like a real audience, don't they?" whispered Mabel. "Go on, Jimmy—don't forget the Merchant has to be pompous and use long words."

Jimmy, enlarged by pillows under Gerald's best overcoat which had been intentionally bought with a view to his probable growth during the two years which it was intended to last him, a Turkish towel turban on his head and an open umbrella over it, opened the first act in a simple and swift soliloquy:

"I am the most unlucky merchant that ever was. I was once the richest merchant in Bagdad, but I lost all my ships, and now I live in a poor house that is all to bits; you can see how the rain comes through the roof, and my daughters take in washing. And—"

The pause might have seemed long, but Gerald rustled in, elegant in Mademoiselle's pink dressing-gown and the character of the eldest daughter.

"A nice drying day," he minced. "Pa dear, put the umbrella the other way up. It'll save us going out in the rain to fetch water. Come on, sisters, dear father's got us a new wash-tub. Here's luxury!"

Round the umbrella, now held the wrong way up, the three sisters knelt and washed imaginary linen. Kathleen wore a violet skirt of Eliza's, a blue blouse of her own, and a cap of knotted handkerchiefs. A white nightdress girt with a white apron and two red carnations in Mabel's black hair left no doubt as to which of the three was Beauty.

The scene went very well. The final dance with waving towels was all that there is of charming, Mademoiselle said; and Eliza was so much amused that, as she said, she got quite a nasty stitch along of laughing so hearty.

You know pretty well what Beauty and the Beast would be like acted by four children who had spent the afternoon in arranging their costumes and so had left no time for rehearsing what they had to say. Yet it delighted them, and it charmed their audience. And what more can any play do, even Shakespeare's? Mabel, in her Princess clothes, was a resplendent Beauty; and Gerald a Beast who wore the drawing-room hearthrugs with an air of indescribable distinction. If Jimmy was not a talkative merchant, he made it up with a stoutness practically unlimited, and Kathleen surprised and delighted even herself by the quickness with which she changed from one to the other of the minor characters—fairies, servants, and messengers. It was at the end of the second act that Mabel, whose costume, having reached the height of elegance, could not be bettered and therefore did not need to be changed, said to Gerald, sweltering under the weighty magnificence of his beast-skin:

"I say, you might let us have the ring back."

"I'm going to," said Gerald, who had quite forgotten it. "I'll give it you in the next scene. Only don't lose it, or go putting it on. You might go out all together and never be seen again, or you might get seven times as visible as anyone else, so that all the rest of us would look like shadows beside you, you'd be so thick, or—"

"Ready!" said Kathleen, bustling in, once more a wicked sister.

Gerald managed to get his hand into his pocket under his hearthrug, and when he rolled his eyes in agonies of sentiment, and said, "Farewell, dear Beauty! Return quickly, for if you remain long absent from your faithful beast he will assuredly perish," he pressed a ring into her hand and added: "This is a magic ring that will give you anything you wish. When you desire to return to your own disinterested beast, put on the ring and utter your wish. Instantly you will be by my side."

Beauty-Mabel took the ring, and it was the ring.

The curtains closed to warm applause from two pairs of hands.

The next scene went splendidly. The sisters were almost too natural in their disagreeableness, and Beauty's annoyance when they splashed her Princess's dress with real soap and water was considered a miracle of good acting. Even the merchant rose to something more than mere pillows, and the curtain fell on his pathetic assurance that in the absence of his dear Beauty he was wasting away to a shadow. And again two pairs of hands applauded.

"Here, Mabel, catch hold," Gerald appealed from under the weight of a towel-horse,* the tea-urn, the tea-tray, and the green baize apron of the boot boy, which together with four red geraniums from the landing, the pampas-grass from the drawing-room fireplace, and the india rubber plants from the drawing-room window were to represent the fountains and garden of the last act. The applause had died away.

"I wish," said Mabel, taking on herself the weight of the tea-urn, "I wish those creatures we made were alive. We should get something like applause then."

"I'm jolly glad they aren't," said Gerald, arranging the baize and the towel-horse. Brutes! It makes me feel quite silly when I catch their paper eyes."

---

* Wooden frame on which towels are hung.

The curtains were drawn back. There lay the hearthrug-coated beast, in flat abandonment among the tropic beauties of the garden, the pampas-grass shrubbery, the india rubber plant bushes, the geranium-trees and the urn fountain. Beauty was ready to make her great entry in all the thrilling splendour of despair. And then suddenly it all happened.

Mademoiselle began it: she applauded the garden scene—with hurried little clappings of her quick French hands. Eliza's fat red palms followed heavily, and then—someone else was clapping, six or seven people, and their clapping made a dull padded sound. Nine faces instead of two were turned towards the stage, and seven out of the nine were painted, pointed paper faces. And every hand and every face was alive. The applause grew louder as Mabel glided forward, and as she paused and looked at the audience her unstudied pose of horror and amazement drew forth applause louder still; but it was not loud enough to drown the shrieks of Mademoiselle and Eliza as they rushed from the room, knocking chairs over and crushing each other in the doorway. Two distant doors banged, Mademoiselle's door and Eliza's door.

"Curtain! curtain! quick!" cried Beauty-Mabel, in a voice that wasn't Mabel's or the Beauty's. "Jerry—those things *have* come alive. Oh, whatever *shall* we do?"

Gerald in his hearthrugs leaped to his feet. Again that flat padded applause marked the swish of cloths on clothes-line as Jimmy and Kathleen drew the curtains.

"What's up?" they asked as they drew.

"You've done it this time!" said Gerald to the pink, perspiring Mabel. "Oh, bother these strings!"

"Can't you burst them? I've done it?" retorted Mabel. "I like that!"

"More than I do," said Gerald.

"Oh, it's all right," said Mabel. "Come on. We must go and pull the things to pieces—then they *can't* go on being alive."

"It's your fault, anyhow," said Gerald with every possible absence of gallantry. "Don't you see? It's turned into a wishing ring. I knew something different was going to happen. Get my knife out of my pocket—this string's in a knot. Jimmy, Cathy, those Ugly-Wuglies have come alive—because Mabel wished it. Cut out and pull them to pieces."

A limp hand gesticulated

Jimmy and Cathy peeped through the curtain and recoiled with white faces and staring eyes. "Not me!" was the brief rejoinder of Jimmy. Cathy said, "Not much!" And she meant it, anyone could see that.

And now, as Gerald, almost free of the hearthrugs, broke his thumb-nail on the stiffest blade of his knife, a thick rustling and a sharp, heavy stumping sounded beyond the curtain.

"They're going out!" screamed Kathleen—"*walking* out—on their umbrella and broomstick legs. You can't stop them, Jerry, they're too awful!"

"Everybody in the town'll be insane by tomorrow night if we don't stop them," cried Gerald. "Here, give me the ring—I'll unwish them."

He caught the ring from the unresisting Mabel, cried, "I wish the Uglies weren't alive," and tore through the door. He saw, in fancy, Mabel's wish undone, and the empty hall strewed with limp bolsters,* hats, umbrellas, coats and gloves, prone abject properties from which the brief life had gone out for ever. But the hall was crowded with live things, strange things—all horribly short as broom sticks and umbrellas are short. A limp hand gesticulated. A pointed white face with red cheeks looked up at him, and wide red lips said something, he could not tell what. The voice reminded him of the old beggar down by the bridge who had no roof to his mouth. These creatures had no roofs to their mouths, of course—they had no—

"Aa oo ré o me me oo a oo ho el?" said the voice again. And it had said it four times before Gerald could collect himself sufficiently to understand that this horror—alive, and most likely quite uncontrollable—was saying, with a dreadful calm, polite persistence:

"Can you recommend me to a good hotel?"

---

* Long stuffed pillows.

CHAPTER VII

"Can you recommend me to a good hotel?" The speaker had no inside to his head. Gerald had the best of reasons for knowing it. The speaker's coat had no shoulders inside it—only the cross-bar that a jacket is slung on by careful ladies. The hand raised in interrogation was not a hand at all; it was a glove lumpily stuffed with pocket-handkerchiefs; and the arm attached to it was only Kathleen's school umbrella. Yet the whole thing was alive, and was asking a definite, and for anybody else, anybody who really *was* a body, a reasonable question.

With a sensation of inward sinking, Gerald realized that now or never was the time for him to rise to the occasion. And at the thought he inwardly sank more deeply than before. It seemed impossible to rise in the very smallest degree.

"I beg your pardon" was absolutely the best he could do; and the painted, pointed paper face turned to him once more, and once more said:—

"Aa oo ré o me me oo a oo ho el?"

"You want a hotel?" Gerald repeated stupidly, "a *good* hotel?"

"A oo ho el," reiterated the painted lips.

"I'm awfully sorry," Gerald went on—one can always be polite, of course, whatever happens, and politeness came naturally to him—"but all our hotels shut so early—about eight, I think."

"Och em er," said the Ugly-Wugly. Gerald even now does not understand how that practical joke—hastily wrought of hat, overcoat, paper face and limp hands—could have managed, by just being alive, to become perfectly respectable, apparently about fifty years old, and obviously well known and respected in his own suburb—the kind of man who travels first class and smokes expensive cigars. Gerald knew this time, without need of repetition, that the Ugly-Wugly had said:

"Knock 'em up."

"You can't," Gerald explained; "they're all stone deaf—every single person who keeps a hotel in this town. It's—" he wildly plunged—"it's a County Council law. Only deaf people are allowed to keep hotels. It's because of the hops in the beer," he found himself adding; "you know, hops are so good for ear-ache."

"I o wy ollo oo," said the respectable Ugly-Wugly; and Gerald was not surprised to find that the thing did "not quite follow him."

"It is a little difficult at first," he said. The other Ugly-Wuglies were crowding round. The lady in the poke bonnet said—Gerald found he was getting quite clever at understanding the conversation of those who had no roofs to their mouths:

"If not a hotel, a lodging."

"My lodging is on the cold ground," sang itself unbidden and unavailing in Gerald's ear. Yet stay—was it unavailing?

"I do know a lodging," he said slowly, "but—" The tallest of the Ugly-Wuglies pushed forward. He was dressed in the old brown overcoat and top-hat which always hung on the school hat-stand to discourage possible burglars by deluding them into the idea that there was a gentleman-of-the-house, and that he was at home. He had an air at once more sporting and less reserved than that of the first speaker, and anyone could see that he was not quite a gentleman.

"Wa I wo oo oh," he began, but the lady Ugly-Wugly in the flower-wreathed hat interrupted him. She spoke more distinctly than the others, owing, as Gerald found afterwards, to the fact that her mouth had been drawn *open*, and the flap cut from the aperture had been folded back—so that she really had something like a roof to her mouth, though it was only a paper one.

"What I want to know," Gerald understood her to say, "is where are the carriages we ordered?"

"I don't know," said Gerald, "but I'll find out. But we ought to be moving," he added; "you see, the performance is over, and they want to shut up the house and put the lights out. Let's be moving."

"Eh—ech e oo-ig," repeated the respectable Ugly-Wugly, and stepped towards the front door.

"Oo um oo," said the flower-wreathed one; and Gerald assures me that her vermilion lips stretched in a smile.

"I shall be delighted," said Gerald with earnest courtesy, "to do anything, of course. Things do happen so awkwardly when you least expect it. I could go with you, and get you a lodging, if you'd only wait a few moments in the—in the yard. It's quite a superior sort of yard," he went on, as a wave of surprised disdain passed over their white paper faces—"not a common yard, you know; the pump," he added madly, "has just been painted green all over, and the dustbin is enamelled iron."

The Ugly-Wuglies turned to each other in consultation, and Gerald gathered that the greenness of the pump and the enamelled character of the dustbin made, in their opinion, all the difference.

"I'm awfully sorry," he urged eagerly, "to have to ask you to wait, but you see I've got an uncle who's quite mad, and I have to give him his gruel at half-past nine. He won't feed out of any hand but mine." Gerald did not mind what he said. The only people one is allowed to tell lies to are the Ugly-Wuglies; they are all clothes and have no insides, because they are not human beings, but only a sort of very real visions, and therefore cannot be really deceived, though they may seem to be.

Through the back door that has the blue, yellow, red, and green glass in it, down the iron steps into the yard, Gerald led the way, and the Ugly-Wuglies trooped after him. Some of them had boots, but the ones whose feet were only broomsticks or umbrellas found the open-work iron stairs very awkward.

"If you wouldn't mind," said Gerald, "just waiting under the balcony? My uncle is so very mad. If he were to see—see any strangers—I mean, even aristocratic ones—I couldn't answer for the consequences."

"Perhaps," said the flower-hatted lady nervously, "it would be better for us to try and find a lodging ourselves?"

"I wouldn't advise you to," said Gerald as grimly as he knew how; "the police here arrest all strangers. It's the new law the Liberals have just made," he added convincingly, "and you'd get the sort of lodging you wouldn't care for—I couldn't bear to think of you in a prison dungeon," he added tenderly.

"I ah wi oo er papers," said the respectable Ugly-Wugly, and added something that sounded like "disgraceful state of things."

However, they ranged themselves under the iron balcony. Gerald gave one last look at them and wondered, in his secret heart, why he was not frightened, though in his outside mind he was congratulating himself on his bravery. For the things did look rather horrid. In that light it was hard to believe that they were really only clothes and pillows and sticks—with no insides. As he went up the steps he heard them talking among themselves—in that strange language of theirs, all oo's and ah's; and he thought he distinguished the voice of the respectable Ugly-Wugly saying, "Most gentlemanly lad," and the wreathed-hatted lady answering warmly: "Yes, indeed."

The coloured-glass door closed behind him. Behind him was the yard, peopled by seven impossible creatures. Before him lay the silent house, peopled, as he knew very well, by five human beings as frightened as human beings could be. You think, perhaps, that Ugly-Wuglies are nothing to be frightened of. That's only because you have never seen one come alive. You must make one—any old suit of your father's, and a hat that he isn't wearing, a bolster or two, a painted paper face, a few sticks, and a pair of boots will do the trick; get your father to lend you a wishing ring, give it back to him when it has done its work, and see how you feel then.

Of course the reason why Gerald was not afraid was that he had the ring; and, as you have seen, the wearer of that is not frightened by *anything* unless he touches that thing. But Gerald knew well enough how the others must be feeling. That was why he stopped for a moment in the hall to try and imagine what would have been most soothing to him if he had been as terrified as he knew they were.

"Cathy! I say! What ho, Jimmy! Mabel ahoy!" he cried in a loud, cheerful voice that sounded very unreal to himself.

The dining-room door opened a cautious inch.

"I say—such larks!" Gerald went on, shoving gently at the door with his shoulder. "Look out! what are you keeping the door shut for?"

"Are you—alone?" asked Kathleen in hushed, breathless tones.

"Yes, of course. Don't be a duffer!"

The door opened, revealing three scared faces and the disarranged chairs where that odd audience had sat.

"Where are they? Have you unwished them? We heard them talking. Horrible!"

"They're in the yard," said Gerald with the best imitation of joyous excitement that he could manage. "It is such fun! They're just like real people, quite kind and jolly. It's the most ripping lark. Don't let on to Mademoiselle and Eliza. I'll square them. Then Kathleen and Jimmy must go to bed, and I'll see Mabel home, and as soon as we get outside I must find some sort of lodging for the Ugly-Wuglies—they *are* such fun though. I *do* wish you could all go with me."

"Fun?" echoed Kathleen dismally and doubting.

"Perfectly killing," Gerald asserted resolutely. "Now, you just listen to what I say to Mademoiselle and Eliza, and back me up for all you're worth."

"But," said Mabel, "you can't mean that you're going to leave me alone directly we get out, and go off with those horrible creatures. They look like fiends."

"You wait till you've seen them close," Gerald advised. "Why, they're just *ordinary*—the first thing one of them did was to ask me to recommend it to a good hotel! I couldn't understand it at first, because it has no roof to its mouth, of course."

It was a mistake to say that, Gerald knew it at once.

Mabel and Kathleen were holding hands in a way that plainly showed how a few moments ago they had been clinging to each other in an agony of terror. Now they clung again. And Jimmy, who was sitting on the edge of what had been the stage, kicking his boots against the pink counterpane, shuddered visibly.

"It doesn't *matter*," Gerald explained—"about the roofs, I mean; you soon get to understand. I heard them say I was a gentlemanly lad as I was coming away. They wouldn't have cared to notice a little thing like that if they'd been fiends, you know."

"It doesn't matter how gentlemanly they think you; if you don't see me home you *aren't*, that's all. Are you going to?" Mabel demanded.

"Of course I am. We shall have no end of a lark. Now for Mademoiselle."

He had put on his coat as he spoke and now ran up the stairs. The others, herding in the hall, could hear his light-hearted there's-nothing-unusual-the-matter-whatever-did-you-bolt-like-that-for knock at Mademoiselle's door, the reassuring "It's only me—Gerald, you know," the pause, the opening of the door, and the low-voiced parley that followed; then Mademoiselle and Gerald at Eliza's door, voices of reassurance; Eliza's terror, bluntly voluble, tactfully soothed.

"Wonder what lies he's telling them," Jimmy grumbled.

"Oh! not *lies*," said Mabel; "he's only telling them as much of the truth as it's good for them to know."

"I wonder what lies he's telling them"

"If you'd been a man," said Jimmy witheringly, "you'd have been a beastly Jesuit, and hid up chimneys."

"If I were only just a boy," Mabel retorted, "I shouldn't be scared out of my life by a pack of old coats."

"I'm *so* sorry you were frightened," Gerald's honeyed tones floated down the staircase; "we didn't think about you being frightened. And it *was* a good trick, wasn't it?"

"There!" whispered Jimmy, "he's been telling her it was a trick of ours."

"Well, so it was," said Mabel stoutly.

"It was indeed a wonderful trick," said Mademoiselle; "and how did you move the mannikins?"

"Oh, we've often done it—with strings, you know," Gerald explained.

"That's true, too," Kathleen whispered.

"Let us see you do once again this trick so remarkable," said Mademoiselle, arriving at the bottom-stair mat.

"Oh, I've cleared them all out," said Gerald. ("So he has," from Kathleen aside to Jimmy.) "We were so sorry you were startled; we thought you wouldn't like to see them again."

"Then," said Mademoiselle brightly, as she peeped into the untidy dining-room and saw that the figures had indeed vanished, "if we supped and discoursed of your beautiful piece of theatre?"

Gerald explained fully how much his brother and sister would enjoy this. As for him—Mademoiselle would see that it was his duty to escort Mabel home, and kind as it was of Mademoiselle to ask her to stay the night, it could not be, on account of the frenzied and anxious affection of Mabel's aunt. And it was useless to suggest that Eliza should see Mabel home, because Eliza was nervous at night unless accompanied by her gentleman friend.

So Mabel was hatted with her own hat and cloaked with a cloak that was not hers; and she and Gerald went out by the front door, amid kind last words and appointments for the morrow.

The moment that front door was shut Gerald caught Mabel by the arm and led her briskly to the corner of the side street which led to the yard. Just round the corner he stopped.

"Now," he said, "what I want to know is—are you an idiot or aren't you?"

"Idiot yourself!" said Mabel, but mechanically, for she saw that he was in earnest.

"Because I'm not frightened of the Ugly-Wuglies. They're as harmless as tame rabbits. But an idiot might be frightened, and give the whole show away. If you're an idiot, say so, and I'll go back and tell them you're afraid to walk home, and that I'll go and let your aunt know you're stopping."

"I'm not an idiot," said Mabel; "and," she added, glaring round her with the wild gaze of the truly terror-stricken, "I'm not afraid of anything."

"I'm going to let you share my difficulties and dangers," said Gerald; "at least, I'm inclined to let you. I wouldn't do as much for my own brother, I can tell you. And if you queer my pitch I'll never speak to you again or let the others either."

"You're a beast, that's what you are! I don't need to be threatened to make me brave. I am."

"Mabel," said Gerald, in low, thrilling tones, for he saw that the time had come to sound another note, "I know you're brave. I believe in you. That's why I've arranged it like this. I'm certain you've got the heart of a lion under that black-and-white exterior. Can I trust you? To the death?"

Mabel felt that to say anything but "Yes" was to throw away a priceless reputation for courage. So "Yes" was what she said.

"Then wait here. You're close to the lamp. And when you see me coming with them remember they're as harmless as serpents—I mean doves. Talk to them just like you would to anyone else. See?"

He turned to leave her, but stopped at her natural question:

"What hotel did you say you were going to take them to?"

"Oh, Jimminy!" the harassed Gerald caught at his hair with both hands. "There! you see, Mabel, you're a help already;" he had, even at that moment, some tact left. "I clean forgot! I meant to ask you—isn't there any lodge or anything in the Castle grounds where I could put them for the night! The charm will break, you know, some time, like being invisible did, and they'll just be a pack of coats and things that we can easily carry home any day. Is there a lodge or anything?"

"There's a secret passage," Mabel began—but at the moment the yard-door opened and an Ugly-Wugly put out its head and looked anxiously down the street.

"Righto!"—Gerald ran to meet it. It was all Mabel could do not to run in an opposite direction with an opposite motive. It was all she could do, but she did it, and was proud of herself as long as ever she remembered that night.

And now, with all the silent precaution necessitated by the near presence of an extremely insane uncle, the Ugly-Wuglies, a grisly band, trooped out of the yard door.

"Walk on your toes, dear," the bonneted Ugly-Wugly whispered to the one with a wreath; and even at that thrilling crisis Gerald wondered how she could, since the toes of one foot were but the end of a golf club and of the other the end of a hockey-stick.

Mabel felt that there was no shame in retreating to the lamp-post at the street corner, but, once there, she made herself halt—and no one but Mabel will ever know how much making that took. Think of it—to stand there, firm and quiet, and wait for those hollow, unbelievable things to come up to her, clattering on the pavement with their stumpy feet or borne along noiselessly, as in the case of the flower-hatted lady, by a skirt that touched the ground, and had, Mabel knew very well, nothing at all inside it.

She stood very still; the insides of her hands grew cold and damp, but still she stood, saying over and over again: "They're not true—they can't be true. It's only a dream—they aren't really true. They can't be." And then Gerald was there, and all the Ugly-Wuglies crowding round, and Gerald saying:

"This is one of our friends, Mabel—the Princess in the play, you know. Be a man!" he added in a whisper for her ear alone.

Mabel, all her nerves stretched tight as banjo strings, had an awful instant of not knowing whether she would be able to be a man or whether she would be merely a shrieking and running little mad girl. For the respectable Ugly-Wugly shook her limply by the hand ("He *can't* be true," she told herself), and the rose-wreathed one took her arm with a soft-padded glove at the end of an umbrella arm, and said:

"You dear, clever little thing! *Do* walk with me!" in a gushing, girlish way, and in speech almost wholly lacking in consonants.

Then they all walked up the High Street as if, as Gerald said, they were anybody else.

It was a strange procession, but Liddlesby goes early to bed, and the Liddlesby police, in common with those of most other places, wear boots that one can hear a mile off. If such boots had been heard, Gerald would have had time to turn back and head them off. He felt now that he could not resist a flush of pride in Mabel's courage as he heard her polite rejoinders to the still more polite remarks of the amiable Ugly-Wuglies. He did not know how near she was to the scream that would throw away the whole thing and bring the police and the residents out to the ruin of everybody.

They met no one, except one man, who murmured, "Guy

It was a strange procession

Fawkes, swelp me!" and crossed the road hurriedly;[6] and when, next day, he told what he had seen, his wife disbelieved him, and also said it was a judgement on him, which was unreasonable.

Mabel felt as though she were taking part in a very completely arranged nightmare, but Gerald was in it too, Gerald, who had asked if she was an idiot. Well, she wasn't. But she soon would be, she felt. Yet she went on answering the courteous vowel-talk of these impossible people. She had often heard her aunt speak of impossible people. Well, now she knew what they were like.

Summer twilight had melted into summer moonlight. The shadows of the Ugly-Wuglies on the white road were much more horrible than their more solid selves. Mabel wished it had been a dark night, and then corrected the wish with a hasty shudder.

Gerald, submitting to a searching interrogatory from the tall-hatted Ugly-Wugly as to his schools, his sports, pastimes, and ambitions, wondered how long the spell would last. The ring seemed to work in sevens. Would these things have seven hours' life—or fourteen—or twenty-one? His mind lost itself in the intricacies of the seven-times table (a teaser at the best of times) and only found itself with a shock when the procession found itself at the gates of the Castle grounds.

Locked—of course.

"You see," be explained, as the Ugly-Wuglies vainly shook the iron gates with incredible hands; "it's so very late. There is another way. But you have to climb through a hole."

"The ladies," the respectable Ugly-Wugly began objecting; but the ladies with one voice affirmed that they loved adventures. "So frightfully thrilling," added the one who wore roses.

So they went round by the road, and coming to the hole—it was a little difficult to find in the moonlight, which always disguises the most familiar things—Gerald went first with the bicycle lantern which he had snatched as his pilgrims came out of the yard; the shrinking Mabel followed, and then the Ugly-Wuglies, with hollow rattlings of their wooden limbs against the stone, crept through, and with strange vowel-sounds of general amazement, manly courage, and feminine nervousness, followed the light along the passage through the fern-hung cutting and under the arch.

When they emerged on the moonlit enchantment of the Italian garden a quite intelligible "Oh!" of surprised admiration broke from more than one painted paper lip; and the respectable Ugly-Wugly was understood to say that it must be quite a show-place—by George, sir! yes.

Those marble terraces and artfully serpentining gravel walks surely never had echoed to steps so strange. No shadows so wildly unbelievable had, for all its enchantments, ever fallen on those smooth, grey, dewy lawns. Gerald was thinking this, or something like it (what he really thought was, "I bet there never was such ado as this, even here!"), when he saw the statue of Hermes leap from its pedestal and run towards him and his company with all the lively curiosity of a street boy eager to be in at a street fight. He saw, too, that he was the only one who perceived that white advancing presence. And he knew that it was the ring that let him see what by others could not be seen. He slipped it from his finger. Yes; Hermes was on his pedestal, still as the snow man you make in the Christmas holidays. He put the ring on again, and there was Hermes, circling round the group and gazing deep in each unconscious Ugly-Wugly face.

"This seems a very superior hotel," the tall-hatted Ugly-Wugly was saying; "the grounds are laid out with what you might call taste."

"We should have to go in by the back door," said Mabel suddenly. "The front door's locked at half-past nine."

A short, stout Ugly-Wugly in a yellow and blue cricket cap, who had hardly spoken, muttered something about an escapade, and about feeling quite young again.

And now they had skirted the marble-edged pool where the gold fish swam and glimmered, and where the great prehistoric beast had come down to bathe and drink. The water flashed white diamonds in the moonlight, and Gerald alone of them all saw that the scaly-plated vast lizard was even now rolling and wallowing there among the lily pads.

They hastened up the steps of the Temple of Flora. The back of it, where no elegant arch opened to the air, was against one of those sheer hills, almost cliffs, that diversified the landscape of that garden. Mabel passed behind the statue of the goddess, fumbled a little, and then Gerald's lantern, flashing like a searchlight, showed a very high and very narrow doorway: the stone that was the door, and that had closed it, revolved slowly under the touch of Mabel's fingers.

"This way," she said, and panted a little. The back of her neck felt cold and goose-fleshy.

"You lead the way, my lad, with the lantern," said the suburban Ugly-Wugly in his bluff, agreeable way.

"I—I must stay behind to close the door," said Gerald.

"The Princess can do that. We'll help her," said the wreathed one with effusion; and Gerald thought her horribly officious.

He insisted gently that he would be the one responsible for the safe shutting of that door.

"You wouldn't like me to get into trouble, I'm sure," he urged; and the Ugly-Wuglies, for the last time kind and reasonable, agreed that this, of all things, they would most deplore.

"You take it," Gerald urged, pressing the bicycle lamp on the elderly Ugly-Wugly; "you're the natural leader. Go straight ahead. Are there any steps?" he asked Mabel in a whisper.

"Not for ever so long," she whispered back. "It goes on for ages, and then twists round."

"Whispering," said the smallest Ugly-Wugly suddenly, "ain't manners."

"He hasn't any, anyhow," whispered the lady Ugly-Wugly; "don't mind him—quite a self-made man," and squeezed Mabel's arm with horrible confidential flabbiness.

The respectable Ugly-Wugly leading with the lamp, the others following trustfully, one and all disappeared into that narrow doorway; and Gerald and Mabel standing without, hardly daring to breathe lest a breath should retard the procession, almost sobbed with relief. Prematurely, as it turned out. For suddenly there was a rush and a scuffle inside the passage, and as they strove to close the door the Ugly-Wuglies fiercely pressed to open it again. Whether they saw something in the dark passage that alarmed them, whether they took it into their empty heads that this could not be the back way to any really respectable hotel, or whether a convincing sudden instinct warned them that they were being tricked, Mabel and Gerald never knew. But they knew that the Ugly-Wuglies were no longer friendly and commonplace, that a fierce change had come over them. Cries of "No, No!" "We won't go on!" "Make him lead!" broke the dreamy stillness of the perfect night. There were screams from ladies' voices, the hoarse, determined shouts of strong Ugly-Wuglies roused to resistance, and, worse than all, the steady pushing open of that narrow stone door that had almost closed upon the ghastly crew.

Through the chink of it they could be seen, a writhing black crowd against the light of the bicycle lamp; a padded hand reached round the door; stick-boned arms stretched out angrily towards the world that that door, if it closed, would shut them off from for ever. And the tone of their consonantless speech was no longer conciliatory and ordinary; it was threatening, full of the menace of unbearable horrors.

The padded hand fell on Gerald's arm, and instantly all the terrors that he had, so far, only known in imagination became real to him, and he saw, in the sort of flash that shows drowning people their past lives, what it was that he had asked of Mabel, and that she had given.

"Push, push for your life!" he cried, and setting his heel against the pedestal of Flora, pushed manfully.

"I can't any more—oh, I can't!" moaned Mabel, and tried to use her heel likewise, but her legs were too short.

"They mustn't get out, they mustn't!" Gerald panted.

"You'll know it when we do," came from inside the door in tones which fury and mouth-rooflessness would have made unintelligible to any ears but those sharpened by the wild fear of that unspeakable moment.

"What's up, there?" cried suddenly a new voice—a voice with all its consonants comforting, clean-cut, and ringing, and abruptly a new shadow fell on the marble floor of Flora's temple.

"Come and help push!" Gerald's voice only just reached the newcomer. "If they get out they'll kill us all."

A strong, velveteen-covered shoulder pushed suddenly between the shoulders of Gerald and Mabel; a stout man's heel sought the aid of the goddess's pedestal; the heavy, narrow door yielded slowly, it closed, its spring clicked, and the furious, surging, threatening mass of Ugly-Wuglies was shut in, and Gerald and Mabel—oh, incredible relief!—were shut out. Mabel threw herself on the marble floor, sobbing slow, heavy sobs of achievement and exhaustion. If I had been there I should have looked the other way, so as not to see whether Gerald yielded himself to the same abandonment.

The newcomer—he appeared to be a gamekeeper, Gerald decided later—looked down on—well, certainly on Mabel, and said:

"Come on, don't be a little duffer." (He may have said, "a couple of little duffers.") "Who is it, and what's it all about?"

"I can't possibly tell you," Gerald panted.

"We shall have to see about that, shan't we," said the newcomer amiably. "Come out into the moonlight and let's review the situation."

Gerald, even in that topsy-turvy state of his world, found time to think that a gamekeeper who used such words as that had most likely a romantic past. But at the same time he saw that such a man would be far less easy to "square" with an unconvincing tale than Eliza, or Johnson, or even Mademoiselle. In fact, he seemed, with the only tale that they had to tell, practically unsquarable.

Gerald got up—if he was not up already, or still up—and pulled at the limp and now hot hand of the sobbing Mabel; and as he did so the unsquarable one took his hand, and thus led both children out from under the shadow of Flora's dome into the bright white moonlight that carpeted Flora's steps. Here he sat down, a child on each side of him, drew a hand of each through his velveteen arm, pressed them to his velveteen sides in a friendly, reassuring way, and said: "Now then! Go ahead!"

Mabel merely sobbed. We must excuse her. She had been very brave, and I have no doubt that all heroines, from Joan of Arc to Grace Darling, have had their sobbing moments.[7]

But Gerald said: "It's no use. If I made up a story you'd see through it."

"That's a compliment to my discernment, anyhow," said the stranger. "What price telling me the truth?"

"If we told you the truth," said Gerald, "you wouldn't believe it."

"Try me," said the velveteen one. He was clean-shaven, and had large eyes that sparkled when the moonlight touched them.

"I *can't*," said Gerald, and it was plain that he spoke the truth. "You'd either think we were mad, and get us shut up, or else—oh, it's no good. Thank you for helping us, and do let us go home."

"I wonder," said the stranger musingly, "whether you have any imagination."

"Considering that we invented them," Gerald hotly began, and stopped with late prudence.

"If by 'them' you mean the people whom I helped you to imprison in yonder tomb," said the Stranger, loosing Mabel's hand to put his arm round her, "remember that I saw and heard them. And with all respect to your imagination, I doubt whether any invention of yours would be quite so convincing."

Gerald put his elbows on his knees and his chin in his hands.

"Collect yourself," said the one in velveteen; "and while you are collecting, let me just put the thing from my point of view. I think you hardly realize my position. I come down from London to take care of a big estate."

"I thought you were a gamekeeper," put in Gerald.

Mabel put her head on the stranger's shoulder. "Hero in disguise, then, I know," she sniffed.

"Not at all," said he; "bailiff would be nearer the mark. On the very first evening I go out to take the moonlit air, and approaching a white building, hear sounds of an agitated scuffle, accompanied by frenzied appeals for assistance. Carried away by the enthusiasm of the moment, I *do* assist and shut up goodness knows who behind a stone door. Now, is it unreasonable that I should ask who it is that I've shut up—helped to shut up, I mean, and who it is that I've assisted?"

"It's reasonable enough," Gerald admitted.

"Well then," said the stranger.

"Well then," said Gerald, "the fact is—No," he added after a pause, "the fact is, I simply can't tell you."

"Then I must ask the other side," said Velveteens. "Let me go—I'll undo that door and find out for myself."

"Tell him," said Mabel, speaking for the first time. "Never mind if he believes or not. We can't have them let out."

"Very well," said Gerald, "I'll tell him. Now look here, Mr. Bailiff, will you promise us on an English gentleman's word of honour—because, of course, I can see you're *that*, bailiff or not—will you promise that you won't tell any one what we tell you and that you won't have us put in a lunatic asylum, however mad we sound?"

"Yes," said the stranger, "I think I can promise that. But if you've been having a sham fight or anything and shoved the other side into that hole, don't you think you'd better let them out? They'll be most awfully frightened, you know. After all, I suppose they are only children."

"Wait till you hear," Gerald answered. "They're not children—not much! Shall I just tell about them or begin at the beginning?"

"The beginning, of course," said the stranger.

Mabel lifted her head from his velveteen shoulder and said, "Let me begin, then. I found a ring, and I said it would make me invisible. I said it in play. And it did. I was invisible twenty-one hours. Never mind where I got the ring. Now, Gerald, you go on."

Gerald went on; for quite a long time he went on, for the story was a splendid one to tell.

"And so," he ended, "we got them in there; and when seven hours are over, or fourteen, or twenty-one, or something with a seven in it, they'll just be old coats again. They came alive at half-past nine. I think they'll stop being it in seven hours—that's half-past four. Now will you let us go home?"

"I'll see you home," said the stranger in a quite new tone of exasperating gentleness. "Come—let's be going."

"You don't believe us," said Gerald. "Of course you don't. Nobody could. But I could make you believe if I chose."

All three stood up, and the stranger stared in Gerald's eyes till Gerald answered his thought.

"No, I don't look mad, do I?"

"No, you aren't. But, come, you're an extraordinarily sensible boy; don't you think you may be sickening for a fever or something?"

"And Cathy and Jimmy and Mademoiselle and Eliza, and the man who said 'Guy Fawkes, swelp me!' and you, you saw them move—you heard them call out. Are you sickening for anything?"

"No—or at least not for anything but information. Come, and I'll see you home."

"Mabel lives at the Towers," said Gerald, as the stranger turned into the broad drive that leads to the big gate.

"No relation to Lord Yalding," said Mabel hastily—"housekeeper's niece." She was holding on to his hand all the way. At the servants' entrance she put up her face to be kissed, and went in.

"Poor little thing!" said the bailiff, as they went down the drive towards the gate.

He went with Gerald to the door of the school.

"Look here," said Gerald at parting. "I know what you're going to do. You're going to try to undo that door."

"Discerning!" said the stranger.

"Well—don't. Or, any way, wait till daylight and let us be there. We can get there by ten."

"All right—I'll meet you there by ten," answered the stranger. "By George! you're the rummest kids I ever met."

"We are rum," Gerald owned, "but so would you be if—Good-night."

As the four children went over the smooth lawn towards Flora's Temple they talked, as they had talked all the morning, about the adventures of last night and of Mabel's bravery. It was not ten, but half-past twelve; for Eliza, backed by Mademoiselle, had insisted on their "clearing up," and clearing up very thoroughly, the "litter" of last night.

"You're a Victoria Cross heroine,* dear, said Cathy warmly. "You ought to have a statue put up to you."

"It would come alive if you put it here," said Gerald grimly.

"I shouldn't have been afraid," said Jimmy.

"By daylight," Gerald assured him, "everything looks so jolly different."

"I do hope he'll be there," Mabel said; "he *was* such a dear, Cathy—a perfect bailiff, with the soul of a gentleman."

"He isn't there, though," said Jimmy. "I believe you just dreamed him, like you did the statues coming alive."

They went up the marble steps in the sunshine, and it was difficult to believe that this was the place where only in last night's moonlight fear had laid such cold hands on the hearts of Mabel and Gerald.

"Shall we open the door," suggested Kathleen, "and begin to carry home the coats?"

"Let's listen first," said Gerald; "perhaps they aren't only coats yet."

They laid ears to the hinges of the stone door, behind which last night the Ugly-Wuglies had shrieked and threatened. All was still as the sweet morning itself. It was as they turned away that they saw the man they had come to meet. He was on the other side of Flora's pedestal. But he was not standing up. He lay there, quite still, on his back, his arms flung wide.

"Oh, look!" cried Cathy, and pointed. His face was a queer greenish colour, and on his forehead there was a cut; its edges were blue, and a little blood had trickled from it on to the white of the marble.

---

* Recipient of the highest award for gallantry granted to a member of the British and Commonwealth armed forces.

A painted pointed paper face peered out

At the same time Mabel pointed too—but she did not cry out as Cathy had done. And what she pointed at was a big glossy-leaved rhododendron bush, from which a painted pointed paper face peered out—very white, very red, in the sunlight—and, as the children gazed, shrank back into the cover of the shining leaves.

CHAPTER VIII

It was but too plain. The unfortunate bailiff must have opened the door before the spell had faded, while yet the Ugly-Wuglies were something more than mere coats and hats and sticks. They had rushed out upon him, and had done this. He lay there insensible—was it a golf-club or a hockey-stick that had made that horrible cut on his forehead? Gerald wondered. The girls had rushed to the sufferer; already his head was in Mabel's lap. Kathleen had tried to get it on to hers, but Mabel was too quick for her.

Jimmy and Gerald both knew what was the first thing needed by the unconscious, even before Mabel impatiently said: "Water! water!"

"What in?" Jimmy asked, looking doubtfully at his hands, and then down the green slope to the marble-bordered pool where the water-lilies were.

"Your hat—anything," said Mabel.

The two boys turned away.

"Suppose they come after us," said Jimmy.

"*What* come after us?" Gerald snapped rather than asked.

"The Ugly-Wuglies," Jimmy whispered.

"Who's afraid?" Gerald inquired.

But he looked to right and left very carefully, and chose the way that did not lead near the bushes. He scooped water up in his straw hat and returned to Flora's Temple, carrying it carefully in both hands. When he saw how quickly it ran through the straw he pulled his handkerchief from his breast pocket with his teeth and dropped it into the hat. It was with this that the girls wiped the blood from the bailiffs brow.

"We ought to have smelling salts," said Kathleen, half in tears. "I know we ought."

"They would be good," Mabel owned.

"Hasn't your aunt any?"

"Yes, but—"

"Don't be a coward," said Gerald; "think of last night. *They* wouldn't hurt you. He must have insulted them or something. Look here, you run. We'll see that nothing runs after you."

There was no choice but to relinquish the head of the interesting invalid to Kathleen; so Mabel did it, cast one glaring glance round the rhododendron-bordered slope, and fled towards the castle.

The other three bent over the still unconscious bailiff.

"He's not dead, is he?" asked Jimmy anxiously.

"No," Kathleen reassured him, "his heart's beating. Mabel and I felt it in his wrist, where doctors do. How frightfully good-looking he is!"

"Not so dusty," Gerald admitted.

"I never know what you mean by good-looking," said Jimmy, and suddenly a shadow fell on the marble beside them and a fourth voice spoke—not Mabel's; her hurrying figure, though still in sight, was far away.

"Quite a personable young man," it said.

The children looked up—into the face of the eldest of the Ugly-Wuglies, the respectable one. Jimmy and Kathleen screamed. I am sorry, but they did.

"Hush!" said Gerald savagely: he was still wearing the ring. "Hold your tongues! I'll get him away," he added in a whisper.

"Very sad affair this," said the respectable Ugly-Wugly. He spoke with a curious accent; there was something odd about his r's, and his m's and n's were those of a person labouring under an almost intolerable cold in the head. But it was not the dreadful "oo" and "ah" voice of the night before. Kathleen and Jimmy stooped over the bailiff. Even that prostrate form, being human, seemed some little protection. But Gerald, strong in the fearlessness that the ring gave to its wearer, looked full into the face of the Ugly-Wugly—and started. For though the face was almost the same as the face he had himself painted on the school drawing-paper, it was not the same. For it was no longer paper. It was a real face, and the hands, lean and almost transparent as they were, were real hands. As it moved a little to get a better view of the bailiff it was plain that it had legs, arms—live legs and arms, and a self-supporting backbone. It was alive indeed—with a vengeance.

"How did it happen?" Gerald asked with an effort at calmness—a successful effort.

"Most regrettable," said the Ugly-Wugly. "The others must have missed the way last night in the passage. They never found the hotel."

"Did *you*?" asked Gerald blankly.

"Of course," said the Ugly-Wugly. "Most respectable, exactly as you said. Then when I came away—I didn't come the front way because I wanted to revisit this sylvan scene by daylight, and the hotel people didn't seem to know how to direct me to it—I found the others all at this door, very angry. They'd been here all night, trying to get out. Then the door opened—this gentleman must have opened it—and before I could protect him, that underbred man in the high hat—you remember—"

Gerald remembered.

"Hit him on the head, and he fell where you see him. The others dispersed, and I myself was just going for assistance when I saw you."

Here Jimmy was discovered to be in tears and Kathleen white as any drawing-paper.

"What's the matter, my little man?" said the respectable Ugly-Wugly kindly. Jimmy passed instantly from tears to yells.

"Here, take the ring!" said Gerald in a furious whisper, and thrust it on to Jimmy's hot, damp, resisting finger. Jimmy's voice stopped short in the middle of a howl. And Gerald in a cold flash realized what it was that Mabel had gone through the night before. But it was daylight, and Gerald was not a coward.

"We must find the others," he said.

"I imagine," said the elderly Ugly-Wugly, "that they have gone to bathe. Their clothes are in the wood."

He pointed stiffly.

"You two go and see," said Gerald. "I'll go on dabbing this chap's head."

In the wood Jimmy, now fearless as any lion, discovered four heaps of clothing, with broomsticks, hockey-sticks, and masks complete, all that had gone to make up the gentlemen Ugly-Wuglies of the night before. On a stone seat well in the sun sat the two lady Ugly-Wuglies, and Kathleen approached them gingerly. Valour is easier in the sunshine than at night, as we all know. When she and Jimmy came close to the bench, they saw that the Ugly-Wuglies were only Ugly-Wuglies such as they had often made. There was no life in them. Jimmy shook them to pieces, and a sigh of relief burst from Kathleen.

Jimmy shook them to pieces

"The spell's broken, you see," she said; "and that old gentleman, he's real. He only happens to be like the Ugly-Wugly we made."

"He's got the coat that hung in the hall on, anyway," said Jimmy.

"No, it's only like it. Let's get back to the unconscious stranger."

They did, and Gerald begged the elderly Ugly-Wugly to retire among the bushes with Jimmy; "because," said he, "I think the poor bailiff's coming round, and it might upset him to see strangers—and Jimmy'll keep you company. He's the best one of us to go with you," he added hastily.

And this, since Jimmy had the ring, was certainly true.

So the two disappeared behind the rhododendrons. Mabel came back with the salts just as the bailiff opened his eyes.

"It's just like life," she said; "I might just as well not have gone. However——" She knelt down at once and held the bottle under the sufferer's nose till he sneezed and feebly pushed her hand away with the faint question:

"What's up now?"

"You've hurt your head," said Gerald. "Lie still."

"No—more—smelling-bottle," he said weakly, and lay.

Quite soon he sat up and looked round him. There was an anxious silence. Here was a grown-up who knew last night's secret, and none of the children were at all sure what the utmost rigour of the law might be in a case where people, no matter how young, made Ugly-Wuglies, and brought them to life—dangerous, fighting, angry life. What would he say—what would he do? He said: "What an odd thing! Have I been insensible long?"

"Hours," said Mabel earnestly.

"Not long," said Kathleen.

"We don't know. We found you like it," said Gerald.

"I'm all right now," said the bailiff, and his eye fell on the blood-stained handkerchief. "I say, I did give my head a bang. And you've been giving me first aid. Thank you most awfully. But it is rum."

"What's rum?" politeness obliged Gerald to ask.

"Well, I suppose it isn't really rum—I expect I saw you just before I fainted, or whatever it was—but I've dreamed the most extraordinary dream while I've been insensible and you were in it."

"Nothing but us?" asked Mabel breathlessly.

"Oh, lots of things—impossible things—but you were real enough."

Everyone breathed deeply in relief. It was indeed, as they agreed later, a lucky let-off.

"Are you sure you're all right?" they all asked, as he got on his feet.

"Perfectly, thank you." He glanced behind Flora's statue as he spoke. "Do you know, I dreamed there was a door there, but of course there isn't. I don't know how to thank you," he added, looking at them with what the girls called his beautiful, kind eyes; "it's lucky for me you came along. You come here whenever you like, you know," he added. "I give you the freedom of the place."

"You're the new bailiff, aren't you?" said Mabel.

"Yes. How did you know?" he asked quickly; but they did not tell him how they knew. Instead, they found out which way he was going, and went the other way after warm handshakes and hopes on both sides that they would meet again soon.

"I'll tell you what," said Gerald, as they watched the tall, broad figure of the bailiff grow smaller across the hot green of the grass slope, "have you got any idea of how we're going to spend the day? Because I have."

The others hadn't.

"We'll get rid of that Ugly-Wugly—oh, we'll find a way right enough—and directly we've done it we'll go home and seal up the ring in an envelope so that its teeth'll be drawn and it'll be powerless to have unforeseen larks with us. Then we'll get out on the roof, and have a quiet day—books and apples. I'm about fed up with adventures, so I tell you."

The others told him the same thing.

"Now, think," said he—"think as you never thought before—how to get rid of that Ugly-Wugly."

Everyone thought, but their brains were tired with anxiety and distress, and the thoughts they thought were, as Mabel said, not worth thinking, let alone saying.

"I suppose Jimmy's all right," said Kathleen anxiously.

"Oh, he's all right: he's got the ring," said Gerald.

"I hope he won't go wishing anything rotten," said Mabel, but Gerald urged her to shut up and let him think.

"I think I think best sitting down," he said, and sat; "and sometimes you can think best aloud. The Ugly-Wugly's real—don't make any mistake about that. And he got made real inside that passage. If we could get him back there he might get changed again, and then we could take the coats and things back."

"Isn't there any other way?" Kathleen asked; and Mabel, more candid, said bluntly: "I'm not going into that passage, so there!"

"Afraid! In broad daylight," Gerald sneered.

"It wouldn't be broad daylight in there," said Mabel, and Kathleen shivered.

"If we went to him and suddenly tore his coat off," said she—"he *is* only coats—he couldn't go on being real then."

"*Couldn't* he!" said Gerald. "You don't know what he's like under the coat."

Kathleen shivered again. And all this time the sun was shining gaily and the white statues and the green trees and the fountains and terraces looked as cheerfully romantic as a scene in a play.

"Anyway," said Gerald, "we'll try to get him back, and shut the door. That's the most we can hope for. And then apples, and *Robinson Crusoe* or the *Swiss Family*, or any book you like that's got no magic in it.[8] Now, we've just got to do it. And he's not horrid now; *really* he isn't. He's real, you see."

"I suppose that makes all the difference," said Mabel, and tried to feel that perhaps it did.

"And it's broad daylight—just look at the sun," Gerald insisted. "Come on!"

He took a hand of each, and they walked resolutely towards the bank of rhododendrons behind which Jimmy and the Ugly-Wugly had been told to wait, and as they went Gerald said: "He's real"—"The sun's shining"—"It'll all be over in a minute." And he said these things again and again, so that there should be no mistake about them.

As they neared the bushes the shining leaves rustled, shivered, and parted, and before the girls had time to begin to hang back Jimmy came blinking out into the sunlight. The boughs closed behind him, and they did not stir or rustle for the appearance of anyone else. Jimmy was alone.

"Where is it?" asked the girls in one breath.

"Walking up and down in a fir-walk," said Jimmy, "doing sums in a book. He says he's most frightfully rich, and he's got to get up to town to the Stocks or something—where they change papers into gold if you're clever, he says. I should like to go to the Stocks-change, wouldn't you?"

"I don't seem to care very much about changes," said Gerald. "I've had enough. Show us where he is—we must get rid of him."

"He's got a motor-car," Jimmy went on, parting the warm varnished-looking rhododendron leaves, "and a garden with a tennis-court and a lake and a carriage and pair, and he goes to Athens for his holiday sometimes, just like other people go to Margate."

"The best thing," said Gerald, following through the bushes, "will be to tell him the shortest way out is through that hotel that he thinks he found last night. Then we get him into the passage, give him a push, fly back, and shut the door."

"He'll starve to death in there," said Kathleen, "if he's really real."

"I expect it doesn't last long, the ring magics don't—anyway, it's the only thing I can think of."

"He's frightfully rich," Jimmy went on unheeding amid the cracking of the bushes; "he's building a public library for the people where he lives, and having his portrait painted to put in it. He thinks they'll like that."

The belt of rhododendrons was passed, and the children had reached a smooth grass walk bordered by tall pines and firs of strange, different kinds. "He's just round that corner," said Jimmy. "He's simply rolling in money. He doesn't know what to do with it. He's been building a horse-trough and drinking fountain with a bust of himself on top. Why doesn't he build a private swimming-bath close to his bed, so that he can just roll off into it of a morning? I wish I was rich; I'd soon show him—"

"That's a sensible wish," said Gerald. "I wonder we didn't think of doing that. Oh, criky!" he added, and with reason. For there, in the green shadows of the pine-walk, in the woodland silence, broken only by rustling leaves and the agitated breathing of the three unhappy others, Jimmy got his wish. By quick but perfectly plain-to-be-seen degrees Jimmy became rich. And the horrible thing was that though they could see it happening they did not know what was happening, and could not have stopped it if they had. All they could see was Jimmy, their own Jimmy, whom they had larked with and quarrelled with and made it up with ever since they could remember, Jimmy continuously and horribly growing old. The whole thing was over in a few seconds. Yet in those few seconds they saw him grow to a youth, a young man, a middle-aged man; and then, with a sort of shivering shock, unspeakably horrible and definite, he seemed to settle down into an elderly gentleman, handsomely but rather dowdily dressed, who was looking down at them through spectacles and asking them the nearest way to the railway-station. If they had not seen the change take place, in all its awful details, they would never have guessed that this stout, prosperous, elderly gentleman with the high hat, the frock-coat, and the large red seal dangling from the curve of a portly waistcoat, was their own Jimmy. But, as they *had* seen it, they knew the dreadful truth.

"Oh, Jimmy, *don't!*" cried Mabel desperately.

Gerald said: "This is perfectly beastly," and Kathleen broke into wild weeping.

"Don't cry, little girl!" said That-which-had-been Jimmy; "and you, boy, can't you give a civil answer to a civil question?"

"He doesn't know us!" wailed Kathleen.

"Who doesn't know you?" said That-which-had-been impatiently.

"You—y-you don't!" Kathleen sobbed.

"I certainly don't," returned That-which—"but surely that need not distress you so deeply."

"Oh, Jimmy. Jimmy, Jimmy!" Kathleen sobbed louder than before.

"He *doesn't* know us," Gerald owned, "or—look here, Jimmy, y-you aren't kidding, are you? Because if you are it's simply abject rot—"

"My name is Mr. ——," said That-which-had-been-Jimmy, and gave the name correctly. By the way, it will perhaps be shorter to call this elderly stout person who was Jimmy grown rich by some simpler name than I have just used. Let us call him "That"—short for "That-which-had-been Jimmy."

"What *are* we to do?" whispered Mabel, awestruck; and aloud she said: "Oh, Mr. James, or whatever you call yourself, *do* give me the ring." For on That's finger the fatal ring showed plain.

"Certainly not," said That firmly. "You appear to be a very grasping child."

"But what are you going to *do?*" Gerald asked in the flat tones of complete hopelessness.

"Your interest is very flattering," said That. "Will you tell me, or won't you, the way to the nearest railway-station?"

"No," said Gerald, "we won't."

"Then," said That, still politely, though quite plainly furious, "perhaps you'll tell me the way to the nearest lunatic asylum?"

"Oh, no, no, no!" cried Kathleen. "You're not so bad as that."

"Perhaps not. But *you* are," That retorted; "if you're not lunatics you're idiots. However, I see a gentleman ahead who is perhaps sane.

Two hats were raised

In fact, I seem to recognize him." A gentleman, indeed, was now to be seen approaching. It was the elderly Ugly-Wugly.

"Oh! don't you remember Jerry?" Kathleen cried, "and Cathy, your own Cathy Puss Cat? Dear, dear Jimmy, *don't* be so silly!"

"Little girl," said That, looking at her crossly through his spectacles, "I am sorry you have not been better brought up." And he walked stiffly towards the Ugly-Wugly. Two hats were raised, a few words were exchanged, and two elderly figures walked side by side down the green pine-walk, followed by three miserable children, horrified, bewildered, alarmed, and, what is really worse than anything, quite at their wits' end.

"He wished to be rich, so of course he is," said Gerald; "he'll have money for tickets and everything."

"And when the spell breaks—it's sure to break, isn't it?—he'll find himself somewhere awful—perhaps in a really good hotel—and not know how he got there."

"I wonder how long the Ugly-Wuglies lasted," said Mabel.

"Yes," Gerald answered, "that reminds me. You two must collect the coats and things. Hide them, anywhere you like, and we'll carry them home tomorrow—if there is any tomorrow," he added darkly.

"Oh, don't!" said Kathleen, once more breathing heavily on the verge of tears: "you wouldn't think everything could be so awful, and the sun shining like it does."

"Look here," said Gerald, "of course I must stick to Jimmy. You two must go home to Mademoiselle and tell her Jimmy and I have gone off in the train with a gentleman—say he looked like an uncle. He does—some kind of uncle. There'll be a beastly row afterwards, but it's got to be done."

"It all seems thick with lies," said Kathleen; "you don't seem to be able to get a word of truth in edgewise hardly."

"Don't you worry," said her brother; "they aren't lies—they're as true as anything else in this magic rot we've got mixed up in. It's like telling lies in a dream; you can't help it."

"Well, all I know is I wish it would stop."

"Lot of use your wishing that is," said Gerald, exasperated. "So long. I've got to go, and you've got to stay. If it's any comfort to you, I don't believe any of it's real: it can't be; it's too thick. Tell Mademoiselle Jimmy and I will be back to tea. If we don't happen to be I can't help it. I can't help anything, except perhaps Jimmy." He started to run, for the girls had lagged, and the Ugly-Wugly and That (late Jimmy) had quickened their pace.

The girls were left looking after them.

"We've got to find these clothes," said Mabel, "simply got to. I used to want to be a heroine. It's different when it really comes to being, isn't it?"

"Yes, very," said Kathleen. "Where shall we hide the clothes when we've got them? Not—not that passage?"

"Never!" said Mabel firmly; "we'll hide them inside the great stone dinosaurus. He's hollow."

"He comes alive—in his stone," said Kathleen.

"Not in the sunshine he doesn't," Mabel told her confidently, "and not without the ring."

"There won't be any apples and books today," said Kathleen.

"No, but we'll do the babiest thing we can do the minute we get home. We'll have a dolls' tea-party. That'll make us feel as if there wasn't really any magic."

"It'll have to be a very strong tea party, then," said Kathleen doubtfully.

And now we see Gerald, a small but quite determined figure, paddling along in the soft white dust of the sunny road, in the wake of two elderly gentlemen. His hand, in his trousers pocket, buries itself with a feeling of satisfaction in the heavy mixed coinage that is his share of the profits of his conjuring at the fair. His noiseless tennis-shoes bear him to the station, where, unobserved, he listens at the ticket office to the voice of That-which-was-James. "One first London," it says and Gerald, waiting till That and the Ugly-Wugly have strolled on to the platform, politely conversing of politics and the Kaffir market,* takes a third return to London. The train strides in, squeaking and puffing. The watched take their seats in a carriage blue-lined. The watcher springs into a yellow wooden compartment. A whistle sounds, a flag is waved. The train pulls itself together, strains, jerks, and starts.

"I don't understand," says Gerald, alone in his third-class carriage, "how railway trains and magic can go on at the same time."

And yet they do.

Mabel and Kathleen, nervously peering among the rhododendron bushes and the bracken and the fancy fir-trees, find six several heaps of coats, hats, skirts, gloves, golf-clubs, hockey-sticks, broom-handles. They carry them, panting and damp, for the mid-day sun is pitiless, up the hill to where the stone dinosaurus looms immense among a forest of larches. The dinosaurus has a hole in his stomach. Kathleen

---

* Stock exchange term for South African mine shares.

Mabel hands up the clothes and the sticks

shows Mabel how to "make a back" and climbs up on it into the cold, stony inside of the monster. Mabel hands up the clothes and the sticks.

"There's lots of room," says Kathleen; "its tail goes down into the ground. It's like a secret passage."

"Suppose something comes out of it and jumps out at you," says Mabel, and Kathleen hurriedly descends.

The explanations to Mademoiselle promise to be difficult, but, as Kathleen said afterwards, any little thing is enough to take a grown-up's attention off. A figure passes the window just as they are explaining that it really did look exactly like an uncle that the boys have gone to London with.

"Who's that?" says Mademoiselle suddenly, pointing, too, which everyone knows is not manners.

It is the bailiff coming back from the doctor's with antiseptic plaster on that nasty cut that took so long a-bathing this morning. They tell her it is the bailiff at Yalding Towers, and she says. "Sky!" (Ciel!) and asks no more awkward questions about the boys. Lunch—very late—is a silent meal. After lunch Mademoiselle goes out, in a hat with many pink roses, carrying a rose-lined parasol. The girls, in dead silence, organize a dolls' tea-party, with real tea. At the second cup Kathleen bursts into tears. Mabel, also weeping, embraces her.

"I wish," sobs Kathleen, "oh, I do wish I knew where the boys were! It would be such a comfort."

Gerald knew where the boys were, and it was no comfort to him at all. If you come to think of it, he was the only person who could know where they were, because Jimmy didn't know that he was a boy—and indeed he wasn't really—and the Ugly-Wugly couldn't be expected to know anything real, such as where boys were. At the moment when the second cup of dolls' tea—very strong, but not strong enough to drown care in—was being poured out by the trembling hand of Kathleen, Gerald was lurking—there really is no other word for it—on the staircase of Aldermanbury Buildings, Old Broad Street. On the floor below him was a door bearing the legend "MR. U. W. UGLI, Stock and Share Broker. And at the Stock Exchange," and on the floor above was another door, on which was the name of Gerald's little brother, now grown suddenly rich in so magic and tragic a way. There were no explaining words under Jimmy's name. Gerald could not guess what walk in life it was to which That (which had been Jimmy) owed its affluence. He had seen, when the door opened to admit his brother, a tangle of clerks and mahogany desks. Evidently That had a large business.

What was Gerald to do? What could he do?

It is almost impossible, especially for one so young as Gerald, to enter a large London office and explain that the elderly and respected head of it is not what he seems, but is really your little brother, who has been suddenly advanced to age and wealth by a tricky wishing ring. If you think it's a possible thing, try it, that's all. Nor could he knock at the door of Mr. U. W. Ugli, Stock and Share Broker (and at the Stock Exchange), and inform his clerks that their chief was really nothing but old clothes that had accidentally come alive, and by some magic, which he couldn't attempt to explain, become real during a night spent at a really good hotel which had no existence.

The situation bristled, as you see, with difficulties. And it was so long past Gerald's proper dinner-time that his increasing hunger was rapidly growing to seem the most important difficulty of all. It is quite possible to starve to death on the staircase of a London building if the people you are watching for only stay long enough in their offices. The truth of this came home to Gerald more and more painfully.

A boy with hair like a new front door mat came whistling up the stairs. He had a dark blue bag in his hands.

"I'll give you a tanner* for yourself if you'll get me a tanner's worth of buns," said Gerald, with that prompt decision common to all great commanders.

"Show us yer tanners," the boy rejoined with at least equal promptness. Gerald showed them. "All right; hand over."

"Payment on delivery," said Gerald, using words from the drapers which he had never thought to use.

The boy grinned admiringly.

"Knows 'is wy abaht," he said; "ain't no flies on 'im."

"Not many," Gerald owned with modest pride. "Cut along, there's a good chap. I've got to wait here. I'll take care of your bag if you like."

"Nor yet there ain't no flies on me neither," remarked the boy, shouldering it. "I been up to the confidence trick for years—ever since I was your age."

With this parting shot he went; and returned in due course bunladen. Gerald gave the sixpence and took the buns. When the boy, a minute later, emerged from the door of Mr. U. W. Ugli, Stock and Share Broker (and at the Stock Exchange), Gerald stopped him.

"What sort of chap's that?" he asked, pointing the question with a jerk of an explaining thumb.

"Awful big pot,"† said the boy; "up to his eyes in oof.‡ Motor and all that."

"Know anything about the one on the next landing?"

"He's bigger than what this one is. Very old firm—special cellar in the Bank of England to put his chink in—all in bins like against the wall at the corn-chandler's. Jimminy, I wouldn't mind 'alf an hour in there, and the doors open and the police away at a beano.§ Not much! Neither. You'll bust if you eat all them buns."

---

* Sixpence (slang).

† Big pile of money (slang).

‡ Money (slang).

§ Festive gathering (slang).

"Have one?" Gerald responded, and held out the bag.

"They say in our office," said the boy, paying for the bun honourably with unasked information, "as these two is all for cutting each other's throats—oh, only in the way of business—been at it for years."

Gerald wildly wondered what magic and how much had been needed to give history and a past to these two things of yesterday, the rich Jimmy and the Ugly-Wugly. If he could get them away would all memory of them fade—in this boy's mind, for instance, in the minds of all the people who did business with them in the City? Would the mahogany-and-clerk-furnished offices fade away? Were the clerks real? Was the mahogany? Was he himself real? Was the boy?

"Can you keep a secret?" he asked the other boy. "Are you on for a lark?"

"I ought to be getting back to the office," said the boy.

"Get then!" said Gerald.

"Don't you get stuffy," said the boy. "I was just a-going to say it didn't matter. I know how to make my nose bleed if I'm a bit late."

Gerald congratulated him on this accomplishment, at once so useful and so graceful, and then said:

"Look here. I'll give you five bob*—honest."

"What for?" was the boy's natural question.

"If you'll help me."

"Fire ahead."

"I'm a private inquiry," said Gerald.

"Tec? You don't look it."

"What's the good of being one if you look it?" Gerald asked impatiently, beginning on another bun. "That old chap on the floor above—he's *wanted*."

"Police?" asked the boy with fine carelessness.

"No—sorrowing relations."

" 'Return to,' " said the boy; " 'all forgotten and forgiven.' I see."

"And I've got to get him to them, somehow. Now, if you could go in and give him a message from someone who wanted to meet him on business—"

---

* 5 shillings (slang).

"Hold on!" said the boy. "I know a trick worth two of that. You go in and see old Ugli. He'd give his ears to have the old boy out of the way for a day or two. They were saying so in our office only this morning."

"Let me think," said Gerald, laying down the last bun on his knee expressly to hold his head in his hands.

"Don't you forget to think about my five bob," said the boy.

Then there was a silence on the stairs, broken only by the cough of a clerk in That's office, and the clickety-clack of a typewriter in the office of Mr. U. W. Ugli.

Then Gerald rose up and finished the bun.

"You're right," he said. "I'll chance it. Here's your five bob."

He brushed the bun crumbs from his front, cleared his throat, and knocked at the door of Mr. U. W. Ugli. It opened and he entered.

The door-mat boy lingered, secure in his power to account for his long absence by means of his well-trained nose, and his waiting was rewarded. He went down a few steps, round the bend of the stairs, and heard the voice of Mr. U. W. Ugli, so well known on that staircase (and on the Stock Exchange) say in soft, cautious accents:

"Then I'll ask him to let me look at the ring—and I'll drop it. You pick it up. But remember, it's a pure accident, and you don't know me. I can't have my name mixed up in a thing like this. You're *sure* he's really unhinged?"

"Quite," said Gerald; "he's quite mad about that ring. He'll follow it anywhere. I know he will. And think of his sorrowing relations."

"I do—I do," said Mr. Ugli kindly; "that's all I *do* think of, of course."

He went up the stairs to the other office, and Gerald heard the voice of That telling his clerks that he was going out to lunch. Then the horrible Ugly-Wugly and Jimmy, hardly less horrible in the eyes of Gerald, passed down the stairs where, in the dusk of the lower landing, two boys were making themselves as undistinguishable as possible, and so out into the street, talking of stocks and shares, bears and bulls. The two boys followed.

"I say," the door-mat-headed boy whispered admiringly, "whatever are you up to?"

"You'll see," said Gerald recklessly. "Come on!"

"You tell me. I must be getting back."

"Well, I'll tell you, but you won't believe me. That old gentleman's not really old at all—he's my young brother suddenly turned into what you see. The other's not real at all. He's only just old clothes and nothing inside."

"He looks it, I must say," the boy admitted; "but I say—you do stick it on, don't you?"

"Well, my brother was turned like that by a magic ring."

"There ain't no such thing as magic," said the boy. "I learnt that at school."

"All right," said Gerald. "Good-bye."

"Oh, go ahead!" said the boy; "you do stick it on, though."

"Well, that magic ring. If I can get hold of it I shall just wish we were all in a certain place. And we shall be. And then I can deal with both of them."

"Deal?"

"Yes, the ring won't unwish anything you've wished. That undoes itself with time, like a spring uncoiling. But it'll give you a brand-new wish—I'm almost certain of it. Anyhow, I'm going to chance it."

"You are a rotter, aren't you?" said the boy respectfully.

"You wait and see," Gerald repeated.

"I say, you aren't going into this swell place? You *can't*!"

The boy paused, appalled at the majesty of Pym's.

"Yes, I am—they can't turn us out as long as we behave. You come along, too. I'll stand lunch."

I don't know why Gerald clung so to this boy. He wasn't a very nice boy. Perhaps it was because he was the only person Gerald knew in London, to speak to—except That-which-had-been-Jimmy and the Ugly-Wugly; and he did not want to talk to either of them.

What happened next happened so quickly that, as Gerald said later, it was "just like magic." The restaurant was crowded—busy men were hastily bolting the food hurriedly brought by busy waitresses. There was a clink of forks and plates, the gurgle of beer from bottles, the hum of talk, and the smell of many good things to eat.

"Two chops, please," Gerald had just said, playing with a plainly shown handful of money, so as to leave no doubt of his honourable intentions. Then at the next table he heard the words, "Ah, yes, curious old family heirloom," the ring was drawn off the finger of That, and Mr. U. W. Ugli, murmuring something about a unique curio, reached his impossible hand out for it. The door-mat-headed boy was watching breathlessly.

"There's a ring right enough," he owned. And then the ring slipped from the hand of Mr. U. W. Ugli and skidded along the floor. Gerald pounced on it like a greyhound on a hare. He thrust the dull circlet on his finger and cried out aloud in that crowded place:

"I wish Jimmy and I were inside that door behind the statue of Flora."

It was the only safe place he could think of.

The lights and sounds and scents of the restaurant died away as a wax-drop dies in fire—a rain-drop in water. I don't know, and Gerald never knew, what happened in that restaurant. There was nothing about it in the papers, though Gerald looked anxiously for "Extraordinary Disappearance of well-known City Man." What the door-mat-headed boy did or thought I don't know either. No more does Gerald. But he would like to know, whereas I don't care tuppence.* The world went on all right, anyhow, whatever he thought or did. The lights and the sounds and the scents of Pym's died out. In place of the light there was darkness; in place of the sounds there was silence; and in place of the scent of beef, pork, mutton, fish, veal, cabbage, onions, carrots, beer, and tobacco there was the musty, damp scent of a place underground that has been long shut up.

Gerald felt sick and giddy, and there was something at the back of his mind that he knew would make him feel sicker and giddier as soon as he should have the sense to remember what it was. Meantime it was important to think of proper words to soothe the City man that had once been Jimmy—to keep him quiet till Time, like a spring uncoiling, should bring the reversal of the spell—make all things as they were and as they ought to be. But he fought in vain for words. There were none. Nor were they needed. For through the deep darkness came a voice—and it was not the voice of that City man who had been Jimmy, but the voice of that very Jimmy who was Gerald's little brother, and who had wished that unlucky wish for riches that could only be answered by changing all that was Jimmy, young and poor,

---

* Twopence; that is, I couldn't care less.

He cried out aloud in that crowded place

to all that Jimmy, rich and old, would have been. Another voice said: "Jerry, Jerry! Are you awake?—I've had such a rum dream."

And then there was a moment when nothing was said or done.

Gerald felt through the thick darkness, and the thick silence, and the thick scent of old earth shut up, and he got hold of Jimmy's hand.

"It's all right, Jimmy, old chap," he said; "it's not a dream now. It's that beastly ring again. I had to wish us here, to get you back at all out of your dream."

"Wish us where?" Jimmy held on to the hand in a way that in the daylight of life he would have been the first to call babyish.

"Inside the passage—behind the Flora statue," said Gerald, adding, "it's all right, really."

"Oh, I dare say it's all right," Jimmy answered through the dark, with an irritation not strong enough to make him loosen his hold of his brother's hand. "But how are we going to get out?"

Then Gerald knew what it was that was waiting to make him feel more giddy than the lightning flight from Cheapside* to Yalding Towers had been able to make him. But he said stoutly:

"I'll wish us out, of course." Though all the time he knew that the ring would not undo its given wishes.

It didn't.

Gerald wished. He handed the ring carefully to Jimmy, through the thick darkness. And Jimmy wished.

And there they still were, in that black passage behind Flora, that had led—in the case of one Ugly-Wugly at least—to "a good hotel." And the stone door was shut. And they did not know even which way to turn to it.

"If I only had some matches!" said Gerald.

"Why didn't you leave me in the dream?" Jimmy almost whimpered. "It was light there, and I was just going to have salmon and cucumber."

"I," rejoined Gerald in gloom, "was just going to have steak and fried potatoes."

The silence, and the darkness, and the earthy scent were all they had now.

"I always wondered what it would be like," said Jimmy in low, even tones, "to be buried alive. And now I know! Oh!" his voice suddenly rose to a shriek, "it isn't true, it isn't! It's a dream—that's what it is!"

There was a pause while you could have counted ten. Then—

"Yes," said Gerald bravely, through the scent and the silence and the darkness, "it's just a dream, Jimmy, old chap. We'll just hold on, and call out now and then just for the lark of the thing. But it's really only a dream, of course."

"Of course," said Jimmy in the silence and the darkness and the scent of old earth.

---

* Street in London.

CHAPTER IX

There is a curtain, thin as gossamer, clear as glass, strong as iron, that hangs for ever between the world of magic and the world that seems to us to be real. And when once people have found one of the little weak spots in that curtain which are marked by magic rings, and amulets, and the like, almost anything may happen. Thus it is not surprising that Mabel and Kathleen, conscientiously conducting one of the dullest dolls' tea-parties at which either had ever assisted, should suddenly, and both at once, have felt a strange, unreasonable, but quite irresistible desire to return instantly to the Temple of Flora—even at the cost of leaving the dolls' tea-service in an unwashed state, and only half the raisins eaten. They went—as one has to go when the magic impulse drives one—against their better judgement, against their wills almost.

And the nearer they came to the Temple of Flora, in the golden hush of the afternoon, the more certain each was that they could not possibly have done otherwise.

And this explains exactly how it was that when Gerald and Jimmy, holding hands in the darkness of the passage, uttered their first concerted yell, "just for the lark of the thing," that yell was instantly answered from outside.

A crack of light showed in that part of the passage where they had least expected the door to be. The stone door itself swung slowly open, and they were out of it, in the Temple of Flora, blinking in the good daylight, an unresisting prey to Kathleen's embraces and the questionings of Mabel.

"And you left that Ugly-Wugly loose in London," Mabel pointed out; "you might have wished it to be with you, too."

"It's all right where it is," said Gerald. "I couldn't think of everything. And besides, no, thank you! Now we'll go home and seal up the ring in an envelope."

"I haven't done anything with the ring yet," said Kathleen.

"I shouldn't think you'd want to when you see the sort of things it does with you," said Gerald.

"It wouldn't do things like that if I was wishing with it," Kathleen protested.

"Look here," said Mabel, "let's just put it back in the treasure-room and have done with it. I oughtn't ever to have taken it away, really. It's a sort of stealing. It's quite as bad, really, as Eliza borrowing it to astonish her gentleman friend with."

"I don't mind putting it back if you like," said Gerald, "only if any of us do think of a sensible wish you'll let us have it out again, of course?"

"Of course, of course," Mabel agreed.

So they trooped up to the castle, and Mabel once more worked the spring that let down the panelling and showed the jewels, and the ring was put back among the odd dull ornaments that Mabel had once said were magic.

"How innocent it looks!" said Gerald. "You wouldn't think there was any magic about it. It's just like an old silly ring. I wonder if what Mabel said about the other things is true! Suppose we try."

"Don't!" said Kathleen. "I think magic things are spiteful. They just enjoy getting you into tight places."

"I'd like to try," said Mabel, "only—well, everything's been rather upsetting, and I've forgotten what I said anything was."

So had the others. Perhaps that was why, when Gerald said that a bronze buckle laid on the foot would have the effect of seven-league boots, it didn't; when Jimmy, a little of the City man he had been clinging to him still, said that the steel collar would ensure your always having money in your pockets, his own remained empty; and when Mabel and Kathleen invented qualities of the most delightful nature for various rings and chains and brooches, nothing at all happened.

"It's only the ring that's magic," said Mabel at last; "and, I say!" she added, in quite a different voice.

"What?"

"Suppose even the ring isn't!"

"But we know it is."

"I don't," said Mabel. "I believe it's not today at all. I believe it's the other day—we've just dreamed all these things. It's the day I made up that nonsense about the ring."

"No, it isn't," said Gerald; "you were in your Princess-clothes then."

"What Princess-clothes?" said Mabel, opening her dark eyes very wide.

"Oh, don't be silly," said Gerald wearily.

"I'm not silly," said Mabel; "and I think it's time you went. I'm sure Jimmy wants his tea."

"Of course I do," said Jimmy. "But you had got the Princess-clothes that day. Come along; let's shut up the shutters and leave the ring in its long home."

"What ring?" said Mabel.

"Don't take any notice of her," said Gerald. "She's only trying to be funny."

"No, I'm not," said Mabel; "but I'm inspired like a Python or a Sibylline lady.* What ring?"

"The wishing-ring," said Kathleen; "the invisibility ring."

"Don't you see *now*," said Mabel, her eyes wider than ever, "the ring's what you *say* it is? That's how it came to make us invisible—I just said it. Oh, we can't leave it here, if that's what it is. It isn't steal-ing, really, when it's as valuable as that, you see. Say what it is."

"It's a wishing-ring," said Jimmy.

"We've had that before and you had your silly wish," said Mabel, more and more excited. "I say it isn't a wishing-ring. I say it's a ring that makes the wearer four yards high."

She had caught up the ring as she spoke, and even as she spoke the ring showed high above the children's heads on the finger of an impossible Mabel, who was, indeed, twelve feet high.

"Now you've done it!" said Gerald—and he was right. It was in vain that Mabel asserted that the ring was a wishing-ring. It quite clearly wasn't; it was what she had said it was.

"And you can't tell at all how long the effect will last," said Ger-ald. "Look at the invisibleness." This is difficult to do, but the others understood him.

---

* Female oracles: The Pithia (named after the Python slain by Apollo) is the Oracle at Delphi; the Sibyl lived in caves, the most respected in Cumae near Naples.

"It may last for days," said Kathleen. "Oh, Mabel, it *was* silly of you!"

"That's right, rub it in," said Mabel bitterly; "you should have believed me when I said it was what I said it was. Then I shouldn't have had to show you, and I shouldn't be this silly size. What am I to do now, I should like to know?"

"We must conceal you till you get your right size again—that's all," said Gerald practically.

"Yes—but *where*?" said Mabel, stamping a foot twenty-four inches long.

"In one of the empty rooms. You wouldn't be afraid?"

"Of course not," said Mabel. "Oh, I do wish we'd just put the ring back and left it."

"Well, it wasn't us that didn't," said Jimmy, with more truth than grammar.

"I shall put it back now," said Mabel, tugging at it.

"I wouldn't if I were you," said Gerald thoughtfully. "You don't want to stay that length, do you? And unless the ring's on your finger when the time's up, I dare say it wouldn't act."

The exalted Mabel sullenly touched the spring. The panels slowly slid into place, and all the bright jewels were hidden. Once more the room was merely eight-sided, panelled, sunlit, and unfurnished.

"Now," said Mabel, "where am I to hide? It's a good thing auntie gave me leave to stay the night with you. As it is, one of you will have to stay the night with me. I'm not going to be left alone, the silly height I am."

Height was the right word; Mabel had said "four yards high"— and she *was* four yards high. But she was hardly any thicker than when her height was four feet seven, and the effect was, as Gerald remarked, "wonderfully worm-like." Her clothes had, of course, grown with her, and she looked like a little girl reflected in one of those long bent mirrors at Rosherville Gardens, that make stout people look so happily slender, and slender people so sadly scraggy.[9] She sat down suddenly on the floor, and it was like a four-fold foot-rule folding itself up.

"It's no use sitting there, girl," said Gerald.

"I'm not sitting here," retorted Mabel; "I only got down so as to

She sat down suddenly on the floor

be able to get through the door. It'll have to be hands and knees through most places for me now, I suppose."

"Aren't you hungry?" Jimmy asked suddenly.

"I don't know," said Mabel desolately; "it's—it's such a long way off!"

"Well, I'll scout," said Gerald; "if the coast's clear—"

"Look here," said Mabel, "I think I'd rather be out of doors till it gets dark."

"You can't. Someone's certain to see you."

"Not if I go through the yew-hedge," said Mabel. "There's a yew-hedge with a passage along its inside like the box-hedge in *The Luck of the Vails*.*

"In *what?*"

"*The Luck of the Vails*. It's a ripping book. It was that book first set me on to hunt for hidden doors in panels and things. If I crept along that on my front, like a serpent—it comes out amongst the rhododendrons, close by the dinosaurus—we could camp there."

"There's tea," said Gerald, who had had no dinner.

"That's just what there isn't," said Jimmy, who had had none either.

"Oh, you *won't* desert me!" said Mabel. "Look here—I'll write to auntie. She'll give you the things for a picnic, if she's there and awake. If she isn't, one of the maids will."

So she wrote on a leaf of Gerald's invaluable pocket-book:—

"*Dearest Auntie,*—

"*Please may we have some things for a picnic? Gerald will bring them. I would come myself, but I am a little tired. I think I have been growing rather fast.—Your loving niece,*

"*Mabel.*

"*P.S.—Lots, please, because some of us are very hungry.*"

It was found difficult, but possible, for Mabel to creep along the tunnel in the yew-hedge. Possible, but slow, so that the three had

---

* Mystery novel (1901), by E. F. Benson (1867–1940), set among the English aristocracy.

hardly had time to settle themselves among the rhododendrons and to wonder bitterly what on earth Gerald was up to, to be such a time gone, when he returned, panting under the weight of a covered basket. He dumped it down on the fine grass carpet, groaned, and added, "But it's worth it. Where's our Mabel?"

The long, pale face of Mabel peered out from rhododendron leaves, very near the ground.

"I look just like anybody else like this, don't I?" she asked anxiously; "all the rest of me's miles away, under different bushes."

"We've covered up the bits between the bushes with bracken and leaves," said Kathleen, avoiding the question; "don't wriggle, Mabel, or you'll waggle them off."

Jimmy was eagerly unpacking the basket. It was a generous tea. A long loaf, butter in a cabbage-leaf, a bottle of milk, a bottle of water, cake, and large, smooth, yellow gooseberries in a box that had once held an extra-sized bottle of somebody's matchless something for the hair and moustache. Mabel cautiously advanced her incredible arms from the rhododendron and leaned on one of her spindly elbows, Gerald cut bread and butter, while Kathleen obligingly ran round, at Mabel's request, to see that the green coverings had not dropped from any of the remoter parts of Mabel's person. Then there was a happy, hungry silence, broken only by those brief, impassioned suggestions natural to such an occasion:

"More cake, please."

"Milk ahoy, there."

"Chuck us the goosegogs."*

Everyone grew calmer—more contented with their lot. A pleasant feeling, half tiredness and half restfulness, crept to the extremities of the party. Even the unfortunate Mabel was conscious of it in her remote feet, that lay crossed under the third rhododendron to the north-north-west of the tea-party. Gerald did but voice the feelings of the others when he said, not without regret:

"Well, I'm a new man, but I couldn't eat so much as another goosegog if you paid me."

"I could," said Mabel; "yes, I know they're all gone, and I've had my share. But I *could*. It's me being so long, I suppose."

---

* Gooseberries (dialect).

A delicious after-food peace filled the summer air. At a little distance the green-lichened grey of the vast stone dinosaurus showed through the shrubs. He, too, seemed peaceful and happy. Gerald caught his stone eye through a gap in the foliage. His glance seemed somehow sympathetic.

"I dare say he liked a good meal in his day," said Gerald, stretching luxuriously.

"Who did?"

"The dino what's-his-name," said Gerald.

"He had a meal today," said Kathleen, and giggled.

"Yes—didn't he?" said Mabel, giggling also.

"You mustn't laugh lower than your chest," said Kathleen anxiously, "or your green stuff will joggle off."

"What do you mean—a meal?" Jimmy asked suspiciously. "What are you sniggering about?"

"He had a meal. Things to put in his inside," said Kathleen, still giggling.

"Oh, be funny if you want to," said Jimmy, suddenly cross. "We don't want to know—do we, Jerry?"

"I do," said Gerald witheringly; "I'm dying to know. Wake me, you girls, when you've finished pretending you're not going to tell."

He tilted his hat over his eyes, and lay back in the attitude of slumber.

"Oh, don't be stupid!" said Kathleen hastily. "It's only that we fed the dinosaurus through the hole in his stomach with the clothes the Ugly-Wuglies were made of!"

"We can take them home with us, then," said Gerald, chewing the white end of a grass stalk, "so that's all right."

"Look here," said Kathleen suddenly; "I've got an idea. Let me have the ring a bit. I won't say what the idea is, in case it doesn't come off, and then you'd say I was silly. I'll give it back before we go."

"Oh, but you aren't going yet!" said Mabel, pleading. She pulled off the ring. "Of course," she added earnestly, "I'm only too glad for you to try any idea, however silly it is."

Now, Kathleen's idea was quite simple. It was only that perhaps the ring would change its powers if someone else renamed it— someone who was not under the power of its enchantment. So the moment it had passed from the long, pale hand of Mabel to one of her own fat, warm, red paws, she jumped up, crying, "Let's go and empty the dinosaurus *now*," and started to run swiftly towards that prehistoric monster. She had a good start. She wanted to say aloud, yet so that the others could not hear her, "This is a wishing-ring. It gives you any wish you choose." And she did say it. And no one heard her, except the birds and a squirrel or two, and perhaps a stone faun, whose pretty face seemed to turn a laughing look on her as she raced past its pedestal.

The way was uphill; it was sunny, and Kathleen had run her hardest, though her brothers caught her up before she reached the great black shadow of the dinosaurus. So that when she did reach that shadow she was very hot indeed and not in any state to decide calmly on the best wish to ask for.

"I'll get up and move the things down, because I know exactly where I put them," she said.

Gerald made a back, Jimmy assisted her to climb up, and she disappeared through the hole into the dark inside of the monster. In a moment a shower began to descend from the opening—a shower of empty waist-coats, trousers with wildly waving legs, and coats with sleeves uncontrolled.

"Heads below!" called Kathleen, and down came walking-sticks and golf-sticks and hockey-sticks and broom-sticks, rattling and chattering to each other as they came.

"Come on," said Jimmy.

"Hold on a bit," said Gerald. "I'm coming up." He caught the edge of the hole above in his hands and jumped. Just as he got his shoulders through the opening and his knees on the edge he heard Kathleen's boots on the floor of the dinosaurus's inside, and Kathleen's voice saying:

"Isn't it jolly cool in here? I suppose statues are always cool. I do wish I was a statue. Oh!"

The "oh" was a cry of horror and anguish. And it seemed to be cut off very short by a dreadful stony silence.

"What's up?" Gerald asked. But in his heart he knew. He climbed up into the great hollow. In the little light that came up through the hole he could see something white against the grey of the creature's sides. He felt in his pockets, still kneeling, struck a match, and when the blue of its flame changed to clear yellow he looked up to see what

Kathleen had her wish: she was a statue

he had known he would see—the face of Kathleen, white, stony, and lifeless. Her hair was white, too, and her hands, clothes, shoes— everything was white, with the hard, cold whiteness of marble. Kathleen had her wish: she was a statue. There was a long moment of perfect stillness in the inside of the dinosaurus. Gerald could not speak. It was too sudden, too terrible. It was worse than anything that had happened yet. Then he turned and spoke down out of that cold, stony silence to Jimmy, in the green, sunny, rustling, live world outside.

"Jimmy," he said, in tones perfectly ordinary and matter of fact, "Kathleen's gone and said that ring was a wishing-ring. And so it was, of course. I see now what she was up to, running like that. And then the young duffer went and wished she was a statue."

"And she is?" asked Jimmy, below.

"Come up and have a look," said Gerald. And Jimmy came, partly with a pull from Gerald and partly with a jump of his own.

"She's a statue, right enough," he said, in awestruck tones. "Isn't it awful!"

"Not at all," said Gerald firmly. "Come on—let's go and tell Mabel."

To Mabel, therefore, who had discreetly remained with her long length screened by rhododendrons, the two boys returned and broke the news. They broke it as one breaks a bottle with a pistol-shot.

"Oh, my goodness!" said Mabel, and writhed through her long length so that the leaves and fern tumbled off in little showers, and she felt the sun suddenly hot on the backs of her legs. "What next? Oh, my goodness!"

"She'll come all right," said Gerald, with outward calm.

"Yes; but what about me?" Mabel urged. "I haven't got the ring. And my time will be up before hers is. Couldn't you get it back? Can't you get it off her hand? I'd put it back on her hand the very minute I was my right size again—faithfully I would."

"Well, it's nothing to blub about," said Jimmy, answering the sniffs that had served her in this speech for commas and full-stops; "not for you, anyway."

"Ah! you don't know," said Mabel; "you don't know what it is to be as long as I am. Do—do try and get the ring. After all, it is my ring more than any of the rest of yours, anyhow, because I did find it, and I did say it was magic."

The sense of justice always present in the breast of Gerald awoke to this appeal.

"I expect the ring's turned to stone—her boots have, and all her clothes. But I'll go and see. Only if I can't, I can't, and it's no use your making a silly fuss."

The first match lighted inside the dinosaurus showed the ring dark on the white hand of the Statuesque Kathleen.

The fingers were stretched straight out. Gerald took hold of the ring, and, to his surprise, it slipped easily off the cold, smooth marble finger.

"I say, Cathy, old girl, I am sorry," he said, and gave the marble hand a squeeze. Then it came to him that perhaps she could hear him. So he told the statue exactly what he and the others meant to do. This helped to clear up his ideas as to what he and the others did mean to do. So that when, after thumping the statue hearteningly on its marble back, he returned to the rhododendrons, he was able to give his orders with the clear precision of a born leader, as he later said. And since the others had, neither of them, thought of any plan, his plan was accepted, as the plans of born leaders are apt to be.

"Here's your precious ring," he said to Mabel. "Now you're not frightened of anything, are you?"

"No," said Mabel, in surprise. "I'd forgotten that. Look here, I'll stay here or farther up in the wood if you'll leave me all the coats, so that I sha'n't be cold in the night. Then I shall be here when Kathleen comes out of the stone again."

"Yes," said Gerald, "that was exactly the born leader's idea."

"You two go home and tell Mademoiselle that Kathleen's staying at the Towers. She is."

"Yes," said Jimmy, "she certainly is."

"The magic goes in seven-hour lots," said Gerald; "your invisibility was twenty-one hours, mine fourteen, Eliza's seven. When it was a wishing-ring it began with seven. But there's no knowing what number it will be really. So there's no knowing which of you will come right first. Anyhow, we'll sneak out by the cistern window and come down the trellis, after we've said good night to Mademoiselle, and come and have a look at you before we go to bed. I think you'd better come close up to the dinosaurus and we'll leaf you over before we go."

Mabel crawled into cover of the taller trees, and there stood up looking as slender as a poplar and as unreal as the wrong answer to a sum in long division. It was to her an easy matter to crouch beneath the dinosaurus, to put her head up through the opening, and thus to behold the white form of Kathleen.

"It's all right, dear," she told the stone image; "I shall be quite close to you. You call me as soon as you feel you're coming right again."

The statue remained motionless, as statues usually do, and Mabel withdrew her head, lay down, was covered up, and left. The boys went home. It was the only reasonable thing to do. It would never have done for Mademoiselle to become anxious and set the police on their track. Everyone felt that. The shock of discovering the missing Kathleen, not only in a dinosaurus's stomach, but, further, in a stone statue of herself, might well have unhinged the mind of any constable, to say nothing of the mind of Mademoiselle, which, being foreign, would necessarily be a mind more light and easy to upset. While as for Mabel—

"Well, to look at her as she is now," said Gerald, "why, it would send any one off their chump* except us."

"We're different," said Jimmy; "our chumps have had to jolly well get used to things. It would take a lot to upset us now."

"Poor old Cathy! all the same," said Gerald.

"Yes, of course," said Jimmy.

The sun had died away behind the black trees and the moon was rising. Mabel, her preposterous length covered with coats, waistcoats, and trousers laid along it, slept peacefully in the chill of the evening. Inside the dinosaurus Kathleen, alive in her marble, slept too. She had heard Gerald's words—had seen the lighted matches. She was Kathleen just the same as ever only she was Kathleen in a case of marble that would not let her move. It would not have let her cry, even if she wanted to. But she had not wanted to cry. Inside, the marble was not cold or hard. It seemed, somehow, to be softly lined with warmth and pleasantness and safety. Her back did not ache with stooping. Her limbs were not stiff with the hours that they had stayed moveless. Everything was well—better than well. One had only to wait quietly and quite comfortably and one would come out of this stone case, and once more be the Kathleen one had always been used to being. So she waited happily and calmly, and presently waiting changed to not waiting—to not anything; and, close held in the soft inwardness

---

* Out of their senses (slang).

Mabel lay down, was covered up, and left

of the marble, she slept as peacefully and calmly as though she had been lying in her own bed.

She was awakened by the fact that she was not lying in her own bed—was not, indeed, lying at all—by the fact that she was standing and that her feet had pins and needles in them. Her arms, too, held out in that odd way, were stiff and tired. She rubbed her eyes, yawned, and remembered. She had been a statue, a statue inside the stone dinosaurus.

"Now I'm alive again," was her instant conclusion, "and I'll get out of it."

She sat down, put her feet through the hole that showed faintly grey in the stone beast's underside, and as she did so a long, slow lurch threw her sideways on the stone where she sat. *The dinosaurus was moving!*

"*Oh!*" said Kathleen inside it, "how dreadful! It must be moonlight, and it's come alive, like Gerald said."

It was indeed moving. She could see through the hole the changing surface of grass and bracken and moss as it waddled heavily along. She dared not drop through the hole while it moved, for fear it should crush her to death with its gigantic feet. And with that thought came another: where was Mabel? Somewhere—somewhere near? Suppose one of the great feet planted itself on some part of Mabel's inconvenient length? Mabel being the size she was now it would be quite difficult not to step on some part or other of her, if she should happen to be in one's way—quite difficult, however much one tried. And the dinosaurus would not try: Why should it? Kathleen hung in an agony over the round opening. The huge beast swung from side to side. It was going faster; it was no good, she dared not jump out. Anyhow, they must be quite away from Mabel by now. Faster and faster went the dinosaurus. The floor of its stomach sloped. They were going downhill. Twigs cracked and broke as it pushed through a belt of evergreen oaks; gravel crunched, ground beneath its stony feet. Then stone met stone. There was a pause. A splash! They were close to water—the lake where by moonlight Hermes fluttered and Janus* and the dinosaurus swam together. Kathleen dropped swiftly through the hole on to the flat marble that edged the basin, rushed sideways, and stood panting in the shadow of a statue's pedestal. Not a moment too soon, for even as she crouched the monster lizard slipped heavily into the water, drowning a thousand smooth, shining lily pads, and swam away towards the central island.

"Be still, little lady. I leap!" The voice came from the pedestal, and next moment Phoebus had jumped from the pedestal in his little temple, clearing the steps, and landing a couple of yards away.

"You are new," said Phoebus over his graceful shoulder. "I should not have forgotten you if once I had seen you."

---

* Roman god of gates and doors, beginnings and endings, and major transitions in individual and social life; the month of January is named for him.

The monster lizard slipped heavily into the water

"I am," said Kathleen, "quite, quite new. And I didn't know you could talk."

"Why not?" Phoebus laughed. "You can talk."

"But I'm alive."

"Am not I?" he asked.

"Oh, yes, I suppose so," said Kathleen, distracted, but not afraid; "only I thought you had to have the ring on before one could even see you move."

Phoebus seemed to understand her, which was rather to his credit, for she had certainly not expressed herself with clearness.

"Ah! that's for mortals," he said. "*We* can hear and see each other in the few moments when life is ours. That is a part of the beautiful enchantment."

"But I am a mortal," said Kathleen.

"You are as modest as you are charming," said Phoebus Apollo absently; "the white water calls me! I go," and the next moment rings of liquid silver spread across the lake, widening and widening, from the spot where the white joined hands of the Sun-god had struck the water as he dived.

Kathleen turned and went up the hill towards the rhododendron bushes. She must find Mabel, and they must go home at once. If only Mabel was of a size that one could conveniently take home with one! Most likely, at this hour of enchantments, she was. Kathleen, heartened by the thought, hurried on. She passed through the rhododendron bushes, remembered the pointed painted paper face that had looked out from the glossy leaves, expected to be frightened—and wasn't. She found Mabel easily enough, and much more easily than she would have done had Mabel been as she wished to find her. For quite a long way off in the moonlight, she could see that long and worm-like form, extended to its full twelve feet—and covered with coats and trousers and waist-coats. Mabel looked like a drain-pipe that has been covered in sacks in frosty weather. Kathleen touched her long cheek gently, and she woke.

"What's up?" she said sleepily.

"It's only me," Kathleen explained.

"How cold your hands are!" said Mabel.

"Wake up," said Kathleen, "and let's talk."

"Can't we go home now? I'm awfully tired, and it's so long since tea-time."

"*You're* too long to go home yet," said Kathleen sadly, and then Mabel remembered.

She lay with closed eyes—then suddenly she stirred and cried out:

"Oh! Cathy, I feel so funny—like one of those horn snakes when you make it go short to get it into its box. I am—yes—I know I am—"

She was; and Kathleen, watching her, agreed that it was exactly like the shortening of a horn spiral snake between the closing hands

"What is it?" she asked, beginning to tremble

of a child. Mabel's distant feet drew near—Mabel's long, lean arms grew shorter—Mabel's face was no longer half a yard long.

"You're coming right—you are! Oh, I am so glad!" cried Kathleen.

"I know I am," said Mabel; and as she said it she became once more Mabel, not only in herself which, of course, she had been all the time, but in her outward appearance.

"You are all right. Oh, hooray! hooray! I *am* so glad!" said Kathleen kindly; "and now we'll go home at once, dear."

"Go home?" said Mabel, slowly sitting up and staring at Kathleen with her big dark eyes. "Go home—like that?"

"Like what?" Kathleen asked impatiently.

"Why, *you*," was Mabel's odd reply.

"I'm all right," said Kathleen. "Come on."

"Do you mean to say you don't know?" said Mabel. "Look at yourself—your hands—your dress—everything."

Kathleen looked at her hands. They were of marble whiteness. Her dress, too—her shoes, her stockings, even the ends of her hair. She was white as new-fallen snow.

"What is it?" she asked, beginning to tremble. "What am I all this horrid colour for?"

"Don't you see? Oh, Cathy, don't you see? You've *not* come right. You're a statue still."

"I'm not—I'm alive—I'm talking to you."

"I know you are, darling," said Mabel, soothing her as one soothes a fractious child. "That's because it's moonlight."

"But you can see I'm alive."

"Of course I can. I've got the ring."

"But I'm all right; I *know* I am."

"Don't you see," said Mabel gently, taking her white marble hand, "you're not all right? It's moonlight, and you're a statue, and you've just come alive with all the other statues. And when the moon goes down you'll just be a statue again. *That's* the difficulty, dear, about our going home again. You're just a statue still, only you've come alive with the other marble things. Where's the dinosaurus?"

"In his bath," said Kathleen, "and so are all the other stone beasts."

"Well," said Mabel, trying to look on the bright side of things, "then we've got one thing, at any rate, to be thankful for!"

CHAPTER X

"I f," said Kathleen, sitting disconsolate in her marble, "if I am really a statue come alive, I wonder you're not afraid of me."

"I've got the ring," said Mabel with decision. "Cheer up, dear! you will soon be better. Try not to think about it."

She spoke as you speak to a child that has cut its finger, or fallen down on the garden path, and rises up with grazed knees to which gravel sticks intimately.

"I know," Kathleen absently answered.

"And I've been thinking," said Mabel brightly, "we might find out a lot about this magic place, if the other statues aren't too proud to talk to us."

"They aren't," Kathleen assured her; "at least, Phoebus wasn't. He was most awfully polite and nice."

"Where is he?" Mabel asked.

"In the lake—he was," said Kathleen.

"Then let's go down there," said Mabel. "Oh, Cathy! it is jolly being your own proper thickness again." She jumped up, and the withered ferns and branches that had covered her long length and had been gathered closely upon her as she shrank to her proper size fell as forest leaves do when sudden storms tear them. But the white Kathleen did not move.

The two sat on the grey moonlit grass with the quiet of the night all about them. The great park was still as a painted picture; only the splash of the fountains and the far-off whistle of the Western express broke the silence, which, at the same time, then deepened.

"What cheer, little sister!" said a voice behind them—a golden voice. They turned quick, startled heads, as birds, surprised, might turn. There in the moonlight stood Phoebus, dripping still from the lake, and smiling at them, very gentle, very friendly.

"Oh, it's you!" said Kathleen.

"None other," said Phoebus cheerfully. "Who is your friend, the earth-child?"

"This is Mabel," said Kathleen.

Mabel got up and bowed, hesitated, and held out a hand.

"I am your slave, little lady," said Phoebus, enclosing it in marble fingers. "But I fail to understand how you can see us, and why you do not fear."

Mabel held up the hand that wore the ring.

"Quite sufficient explanation," said Phoebus; "but since you have that, why retain your mottled earthy appearance? Become a statue, and swim with us in the lake."

"I can't swim," said Mabel evasively.

"Nor yet me," said Kathleen.

"You can," said Phoebus. "All Statues that come to life are proficient in all athletic exercises. And you, child of the dark eyes and hair like night, wish yourself a statue and join our revels."

"I'd rather not, if you will excuse me," said Mabel—cautiously. "You see . . . this ring . . . you wish for things, and you never know how long they're going to last. It would be jolly and all that to be a statue now, but in the morning I should wish I hadn't."

"Earth-folk often do, they say," mused Phoebus. "But, child, you seem ignorant of the powers of your ring. Wish exactly, and the ring will exactly perform. If you give no limit of time, strange enchantments woven by Arithmos the outcast god of numbers will creep in and spoil the spell. Say thus: 'I wish that till the dawn I may be a statue of living marble, even as my child friend, and that after that time I may be as before, Mabel of the dark eyes and night-coloured hair.' "

"Oh, yes, do, it would be so jolly!" cried Kathleen. "Do, Mabel! And if we're both statues, shall we be afraid of the dinosaurus?"

"In the world of living marble fear is not," said Phoebus. "Are we not brothers, we and the dinosaurus, brethren alike wrought of stone and life?"

"And could I swim if I did?"

"Swim, and float, and dive—and with the ladies of Olympus spread the nightly feast, eat of the food of the gods, drink their cup, listen to the song that is undying, and catch the laughter of immortal lips."

"A feast!" said Kathleen. "Oh, Mabel, do! You would if you were as hungry as I am."

"But it won't be real food," urged Mabel.

"It will be real to you, as to us," said Phoebus; "there is no other realness even in your many-coloured world."

Still Mabel hesitated. Then she looked at Kathleen's legs and suddenly said:

"Very well, I will. But first I'll take off my shoes and stockings. Marble boots look simply awful—especially the laces. And a marble stocking that's coming down—and mine *do!*"

She had pulled off shoes and stockings and pinafore.

"Mabel has the sense of beauty," said Phoebus approvingly. "Speak the spell, child, and I will lead you to the ladies of Olympus."

Mabel, trembling a little, spoke it, and there were two little live statues in the moonlit glade. Tall Phoebus took a hand of each.

"Come—run!" he cried. And they ran.

"Oh—it is jolly!" Mabel panted. "Look at my white feet in the grass! I thought it would feel stiff to be a statue, but it doesn't."

"There is no stiffness about the immortals," laughed the Sun-god. "For tonight you are one of us."

And with that they ran down the slope to the lake.

"Jump!" he cried, and they jumped, and the water splashed up round three white, gleaming shapes.

"Oh! I *can* swim!" breathed Kathleen.

"So can I," said Mabel.

"Of course you can," said Phoebus. "Now three times round the lake, and then make for the island."

Side by side the three swam, Phoebus swimming gently to keep pace with the children. Their marble clothes did not seem to interfere at all with their swimming, as your clothes would if you suddenly jumped into the basin of the Trafalgar Square* fountains and tried to swim there. And they swam most beautifully, with that perfect ease and absence of effort or tiredness which you must have noticed about your own swimming—in dreams. And it was the most lovely place to swim in; the water-lilies, whose long, snaky stalks are so inconvenient to ordinary swimmers, did not in the least interfere with the movements of marble arms and legs. The moon was high in the clear sky-dome. The weeping willows, cypresses, temples, terraces, banks of trees and shrubs, and the wonderful old house, all added to the romantic charm of the scene.

---

* Major plaza in central London commemorating the 1805 British naval victory over the French at the Battle of Trafalgar.

Side by side the three swam

"This is the nicest thing the ring has brought us yet," said Mabel, through a languid but perfect side-stroke.

"I thought you'd enjoy it," said Phoebus kindly; "now once more round, and then the island."

They landed on the island amid a fringe of rushes, yarrow, willow-herb, loose-strife, and a few late, scented, powdery, creamy heads of meadow-sweet. The island was bigger than it looked from the bank, and it seemed covered with trees and shrubs. But when, Phoebus leading the way, they went into the shadow of these, they perceived that beyond the trees lay a light, much nearer to them than the other side of the island could possibly be. And almost at once they were through the belt of trees, and could see where the light came from. The trees they had just passed among made a dark circle round a big cleared space, standing up thick and dark, like a crowd round a football field, as Kathleen remarked.

First came a wide, smooth ring of lawn, then marble steps going down to a round pool, where there were no water-lilies, only gold and silver fish that darted here and there like flashes of quicksilver and dark flames. And the enclosed space of water and marble and grass was lighted with a clear, white, radiant light, seven times stronger than the whitest moonlight, and in the still waters of the pool seven moons lay reflected. One could see that they were only reflections by the way their shape broke and changed as the gold and silver fish rippled the water with moving fin and tail that steered.

The girls looked up at the sky, almost expecting to see seven moons there. But no, the old moon shone alone, as she had always shone on them.

"There are seven moons," said Mabel blankly, and pointed, which is not manners.

"Of course," said Phoebus kindly; "everything in our world is seven times as much so as in yours."

"But there aren't seven of you," said Mabel.

"No, but I am seven times as much," said the Sun-god. "You see, there's numbers, and there's quantity, to say nothing of quality. You see that, I'm sure."

"Not quite," said Kathleen.

"Explanations always weary me," Phoebus interrupted. "Shall we join the ladies?"

On the further side of the pool was a large group, so white that it seemed to make a great white hole in the trees. Some twenty or thirty figures there were in the group—all statues and all alive. Some were dipping their white feet among the gold and silver fish, and sending ripples across the faces of the seven moons. Some were pelting each other with roses—roses so sweet that the girls could smell them even across the pool. Others were holding hands and dancing in a ring, and two were sitting on the steps playing cat's-cradle—which is a very ancient game indeed—with a thread of white marble.

As the new-comers advanced a shout of greeting and gay laughter went up.

"Late again, Phoebus!" someone called out. And another: "Did one of your horses cast a shoe?" And yet another called out something about laurels.

"I bring two guests," said Phoebus, and instantly the statues crowded round, stroking the girls' hair, patting their cheeks, and calling them the prettiest love-names.

"Are the wreaths ready, Hebe?" the tallest and most splendid of the ladies called out. "Make two more!"

And almost directly Hebe came down the steps, her round arms hung thick with rose-wreaths. There was one for each marble head.

Everyone now looked seven times more beautiful than before, which, in the case of the gods and goddesses, is saying a good deal. The children remembered how at the raspberry vinegar feast Mademoiselle had said that gods and goddesses always wore wreaths for meals.

Hebe herself arranged the roses on the girls' heads—and Aphrodite Urania,* the dearest lady in the world, with a voice like mother's at those moments when you love her most, took them by the hands and said:

"Come, we must get the feast ready. Eros†—Psyche—Hebe—Ganymede—all you young people can arrange the fruit."[10]

"I don't see any fruit," said Kathleen, as four slender forms disengaged themselves from the white crowd and came towards them.

---

* Celestial Aphrodite; a particular vision of Aphrodite as the Greek goddess of spiritual as opposed to merely sensual love.

† Eros: Greek god of love; Psyche: princess in Roman mythology who marries Cupid (Eros); Hebe: Greek goddess of youth; Ganymede: in Greek myth, the Trojan prince who is carried off to become cupbearer of the gods. See also endnote 10.

"You will though," said Eros, a really nice boy, as the girls instantly agreed; "you've only got to pick it."

"Like this," said Psyche, lifting her marble arms to a willow branch. She reached out her hand to the children—it held a ripe pomegranate.

"I see," said Mabel. "You just—" She laid her fingers to the willow branch and the firm softness of a big peach was within them.

"Yes, just that," laughed Psyche, who was a darling, as any one could see.

After this Hebe gathered a few silver baskets from a convenient alder, and the four picked fruit industriously. Meanwhile the elder statues were busy plucking golden goblets and jugs and dishes from the branches of ash-trees and young oaks and filling them with everything nice to eat and drink that anyone could possibly want, and these were spread on the steps. It was a celestial picnic. Then everyone sat or lay down and the feast began. And oh! the taste of the food served on those dishes, the sweet wonder of the drink that melted from those gold cups on the white lips of the company! And the fruit—there is no fruit like it grown on earth, just as there is no laughter like the laughter of those lips, no songs like the songs that stirred the silence of that night of wonder.

"Oh!" cried Kathleen, and through her fingers the juice of her third peach fell like tears on the marble steps. "I do wish the boys were here!"

"I do wonder what they're doing," said Mabel.

"At this moment," said Hermes, who had just made a wide ring of flight, as a pigeon does, and come back into the circle—"at this moment they are wandering desolately near the home of the dinosaurus, having escaped from their home by a window, in search of you. They fear that you have perished, and they would weep if they did not know that tears do not become a man, however youthful."

Kathleen stood up and brushed the crumbs of ambrosia from her marble lap.

"Thank you all very much," she said. "It was very kind of you to have us, and we've enjoyed ourselves very much, but I think we ought to go now, please."

"If it is anxiety about your brothers," said Phoebus obligingly, "it is the easiest thing in the world for them to join you. Lend me your ring a moment."

He took it from Kathleen's half-reluctant hand, dipped it in the re-

It was a celestial picnic

flection of one of the seven moons, and gave it back. She clutched it. "Now," said the Sun-god, "wish for them that which Mabel wished for herself. Say—"

"I know," Kathleen interrupted. "I wish that the boys may be statues of living marble like Mabel and me till dawn, and afterwards be like they are now."

"If you hadn't interrupted," said Phoebus—"but there, we can't expect old heads on shoulders of young marble. You should have wished them *here*—and—but no matter. Hermes, old chap, cut across and fetch them, and explain things as you come."

He dipped the ring again in one of the reflected moons before he gave it back to Kathleen.

"There," he said, "now it's washed clean ready for the next magic."

"It is not our custom to question guests," said Hera* the queen, turning her great eyes on the children; but that ring excites, I am sure, the interest of us all."

"It is *the* ring," said Phoebus.

"That, of course," said Hera; "but if it were not inhospitable to ask questions I should ask, How came it into the hands of these earth-children?"

"That," said Phoebus, "is a long tale. After the feast the story, and after the story the song."

Hermes seemed to have "explained everything" quite fully; for when Gerald and Jimmy in marble whiteness arrived, each clinging to one of the god's winged feet, and so borne through the air, they were certainly quite at ease. They made their best bows to the goddesses and took their places as unembarrassed as though they had had Olympian suppers every night of their lives. Hebe had woven wreaths of roses ready for them, and as Kathleen watched them eating and drinking, perfectly at home in their marble, she was very glad that amid the welling springs of immortal peach-juice she had not forgotten her brothers.

"And now," said Hera, when the boys had been supplied with everything they could possibly desire, and more than they could eat— "now for the story."

"Yes," said Mabel intensely; and Kathleen said, "Oh *yes*; now for the story. How splendid!"

"The story," said Phoebus unexpectedly, "will be told by our guests."

"Oh *no!*" said Kathleen, shrinking.

"The lads, maybe, are bolder," said Zeus the king,[†] taking off his rose-wreath, which was a little tight, and rubbing his compressed ears.

---

* Greek goddess of marriage; wife and sister of Zeus.

† Ruler of the gods, and god of the sky and weather.

"I really can't," said Gerald; "besides, I don't know any stories."

"Nor yet me," said Jimmy.

"It's the story of how we got the ring that they want," said Mabel in a hurry. "I'll tell it if you like. Once upon a time there was a little girl called Mabel," she added yet more hastily, and went on with the tale— all the tale of the enchanted castle, or almost all, that you have read in these pages. The marble Olympians listened enchanted—almost as enchanted as the castle itself, and the soft moonlit moments fell past like pearls dropping into a deep pool.

"And so," Mabel ended abruptly, "Kathleen wished for the boys and the Lord Hermes fetched them and here we all are."

A burst of interested comment and question blossomed out round the end of the story, suddenly broken off short by Mabel.

"But," said she, brushing it aside, as it grew thinner, "now we want you to tell us."

"To tell you—?"

"How you come to be alive, and how you know about the ring— and everything you *do* know."

"Everything I know?" Phoebus laughed—it was to him that she had spoken—and not his lips only but all the white lips curled in laughter. "The span of your life, my earth-child, would not contain the words I should speak, to tell you all I know."

"Well, about the ring anyhow, and how you come alive," said Gerald; "you see, it's very puzzling to us."

"Tell them, Phoebus," said the dearest lady in the world; "don't tease the children."

So Phoebus, leaning back against a heap of leopard-skins that Dionysus had lavishly plucked from a spruce fir, told.

"All statues," he said, "can come alive when the moon shines, if they so choose. But statues that are placed in ugly cities do not choose. Why should they weary themselves with the contemplation of the hideous?"

"Quite so," said Gerald politely, to fill the pause.

"In your beautiful temples," the Sun-god went on, "the images of your priests and of your warriors who lie cross-legged on their tombs come alive and walk in their marble about their temples, and through the woods and fields. But only on one night in all the year can any see them. You have beheld us because you held the ring, and are of one brotherhood with us in your marble, but on that one night all may behold us."

"And when is that?" Gerald asked, again polite, in a pause.

"At the festival of the harvest," said Phoebus. "On that night as the moon rises it strikes one beam of perfect light on to the altar in certain temples. One of these temples is in Hellas,* buried under the fall of a mountain which Zeus, being angry, hurled down upon it. One is in this land; it is in this great garden."

"Then," said Gerald, much interested, "if we were to come up to that temple on that night, we could see you, even without being statues or having the ring?"

"Even so," said Phoebus. "More, any question asked by a mortal we are on that night bound to answer."

"And the night is—when?"

"Ah!" said Phoebus, and laughed. "Wouldn't you like to know!"

Then the great marble King of the Gods yawned, stroked his long beard, and said: "Enough of stories, Phoebus. Tune your lyre."

"But the ring," said Mabel in a whisper, as the Sun-god tuned the white strings of a sort of marble harp that lay at his feet—"about how you know all about the ring?"

"Presently," the Sun-god whispered back. "Zeus must be obeyed; but ask me again before dawn, and I will tell you all I know of it." Mabel drew back, and leaned against the comfortable knees of one Demeter†— Kathleen and Psyche sat holding hands. Gerald and Jimmy lay at full length, chins on elbows, gazing at the Sun-god; and even as he held the lyre, before ever his fingers began to sweep the strings, the spirit of music hung in the air, enchanting, enslaving, silencing all thought but the thought of itself, all desire but the desire to listen to it.

Then Phoebus struck the strings and softly plucked melody from them, and all the beautiful dreams of all the world came fluttering close with wings like doves' wings; and all the lovely thoughts that sometimes hover near, but not so near that you can catch them, now came home as to their nests in the hearts of those who listened. And those who listened forgot time and space, and how to be sad, and how to be naughty,

---

* Greece.

† Greek goddess of agriculture.

and it seemed that the whole world lay like a magic apple in the hand of each listener, and that the whole world was good and beautiful.

And then, suddenly, the spell was shattered. Phoebus struck a broken chord, followed by an instant of silence; then he sprang up, crying, "The dawn! the dawn! To your pedestals, O gods!"

In an instant the whole crowd of beautiful marble people had leaped to its feet, had rushed through the belt of wood that cracked and rustled as they went, and the children heard them splash in the water beyond. They heard, too, the gurgling breathing of a great beast, and knew that the dinosaurus, too, was returning to his own place.

Only Hermes had time, since one flies more swiftly than one swims, to hover above them for one moment, and to whisper with a mischievous laugh:

"In fourteen days from now, at the Temple of Strange Stones."

"What's the secret of the ring?" gasped Mabel.

"The ring is the heart of the magic," said Hermes. "Ask at the moonrise on the fourteenth day, and you shall know all."

With that he waved the snowy caduceus* and rose in the air supported by his winged feet. And as he went the seven reflected moons died out and a chill wind began to blow, a grey light grew and grew, the birds stirred and twittered, and the marble slipped away from the children like a skin that shrivels in fire, and they were statues no more, but flesh and blood children as they used to be, standing knee-deep in brambles and long coarse grass. There was no smooth lawn, no marble steps, no seven-mooned fish-pond. The dew lay thick on the grass and the brambles, and it was very cold.

"We ought to have gone with them," said Mabel with chattering teeth. "We can't swim now we're not marble. And I suppose this is the island?"

It was—and they couldn't swim.

They knew it. One always knows those sort of things somehow without trying. For instance, you know perfectly that you can't fly. There are some things that there is no mistake about.

The dawn grew brighter and the outlook more black every moment.

---

* Staff entwined with two snakes; traditionally associated with Hermes (Mercury).

"There isn't a boat, I suppose?" Jimmy asked.

"No," said Mabel, "not on this side of the lake; there's one in the boat-house, of course—if you could swim there."

"You know I can't," said Jimmy.

"Can't anyone think of anything?" Gerald asked, shivering.

"When they find we've disappeared they'll drag all the water for miles round," said Jimmy hopefully, "in case we've fallen in and sunk to the bottom. When they come to drag this we can yell and be rescued."

"Yes, dear, that will be nice," was Gerald's bitter comment.

"Don't be so disagreeable," said Mabel with a tone so strangely cheerful that the rest stared at her in amazement.

"The ring," she said. "Of course we've only got to wish ourselves home with it. Phoebus washed it in the moon ready for the next wish."

"You didn't tell us about that," said Gerald in accents of perfect good temper. "Never mind. Where is the ring?"

"You had it," Mabel reminded Kathleen.

"I know I had," said that child in stricken tones, "but I gave it to Psyche to look at—and—and she's got it on her finger!"

Everyone tried not to be angry with Kathleen. All partly succeeded.

"If we ever get off this beastly island," said Gerald, "I suppose you can find Psyche's statue and get it off again?"

"No I can't," Mabel moaned. "I don't know where the statue is. I've never seen it. It may be in Hellas, wherever that is—or anywhere, for anything I know."

No one had anything kind to say, and it is pleasant to record that nobody said anything. And now it was grey daylight, and the sky to the north was flushing in pale pink and lavender.

The boys stood moodily, hands in pockets. Mabel and Kathleen seemed to find it impossible not to cling together, and all about their legs the long grass was icy with dew.

A faint sniff and a caught breath broke the silence.

"Now, look here," said Gerald briskly, "I won't have it. Do you hear? Snivelling's no good at all. No, I'm not a pig. It's for your own good. Let's make a tour of the island. Perhaps there's a boat hidden somewhere among the overhanging boughs."

"How could there be?" Mabel asked.

"Someone might have left it there, I suppose," said Gerald.

"But how would they have got off the island?"

"In another boat, of course," said Gerald; "come on."

Downheartedly, and quite sure that there wasn't and couldn't be any boat, the four children started to explore the island. How often each one of them had dreamed of islands, how often wished to be stranded on one! Well, now they were. Reality is sometimes quite different from dreams, and not half so nice. It was worst of all for Mabel, whose shoes and stockings were far away on the mainland. The coarse grass and brambles were very cruel to bare legs and feet.

They stumbled through the wood to the edge of the water, but it was impossible to keep close to the edge of the island, the branches grew too thickly. There was a narrow, grassy path that wound in and out among the trees, and this they followed, dejected and mournful. Every moment made it less possible for them to hope to get back to the school-house unnoticed. And if they were missed and beds found in their present unslept-in state—well, there would be a row of some sort, and, as Gerald said, "Farewell to liberty!"

"Of course we can get off all right," said Gerald. "Just all shout when we see a gardener or a keeper on the mainland. But if we do, concealment is at an end and all is absolutely up!"

"Yes," said everyone gloomily.

"Come, buck up!" said Gerald, the spirit of the born general beginning to reawaken in him. "We shall get out of this scrape all right, as we've got out of others; you know we shall. See, the sun's coming out. You feel all right and jolly now, don't you?"

"Yes, oh yes!" said everyone, in tones of unmixed misery.

The sun was now risen, and through a deep cleft in the hills it sent a strong shaft of light straight at the island. The yellow light, almost level, struck through the stems of the trees and dazzled the children's eyes. This, with the fact that he was not looking where he was going, as Jimmy did not fail to point out later, was enough to account for what now happened to Gerald, who was leading the melancholy little procession. He stumbled, clutched at a tree-trunk, missed his clutch, and disappeared, with a yell and a clatter; and Mabel, who came next, only pulled herself up just in time not to fall down a steep flight of moss-grown steps that seemed to open suddenly in the ground at her feet.

"Oh, Gerald!" she called down the steps; "are you hurt?"

"No," said Gerald, out of sight and crossly, for he *was* hurt, rather severely; "it's steps, and there's a passage."

"There always is," said Jimmy.

"I knew there was a passage," said Mabel; "it goes under the water and comes out at the Temple of Flora. Even the gardeners know that, but they won't go down, for fear of snakes."

"Then we can get out that way—I do think you might have said so," Gerald's voice came up to say.

"I didn't think of it," said Mabel. "At least—And I suppose it goes past the place where the Ugly-Wugly found its good hotel."

"I'm not going," said Kathleen positively, "not in the dark, I'm not. So I tell you!"

"Very well, baby," said Gerald sternly, and his head appeared from below very suddenly through interlacing brambles. "No one asked you to go in the dark. We'll leave you here if you like, and return and rescue you with a boat. Jimmy, the bicycle lamp!" He reached up a hand for it.

Jimmy produced from his bosom, the place where lamps are always kept in fairy stories—see Aladdin and others—a bicycle lamp.

"We brought it," he explained, "so as not to break our shins over bits of long Mabel among the rhododendrons."

"Now," said Gerald very firmly, striking a match and opening the thick, rounded glass front of the bicycle lamp, "I don't know what the rest of you are going to do, but I'm going down these steps and along this passage. If we find the good hotel—a good hotel never hurt anyone yet."

"It's no good, you know," said Jimmy weakly; "you know jolly well you can't get out of that Temple of Flora door, even if you get to it."

"I don't know," said Gerald, still brisk and commander-like; "there's a secret spring inside that door most likely. We hadn't a lamp last time to look for it, remember."

"If there's one thing I do hate its undergroundness," said Mabel.

"You're not a coward," said Gerald, with what is known as diplomacy. "You're brave, Mabel. Don't I know it! You hold Jimmy's hand and I'll hold Cathy's. Now then."

"I won't have my hand held," said Jimmy, of course. "I'm not a kid."

"Well, Cathy will. Poor little Cathy! Nice brother Jerry'll hold poor Cathy's hand."

Gerald's bitter sarcasm missed fire here, for Cathy gratefully caught the hand he held out in mockery. She was too miserable to read his mood, as she mostly did. "Oh, thank you, Jerry dear," she said gratefully;

"you *are* a dear, and I will try not to be frightened." And for quite a minute Gerald shamedly felt that he had not been quite, quite kind.

So now, leaving the growing goldness of the sunrise, the four went down the stone steps that led to the underground and underwater passage, and everything seemed to grow dark and then to grow into a poor pretence of light again, as the splendour of dawn gave place to the small dogged lighting of the bicycle lamp. The steps did indeed lead to a passage, the beginnings of it choked with the drifted dead leaves of many old autumns. But presently the passage took a turn, there were more steps, down, down, and then the passage was empty and straight—lined above and below and on each side with slabs of marble, very clear and clean. Gerald held Cathy's hand with more of kindness and less of exasperation than he had supposed possible.

And Cathy, on her part, was surprised to find it possible to be so much less frightened than she expected.

The flame of the bull's-eye threw ahead a soft circle of misty light— the children followed it silently. Till, silently and suddenly, the light of the bull's-eye behaved as the flame of a candle does when you take it out into the sunlight to light a bonfire, or explode a train of gunpowder, or what not. Because now, with feelings mixed indeed, of wonder, and interest, and awe, but no fear, the children found themselves in a great hall, whose arched roof was held up by two rows of round pillars, and whose every corner was filled with a soft, searching, lovely light, filling every cranny, as water fills the rocky secrecies of hidden sea-caves.

"How beautiful!" Kathleen whispered, breathing hard into the tickled ear of her brother, and Mabel caught the hand of Jimmy and whispered, "I must hold your hand—I must hold on to something silly, or I shan't believe it's real."

For this hall in which the children found themselves was the most beautiful place in the world. I won't describe it, because it does not look the same to any two people, and you wouldn't understand me if I tried to tell you how it looked to any one of these four. But to each it seemed the most perfect thing possible. I will only say that all round it were great arches. Kathleen saw them as Moorish, Mabel as Tudor, Gerald as Norman, and Jimmy as Churchwarden Gothic. (If you don't know what these are, ask your uncle who collects brasses, and he will explain, or perhaps Mr. Millar will draw the different kinds of arches for you.[11]) And through these arches one could see many things—oh! but many things. Through one appeared an olive garden, and in it two lovers who held each other's hands, under an Italian moon; through another a wild sea, and a ship to whom the wild, racing sea was slave. A third showed a king on his throne, his courtiers obsequious about him; and yet a fourth showed a really good hotel, with the respectable Ugly-Wugly sunning himself on the front doorsteps. There was a mother, bending over a wooden cradle. There was an artist gazing entranced on the picture his wet brush seemed to have that moment completed, a general dying on a field where Victory had planted the standard he loved, and these things were not pictures, but the truest truths, alive, and, as anyone could see, immortal.

Many other pictures there were that these arches framed. And all showed some moment when life had sprung to fire and flower—the best that the soul of man could ask or man's destiny grant. And the really good hotel had its place here too, because there are some souls that ask no higher thing of life than "a really good hotel."

"Oh, I am glad we came; I am, I am!" Kathleen murmured, and held fast to her brother's hand.

They went slowly up the hall, the ineffectual bull's-eye, held by Jimmy, very crooked indeed, showing almost as a shadow in this big, glorious light.

And then, when the hall's end was almost reached, the children saw where the light came from. It glowed and spread itself from one place, and in that place stood the one statue that Mabel "did not know where to find"—the statue of Psyche. They went on, slowly, quite happy, quite bewildered. And when they came close to Psyche they saw that on her raised hand the ring showed dark.

Gerald let go Kathleen's hand, put his foot on the pediment, his knee on the pedestal. He stood up, dark and human, beside the white girl with the butterfly wings.

"I do hope you don't mind," he said, and drew the ring off very gently. Then, as he dropped to the ground, "Not here," he said. "I don't know why, but not here."

And they all passed behind the white Psyche, and once more the bicycle lamp seemed suddenly to come to life again as Gerald held it in front of him, to be the pioneer in the dark passage that led from the Hall of ——, but they did not know, then, what it was the Hall of.

Then, as the twisting passage shut in on them with a darkness that pressed close against the little light of the bicycle lamp, Kathleen said, "Give me the ring. I know exactly what to say."

Gerald gave it with not extreme readiness.

"I wish," said Kathleen slowly, "that no one at home may know that we've been out tonight, and I wish we were safe in our own beds, undressed, and in our nightgowns, and asleep."

And the next thing any of them knew, it was good, strong, ordinary daylight—not just sunrise, but the kind of daylight you are used to being called in, and all were in their own beds. Kathleen had framed the wish most sensibly. The only mistake had been in saying "in our own beds," because, of course, Mabel's own bed was at Yalding Towers, and to this day Mabel's drab-haired aunt cannot understand how Mabel, who was staying the night with that child in the town she was so taken up with, hadn't come home at eleven, when the aunt locked up, and yet she was in her bed in the morning. For though not a clever woman, she was not stupid enough to be able to believe any one of the eleven fancy explanations which the distracted Mabel offered in the course of the morning. The first (which makes twelve) of these explanations was The Truth, and of course the aunt was far too clever to believe That!

CHAPTER XI

It was show-day at Yalding Castle, and it seemed good to the children to go and visit Mabel, and, as Gerald put it, to mingle unsuspected with the crowd; to gloat over all the things which they knew and which the crowd didn't know about the castle and the sliding panels, the magic ring and the statues that came alive. Perhaps one of the pleasantest things about magic happenings is the feeling which they give you of knowing what other people not only don't know but wouldn't, so to speak, believe if they did.

On the white road outside the gates of the castle was a dark spattering of breaks and wagonettes and dog-carts. Three or four waiting motor-cars puffed fatly where they stood, and bicycles sprawled in heaps along the grassy hollow by the red brick wall. And the people who had been brought to the castle by the breaks and wagonettes, and dog-carts and bicycles and motors, as well as those who had walked there on their own unaided feet, were scattered about the grounds, or being shown over those parts of the castle which were, on this one day of the week, thrown open to visitors.

There were more visitors than usual today because it had somehow been whispered about that Lord Yalding was down, and that the holland covers were to be taken off the state furniture so that a rich American who wished to rent the castle, to live in, might see the place in all its glory.

It certainly did look very splendid. The embroidered satin, gilded leather and tapestry of the chairs, which had been hidden by brown holland, gave to the rooms a pleasant air of being lived in. There were flowering plants and pots of roses here and there on tables or window-ledges. Mabel's aunt prided herself on her tasteful touch in the home, and had studied the arrangement of flowers in a series of articles in *Home Drivel* called "How to Make Home High-class on Nine-pence a Week."

The great crystal chandeliers, released from the bags that at ordinary times shrouded them, gleamed with grey and purple splendour. The brown linen sheets had been taken off the state beds, and the red ropes that usually kept the low crowd in its proper place had been rolled up and hidden away.

"It's exactly as if we were calling on the family," said the grocer's daughter from Salisbury to her friend who was in the millinery.

"If the Yankee doesn't take it, what do you say to you and me setting up here when we get spliced?" the draper's assistant asked his sweetheart. And she said: "Oh, Reggie, how can you! you are too funny."

All the afternoon the crowd in its smart holiday clothes, pink blouses, and light-coloured suits, flowery hats, and scarves beyond description passed through and through the dark hall, the magnificent drawing-rooms and boudoirs and picture-galleries. The chattering crowd was awed into something like quiet by the calm, stately bedchambers, where men had been born, and died; where royal guests had lain in long-ago summer nights, with big bow-pots of elder-flowers set on the hearth to ward off fever and evil spells. The terrace, where in old days dames in ruffs had sniffed the sweet-brier and southernwood of the borders below, and ladies, bright with rouge and powder and brocade, had walked in the swing of their hooped skirts—the terrace now echoed to the sound of brown boots, and the tap-tap of high-heeled shoes at two and eleven three, and high laughter and chattering voices that said nothing that the children wanted to hear. These spoiled for them the quiet of the enchanted castle, and outraged the peace of the garden of enchantments.

"It isn't such a lark after all," Gerald admitted, as from the window of the stone summer-house at the end of the terrace they watched the loud colours and heard the loud laughter. "I do hate to see all these people in our garden."

"I said that to that nice bailiff-man this morning," said Mabel, setting herself on the stone floor, "and he said it wasn't much to let them come once a week. He said Lord Yalding ought to let them come when they liked—said he would if he lived there."

"That's all he knows!" said Jimmy. "Did he say anything else?"

"Lots," said Mabel. "I do like him! I told him—"

"You didn't!"

"Yes. I told him lots about our adventures. The humble bailiff is a beautiful listener."

"We shall be locked up for beautiful lunatics if you let your jaw get the better of you, my Mabel child."

"Not us!" said Mabel. "I told it—you know the way—every word true, and yet so that nobody believes any of it. When I'd quite done he said I'd got a real littery talent, and I promised to put his name on the beginning of the first book I write when I grow up."

"You don't know his name," said Kathleen. "Let's do something with the ring."

"Imposs!" said Gerald. "I forgot to tell you, but I met Mademoiselle when I went back for my garters—and she's coming to meet us and walk back with us."

"What did you say?"

"I said," said Gerald deliberately, "that it was very kind of her. And so it was. Us not wanting her doesn't make it not kind her coming—"

"It may be kind, but it's sickening too," said Mabel, "because now I suppose we shall have to stick here and wait for her; and I promised we'd meet the bailiff-man. He's going to bring things in a basket and have a picnic-tea with us."

"Where?"

"Beyond the dinosaurus. He said he'd tell me all about the anteddy-something animals—it means before Noah's Ark; there are lots besides the dinosaurus—in return for me telling him my agreeable fictions. Yes, he called them that."

"When?"

"As soon as the gates shut. That's five."

"We might take Mademoiselle along," suggested Gerald.

"She'd be too proud to have tea with a bailiff, I expect; you never know how grown-ups will take the simplest things." It was Kathleen who said this.

"Well, I'll tell you what," said Gerald, lazily turning on the stone bench. "You all go along, and meet your bailiff. A picnic's a picnic. And I'll wait for Mademoiselle."

Mabel remarked joyously that this was jolly decent of Gerald, to which he modestly replied: "Oh, rot!"

Jimmy added that Gerald rather liked sucking-up to people.

"Little boys don't understand diplomacy," said Gerald calmly;

"sucking-up is simply silly. But it's better to be good than pretty and—"

"How do you know?" Jimmy asked.

"And," his brother went on, "you never know when a grown-up may come in useful. Besides, they *like* it. You must give them *some* little pleasures. Think how awful it must be to be old. My hat!"

"I hope I shan't be an old maid," said Kathleen.

"I don't *mean* to be," said Mabel briskly. "I'd rather marry a travelling tinker."

"It would be rather nice," Kathleen mused, "to marry the Gipsy King and go about in a caravan telling fortunes and hung round with baskets and brooms."

"Oh, if I could choose," said Mabel, "of course I'd marry a brigand, and live in his mountain fastnesses, and be kind to his captives and help them to escape and—"

"You'll be a real treasure to your husband," said Gerald.

"Yes," said Kathleen, "or a sailor would be nice. You'd watch for his ship coming home and set the lamp in the dormer window to light him home through the storm; and when he was drowned at sea you'd be most frightfully sorry, and go every day to lay flowers on his daisied grave."

"Yes," Mabel hastened to say, "or a soldier, and then you'd go to the wars with short petticoats and a cocked hat and a barrel round your neck like a St. Bernard dog. There's a picture of a soldier's wife on a song auntie's got. It's called 'The Veevandyear.' "*

"When I marry—" Kathleen quickly said.

"When I marry," said Gerald, "I'll marry a dumb girl, or else get the ring to make her so that she can't speak unless she's spoken to. Let's have a squint."

He applied his eye to the stone lattice.

"They're moving off," he said. "Those pink and purple hats are nodding off in the distant prospect; and the funny little man with the beard like a goat is going a different way from everyone else—the gardeners will have to head him off. I don't see Mademoiselle, though. The rest of you had better bunk. It doesn't do to run any risks

---

* From *vivandiere*, a woman who accompanies troops to sell them supplies (French).

with picnics. The deserted hero of our tale, alone and unsupported, urged on his brave followers to pursue the commissariat waggons, he himself remaining at the post of danger and difficulty, because he was born to stand on burning decks whence all but he had fled, and to lead forlorn hopes when despaired of by the human race!"

"I think I'll marry a dumb husband," said Mabel, "and there shan't be any heroes in my books when I write them, only a heroine. Come on, Cathy."

Coming out of that cool, shadowy summer-house into the sunshine was like stepping into an oven, and the stone of the terrace was burning to the children's feet.

"I know now what a cat on hot bricks feels like," said Jimmy.

The antediluvian animals are set in a beech-wood on a slope at least half a mile across the park from the castle. The grandfather of the present Lord Yalding had them set there in the middle of last century, in the great days of the late Prince Consort,* the Exhibition of 1851, Sir Joseph Paxton,† and the Crystal Palace. Their stone flanks, their wide, ungainly wings, their lozenged crocodile-like backs show grey through the trees a long way off.

Most people think that noon is the hottest time of the day. They are wrong. A cloudless sky gets hotter and hotter all the afternoon, and reaches its very hottest at five. I am sure you must all have noticed this when you are going out to tea anywhere in your best clothes, especially if your clothes are starched and you happen to have a rather long and shadeless walk.

Kathleen, Mabel, and Jimmy got hotter and hotter, and went more and more slowly. They had almost reached that stage of resentment and discomfort when one "wishes one hadn't come" before they saw, below the edge of the beech-wood, the white waved handkerchief of the bailiff.

That banner, eloquent of tea, shade, and being able to sit down, put new heart into them. They mended their pace, and a final desperate run landed them among the drifted coppery leaves and bare grey and green roots of the beech-wood.

---

* Prince Albert (1819–1861), husband of Queen Victoria.

† Famed British gardener and hothouse designer who was the architect of the Crystal Palace (see endnote 5 to *Five Children and It*).

"Oh, glory!" said Jimmy, throwing himself down. "How do you do?"

The bailiff looked very nice, the girls thought. He was not wearing his velveteens, but a grey flannel suit that an Earl need not have scorned; and his straw hat would have done no discredit to a Duke; and a Prince could not have worn a prettier green tie. He welcomed the children warmly. And there were two baskets dumped heavy and promising among the beech-leaves.

He was a man of tact. The hot, instructive tour of the stone antediluvians, which had loomed with ever-lessening charm before the children, was not even mentioned.

"You must be desert-dry," he said, "and you'll be hungry, too, when you've done being thirsty. I put on the kettle as soon as I discerned the form of my fair romancer in the extreme offing."

The kettle introduced itself with puffings and bubblings from the hollow between two grey roots where it sat on a spirit-lamp.

"Take off your shoes and stockings, won't you?" said the bailiff in matter-of-course tones, just as old ladies ask each other to take off their bonnets; "there's a little baby canal just over the ridge."

The joys of dipping one's feet in cool running water after a hot walk have yet to be described. I could write pages about them. There was a mill-stream when I was young with little fishes in it, and dropped leaves that spun round, and willows and alders that leaned over it and kept it cool, and—but this is not the story of my life.

When they came back, on rested, damp, pink feet, tea was made and poured out, delicious tea with as much milk as ever you wanted, out of a beer bottle with a screw top, and cakes, and gingerbread, and plums, and a big melon with a lump of ice in its heart—a tea for the gods!

This thought must have come to Jimmy, for he said suddenly, removing his face from inside a wide-bitten crescent of melon-rind:

"Your feast's as good as the feast of the Immortals, almost."

"Explain your recondite allusion," said the grey-flannelled host; and Jimmy, understanding him to say, "What do you mean?" replied with the whole tale of that wonderful night when the statues came alive, and a banquet of unearthly splendour and deliciousness was plucked by marble hands from the trees of the lake island.

When he had done the bailiff said:

The joys of dipping one's feet in cool running water

"Did you get all this out of a book?"

"No," said Jimmy, "it happened."

"You are an imaginative set of young dreamers, aren't you?" the bailiff asked, handing the plums to Kathleen, who smiled, friendly but embarrassed. Why couldn't Jimmy have held his tongue?

"No, we're not," said that indiscreet one obstinately; "everything I've told you *did* happen, and so did the things Mabel told you."

The bailiff looked a little uncomfortable. "All right, old chap," he said. And there was a short, uneasy silence. "Look here," said Jimmy, who seemed for once to have got the bit between his teeth, "do you believe me or not?"

"Don't be silly, Jimmy!" Kathleen whispered. "Because, if you don't I'll *make* you believe."

"Don't!" said Mabel and Kathleen together.

"Do you or don't you?" Jimmy insisted, lying on his front with his chin on his hands, his elbows on a moss-cushion, and his bare legs kicking among the beech-leaves.

"I think you tell adventures awfully well," said the bailiff cautiously.

"Very well," said Jimmy, abruptly sitting up, "you don't believe me. Nonsense, Cathy! he's a gentleman, even if he is a bailiff."

"Thank you!" said the bailiff with eyes that twinkled.

"You won't tell, will you?" Jimmy urged.

"Tell what?"

"*Anything.*"

"Certainly not. I am, as you say, the soul of honour."

"Then—Cathy, give me the ring."

"Oh, *no!*" said the girls together.

Kathleen did not mean to give up the ring; Mabel did not mean that she should; Jimmy certainly used no force. Yet presently he held it in his hand. It was his hour. There are times like that for all of us, when what we say shall be done *is* done.

"Now," said Jimmy, "this is the ring Mabel told you about. I say it is a wishing-ring. And if you will put it on your hand and wish, whatever you wish will happen."

"Must I wish out loud?"

"Yes—I think so."

"Don't wish for anything silly," said Kathleen, making the best of the situation, "like its being fine on Tuesday or its being your favourite pudding for dinner tomorrow. Wish for something you really want."

"I will," said the bailiff. "I'll wish for the only thing I really want. I wish my—I wish my friend were here."

The three who knew the power of the ring looked round to see the bailiff's friend appear; a surprised man that friend would be, they thought, and perhaps a frightened one. They had all risen, and stood ready to soothe and reassure the newcomer. But no startled gentleman appeared in the wood, only, coming quietly through the dappled sun and shadow under the beech-trees, Mademoiselle and Gerald, Mademoiselle in a white gown, looking quite nice and like a picture, Gerald hot and polite.

"Good afternoon," said that dauntless leader of forlorn hopes. "I persuaded Mademoiselle—"

That sentence was never finished, for the bailiff and the French governess were looking at each other with the eyes of tired travellers who find, quite without expecting it, the desired end of a very long journey. And the children saw that even if they spoke it would not make any difference.

"You!" said the bailiff.

"Mais . . . c'est donc vous,"* said Mademoiselle, in a funny choky voice.

And they stood still and looked at each other, "like stuck pigs," as Jimmy said later, for quite a long time.

"Is *she* your friend?" Jimmy asked.

"Yes—oh yes," said the bailiff. "You are my friend, are you not?"

"But yes," Mademoiselle said softly. "I am your friend."

"There! you see," said Jimmy, "the ring *does* do what I said."

"We won't quarrel about that," said the bailiff. "You can say it's the ring. For me—it's a coincidence—the happiest, the dearest—"

"Then you—?" said the French governess.

"Of course," said the bailiff. "Jimmy, give your brother some tea. Mademoiselle, come and walk in the woods: there are a thousand things to say."

"Eat then, my Gerald," said Mademoiselle, now grown young, and astonishingly like a fairy princess. "I return all at the hour, and we re-enter together. It is that we must speak each other. It is long time that we have not seen us, me and Lord Yalding!"

"So he was Lord Yalding all the time," said Jimmy, breaking a stupefied silence as the white gown and the grey flannels disappeared among the beech-trunks. "Landscape painter sort of dodge—silly, I call it. And fancy her being a friend of his, and his wishing she was here! Different from us, eh? Good old ring!"

"His friend!" said Mabel with strong scorn; "don't you see she's

---

* But . . . so it's you (French).

They stood still and looked at each other

his lover? Don't you see she's the lady that was bricked up in the convent, because he was so poor, and he couldn't find her. And now the ring's made them live happy ever after. I *am* glad! Aren't you, Cathy?"

"Rather!" said Kathleen; "it's as good as marrying a sailor or a bandit."

"It's the ring did it," said Jimmy. "If the American takes the house he'll pay lots of rent, and they can live on that."

"I wonder if they'll be married tomorrow!" said Mabel.

"Wouldn't if be fun if we were bridesmaids," said Cathy.

"May I trouble you for the melon," said Gerald. "Thanks! Why didn't we know he was Lord Yalding? Apes and moles that we were!"

"I've known since last night," said Mabel calmly; "only I promised not to tell. I *can* keep a secret, can't I?"

"Too jolly well," said Kathleen, a little aggrieved.

"He was disguised as a bailiff," said Jimmy; "that's why we didn't know."

"Disguised as a fiddle-stick-end,"* said Gerald. "Ha, ha! I see something old Sherlock Holmes never saw, nor that idiot Watson, either. If you want a really impenetrable disguise, you ought to disguise yourself as what you really are. I'll remember that."

"It's like Mabel, telling things so that you can't believe them," said Cathy.

"I think Mademoiselle's jolly lucky," said Mabel.

"She's not so bad. He might have done worse," said Gerald. "Plums, please!"

There was quite plainly magic at work. Mademoiselle next morning was a changed governess. Her cheeks were pink, her lips were red, her eyes were larger and brighter, and she had done her hair in an entirely new way, rather frivolous and very becoming.

"Mam'selle's coming out!" Eliza remarked.

Immediately after breakfast Lord Yalding called with a wagonette that wore a smart blue cloth coat, and was drawn by two horses whose coats were brown and shining and fitted them even better than

---

* Phrase that replaces other words when one derisively repeats a statement.

the blue cloth coat fitted the wagonette, and the whole party drove in state and splendour to Yalding Towers.

Arrived there, the children clamoured for permission to explore the castle thoroughly, a thing that had never yet been possible. Lord Yalding, a little absent in manner, but yet quite cordial, consented. Mabel showed the others all the secret doors and unlikely passages and stairs that she had discovered. It was a glorious morning. Lord Yalding and Mademoiselle went through the house, it is true, but in a rather half-hearted way. Quite soon they were tired, and went out through the French windows of the drawing-room and through the rose garden, to sit on the curved stone seat in the middle of the maze, where once, at the beginning of things, Gerald, Kathleen, and Jimmy had found the sleeping Princess who wore pink silk and diamonds.

The children felt that their going left to the castle a more spacious freedom, and explored with more than Arctic enthusiasm. It was as they emerged from the little rickety secret staircase that led from the powdering-room of the state suite to the gallery of the hall that they came suddenly face to face with the odd little man who had a beard like a goat and had taken the wrong turning yesterday.

"This part of the castle is private," said Mabel, with great presence of mind, and shut the door behind her.

"I am aware of it," said the goat-faced stranger, "but I have the permission of the Earl of Yalding to examine the house *at* my leisure."

"Oh!" said Mabel. "I beg your pardon. We all do. We didn't know."

"You are relatives of his lordship, I should surmise?" asked the goat-faced.

"Not exactly," said Gerald. "Friends."

The gentleman was thin and very neatly dressed; he had small, merry eyes and a face that was brown and dry-looking.

"You are playing some game, I should suppose?"

"No, sir," said Gerald, "only exploring."

"May a stranger propose himself as a member of your Exploring Expedition?" asked the gentleman, smiling a tight but kind smile.

The children looked at each other.

"You see," said Gerald, "it's rather difficult to explain—but—you see what I mean, don't you?"

"He means," said Jimmy, "that we can't take you into an exploring party without we know what you want to go for."

"Are you a photographer?" asked Mabel, "or is it some newspaper's sent you to write about the Towers?"

"I understand your position," said the gentleman. "I am not a photographer, nor am I engaged by any journal. I am a man of independent means, travelling in this country with the intention of renting a residence. My name is Jefferson D. Conway."

"Oh!" said Mabel; "then you're the American millionaire."

"I do not like the description, young lady," said Mr. Jefferson D. Conway. "I am an American citizen, and I am not without means. This is a fine property—a very fine property. If it were for sale—"

"It isn't, it can't be," Mabel hastened to explain. "The lawyers have put it in a tale, so Lord Yalding can't sell it. But you could take it to live in, and pay Lord Yalding a good millionairish rent, and then he could marry the French governess—"

"Shish!" said Kathleen and Mr. Jefferson D. Conway together, and he added:

"Lead the way, please; and I should suggest that the exploration be complete and exhaustive."

Thus encouraged, Mabel led the millionaire through all the castle. He seemed pleased, yet disappointed too.

"It is a fine mansion," he said at last when they had come back to the point from which they had started; "but I should suppose, in a house this size, there would mostly be a secret stairway, or a priests' hiding place, or a ghost?"

"There are," said Mabel briefly, "but I thought Americans didn't believe in anything but machinery and newspapers." She touched the spring of the panel behind her, and displayed the little tottery staircase to the American. The sight of it worked a wonderful transformation in him. He became eager, alert, very keen.

"Say!" he cried, over and over again, standing in the door that led from the powdering-room to the state bed-chamber. "But this is great—great!"

The hopes of everyone ran high. It seemed almost certain that the castle would be let for a millionairish rent and Lord Yalding be made affluent to the point of marriage.

"If there were a ghost located in this ancestral pile, I'd close with

He became eager, alert, very keen

the Earl of Yalding today, now, on the nail," Mr. Jefferson D. Conway went on.

"If you were to stay till tomorrow, and sleep in this room, I expect you'd see the ghost," said Mabel.

"There is a ghost located here then?" he said joyously.

"They say," Mabel answered, "that old Sir Rupert, who lost his head in Henry the Eighth's time, walks of a night here, with his head under his arm. But we've not seen that. What we have seen is the lady in a pink dress with diamonds in her hair. She carries a lighted taper," Mabel hastily added. The others, now suddenly aware of Mabel's plan, hastened to assure the American in accents of earnest truth that they had all seen the lady with the pink gown.

He looked at them with half-closed eyes that twinkled.

"Well," he said, "I calculate to ask the Earl of Yalding to permit me to pass a night in his ancestral best bed-chamber. And if I hear so much as a phantom footstep, or hear so much as a ghostly sigh, I'll take the place."

"I *am* glad!" said Cathy.

"You appear to be very certain of your ghost," said the American, still fixing them with little eyes that shone. "Let me tell you, young gentlemen, that I carry a gun, and when I see a ghost, I shoot."

He pulled a pistol out of his hip-pocket, and looked at it lovingly.

"And I am a fair average shot," he went on, walking across the shiny floor of the state bed-chamber to the open window. "See that big red rose, like a tea-saucer?"

They saw.

The next moment a loud report broke the stillness, and the red petals of the shattered rose strewed balustrade and terrace.

The American looked from one child to another. Every face was perfectly white.

"Jefferson D. Conway made his little pile by strict attention to business, and keeping his eyes skinned," he added. "Thank you for all your kindness."

"Suppose you'd done it, and he'd shot you!" said Jimmy cheerfully. "That *would* have been an adventure, wouldn't it?"

"I'm going to do it still," said Mabel, pale and defiant. "Let's find Lord Yalding and get the ring back."

Lord Yalding had had an interview with Mabel's aunt, and lunch for six was laid in the great dark hall, among the armour and the oak furniture—a beautiful lunch served on silver dishes. Mademoiselle, becoming every moment younger and more like a Princess, was moved to tears when Gerald rose, lemonade-glass in hand, and proposed the health of "Lord and Lady Yalding."

When Lord Yalding had returned thanks in a speech full of agreeable jokes the moment seemed to Gerald propitious, and he said:

"The ring, you know—you don't believe in it, but we do. May we have it back?"

And got it.

Then, after a hasty council, held in the panelled jewel-room, Mabel said: "This is a wishing-ring, and I wish all the American's weapons of all sorts were here."

Instantly the room was full—six feet up the wall—of a tangle and mass of weapons, swords, spears, arrows, tomahawks, fowling pieces, blunderbusses, pistols, revolvers, scimitars, kreeses—every kind of weapon you can think of—and the four children wedged in among all these weapons of death hardly dared to breathe.

"He collects arms, I expect," said Gerald, "and the arrows are poisoned, I shouldn't wonder. Wish them back where they came from, Mabel, for goodness' sake, and try again."

Mabel wished the weapons away, and at once the four children stood safe in a bare panelled room. But—

"No," Mabel said, "I can't stand it. We'll work the ghost another way. I wish the American may think he sees a ghost when he goes to bed. Sir Rupert with his head under his arm will do."

"Is it tonight he sleeps there?"

"I don't know. I wish he may see Sir Rupert every night—that'll make it all serene."

"It's rather dull," said Gerald; "we shan't know whether he's seen Sir Rupert or not."

"We shall know in the morning, when he takes the house."

This being settled, Mabel's aunt was found to be desirous of Mabel's company, so the others went home.

It was when they were at supper that Lord Yalding suddenly appeared, and said:

"Mr. Jefferson Conway wants you boys to spend the night with him in the state chamber. I've had beds put up. You don't mind, do you? He seems to think you've got some idea of playing ghost-tricks on him."

It was difficult to refuse, so difficult that it proved impossible.

Ten o'clock found the boys each in a narrow white bed that looked quite absurdly small in that high, dark chamber, and in face of that tall gaunt four-poster hung with tapestry and ornamented with funereal-looking plumes.

"I hope to goodness there isn't a *real* ghost," Jimmy whispered.

"Not likely," Gerald whispered back.

"But I don't want to see Sir Rupert's ghost with its head under its arm," Jimmy insisted.

"You won't. The most you'll see'll be the millionaire seeing it. Mabel said he was to see it, not us. Very likely you'll sleep all night and not see anything. Shut your eyes and count up to a million and don't be a goat!"

But he was reckoning without Mabel and the ring. As soon as Mabel had learned from her drab-haired aunt that this was indeed the night when Mr. Jefferson D. Conway would sleep at the castle she had hastened to add a wish, "that Sir Rupert and his head may appear tonight in the state bedroom."

Jimmy shut his eyes and began to count a million. Before he had counted it he fell asleep. So did his brother.

They were awakened by the loud echoing bang of a pistol shot. Each thought of the shot that had been fired that morning, and opened eyes that expected to see a sunshiny terrace and red-rose petals strewn upon warm white stone.

Instead, there was the dark, lofty state chamber, lighted but little by six tall candles; there was the American in shirt and trousers, a smoking pistol in his hand; and there, advancing from the door of the powdering-room, a figure in doublet and hose, a ruff round its neck—and no head! The head, sure enough, was there; but it was under the right arm, held close in the slashed-velvet sleeve of the doublet. The face looking from under the arm wore a pleasant smile. Both boys, I am sorry to say, screamed. The American fired again. The bullet passed through Sir Rupert, who advanced without appearing to notice it.

Then, suddenly, the lights went out. The next thing the boys knew it was morning. A grey daylight shone blankly through the tall windows—and wild rain was beating upon the glass, and the American was gone.

"Where are we?" said Jimmy, sitting up with tangled hair and looking round him. "Oh, I remember. Ugh! it was horrid. I'm about fed up with that ring, so I don't mind telling you."

"Nonsense!" said Gerald. "I enjoyed it. I wasn't a bit frightened, were you?"

"No," said Jimmy, "of course I wasn't."

*   *   *

The American fired again

"We've done the trick," said Gerald later when they learned that the American had breakfasted early with Lord Yalding and taken the first train to London; "he's gone to get rid of his other house, and take this one. The old ring's beginning to do really useful things."

"Perhaps you'll believe in the ring now," said Jimmy to Lord Yalding, whom he met later on in the picture-gallery; "it's all our doing that

Mr. Jefferson saw the ghost. He told us he'd take the house if he saw a ghost, so of course we took care he did see one."

"Oh, you did, did you?" said Lord Yalding in rather an odd voice. "I'm very much obliged, I'm sure."

"Don't mention it," said Jimmy kindly. "I thought you'd be pleased and him too."

"Perhaps you'll be interested to learn," said Lord Yalding, putting his hands in his pockets and staring down at Jimmy, "that Mr. Jefferson D. Conway was so pleased with your ghost that he got me out of bed at six o'clock this morning to talk about it."

"Oh, ripping!" said Jimmy. "What did he say?"

"He said, as far as I can remember," said Lord Yalding, still in the same strange voice—"he said: 'My lord, your ancestral pile is A1. It is, in fact, The Limit. Its luxury is palatial, its grounds are nothing short of Edenesque. No expense has been spared, I should surmise. Your ancestors were whole-hoggers. They have done the thing as it should be done—every detail attended to. I like your tapestry, and I like your oak, and I like your secret stairs. But I think your ancestors should have left well enough alone, and stopped at that.' So I said they had, as far as I knew, and he shook his head and said:

"'No, Sir. Your ancestors take the air of a night with their heads under their arms. A ghost that sighed or glided or rustled I could have stood, and thanked you for it, and considered it in the rent. But a ghost that bullets go through while it stands grinning with a bare neck and its head loose under its own arm and little boys screaming and fainting in their beds—no! What I say is, if this is a British hereditary high-toned family ghost, excuse me!' And he went off by the early train."

"I say," the stricken Jimmy remarked, "I *am* sorry, and I don't think we did faint, really I don't—but we thought it would be just what you wanted. And perhaps someone else will take the house."

"I don't know anyone else rich enough," said Lord Yalding. "Mr. Conway came the day before he said he would, or you'd never have got hold of him. And I don't know how you did it, and I don't want to know. It was a rather silly trick."

There was a gloomy pause. The rain beat against the long windows.

"I say"—Jimmy looked up at Lord Yalding with the light of a

new idea in his round face. "I say, if you're hard up, why don't you sell your jewels?"

"I haven't any jewels, you meddlesome young duffer," said Lord Yalding quite crossly; and taking his hands out of his pockets, he began to walk away.

"I mean the ones in the panelled room with the stars in the ceiling," Jimmy insisted, following him.

"There aren't any," said Lord Yalding shortly; "and if this is some more ring-nonsense I advise you to be careful, young man. I've had about as much as I care for."

"It's not ring-nonsense," said Jimmy: "there are shelves and shelves of beautiful family jewels. You can sell them and—"

"Oh, no!" cried Mademoiselle, appearing like an oleograph of a duchess in the door of the picture-gallery; "don't sell the family jewels—"

"There aren't any, my lady," said Lord Yalding, going towards her. "I thought you were never coming."

"Oh, aren't there!" said Mabel, who had followed Mademoiselle. "You just come and see."

"Let us see what they will to show us," cried Mademoiselle, for Lord Yalding did not move; "it should at least be amusing."

"It is," said Jimmy.

So they went, Mabel and Jimmy leading, while Mademoiselle and Lord Yalding followed, hand in hand.

"It's much safer to walk hand in hand," said Lord Yalding; "with these children at large one never knows what may happen next."

CHAPTER XII

It would be interesting, no doubt, to describe the feelings of Lord Yalding as he followed Mabel and Jimmy through his ancestral halls, but I have no means of knowing at all what he felt. Yet one must suppose that he felt something: bewilderment, perhaps, mixed with a faint wonder, and a desire to pinch himself to see if he were dreaming. Or he may have pondered the rival questions, "Am I mad?" "Are they mad?" without being at all able to decide which he ought to try to answer, let alone deciding what, in either case, the answer ought to be. You see, the children did seem to believe in the odd stories they told—and the wish had come true, and the ghost *had* appeared. He must have thought—but all this is vain; I don't *really* know what he thought any more than you do.

Nor can I give you any clue to the thoughts and feelings of Mademoiselle. I only know that she was very happy, but anyone would have known that if they had seen her face. Perhaps this is as good a moment as any to explain that when her guardian had put her in a convent so that she should not sacrifice her fortune by marrying a poor lord, her guardian had secured that fortune (to himself) by going off with it to South America. Then, having no money left, Mademoiselle had to work for it. So she went out as governess, and took the situation she did take because it was near Lord Yalding's home. She wanted to see him, even though she thought he had forsaken her and did not love her any more. And now she had seen him. I dare say she thought about some of these things as she went along through his house, her hand held in his. But of course I can't be sure.

Jimmy's thoughts, of course, I can read like any old book. He thought, "Now he'll *have* to believe me." That Lord Yalding should believe him had become, quite unreasonably, the most important thing in the world to Jimmy. He wished that Gerald and Kathleen were there to share his triumph, but they were helping Mabel's aunt to cover the grand furniture up, and so were out of what followed. Not that they missed much, for when Mabel proudly said, "Now you'll see," and the others came close round her in the little panelled room, there was a pause, and then—nothing happened at all!

"There's a secret spring here somewhere," said Mabel, fumbling with fingers that had suddenly grown hot and damp.

"Where?" said Lord Yalding.

"*Here*," said Mabel impatiently, "only I can't find it."

And she couldn't. She found the spring of the secret panel under the window all right, but that seemed to everyone dull compared with the jewels that everyone had pictured and two at least had seen. But the spring that made the oak panelling slide away and displayed jewels plainly to any eye worth a king's ransom—this could not be found. More, it was simply not there. There could be no doubt of that. Every inch of the panelling was felt by careful fingers. The earnest protests of Mabel and Jimmy died away presently in a silence made painful by the hotness of one's ears, the discomfort of not liking to meet anyone's eyes, and the resentful feeling that the spring was not behaving in at all a sportsmanlike way, and that, in a word, this was not cricket.

"You see!" said Lord Yalding severely. "Now you've had your joke, if you call it a joke, and I've had enough of the whole silly business. Give me the ring—it's mine, I suppose, since you say you found it somewhere here—and don't let's hear another word about all this rubbish of magic and enchantment."

"Gerald's got the ring," said Mabel miserably.

"Then go and fetch him," said Lord Yalding—"both of you."

The melancholy pair retired, and Lord Yalding spent the time of their absence in explaining to Mademoiselle how very unimportant jewels were compared with other things.

The four children came back together.

"We've had enough of this ring business," said Lord Yalding. "Give it to me and we'll say no more about it."

"I—I can't get it off," said Gerald. "It—it always did have a will of its own."

"I'll soon get it off," said Lord Yalding. But he didn't. "We'll try soap," he said firmly. Four out of his five hearers knew just exactly how much use soap would be.

"They won't believe about the jewels," wailed Mabel, suddenly dissolved in tears, "and I can't find the spring. I've felt all over—we all have—it was just here, and—"

Her fingers felt it as she spoke; and as she ceased to speak the carved panels slid away, and the blue velvet shelves laden with jewels were disclosed to the unbelieving eyes of Lord Yalding and the lady who was to be his wife.

"Jove!" said Lord Yalding.

"*Miséricorde!*"* said the lady.

"But why *now?*" gasped Mabel. "Why not before?"

"I expect it's magic," said Gerald. "There's no real spring here, and it couldn't act because the ring wasn't here. You know Phoebus told us the ring was the heart of all the magic."

"Shut it up and take the ring away and see."

They did, and Gerald was (as usual, he himself pointed out) proved to be right. When the ring was away there was no spring; when the ring was in the room there (as Mabel urged) was the spring all right enough.

"So you see," said Mabel to Lord Yalding.

"I see that the spring's very artfully concealed," said that dense peer. "I think it was very clever indeed of you to find it. And if those jewels are real—"

"Of course they're real," said Mabel indignantly.

"Well, anyway," said Lord Yalding, "thank you all very much. I think it's clearing up. I'll send the wagonette home with you after lunch. And if you don't mind, I'll have the ring."

Half an hour of soap and water produced no effect whatever, except to make the finger of Gerald very red and very sore. Then Lord Yalding said something very impatient indeed, and then Gerald suddenly became angry and said: "Well, I'm sure I wish it would come off," and of course instantly, "slick as butter," as he later pointed out, off it came.

"Thank you," said Lord Yalding.

"And I believe now he thinks I kept it on on purpose," said Gerald afterwards when, at ease on the leads at home, they talked the whole thing out over a tin of preserved pineapple and a bottle of ginger-beer apiece. "There's no pleasing some people. He wasn't in such a fiery hurry to order that wagonette after he found that Made-

---

* Mercy! (French).

moiselle meant to go when we did. But I liked him better when he was a humble bailiff. Take him for all in all, he does not look as if we should like him again."

"He doesn't know what's the matter with him," said Kathleen, leaning back against the tiled roof; "it's really the magic—it's like sickening with measles. Don't you remember how cross Mabel was at first about the invisibleness?"

"Rather!" said Jimmy.

"It's partly that," said Gerald, trying to be fair, "and partly it's the being in love. It always makes people like idiots—a chap at school told me. His sister was like that—quite rotten, you know. And she used to be quite a decent sort before she was engaged."

At tea and at supper Mademoiselle was radiant—as attractive as a lady on a Christmas card, as merry as a marmoset, and as kind as you would always be yourself if you could take the trouble. At breakfast, an equal radiance, kindness, attraction, merriment. Then Lord Yalding came to see her. The meeting took place in the drawing-room; the children with deep discreetness remained shut in the school-room till Gerald, going up to his room for a pencil, surprised Eliza with her ear glued to the drawing-room key-hole.

After that Gerald sat on the top stair with a book. He could not hear any of the conversation in the drawing-room, but he could command a view of the door, and in this way be certain that no one else heard any of it. Thus it was that when the drawing-room door opened Gerald was in a position to see Lord Yalding come out. "Our young hero," as he said later, "coughed with infinite tact to show that he was there," but Lord Yalding did not seem to notice. He walked in a blind sort of way to the hat-stand, fumbled clumsily with the umbrellas and macintoshes, found his straw hat and looked at it gloomily, crammed it on his head and went out, banging the door behind him in the most reckless way.

He left the drawing-room door open, and Gerald, though he had purposely put himself in a position where one could hear nothing from the drawing-room when the door was shut, could hear something quite plainly now that the door was open. That something, he noticed with deep distress and disgust, was the sound of sobs and sniffs. Mademoiselle was quite certainly crying.

"Jimminy!" he remarked to himself, "they haven't lost much

time. Fancy their beginning to quarrel *already*! I hope I'll never have to be anybody's lover."

But this was no time to brood on the terrors of his own future. Eliza might at any time occur. She would not for a moment hesitate to go through that open door, and push herself into the very secret sacred heart of Mademoiselle's grief. It seemed to Gerald better that he should be the one to do this. So he went softly down the worn green Dutch carpet of the stairs and into the drawing-room, shutting the door softly and securely behind him.

"It is all over," Mademoiselle was saying, her face buried in the beady arum-lilies on a red ground worked for a cushion cover by a former pupil: "he will not marry me!"

Do not ask me how Gerald had gained the lady's confidence. He had, as I think I said almost at the beginning, very pretty ways with grown-ups, when he chose. Anyway, he was holding her hand, almost as affectionately as if she had been his mother with a headache, and saying "Don't!" and "Don't cry!" and "It'll be all right, you see if it isn't" in the most comforting way you can imagine, varying the treatment with gentle thumps on the back and entreaties to her to tell him all about it.

This wasn't mere curiosity, as you might think. The entreaties were prompted by Gerald's growing certainty that whatever was the matter was somehow the fault of that ring. And in this Gerald was ("once more," as he told himself) right.

The tale, as told by Mademoiselle, was certainly an unusual one. Lord Yalding, last night after dinner, had walked in the park "to think of—"

"Yes, I know," said Gerald; "and he had the ring on. And he saw—"

"He saw the monuments become alive," sobbed Mademoiselle; "his brain was troubled by the ridiculous accounts of fairies that you tell him. He sees Apollon and Aphrodité alive on their marble. He remembers him of your story. He wish himself a statue. Then he becomes mad—imagines to himself that your story of the island is true, plunges in the lake, swims among the beasts of the Ark of Noé, feeds with gods on an island. At dawn the madness become less. He think the Panthéon vanish. But him, no—he thinks himself statue, hiding from gardeners in his garden till nine less a quarter. Then he thinks to wish himself no more a statue and perceives that he is flesh and blood. A bad dream, but he has lost the head with the tales you tell. He say it is no dream but he is fool—mad—how you say? And a mad man must not marry. There is no hope. I am at despair! And the life is vain!"

"There is," said Gerald earnestly. "I assure you there is—hope, I mean. And life's as right as rain really. And there's nothing to despair about. He's *not* mad, and it's *not* a dream. It's magic. It really and truly is."

"The magic exists not," Mademoiselle moaned; "it is that he is mad. It is the joy to re-see me after so many days. Oh, la-la-la-la-la!"

"Did he talk to the gods?" Gerald asked gently.

"It is there the most mad of all his ideas. He say that Mercure give him rendezvous at some temple tomorrow when the moon raise herself."

"Right," cried Gerald, "righto! Dear nice, kind, pretty Mademoiselle Rapunzel, don't be a silly little duffer"—he lost himself for a moment among the consoling endearments he was accustomed to offer to Kathleen in moments of grief and emotion, but hastily added: "I mean, do not be a lady who weeps causelessly. Tomorrow he will go to that temple. I will go. Thou shalt go—he will go. We will go—you will go—let 'em all go! And, you see, it's going to be absolutely all right. He'll see he isn't mad, and you'll understand all about everything. Take my handkerchief, it's quite a clean one as it happens; I haven't even unfolded it. Oh! do stop crying, there's a dear, darling, long-lost lover."

This flood of eloquence was not without effect. She took his handkerchief, sobbed, half smiled, dabbed at her eyes, and said: "Oh, naughty! Is it some trick you play him, like the ghost?"

"I can't explain," said Gerald, "but I give you my word of honour—you know what an Englishman's word of honour is, don't you? even if you *are* French—that everything is going to be exactly what you wish. I've never told you a lie. Believe me!"

"It is curious," said she, drying her eyes, "but I do." And once again, so suddenly that he could not have resisted, she kissed him. I think, however, that in this her hour of sorrow he would have thought it mean to resist.

"It pleases her and it doesn't hurt me—much," would have been his thought.

* * *

And now it is near moonrise. The French governess, half-doubting, half-hoping, but wholly longing to be near Lord Yalding even if he be as mad as a March hare, and the four children—they have collected Mabel by an urgent letter-card posted the day before—are going over the dewy grass. The moon has not yet risen, but her light is in the sky mixed with the pink and purple of the sunset. The west is heavy with ink-clouds and rich colour, but the east, where the moon rises, is clear as a rock-pool.

They go across the lawn and through the beech-wood and come at last, through a tangle of underwood and bramble, to a little level tableland that rises out of the flat hill-top—one tableland out of another. Here is the ring of vast rugged stones, one pierced with a curious round hole, worn smooth at its edges. In the middle of the circle is a great flat stone, alone, desolate, full of meaning—a stone that is covered thick with the memory of old faiths and creeds long since forgotten. Something dark moves in the circle. The French girl breaks from the children, goes to it, clings to its arm. It is Lord Yalding, and he is telling her to go.

"Never of the life!" she cries. "If you are mad I am mad too, for I believe the tale these children tell. And I am here to be with thee and see with thee—whatever the rising moon shall show us."

The children, holding hands by the flat stone, more moved by the magic in the girl's voice than by any magic of enchanted rings, listen, trying not to listen.

"Are you not afraid?" Lord Yalding is saying.

"Afraid? With you?" she laughs. He put his arm round her. The children hear her sigh.

"Are you afraid," he says, "my darling?"

Gerald goes across the wide turf ring expressly to say:

"You can't be afraid if you are wearing the ring. And I'm sorry, but we can hear every word you say."

She laughs again. "It makes nothing," she says "you know already if we love each other."

Then he puts the ring on her finger, and they stand together. The white of his flannel coat sleeve marks no line on the white of her dress; they stand as though cut out of one block of marble.

Then a faint greyness touches the top of that round hole, creeps up the side. Then the hole is a disc of light—a moonbeam strikes straight through it across the grey green of the circle that the stones mark, and as the moon rises the moonbeam slants downward. The children have drawn back till they stand close to the lovers. The moonbeam slants more and more; now it touches the far end of the stone, now it draws nearer and nearer to the middle of it, now at last it touches the very heart and centre of that central stone. And then it is as though a spring were touched, a fountain of light released. Everything changes. Or, rather, everything is revealed. There are no more secrets. The plan of the world seems plain, like an easy sum that one writes in big figures on a child's slate. One wonders how one can ever have wondered about anything. Space is not; every place that one has seen or dreamed of is here. Time is not; into this instant is crowded all that one has ever done or dreamed of doing. It is a moment and it is eternity. It is the centre of the universe and it is the universe itself. The eternal light rests on and illuminates the eternal heart of things.

None of the six human beings who saw that moon-rising were ever able to think about it as having anything to do with time. Only for one instant could that moonray have rested full on the centre of that stone. And yet there was time for many happenings.

From that height one could see far out over the quiet park and sleeping gardens, and through the grey green of them shapes moved, approaching.

The great beasts came first, strange forms that were when the world was new—gigantic lizards with wings—dragons they lived as in men's memories—mammoths, strange vast birds, they crawled up the hill and ranged themselves outside the circle. Then, not from the garden but from very far away, came the stone gods of Egypt and Assyria—bull-bodied, bird-winged, hawk-headed, cat-headed, all in stone, and all alive and alert; strange, grotesque figures from the towers of cathedrals—figures of angels with folded wings, figures of beasts with wings wide spread; sphinxes; uncouth idols from Southern palm-fringed islands; and, last of all, the beautiful marble shapes of the gods and goddesses who had held their festival on the lake-island, and bidden Lord Yalding and the children to this meeting.

Not a word was spoken. Each stone shape came gladly and quietly into the circle of light and understanding, as children, tired with a long ramble, creep quietly through the open door into the firelit welcome of home.

The children had thought to ask many questions. And it had been promised that the questions should be answered. Yet now no one spoke a word, because all had come into the circle of the real magic where all things are understood without speech.

Afterwards none of them could ever remember at all what had happened. But they never forgot that they had been somewhere where everything was easy and beautiful. And people who can remember even that much are never quite the same again. And when they came to talk of it next day they found that to each some little part of that night's great enlightenment was left.

All the stone creatures drew closer round the stone—the light where the moonbeam struck it seemed to break away in spray such as water makes when it falls from a height. All the crowd was bathed in whiteness. A deep hush lay over the vast assembly.

Then a wave of intention swept over the mighty crowd. All the faces, bird, beast, Greek statue, Babylonian monster, human child, and human lover, turned upward, the radiant light illumined them and one word broke from all.

"The light!" they cried, and the sound of their voice was like the sound of a great wave; "the light! the light—"

And then the light was not any more, and, soft as floating thistledown, sleep was laid on the eyes of all but the immortals.

The grass was chill and dewy and the clouds had veiled the moon. The lovers and the children were standing together, all clinging close, not for fear, but for love.

"I want," said the French girl softly, "to go to the cave on the island."

Very quietly through the gentle brooding night they went down to the boat-house, loosed the clanking chain, and dipped oars among the drowned stars and lilies. They came to the island, and found the steps.

"I brought candles," said Gerald, "in case."

So, lighted by Gerald's candles, they went down into the Hall of Psyche and there glowed the light spread from her statue, and all was as the children had seen it before.

It is the Hall of Granted Wishes.

"The ring," said Lord Yalding.

"The ring," said his lover, "is the magic ring given long ago to a mortal, and it is what you say it is. It was given to your ancestor by a lady of my house that he might build her a garden and a house like her own palace and garden in her own land. So that this place is built partly by his love and partly by that magic. She never lived to see it; that was the price of the magic."

It must have been English that she spoke, for otherwise how could the children have understood her? Yet the words were not like Mademoiselle's way of speaking.

"Except from children," her voice went on, "the ring exacts a payment. You paid for me, when I came by your wish, by this terror of madness that you have since known. Only one wish is free."

"And that wish is—"

"The last," she said. "Shall I wish?"

"Yes—wish," they said, all of them.

"I wish, then," said Lord Yalding's lover, "that all the magic this ring has wrought may be undone, and that the ring itself may be no more and no less than a charm to bind thee and me together for evermore."

She ceased. And as she ceased the enchanted light died away, the windows of granted wishes went out, like magic-lantern pictures. Gerald's candle faintly lighted a rudely arched cave, and where Psyche's statue had been was a stone with something carved on it.

Gerald held the light low.

"It is her grave," the girl said.

Next day no one could remember anything at all exactly. But a good many things were changed. There was no ring but the plain gold ring that Mademoiselle found clasped in her hand when she woke in her own bed in the morning. More than half the jewels in the panelled room were gone, and those that remained had no panelling to cover them; they just lay—bare on the velvet-covered shelves. There was no passage at the back of the Temple of Flora. Quite a lot of the secret passages and hidden rooms had disappeared. And there were not nearly so many statues in the garden as everyone had supposed. And large pieces of the castle were missing and had to be replaced at great expense. From which we may conclude that Lord Yalding's ancestor had used the ring a good deal to help him in his building.

However, the jewels that were left were quite enough to pay for everything.

The suddenness with which all the ring-magic was undone was such a shock to everyone concerned that they now almost doubt that any magic ever happened.

But it is certain that Lord Yalding married the French governess and that a plain gold ring was used in the ceremony, and this, if you come to think of it, could be no other than the magic ring, turned, by that last wish, into a charm to keep him and his wife together for ever.

Also, if all this story is nonsense and a make-up—if Gerald and Jimmy and Kathleen and Mabel have merely imposed on my trusting nature by a pack of unlikely inventions, how do you account for the paragraph which appeared in the evening papers the day after the magic of the moon-rising?

"MYSTERIOUS DISAPPEARANCE OF A
WELL-KNOWN CITY MAN,"

it said, and then went on to say how a gentleman, well known and much respected in financial circles, had vanished, leaving no trace.

"Mr. U. W. Ugli," the papers continued, "had remained late, working at his office as was his occasional habit. The office door was found locked, and on its being broken open the clothes of the unfortunate gentleman were found in a heap on the floor, together with an umbrella, a walking stick, a golf club, and, curiously enough, a feather brush, such as housemaids use for dusting. Of his body, however, there was no trace. The police are stated to have a clue."

If they have, they have kept it to themselves. But I do not think they can have a clue, because, of course, that respected gentleman was the Ugly-Wugly who became real when, in search of a really good hotel, he got into the Hall of Granted Wishes. And if none of this story ever happened, how is it that those four children are such friends with Lord and Lady Yalding, and stay at The Towers almost every holidays?

It is all very well for all of them to pretend that the whole of this story is my own invention: facts are facts, and you can't explain them away.

ENDNOTES

Five Children and It

1. (p. 3) *To John Bland*: The "five children" of the novel are loosely based on Nesbit's own. John Bland ("The Lamb") was Nesbit's fifth, born when the others were already in their teens. See the introduction (p. xxii) for an account of the circumstances surrounding his birth.

2. (p. 20) *if you had three wishes given you, and have despised the old man and his wife in the black-pudding story*: In this version of the fairy tale of "the three wishes," a man who dislikes his wife's cooking wishes for a helping of black pudding, to which she reacts by wishing the pudding on his nose. This requires the man to use the third and final wish to undo the effects of the second. See the introduction for a discussion of the significance of this fairy tale, which exists in many versions around the world.

3. (p. 84) *"What was it Sir Philip Sidney said when the soldier wouldn't stand him a drink?"*: Like those of Shakespeare, the sonnets of soldier and states-man Philip Sidney (1554–1586) are considered among the finest of the Elizabethan age. In this passage, Cyril inverts a line attributed to Sidney: Wounded and dying on the battlefield, Sidney supposedly handed his water bottle to another wounded soldier with the words "Thy need is greater than mine."

4. (p. 107) *he began boldly enough, with a sentence straight out of Ralph de Courcy; or, The Boy Crusader*: Ralph de Courcy is a character in *A March on London: Being a Story of Wat Tyler's Insurrection* (1897), by the pro-lific G. A. (George Alfred) Henty (1832–1902). Known as "the boys' own historian," he wrote more than one hundred historical novels featuring young men who learn manly virtues in the heat of signif-icant historical conflicts. The Boy Crusader may be a reference to his *Winning His Spurs: A Tale of the Crusades* (1882), which was republished the following year as *The Boy Knight, Who Won His Spurs Fighting with King Richard of England: A Tale of the Crusaders*.

5. (p. 142) *One gentleman . . . offered Robert, in an obliging whisper, ten pounds a*

week to appear at the Crystal Palace: A huge iron and glass building, the Crystal Palace, designed by Sir Joseph Paxton (1801–1865), originally housed the Great Exhibition of 1851. It was subsequently moved to Sydenham Hill, overlooking London, and expanded; over the years its spectacular exhibits drew many thousands of visitors, including Nesbit and her family. It was destroyed by fire in 1936.

6. (p. 144) "*Robert and I are dressed the same. We'll manage somehow, like Sydney Carton did*": At the end of Charles Dickens's *A Tale of Two Cities* (1859), Sydney Carton contrives an elaborate self-sacrificial plan to rescue his condemned look-alike, Charles Darnay, from a French prison by switching places with him.

7. (p. 182) "*I wish Martha to forget about the diamond ring, and mother to forget about the keeper cleaning the windows.*" "*It's like 'Brass Bottle',*" said Jane: Nesbit is acknowledging the influence of *The Brass Bottle* (1900), a fantasy novel by Thomas Anstey Guthrie (1856–1934), who wrote under the pseudonym F. Anstey. In this novel, a modern architect buys an antique brass bottle and discovers that it contains a genie. The latter's beneficence is so excessive that it backfires at every turn, and the exasperated architect ends up wishing it to "kindly obliterate all recollection of yourself and the brass bottle from the minds of every human being who has had anything to do with you or it" (see *The Brass Bottle*, London: Penguin, 1946, p. 218).

The Enchanted Castle

1. (p. 193) *assuming a gentle, pleading expression, resembling that of the late little Lord Fauntleroy—who must, by the way, be quite old now, and an awful prig*: A novel by Frances Hodgson Burnett (1849–1924), *Little Lord Fauntleroy* (1886) was immensely popular in its time. The book's title character later came to epitomize (somewhat unfairly) a certain type of overdressed and insufferably polite young man.

2. (p. 205) *Beyond the rose garden was a yew hedge with an arch cut in it, and it was the beginning of a maze like the one in Hampton Court*: The renowned hedge maze at Hampton Court, a former royal palace in an outer borough of London, was planted for William of Orange between 1689 and 1695.

3. (p. 225) "*I was playing at Fair Rosamond first, and then I heard you talking in the* *maze*": Rosamond, or Rosamund, Clifford (c.1140–c.1176) was a mistress of Henry II (1133–1189). According to one legend, she was hidden in the labyrinthine bower of a secret garden, but was tracked down and killed by Henry's jealous wife, Eleanor of Aquitane (c.1122–1204). In one version of the story, it is the equivalent of Ariadne's thread that enables the Queen and her henchman to penetrate the maze.

4. (p. 240) *"Like La Belle Dame Sans Merci, and he does not want to be found in future ages alone and palely loitering in the middle of sedge and things"*: John Keats's 1819 ballad describes an encounter between a man and an enchanted beauty who has left him, like others before him, in a forlorn state. Gerald's reference to being found alone in the sedge recalls the last lines of the first and final stanzas: "Alone and palely loitering? / The sedge has wither'd from the lake, / And no birds sing."

5. (p. 265) *"The melancholy Mabel will await the tryst without success, as far as this one is concerned. 'Fish, fish, other fish—other fish I fry!'" he warbled to the tune of "Cherry Ripe"*: Gerald is parodying a love poem by Robert Herrick (1591–1674); its first line is "Cherry-ripe, ripe, ripe, I cry." The rest of Gerald's song echoes the finale: "Where my Julia's lips do smile; / There's the land, or cherry-isle, / Whose plantations fully show / All the year where cherries grow."

6. (pp. 313, 315) *They met no one, except one man, who murmured, "Guy Fawkes, swelp me!" and crossed the road hurriedly*: Guy Fawkes (1570–1606) was the best-known member of a group of Catholic conspirators who attempted to blow up England's Houses of Parliament and kill the king in 1605. The plot was uncovered, and Fawkes and the others were tried and executed. Guy Fawkes Day is celebrated annually on November 5 with fireworks and the burning of Fawkes in effigy.

7. (p. 319) *We must excuse her. She had been very brave, and I have no doubt that all heroines, from Joan of Arc to Grace Darling, have had their sobbing moments*: Grace Darling (1815–1842) was the daughter of a lighthouse keeper in Northumberland, England, who became a national heroine after September 1838, when she and her father rescued survivors of a ship, the *Forfarshire*, that had run aground on a nearby island.

8. (p. 330) *"Anyway," said Gerald, "we'll try to get him back, and shut the door. That's the most we can hope for. And then apples, and Robinson Crusoe or the Swiss Family, or any book you like that's got no magic in it"*: The popular adventure novel *Robinson Crusoe* (1719), by Daniel Defoe (1660–1731), inspired

similar castaway narratives, perhaps the most famous of which is *The Swiss Family Robinson* (1814), by Johann David Wyss (1743–1818). As Gerald indicates, these tales of shipwrecked individuals and families, known for their realistic adventures, are devoid of magic and enchantment.

9. (p. 348) *she looked like a little girl reflected in one of those long bent mirrors at Rosherville Gardens that make stout people look so happily slender, and slender people so sadly scraggy:* Rosherville Gardens, a riverside resort in Northfleet, England, opened in the early 1840s. For a time a popular destination for Londoners, who reached it by steamboat, the resort featured a bear pit, zoo, aviary, botanical gardens, maze, open-air theaters, and tea rooms.

10. (p. 369) *"Come, we must get the feast ready. Eros—Psyche—Hebe—Ganymede— all you young people can arrange the fruit":* In classical mythology, Psyche (which means "soul" in Greek) is the princess who married Cupid, the god of love. As a result of her failure of trust, she is compelled to leave her husband's castle, but after enduring many trials and a long separation, she is reunited with the god and made immortal. The myth of Psyche and Cupid can be seen as an allegory of the soul transfigured by love. In chapter 6, the children act out a fairy-tale version of this myth in the story of *Beauty and the Beast.* See the introduction for an account of the increasingly significant, if never explicitly stated, role of the myth and the fairy tale in the second half of *The Enchanted Castle.*

11. (p. 379) *perhaps Mr. Millar will draw the different kinds of arches for you:* H. R. Millar (1869–1942) worked as an illustrator for *The Strand Magazine* as well as other publications. His collaboration with Nesbit began in 1899 with the illustrations for *The Book of Dragons,* which originally appeared in *The Strand,* and they continued to work together until her relationship with the magazine ended in 1913.

INSPIRED BY THE ENCHANTED CASTLE AND FIVE CHILDREN AND IT

British author J. K. Rowling frequently identifies Edith Nesbit as a major inspiration for her immensely popular Harry Potter novels. Therefore, it may be no coincidence that in the wave of excitement surrounding the Harry Potter phenomenon, a major film adaptation of Nesbit's Five Children and It has also appeared. Surprisingly, John Stephenson's Five Children and It (2004) is only the third Nesbit novel to appear on the large screen, following The Railway Children (1970) and The Phoenix and the Magic Carpet (1995). The film stars Kenneth Branagh as Uncle Albert, Zoe Wannamaker as Martha the housekeeper (Wannamaker also appeared in the second Harry Potter film), Eddie Izzard as the voice of the Psammead, Freddie Highmore as Robert, the narrator, and four other child actors. Produced in conjunction with Jim Henson's Creature Shop, the film uses a combination of computer-generated special effects, animatronics, and live action to bring Nesbit's story to life.

Works by Nesbit have appeared more often on television, at least in the United Kingdom. In addition to TV movies and serial adaptations of The Story of the Treasure Seekers (released as Treasure Seekers in 1996), The Phoenix and the Carpet (1976 and 1997), and The Railway Children (1951, 1957, and 2000), a six-episode miniseries of The Enchanted Castle aired on British television in 1979, and a similar serialization of Five Children and It (retitled The Sand Fairy for U.S. distribution) was broadcast in 1991. Nesbit herself was the subject of a television play that was shown on BBC television in 1972 as part of the series The Edwardians.

For a discussion of authors inspired by Nesbit, see part VI of the introduction to this volume.

COMMENTS & QUESTIONS

In this section, we aim to provide the reader with an array of perspectives on the text, as well as questions that challenge those perspectives. The commentary has been culled from sources as diverse as reviews contemporaneous with the work, letters written by the author, literary criticism of later generations, and appreciations written throughout the work's history. Following the commentary, a series of questions seeks to filter Edith Nesbit's The Enchanted Castle and Five Children and It through a variety of points of view and bring about a richer understanding of these enduring works.

Comments

THE NATION

E. Nesbit and W. W. Jacobs are the two contributors who have given a certain cheap magazine some circulation among a constituency at whom, to judge by the rest of its matter, it was not aimed. E. Nesbit is, one may almost say, the only person now telling fairy stories in public for love of the game. "The Enchanted Castle" is a very good example of her craft. Its humor consists in the continual jumbling of the realities of English child life, and the unrealities (or deeper realities) of the land of fancy. The wits of these young Britons are, when they choose, mazed with fairy-lore, and they have the dialect of romance at their tongue's end. Probably no such deep philosophy could be read into their adventures as ingenuity has connected with the exploits of their great progenitor Alice; but the absurdity of the things they do is made delightful by the whimsical air of the writer. In short, the book illustrates once more the English faculty of amusing children without boring one's self.

—August 13, 1908

NEW YORK TIMES

There is great charm in E. Nesbit's book, "The Enchanted Castle." In its general character it is decidedly above the average run of so-called juvenile literature, and should prove vastly entertaining to the imaginative children to whom it is primarily addressed, as well as to grown-up folk who have a liking for books that are quaint, fanciful, and delicately humorous.

—July 11, 1908

THE NATION

If Emil [in Erich Kastner's *Emil and the Detective*] is a real person, the "five children" constitute an equally real family. The public of Mrs. Nesbit, so large and devoted, will rejoice in this American edition of a book which has been making friends everywhere for twenty years. The ingenuity of the author's imagination, her humor, and her charming outlook invest the adventures of her young characters with unceasing interest.

—November 19, 1930

C. S. LEWIS

Much better than either [Sir Arthur Conan Doyle's *Sir Nigel* or Mark Twain's *A Connecticut Yankee in King Arthur's Court*] was E. Nesbit's trilogy, *Five Children and It*, *The Phoenix and the Wishing* [sic] *Carpet*, and *The Amulet*. The last did most for me. It first opened my eyes to antiquity, the 'dark backward and abysm of time.' I can still reread it with delight.

—from *Surprised by Joy* (1955)

GORE VIDAL

After Lewis Carroll, E. Nesbit is the best of the English fabulists who wrote about children (neither wrote for children) and like Carroll she was able to create a world of magic and inverted logic that was entirely her own.

—*New York Review of Books* (December 3, 1964)

J. B. PRIESTLEY

The Edwardian variety of literary interests and abilities can be well illustrated by some mention of the finely-written whimsical tales it has left us, the kind of work later writers have never been able to improve upon or supplant. . . . And I am ready to include in this class Edith Nesbit's entrancing stories about children, which I read and enjoyed as a child and then, enjoying them all over again, praised in print when I was fully adult—but still fascinated by magic.

—from *The Edwardians* (1970)

ALISON LURIE

Though there are foreshadowings of her characteristic manner in Charles Dickens's *Holiday Romance* and Kenneth Grahame's *The Golden Age*, Nesbit was the first to write at length for children as intellectual equals and in their own language. Her books were startlingly innovative in other ways: they took place in contemporary England, and recommended socialist solutions to its problems; they presented a modern view of childhood; and they used magic both as a comic device and as a serious metaphor for the power of the imagination. Every writer of children's fantasy since Nesbit's time is indebted to her—and so are some authors of adult fiction.

—*New York Review of Books* (October 25, 1984)

COLIN MANLOVE

In *The Enchanted Castle* we are more concerned with the inner world of the spirit, than with the outer world of objects and doings. . . . What is solid and real in the earlier books is less certain here. A statue may come alive, a dummy may turn into a half-person, a girl into a princess: nothing is what it seems. We are partly in a world of the imagination, partly in one of magic, and who is to say which it is? Where in the earlier books the imagination became real, here the real becomes the imagination. And where the earlier books took place mainly in the day, these later ones often have nighttime settings. It is as though Nesbit had passed from a materialist to an idealist attitude towards magic.

—from *From Alice to Harry Potter: Children's Fantasy in England* (2003)

NATASHA WALTER

In the tales of Lewis or Rowling or Pullman the children find themselves part of a grand quest, a huge cosmic battle in which they will play a destined role. In Nesbit's work everything is much more anarchic, and the children are always unsure whether they are going to be thrown into the darkest dungeon in Egypt or be sent to bed without supper. For her, magic worlds are as chaotic as real life; there are no Voldemorts or Dumbledores, no forces of pure evil or pure good, in her fantasies. So the children have to muddle through just as they would in everyday life.

—*The Guardian* (October 9, 2004)

Questions

1. Alison Lurie praises Nesbit for writing "at length for children as intellectual equals and in their own language." But Gore Vidal claims that for all her virtues she wasn't really writing "for children." Discuss the voice of the narrator in these novels and the relationship between the narrator and the audience (or audiences) she seems to be addressing.

2. How does Nesbit appropriate traditional folktales, ancient legends, and classical myths in these novels?

3. What are the relative strengths and weaknesses of the looser episodic organization of the early fantasy *Five Children and It*, as compared to the more unified plot of *The Enchanted Castle*, a later work? Which approach do you prefer?

4. Nesbit was known for focusing on a group of children rather than the single protagonist who had prevailed in earlier children's fiction. Discuss the similarities and differences of character in the juvenile ensemble in these novels and the ways they interact with each other and respond to the challenges that come their way.

5. Natasha Walter claims that, compared to the imaginary worlds of C. S. Lewis and other more recent fantasists, Nesbit's works are "much more anarchic" and her "magic worlds are as chaotic as real life." On the other hand, Colin Manlove argues that in her later fantasies Nesbit shifts "from a materialist to an idealist attitude towards magic" and "in *The Enchanted Castle* we are more concerned with the inner world of the spirit, than with the outer world of objects and doings." Compare the kind of magic that appears in *Five Children and It* with the sort that comes to the fore in the second half of *The Enchanted Castle*.

FOR FURTHER READING

Other Children's Books by Edith Nesbit

The Story of the Treasure Seekers: Being the Adventures of the Bastable Children in Search of a Fortune. 1899. London: Puffin Books, 1994. Nesbit's first full-length children's novel.

The Book of Dragons. 1900. New York: Seastar Books, 2001. Still popular, a collection of eight dragon stories.

The Wouldbegoods: Being the Further Adventures of the Treasure Seekers. 1901. London: Puffin Books, 1996. The second volume in the Bastable series.

The Phoenix and the Carpet. 1904. London: Puffin Books, 1994. A sequel to Five Children and It.

The New Treasure Seekers. 1904. London: Puffin Books, 1996. The third volume in the Bastable series.

The Story of the Amulet. 1906. London: Puffin Books, 1996. The third and final volume of the "Five Children" series.

The Railway Children. 1906. London: Puffin Books, 1994. After The Story of the Treasure Seekers, her most popular family adventure novel.

The House of Arden. 1908. New York: Books of Wonder, 1997. The Arden children travel into the past in search of lost family treasure.

Harding's Luck. 1909. New York: Books of Wonder, 1999. A sequel to The House of Arden.

The Magic City. 1910. New York: Seastar Books, 2000. The adventures of two children inside their own toy city.

The Wonderful Garden. 1911. New York: Coward-McCann, 1959. Three children find and plant the seeds of Heart's Desire.

The Magic World. 1912. London: Puffin Books, 1994. A collection of twelve stories.

Wet Magic. 1913. New York: Seastar Books, 2001. Four children help the Merfolk in their struggle against the Underfolk.

Long Ago When I Was Young. 1966. New York: Dial Books for Young Readers, 1991. A series of childhood reminiscences originally published as

"My School-Days" in *The Girl's Own Paper*, October 1896–September 1897.

Biography

Briggs, Julia. *A Woman of Passion: The Life of E. Nesbit, 1858–1924.* 1987. New York: New Amsterdam Books, 2000. A thorough update of Moore's biography with edifying commentary on Nesbit's works.

Moore, Doris Langley. *E. Nesbit: A Biography.* 1933. Revised edition. London: Ernest Benn, 1967. Based on extensive interviews with and letters from Nesbit's family and other acquaintances.

Criticism and Contexts

Bell, Anthea. *E. Nesbit.* 1960. New York: H. Z. Walck, 1964. A succinct overview of her life and works.

Carpenter, Humphrey. *Secret Gardens: A Study of the Golden Age of Children's Literature.* Boston: Houghton Mifflin, 1985. An account of the Anglo-American tradition from the mid-nineteenth to the early twentieth century. The sharply critical chapter on Nesbit questions both her originality and the value of her influence.

Crouch, Marcus. *Treasure Seekers and Borrowers: Children's Books in Britain, 1900–1960.* London: Library Association, 1962. An informative survey that identifies Nesbit as a central figure in the modern British tradition and credits her with reshaping the family story, the fantasy novel, and the historical romance.

————. *The Nesbit Tradition: The Children's Novel in England, 1945–1970.* London: Ernest Benn, 1972. An overview that emphasizes Nesbit's enduring influence on English children's fiction.

Knoepflmacher, U. C. "Of Babylands and Babylons: E. Nesbit and the Reclamation of the Fairy Tale." *Tulsa Studies in Women's Literature* 6:2 (Fall 1987), pp. 299–325. A probing essay that uses Nesbit's autobiographical writings (primarily *Long Ago When I Was Young*) to explore some of the psychological conflicts in her major fiction.

Lochhead, Marion. *Renaissance of Wonder: The Fantasy Worlds of C. S. Lewis, J. R. R.*

Tolkien, George MacDonald, E. Nesbit and Others. San Francisco: Harper and Row, 1977. A historical survey with a chapter devoted to Nesbit.

Manlove, Colin N. From Alice to Harry Potter: Children's Fantasy in England. Christchurch, New Zealand: Cybereditions, 2003. An illuminating tour of the fantasy tradition from the mid-nineteenth century to the present.

Nelson, Claudia. Boys Will Be Girls: The Feminine Ethic and British Children's Fiction, 1857–1917. New Brunswick, NJ: Rutgers University Press, 1991. An analysis of the sanctification of childhood and related changes in gender ideals in the fiction of the era.

Nicholson, Mervyn. "What C. S. Lewis Took from E. Nesbit." Children's Literature Association Quarterly 16 (1991), pp. 16–22. An essay that examines the influence of Nesbit's fantasies on the plot, character, and narrative voice of Lewis's The Chronicles of Narnia, with an analysis of the sections most heavily indebted to her works.

Nikolajeva, Maria. Children's Literature Comes of Age: Toward a New Aesthetic. New York: Garland, 1996. A sophisticated and wide-ranging study that identifies Nesbit as "the key figure of modern fantasy" (p. 159) and highlights her appropriation of other literature from traditional folktales to the novels of H. G. Wells.

Prickett, Stephen. Victorian Fantasy. Hassocks, Sussex: Harvester, 1979. A standard work on the period that concludes with a chapter on Kipling and Nesbit.

Streatfeild, Noel. Magic and the Magician: E. Nesbit and Her Children's Books. New York: Abelard Schumann, 1958. A book-length appreciation by a well-known author of children's literature.